About the Author

David John Adams looks back on a full and interesting life, guided by the often-unseen but always present hand of Almighty God. The ultra-busy English Construction Engineer progressed into the adventures of retirement, balancing the toils and joys of live-in grandparenting with the daily struggles of living in an alien land. Helping Eastern European locals to develop their held-back talents, is as much a privilege as bringing forth this 'book that is in us all', showing that bodily age comes second place to a burning heart!

For Sir Tim Smit,

Jewels of Glory

All great achievements in life have needed a man with vision, who would dare to do what he believed in — thank you for daring!

David D'Olay

David John Adams

Jewels of Glory

Olympia Publishers
London

www.olympiapublishers.com
OLYMPIA PAPERBACK EDITION

Copyright © David John Adams 2020

The right of David John Adams to be identified as author of
this work has been asserted in accordance with sections 77 and 78 of the
Copyright, Designs and Patents Act 1988.

All Rights Reserved

No reproduction, copy or transmission of this publication
may be made without written permission.
No paragraph of this publication may be reproduced,
copied or transmitted save with the written permission of the publisher, or in
accordance with the provisions
of the Copyright Act 1956 (as amended).

Any person who commits any unauthorised act in relation to
this publication may be liable to criminal
prosecution and civil claims for damage.

A CIP catalogue record for this title is
available from the British Library.

ISBN: 978-1-78830-669-0

This is a work of fiction.
Names, characters, places and incidents originate from the writer's imagination.
Any resemblance to actual persons, living or dead, is purely coincidental.

First Published in 2020

Olympia Publishers
Tallis House
2 Tallis Street
London
EC4Y 0AB

Printed in Great Britain

Dedication

This book is dedicated to my wonderful wife, Janet, who is the most-treasured of my 'Jewels of Glory'.

CHAPTER 1

His Royal Highness, Crown Prince Sheikh Abdullah bin Rashid Al Nu'masiq scowled at his country's military attaché at their London embassy, "For what purpose are you employed if not for gaining the maximum advantage for us with these infidels? How dare these pensioned-off soldiers play their infantile games and offer us a meaningless ten per cent reduction off their ridiculously inflated quotation! They have the audacity to demand we reduce our oil prices, then they offer us only miniscule discounts for their ill-designed military hardware! You will negotiate a thirty per cent reduction or you can tell them that we will take our cheque book elsewhere!" The Federation of Non-aligned Arab Emirates' Attaché found Crown Prince Abdullah easy to deal with, requiring only a show of subservience at least until he had returned home to the desert. Putting on his practiced expression for accomplishing favour with Sheikh Abdullah, or any of the other emirs and crown princes of the FNAE, the seasoned diplomat responded, "Certainly, Highness. When the ambassador returns on Wednesday, I will brief him immediately. Naturally, he will want to speak directly to his old Oxford friend, the British foreign secretary. Do not be concerned Highness, all will be well." The man sitting quietly in the corner was unnoticed as he grimaced at his elder brother's typical lecture and the attaché's smoothly worded reply. His Highness Prince Sheikh Salim bin Rashid Al Nu'masiq was of a different temperament to his crown prince brother.

Abdullah visited London infrequently, exercising authority with an assurance of gaining his own way in all matters, be they military, economic or personal. His reputation caused shudders in many quarters, although sometimes with concealed smiles, as with certain ladies of availability who managed to suppress their reactions whilst accepting expensive gifts offered lavishly for their private services.

In contrast, Sheikh Salim had lived and studied for several years in London and preferred its openness and opportunities for meeting with people from the whole world, rather than the preserved aloofness and authority of Middle-Eastern life. Abdullah showed his disdain for Salim's apparent passiveness, "Come, younger brother, give us your 'locally-based' wisdom on this matter."

Salim ignored Abdullah's habitual contempt and replied, "His Highness is far above my own level of knowledge on military purchases. May your bargaining power be demonstrated with success." The attaché thought the quietly-natured Sheikh Salim to be of no consequence, as a lesser son destined to play no part in the FNAE's affairs, relegated to go through life as an unimportant member of the ruling family. Whilst Abdullah had been schooled in military might, Salim had opted for degrees in oil technology at Imperial College and Business Development at the London School of Economics. Their father, as the emir of seventeen years' standing, clearly approved this differential, wanting the future emir to be equipped for ruler-ship, whilst lesser sons could be schooled in subjects useful to a kingdom dependent on rich oil deposits and how to make the most of them. Whilst in London, Sheikh Salim had developed a love for things of natural beauty rather than for money and power. He considered the complicated design of a guided missile to be immensely inferior to that of a fragile flower that grew silently upward, hosting the future display of its glorious colours and perfume before regenerating itself without any need for man's heavy-handed help. Salim relished the peace of Kew Gardens, in which he loved to stroll, far from the pressure of needing to succeed like Abdullah. As a younger son, he accepted his purely reserve role in life, leaving it to elder brothers to play their proper part in the monarchy, politics and military aspects of their father's kingdom. This was one of the five ancient desert monarchies that had chosen not to join the United Arab Emirates, but instead had established the FNAE in the vast wastelands beyond the UAE in what was known as 'The Empty Quarter'. Salim's father, HRH Emir Sheikh Rashid bin Hamad Al Nu'masiq was respected for his evident wisdom and tact within the agglomeration of naturally aggressive Arab sheikdoms, being recognised as the wise leader of the council of the five emirs. He managed to steer the FNAE diplomatically through the frequently torpid currents of Middle Eastern life, but had as yet been unable to demonstrate that the FNAE could be a meaningful player within global politics.

Salim sighed to himself at the irrational and iron thoughts of his brother Abdullah and so many of the world's leaders. How could such single-minded political or religious advocates from the world's various faiths expound that 'might is right'? Why should their own 'rightness' necessitate all others to be 'wrong', even to the extent of using indoctrinated zeal to murder, mutilate, rape and terrorise persons of a different faith or culture, claiming its actions to be '*In God's name!*'? Salim tore his mind away from these troubling thoughts and silently thanked his maker for the peace that enveloped his own life, as Abdullah arrogantly gave his irrelevant younger brother the haughty instruction: "On Tuesday morning at 10-45 you will escort me to the shop in Hatton Garden of those abominable Jewish brothers, Klein, a name well-warranted for their small activities for us! Maybe your knowledge of floral design will assist my choice of jewels for my favourite wives!"

***

Lord Henry Walsham gently stroked Christine's long blonde hair, bending from his ample height to whisper in her ear. Struggling not to lose control of her emotions, Christine Templeton clung onto her notebook and pen, but could not stop herself from turning her face towards her beloved fiancé. She responded to his kiss and the gentle pressure of his arms. The notebook slipped from her grasp, as she decided to postpone her writing and murmured, "Oh Henry, how can such a simple shop-girl like me be so blessed to be loved by such a handsome and wonderful man?"

He replied with typical good humour, "Well, darling, you do actually own the shop and employ the staff! How often I thank my Aunt Matilda for falling so suddenly ill with food poisoning!" Henry relaxed his body and smiled so tenderly at his treasure. "I too thank God that Aunt Matilda succumbed. We'll never forget that momentous day darling! If you hadn't accepted your mother's urgent plea for a companion, we would never have met! But how my heart and mind went into turmoil, as I noticed such a distinguished stranger sitting amongst the rag-trade connoisseurs. Who could he be, and why was he staring so intently at me?"

"All I did was accompany Mother to avoid spoiling her evening. She relished your invitation and so looked forward to seeing some modern designs, and maybe to purchasing a less boring dress or two. How was I to know that a creature immeasurably more beautiful than her creations would be there, sitting in the shadows beyond an endless stream of haughty models pouting at the audience as they paraded their scraps of far too expensive clothing! But she… she turned my legs to water and set my heart on fire, never to be extinguished my love!" The cherished memories led them further away from Christine's note-book and intentions, as they kissed again and again, so contentedly happy and so very much in love. "Now Henry," said Christine, attempting a serious voice. "We simply must agree tonight on the guest list and our prayers; our wedding day is only two months away and you really can't invite the whole British aristocracy! We've agreed on two hundred guests and my meagre gang in suits can't be smothered by yours in ermine robes!"

Henry smiled, "OK, sweetheart, I'll reduce my clientele to a hundred, if you can rustle up the other half."

Christine responded, "But, Darling, I don't even know a hundred people! You stick at a hundred and twenty and I'll do my best to rustle up another eighty." Henry beamed.

"Agreed! and maybe your Amazonian cheer-leader, Susan, will go down with jungle fever, or at least such a sore throat that she can't use her foghorn voice, then it would be seventy-nine!" Christine ignored Henry's comments about her flat-mate, who she knew irritated him on sight a mile away, and continued,

"Now we need to look at our marriage prayer again, because you've just not taking this seriously."

Henry attempted in vain to kiss his determined fiancée, "Well darling, what's so wrong with the good old Book of Common Prayer. It's lasted pretty well for the last few centuries."

Pushing him away, Christine responded, "Exactly Henry! It's so antiquated and boring! We need to inject some life amongst the Shakespearean recitations of the clergy. You know how hard I've tried to find some words that will please them, as well as our Heavenly Father. Let's look at it again my love."

Henry's sweetest smile and surrounding arms reduced Christine's firm resolve to settle this long-running issue, but eventually they realised that their Sunday evening was drawing to a close. "Look, darling," negotiated Christine. "I'll have another look at what I've written out, and bring it with me on Tuesday, as long as you absolutely promise to study it after we finish at the Kleins."

Henry beamed in satisfaction, "Wonderful, my adorable wife- to-be!"

They left Eaton Place at 8.30pm to walk the short distance from Henry's town house to the tube. "I know that you don't like me travelling on the underground as late as this, but I'll be perfectly safe and it's not really very far to Hampstead.

Henry replied, "Well it's not for much longer darling until you'll be safely enthroned as mistress of my Belgravia home."

Christine pouted theatrically, "Excuse me your lordship, but it's only as your wife, and certainly not your mistress, that I've eventually agreed to move into your rented castle!" They agreed once again their arrangements to meet at Klein's Jewellers in Hatton Garden at 11 am sharp on Tuesday, to buy their wedding rings, and then kissed each other 'Goodnight'.

***

"But Uncle Aaron, E X E P T I O N is not how to spell 'exception'! Just because you haven't got a C you can't change the spelling!" Aaron Klein put on an especially disappointed face for his one and only niece.

"OK Ruth, you know that my spelling is not as accurate your mum and dad's. I'm very pleased that you are gradually coming up to their high standards!" Reuben, the elder of the two Klein brothers, with Naomi his wife of twenty years, took little interest in such time-absorbing pursuits as board games. For them, their entire married life had focussed on continuing Reuben's father's well-established jewellery business.

Their family and working lives had been interwoven and aimed solely at this. It was clearly their intention that seventeen-year-old Ruth and her fifteen-year-old brother, Isaac, would be educated and trained only in those particular subjects and interests that nurtured the business. As the Jewish matriarch, Naomi had trained her children to respect and obey their father in all things, including his barely concealed plans for their children.

Aaron, who at thirty-nine years of age was three years junior to his only brother, could see that a storm was slowly developing on the supposedly tranquil family sea. Whilst the rapidly maturing Ruth had a demure and pleasant nature, happy to defer most matters to her parents; the same was obviously not true of young Isaac. Something of his paternal grandfather, Abraham, showed in his intensely independent and forthright nature. These traits had greatly helped war-time Jewish refugees from central Europe, who had worked from dawn to dusk to carve out a niche in the already established Hatton Garden jewellery empire, placing it at the head of the world's love of rare and valuable trinkets. Not surprisingly, Abraham and his wife, Ruth, had died too early, in middle age, but not before they had made 'Kleins' into one of the most respected and trusted jewellers in 'The Garden'. The elder son, Reuben, was destined to continue Abraham's role, but somehow, he lacked the assertiveness and direction of his father's character. This had caused the present generation of Kleins to become 'settled', more interested in percentage successes than taking risks. Although this way of life satisfied Reuben and Naomi, it clearly presented difficulties to Aaron as the obviously 'lesser' of the two business partners. 'Just what was his life all about?' was his constantly repeated question. The same was true of Isaac, with the additional problem that he was developing the volcanic strategy of increasing energy 'below ground' in preparation for a future dramatic, and maybe devastating, outburst.

The lovely Ruth had managed to sail through her childhood in the manner expected of a Jewish maiden, whilst she had been quietly developing her own thoughts on life. Uncle Aaron was her soul-mate. They loved each other's company and shared preferences on most daily aspects of life. Together, they explored the adventures and possibilities of the current and the future, but predominantly in the safety of observing, reading and playing games, which gentle interests provided an outlet for what otherwise could have become rather restricted lives. Aaron appreciated that his wonderfully happy relationship with his adorable and adoring niece could not continue for very much longer. Ruth's physical beauty, mental abilities and emotional charms were bound to conquer some aspiring 'Joshua' or Caleb' of Biblical heroism. He knew that then she would ably devise a gracious method of moving her affections from her beloved uncle to those of the future man of her life, but for now Aaron and Ruth relished their relationship which knew no enemies, had no competitors, hurt nobody else and rested in perfect contentment. Promptly, at 9.00pm, Aaron made his accustomed exit from the Klein's family home above the shop to make the ten minutes' walk to his own comfortable bachelor flat, which eminently suited his gentle nature and love of independence, whilst fitting in to the wider Klein family business, where his was unmistakably the junior role.

***

As soon as Christine had reached home and hung up her coat, Susan Bambridge expostulated her own version of religious zeal in a typical encounter with her landlady and flatmate, "But Chris, you are choosing to ignore one of the Bible's primary instructions: 'Do not be yoked to an unbeliever'. Surely, you must know that your lord and master Henry Walsham will stamp his size twelve aristocratic boots all over your faith in Jesus Christ. He'll act out the dignified religious noble to defend the British heritage of sitting in his own paid-up wooden pew! He'll claim to be a 'pillar of the church' but all he'll do is block the view of anyone looking for Jesus…"

Christine stopped her friend, "No! You can't describe the man I love, and who loves me, in such a tyrannical role! Henry believes assuredly in God and once we are married, he'll grow into a deeper relationship with Jesus."

Susan broke in, "Oh Chris, I wish that could be true, but the evangelical church is full of disillusioned wives who trusted in their own ability to convert their husbands, who demand obedience to the only scripture they can quote: *'Wives must submit to their husbands!'*"

Christine remained calm, replying softly, "It's not in my own ability that I trust, Susan, but in the power of the Holy Spirit and the blood of Jesus. God will never let me down."

Her flatmate took a breath and continued her diatribe unabated, "You really must watch out Christine: most high-Ccurch Anglicans are no better than Catholics, with their bells and smells, statues and fancy-dress clothes! They're just as wrong as all those Mohammedans! And another thing, Christine: why can't you and Henry buy your wedding rings from a respectable English jewellers instead of lining the pockets of those Jews who rejected God's Son?"

Susan stood up, "Steady on Susan or you'll burst one of your Anglo-Saxon blood vessels, be rushed off to hospital by an African ambulance driver and his eastern European nurse, treated by an Indian doctor, given a blood transfusion donated by an assured atheist, and put in a ward with a Hindu, two New Agers and a JW! Now be a good girl and climb down off your religious high horse, please."

Susan calmed down a little, "I'm sorry Chris. You're such a nice girl and I just don't want to see you make such a big mistake, after all there are plenty of other fish in…"

Christine cut through her friend's unbridled intolerance, "Goodnight Susan, that's enough for tonight. I'm going to bed!"

***

Aaron Klein often made a small detour on Sunday evenings to visit his friend Julian Steinburg, rather a flamboyant man with very independent and unusual ways, who was frequently away from his flat on some business or other. Julian was in his mid-thirties, hailed from a rich New York Jewish family, and was quite well known as a resident of 'The Garden' although his actual occupation and situation was not at all clear to most people. Some thought that he represented his father's business interests in London, whilst others believed him to be the black sheep of the family and thereby exiled from the New York scene. His habit of parking his current expensive car outside his flat was disliked by his less-affluent neighbours who possessed more business-like cars. Tonight, Julian was at home and welcomed Aaron into his expensively furnished flat where the atmosphere was so different from that in the Klein's family home. The air temperature was several degrees warmer and Bruckner's Symphony No. 4 was playing a little too loudly on the stereo. Aaron sunk into a commodious armchair and accepted the proffered glass of wine, noticing that Julian was wearing casual but expensive clothes that he had not seen before. The two friends settled immediately into their Sunday evening routine, whenever he was at home, sharing their love of classical music and chess. Aaron had not collected the luxuries that Julian loved to indulge in, such as the antique gold carriage clock adorning the mantle-piece. "Aha!" beamed Julian, "it didn't take you long to spot my new acquisition!"

Aaron smiled. "Well, your glossy objets-d'art are never difficult to notice! Where do you get such things? They look far too expensive for the Portobello Road market. Have you been abroad yet again?"

Julian grinned, "Well, I did pop over the Channel on a little business a few days ago." The friends' Jewish bonds were strong enough, but were not exercised in the same way. Although non-restrictive Jewish practices were part of each of their daily lives, they had long-ago agreed to differ on stronger points of religious theory and practice. Aaron was in no way a weak-minded man, but he kept his religious thoughts and actions mainly to himself, whereas Julian was far louder in his assertions. He was a devoted exponent of Jewish superiority, as the one and only chosen race, being the single object of choice and pleasure for the God of the patriarchs Abraham, Isaac and Jacob. Julian's Jewish fervour included his openly-declared dislike and distrust of Christians and Muslims, such that his acquaintances assumed religious zeal to be the major factor in Julian's otherwise carefully hidden life, of which they had no accurate knowledge whatsoever.

CHAPTER 2

The six persons who had gathered in Klein's Jewellers at 11 o'clock on Tuesday 24th April were each intent on their own thoughts and actions, whilst also being observant of each other. Christine Templeton was supremely happy that Lord Henry Walsham loved her so very much. She was perfectly content and ready to enter into life-long marriage with this good and honourable man, despite her friend Susan's misgivings concerning Henry's less outward-going faith. She had no deep thoughts about the two Klein business partner brothers, other than being pleased with their professionalism and honesty as jewellers and appreciative of their discretion when dealing with rich customers who were in the public's eye. Christine observed that the senior partner Reuben Klein had an inappropriately serious and boring nature for such a front-of-house job, whereas the junior partner Aaron Klein had a rather more alluringly hidden nature, currently more interesting due to his close proximity to her just across the shop counter. She noted that Reuben was beyond Henry to her right-hand side, deep in conversation with the clearly senior of the two Arab sheikhs. Although they were hidden from her view, their voices disclosed the business of purchasing expensive jewels, which Christine assumed were destined for his several wives and lovers. The second sheikh was an enigma, keeping to himself to the far left of her, apparently absorbed in less-valuable yet more picturesque items of jewellery. Among those particular displays, Christine thought that she had spotted some rather small but appealing tie-pins, which could furnish an attractive present for Henry's birthday next month, just a few weeks before their marriage, which remembrance enabled her to refocus her duty on assisting Henry to choose their wedding rings.

Henry was concentrating on the wide selection of wedding rings displayed before himself and his wonderful wife-to-be. It was not many months since he had amazed himself by secretly purchasing the engagement ring, that he had then proffered to Christine as an ardent demonstration of his deep love for her whilst kneeling ardently and proposing marriage to this love-of-his-life. It was her delight in the engagement ring that had led them to this return visit to the Kleins, now to select tokens of love and fidelity very conscientiously, suitable to endorse his firm decision to make this attractive and vibrant young woman his beloved wife and mother to their offspring. Henry approved of Aaron Klein's polite demeanour in standing back just a little way behind the shop counter, thus allowing his fiancée and himself the privacy to make their own choices. Henry had no taste for the assertive sheikh standing to his right engaged in significant purchases of diamonds, gauging that the Arab's blinkered arrogance would not be an economic match for the senior Jew, who was clearly accustomed to negotiating suitably intensified prices with rather difficult but very wealthy men. Henry dismissed the other Arab sheikh as in all probability being a rich dilettante of no real consequence in life.

Reuben Klein was indeed concentrating on achieving amplified success in the ageless eastern manner of bartering with such as Sheikh Abdullah. He was acting a subservient role in the negotiations, diplomatically leading this unholy crown prince to believe himself to be the victor against himself; yet, he recognised the Jew to be an antagonist worthy of further trade.

Reuben needed to ensure that Klein's Jewellers could look forward confidently to lucrative business, once the current emir had handed over his batten posthumously to this exceptionally nasty Sheikh Abdullah. The Arab appeared to be interested in considering only the most expensive items in their stock, thus Reuben concentrated on elevating the sale prices without regard for the onward locations of navels, noses and ears residing in a cosseted harem, or bored European ladies of easy acquaintance. Reuben saw no value in diluting his attention to the curious behaviour of the less-important Arab, who appeared to be perfectly happy to scrutinise less-expensive but pretty jewels on display to the far left of their shop.

Aaron was genuinely pleased to give discreet help to the business-like Lord Walsham and his fiancée, standing so close together across the counter from himself. He had no need or desire to push or persuade this so-obviously happy couple, who were considering marriage tokens that would give them joy for the rest of their lives. He was pleased for them as they stood at the threshold of married life, without the sordidness of the Arabian system, or the antiquated method of parental choice followed in his own Jewish faith's culture. He realised that it was now very many years since his independence of thought had confined him to bachelorhood, rather than a marriage of convenience not of his own choosing. So be it he told himself philosophically, with only a very little regret caused by the beauty of the lady standing so close to him physically, whilst being a million miles from his situation, opportunities and faith. Forcing his attention to less personal considerations, Aaron had only mild puzzlement that the lesser sheikh, standing alone to his right, should be so content in inspecting gems of smaller value than most Arabs that had visited the shop.

His Royal Highness Sheikh Abdullah bin Hamad Al Nu'masiq was absolutely certain of his own prowess to defeat the accursed Jew, Reuben Klein, who appeared not to be negotiating at all, but passively acquiescing to his own proposals. The sheikh's proud self-conceit and total intolerance would never recognise that Jewish jewellers had achieved centuries of success against more obvious contenders for supremacy whilst themselves appearing, erroneously, to be vastly inferior. He could not see the junior but equally despised Jew, standing servant-like behind the shop counter, across from the pompous and outdated infidel and his woman in the centre of the shop. Sheikh Abdullah's interest in the woman was slight, falling into his category of 'not for now but maybe later', assuming naturally that sufficient persuasion would succeed in attracting yet another into his perfumed web of conquest. He ignored his younger brother who stood idly to the far left of the shop, apparently looking incongruously at cheap trinkets.

Abdullah relished the time, which might not be far ahead, when he could dispense permanently with Salim's passivity and worthlessness from his own emirate's court circle.

Uninterested in his elder brother's personal views about himself, Sheikh Salim remained disgusted and embarrassed with Abdullah's unhidden behaviour, so hideously different to the respected diplomacy shown by their father the emir. Salim expected that the senior, rather austere, Klein brother would easily outmatch Abdullah, whilst the younger Klein seemed less officious and more to his liking, appearing to be calm and discrete although probably just as effective in business as his elder brother. The tall military-looking man in the centre of the shop looked rather dull in comparison to the visible vitality and beauty of the young woman, who must be very happily attracted by his hidden virtues.

***

As the unknowingly designated time steadily and quietly approached ten minutes past eleven o'clock on Tuesday 24th April, the entrance door to Klein's Jeweller's shop in Hatton Garden opened and a young man stepped inside. He looked around furtively, registering amazement and confusion that two Arab sheikhs were there, one to his left and one to his right-hand-side, before he resolutely took three further paces forward to stand immediately behind the tall militarily looking man at the shop counter. An unsteady voice came hoarsely from his dry throat, speaking out his so often practised words, *"Death to all Jews and Christians."* Christine Templeton had turned her head when the shop bell tinkled, watching the person enter and approach to be standing exactly behind Henry and herself.

The young man's words galvanised her into spontaneous action, "NO!" she shrieked at the top of her voice, flinging out her left hand at the man's face. His absolute surprise at this well-dressed woman's violent reaction confused him momentarily, such that the additionally intended words in praise of Allah were forgotten, as his shaking hand reached inside his jacket.

When a powerful bomb is detonated, all normality disappears in a moment of time, relegating the normal use of a person's intelligence and the body's built-in response systems into obscurity. Klein's jewellery shop and the people inside it were transformed in such an instant: sight was lost as the immense pressure of exploding air forced eyelids closed and seeing was replaced by hearing, smell and touch. Concentrations of unnatural sounds formed a hideous cacophony as the explosive air shot-blasted everything in its relentless path, intermixing with the orchestral percussion of unknown objects crashing into and through each other. Rudely intruded senses knew that gentility had ceased to exist as a total lack of understanding, incomprehensible feelings and raucous noises were registered collectively as the actuality of awful crashing, hitting, smashing and destroying was taking place. Speech never could begin as smells and tastes from choking air produced a combined inundation similar to that of being caught underwater by a miscalculated surging wave on the beach. This was an environment in which senses failed without attempting to operate. Pain was not accentuated, becoming lost in the complexities of never-before experiences. There was a purely passive realisation that objects and an atmosphere of undeclared things were inundating whatever was 'you', as pieces of shop counters, shelves and fittings, mingled with body parts, exotic jewels, hot blood and weapons of glass destroyed all what was before. Disbelief was smothered by acceptance of something far above yourself, as reaction failed to exist. Unbelief in its happening did not occur, because it was. Amongst the total chaos of a shop and people being blown and smashed to pieces, all minds, hearts and bodies that remained unconquered by death, simply received the information that devastation had occurred. It was an ending, a closing down. Life finished, or gave way to something else. All else stopped.

***

Since Britain's biggest ever robbery in April 2015, there had been many changes at Scotland Yard, the headquarters of the Metropolitan Police and the most well-known and respected police HQ in the world. They had been very embarrassed that a gang of old-aged-pensioners had decided on, planned and carried out their audacious crime only a mile and a half away. The geriatric robbers had spent that Easter weekend drilling through an enormously thick concrete wall, to gain undisturbed entry to the stronghold of London's Hatton Garden diamond Bourse, from which they had calmly robbed scores of safe deposit boxes containing jewels valued in many millions of pounds. Subsequently a host of technical security measures had been installed throughout the hundred and more jewellery shops in 'The Garden' one of which was a type of detector that registered the speed of air movement in front of it. Hence, with these detectors linked to local police centres, immediate notice of unusually dramatic air movement was sent directly to the Metropolitan Police's Bomb Squad's Chief Officer at Scotland Yard. Inspector Alan Harling's office was surprisingly small, sparsely furnished and laid out in the characteristic way of its occupant, with everything in its proper place, without any superfluous trappings or a hint of attractiveness. The cabinets, drawers and files were labelled and cross-referenced systematically and his desk was uncluttered, baring only its essential items. An alarm on the sophisticated communications switchboard, which was his immediate command and control aid, grabbed his instant attention 'EXPLOSION AT 57B HATTON GARDEN'. He flicked a switch, "Harling to teams A, B, C and D. Explosion at 57B Hatton Garden. Teams B and C to scene, liaise immediately with local services. Team D establish base control here. Team A prepare to take me to scene in thirty seconds."

The four current duty officers of his Bomb Squad's teams responded with an immediate, "Yes, Sir!" Harling alerted his boss Chief Superintendent George Price then grabbed his briefcase and marched outside where Team A's Sergeant Dent held the car's door open for him whilst reporting that Station Officer Smithson of London's Fire Service and Station Commander Browning of the Metropolis's Ambulance Service had been informed.

It took barely three minutes for the car to scream along The Strand, up Fetter Lane, cross Holborn Circus and enter Hatton Garden. Quickly becoming aware of the scale of the explosion, Harling gave his first orders, "Dent, tell the local boys to move public segregation out to a hundred metre radius."

As they jumped out opposite what had been the shop window of Klein's Jewellers, the lead officer from the first fire engine to have arrived ran to Harling, "No smell of gas, Sir. Looks like a bomb. Fire at ground and first floors only. Hoses in play. Adjacent properties being evacuated. Smoke too dense for ambulance boys. My chaps with breathing gear are inside now." Further ambulances and fire engines were arriving and preparing for action. A young fireman emerged clasping a person who was immediately shrouded in blankets. Harling registered that the first survivor had been brought out and shepherded to the nearest ambulance, followed within seconds by another being half dragged and half carried by an older fireman. He was bleeding freely from what looked like upper body wounds, but his legs were working. Harling put him down as in his forties and a good possibility to be interviewed after hospital admittance.

Another fire service officer emerged from the shop and spotted Harling, "Need more help, Sir. Woman inside is very bad but alive. Three or four others look dead."

The inspector called sergeants Foster and Baines of his Teams B and C to him. "Foster, deploy local boys behind building. Fire chief has sent an appliance round. Report on situation. Baines, we're going to need an incident base. Spread your boys out to the nearest suitable premises, maybe a café or similar. Ask the managers firmly but gently!" Three firemen emerged with a stretcher, on which was a smashed shape, possibly a woman. It was taken to the next ambulance as Chief Superintendent Price approached Harling's shoulder. "Looks like you're in control Harling. Need any help?" The Inspector reported that there were at least three survivors, each of whom was now on their way to UCLH on the Euston Road. The University College London Hospital was the closest and one of the best prepared hospitals kept in constant readiness for receiving emergencies, as evidenced by the habitual noise of sirens to be heard around the Tottenham Court Road, Gower Street and St. Pancras areas.

"I'll set up a local incident room ASAP, Sir. Request you tell the media to await its location and send my Sergeant Atkinson with his Team D to man it, complete with full communications set up, Sir."

Price responded, "OK Harling. I'll handle the press for now and deal upwards through Associate Commissioner Williams with politicians."

Inspector Harling turned quickly from his boss to hear his eager

Sergeant Baines, "There's a possible place forty metres south, Sir. Owner looks co-operative."

Harling turned, "Good work, take me to him straight-away." The two officers walked quickly from the devastated shop to a restaurant on the opposite side of the street. "Morning, Sir," said Harling to a middle-aged man of middle-eastern origin standing in his restaurant doorway. "It's been a very serious event here, Sir. I need to set up a suitable incident centre for liaising with emergency services, local people, the press and visitors. Could your premises be freed up for me, say for the next two weeks or so, Sir? All loss of revenue will be covered by the police."

The restaurateur responded immediately, "Well Sir, Klein's are a decent firm who've been here much longer than me. I'll be pleased to help them out a bit."

Harling shook his hand, "Thank you very much, Sir. Sergeant Baines will agree details with you for immediate occupancy and establishment of a temporary HQ. Scotland Yard will reimburse all costs and be as thankful as possible."

Inspector Harling returned quickly to the pavement outside the Klein's shop, where Sergeant Foster reported, "The rear entrance to the shop's all clear, Sir. There were four persons, all staff of the Kleins gathered there, very shocked and dazed, but with only superficial injuries. I've got their names. Ambulance boys are giving them a preliminary check before they're taken to UCLH."

Harling was pleased, "OK Foster, I'll check first with the fire chief that the building is not in further danger, then I'm going to UCLH to interview casualties being brought in. We'll need to find out quickly what happened here. Stay right outside the shop and report straight to me about anything that's discovered by the fire boys. Don't let any local police or other persons inside except for emergencies. Get plenty of photos taken of absolutely everything in there, from all directions, right?"

The sergeant answered, "Yes, Sir. The air's very clouded, but I've taken a few chance photos already. You can see a few bodies plus a lot of smaller items, human and otherwise, Sir."

Harling grimaced, "Thanks Foster, stay with it." Harling walked over to Station Officer Smithson of the Fire Service. "What's the situation now John?"

Smithson gave his colleague a résumé, "All live casualties have been removed from the shop and the rear of the building. The fire is largely extinguished on ground and first floors and there's no sign of it progressing seriously upward. The local council's structural engineer is waiting over there for permission to enter and assess the situation."

Inspector Harling signalled to Constable Chapman from his Team A, "Take the engineer inside and stay with him. You've got two minutes maximum for a first structural look. A detailed survey can follow, OK?"

The engineer nodded his understanding and turned to begin his check. Station Commander Browning of the Metropolis's Ambulance Service approached the inspector, "I'm ready to get the bodies removed, if you've finished taking photographs, Harling."

The inspector hesitated, "Thanks Percy, but please wait a moment. Let's you, me and John Smithson make our own quick inspection before anything else changes."

The three emergency services colleagues climbed over the debris outside the missing front windows and into what had been an attractive shop. Inside the chaotic mess of rubble, it was hard to identify anything. They looked from left front to rear right, systematically searching for anything large enough to be of interest. The floor was completely littered with smashed and filthy items, making it impossible to identify any difference between worthless fragments of the shop structure, furnishings, priceless jewels, glass and body parts. Back outside on the pavement again, they drew in fresh air and quickly agreed the next steps, "OK chaps. As soon as my boys have taken enough photos, will John please have all the intact bodies removed first, then the larger identifiable parts, with absolutely all items being put in bin bags with one of my men recording its location in the shop. Percy, please get the bodies, limbs and bigger parts taken to UCLH for identification. Thanks."

The council's engineer approached the inspector, looking very haggard, "The shop's inside rear wall has partially collapsed and it's not entirely load-bearing. The ceiling is mostly intact, apart from a central hole about two metres diameter. The shop's side walls are OK, so there should be no danger to adjacent properties. My main fear is the danger of the first-floor rooms collapsing down into the shop. I'd like to get my council staff to set up some Acrow props to make sure nothing else collapses. No-one must go into the rooms above the shop until that has been done."

Inspector Harling thanked him, "Now, please wait for Sergeant Foster here to give you and your chaps permission to go in and hold up the ceiling. Foster, once the bodies have been removed, let the council chaps in but nothing — and I mean nothing! — must be removed until I get back here from the hospital."

Noddy Foster replied, "Understood Sir!" whilst the engineer went very quickly a few yards away to vomit out some of the horror that he had just witnessed.

Sergeant Walter Baines approached Harling, "Sir, that Arab guy has been extra helpful. He's had his staff empty the restaurant's whole dining room, and move everything possible into rear kitchens and store rooms. Sergeant Atkinson's team has started to arrive. Shall we arrange the room as a type 'Circus' incident room?"

Harling admired his well-trained teams, "Yes, Baines, well done. I'm off to UCLH, but I'll be back within an hour."

***

Inspector Harling and Sergeant Dent were taken through UCLH's A & E rear entrance and escorted straight upstairs to meet the duty registrar, Pawel Jemielity. They shook hands as he explained the situation, "Well Inspector, it's early days of course and others may be brought in, but for now we've received fourteen persons from the Hatton Street incident. Seven of them have nothing seriously wrong, so I've arranged for all of them to wait in one of our meeting rooms, rather than in a public reception area, thinking that you might want to interview them. There were two recognisable bodies plus an assortment of limbs and body parts from two more fatalities, all of which have been put in the morgue ready for investigation. The remaining three persons are serious admissions: an Arab with mostly facial injuries but nothing else obviously wrong externally, a second man with head and upper body injuries and probably broken bones, and a youngish woman in quite a bad state. She's in intensive care and will clearly need a lot of help from Doctor Chaudhary and his team. She's got very nasty head and other injuries and I don't think that she'll be able to talk for many days. She may deteriorate fast, if her internal injuries are more serious than we're guessing now. She may not survive, Inspector. You can speak to the walking wounded as soon as you like, and to the two injured men as long as a doctor or nurse is in attendance please."

Harling appreciated the registrar's efficiency, "Thanks very much for organising things so well, Doctor. I'd like to call in at the group in your meeting room and leave Sergeant Dent with them, while I go straight to see the two male casualties."

The registrar agreed then added, "Certainly Inspector, but please understand that I've given you an entirely unofficial first assessment, just to help you with your investigation. All persons exposed to explosions tend to be seriously affected, mentally as well as physically. Although you might not see significant injuries, explosive effects on internal organs and systems are extremely variable and latent injuries may come into play only after the first round of shock has dissipated."

Inspector Harling spoke briefly to the group of seven waiting together, before leaving Dent to begin gathering statements from them. The two badly-injured men were in separate rooms, remaining under constant observation until a detailed assessment could be made. Doctor Jemielity led Inspector Harling down a corridor and knocked briefly at a door before entering. A nurse stood up and gave the doctor a short report, "The patient is quite calm, though very puzzled about something doctor. He's been talking to himself a bit, but doesn't appear to be alarmed."

The doctor thanked her, adding, "The police inspector can have five minutes now. I will be back after checking on the other persons admitted."

The Inspector noted the Arab's typical 'explosion category four' situation of multiple lacerations and severe shock, "My name is Inspector Harling. Are you able to answer a few short questions please, Sir, to help my initial enquiries?"

The Arab stared at the policeman, nodded his assent and tried to force himself from a sort of dream. "You have been involved in an explosion, Sir, and I need to find out how that happened. Were you inside the jewellery shop?"

Harling waited for the quietly spoken reply to come, "Yes Inspector. I was looking at some jewellery."

The inspector continued, "Please can you describe what happened, as simply as possible?"

Sheikh Salim concentrated hard before speaking, "My brother was negotiating some purchases with one of the shop owners. It was not necessary for me to be involved, so I was on the opposite side of the shop, on my own. Will you tell me what has happened to my brother, Inspector? No-one here has told me."

Harling replied judiciously, "All persons brought here by ambulance are being assessed by the hospital's medical staff, Sir."

The Arab tried to sit up, "But look Inspector, I must know at least if he is dead or alive."

The nurse stretched out a restraining hand as Harling said, "I'm not yet certain, Sir. Please try to say what happened. Who else was in the shop?"

Sheikh Salim obeyed, "My brother and one Mr. Klein were on their own. The other Mr. Klein was behind his counter attending to a couple in the centre of the shop. All was peaceful until the first new person arrived. He came into the shop and stood still. He looked at my brother and myself and appeared confused."

The inspector wrote in his notebook then asked, "What did this man look like and what happened next?"

The Arab looked perplexed as he recalled the events of less than an hour before, "He was a young man with nothing special about him, until he stepped forwards and spoke."

The inspector warmed to his task, "What exactly did he say, Sir?"

The Sheikh remembered, "He didn't shout but simply spoke into the room, '*Death to all Jews and Christians*'."

Harling remained calm, "And what was the reaction inside the shop, Sir?"

Sheikh Salim recalled the terrifying scene, "Only one person moved and spoke. She was the only one who seemed to understand what was happening. She turned towards the young man, hit out at his face and shouted '*No!*' She was so courageous. She tried to knock him down! I couldn't see what he did and then another man ran in right between them.

Then everything was chaotic, an explosion I suppose. I think I fell backwards and passed out. The air smelt horrible and I couldn't see. The dreadful noises confused me. Then someone picked me up and carried me outside. What has happened to my brother, Inspector? He is a Crown Prince of the FNAE. I must know."

The door had just opened and Doctor Jemielity approached them to speak gently to the Arab, "I am sorry, Sir, that a man who was probably your brother was brought here by ambulance. He was not alive. I am very sorry."

Sheikh Salim acknowledged this information without emotion. "My commiserations, Sir," offered Inspector Harling, as he obeyed the doctor's signal and backed respectfully out of the room.

Doctor Jemielity led him to another room, "This one also is in shock and has more injuries to contend with than the Arab. Please keep it brief, Inspector."

The policeman began, "I'm sorry to trouble you, Sir. My name is Inspector Harling of the Metropolitan Police's Bomb Squad. I must ask you please to tell me what happened this morning."

The man who was arraigned with medical drips and appliances drew his thoughts together, "All was quiet until a man walked in who was clearly not a customer. He stood still, then walked towards me and said *'Death to Jews and Christians'*. Miss Templeton seemed to understand that he was a terrorist, but instead of trying to escape she turned to face him and hit out, shouting as she did so. She was heroic, but so was the man who ran in through the open door, right up to them both. Then the shop exploded. What has happened to my brother and Lord Walsham?"

The inspector answered gravely, "I'm sorry to inform you, Sir, that four persons are known to have died in the shop. Your brother may have been one of them. Excuse me, Sir, but are you quite sure that a second man entered the shop?"

Aaron Klein spoke clearly, "Absolutely sure, Inspector."

Harling thanked him and left the room very annoyed that these two otherwise-intelligent men, the Arab and the Jew, had both described seeing a second man rush into the shop. It was a very unwelcome co-incidence, caused by some trick of the light or something. He phoned Chief Superintendent Price, who was preparing to give a simple press statement, and was told to meet him in the Hatton Garden temporary incident room in half an hour.

**

His Highness Prince Salim's mind overcame his physical pains sufficiently to request that two phone calls be arranged shortly. First, he phoned the FNAE embassy and gave the news of the crown prince's death, asking that the ambassador be requested to wait for ten minutes before phoning the emir. Next Salim broke the news to his father, who responded in a stately manner, acknowledging the news without emotion or any comments about the changed monarchical situation and political repercussions. Doctor Jemielity now insisted that the sheikh rest and allow the medical staff to continue their attentions to him. The registrar was not surprised during the afternoon to receive concerning reports from doctors and nurses that the Arab prince was experiencing deteriorating reactions. That frequent response, with explosion victims who had appeared to be miraculously unaffected, was sufficient for Pawel Jemielity to command that Sheikh Salim be given peace.

It was soon confirmed that Aaron Klein had dislocated rather than broken both shoulders, also that his initial scans and X-rays revealed no ruptured organs or internal bleeding, despite his surface wounds looking so bad. That afternoon, a marked deterioration in his blood pressure, temperature and audio/visual responses was noted. He was experiencing constantly reverberating noises and very painful eyes, which symptoms were increasingly worrying him, as was seeing blood stained dressings being removed from his face, upper body and arms. He was becoming alarmed that Reuben's family would not know what had happened, as they had not been at home above the shop at the time and may yet be unaware? These concerns were increasing his blood pressure and anxiety, thus when Doctor Jemielity visited him again, he proposed that Inspector Harling be asked to handle the notification to his brother's wife.

Aaron accepted this advice and Inspector Harling delegated the task of locating Mrs Naomi Klein to advise her of her husband's death and brother-in-law's hospitalisation, to Sergeant Atkinson.

***

Inspector Harling thought hard as he was being driven back to Hatton Garden. It was typical for suicide bombers to act nervously before blowing themselves and their innocent victims to bits, but he had never heard of anyone trying to attack the bomber physically, making this young woman either downright foolish or exceptionally brave. But what about another person rushing up and trying to intervene? That was just ridiculous! "Dent, get onto the hospital morgue and check how many bodies they received: I mean intact persons or obvious heads, trunks and limbs." As he strode into the improvised incident room, he was delighted that Mr Kumai had volunteered so willingly to hand over his restaurant for police use, and he felt real pride in his teams' work during the last hour. Harling went once again to the site of the explosion, wanting to better understand the geography and likely movements of persons, now that the air was clearer, and realising the irony of Muslims being involved as perpetrators, victims, survivors and of giving assistance to the police. The emergency services colleagues conferred and agreed to leave only monitoring fire crews and two ambulances there. Thus satisfied, the inspector marched briskly back to join Chief Superintendent Price at the incident room, reflecting how his well-ordered mind was firmly in control: he had ascertained briefly what had happened at just after 11.00 on this otherwise normal Tuesday, that a young man had entered a smallish jeweller's shop, almost certainly under instructions, had reciting a short prepared message of hatred against Christians and Jews, then detonated his bomb jacket killing himself and three or four other persons and injuring some others. Now his duty was to investigate the perpetrators of this heinous crime and bring them to justice, discouraging further similar attacks of religious hatred.

He had ascertained that the jewellery shop was owned by a Jewish family named Klein, and that the only customers at the time of the incident appeared to have been an English couple and two Arabian men, one of whom was a crown prince of the Federation of Non-aligned Arab Emirates, whatever that mouthful might mean. His 'Copper's nose' smelled trouble with this Arab connection, but in fact it came from a different direction. When the business associates of Lord Henry

Walsham became tired of waiting any longer for him to arrive for his 11.45 meeting, they tried all usual ways to contact him in vain. His private secretary knew of his appointment at Klein jewellers and having heard on the radio of a suspected terrorist attack in that vicinity, she contacted the police. Once the worst had been learned, she passed the information to Henry's father, the Earl of Suffolk, who chose to bully the Met's commissioner by demanding her personal involvement rather than that of a mere inspector. It was as well that Alan Harling's ultra-professional reputation was well known from the bottom right to the top of the Met, with his nick-name 'AH', deriving from his initials, often producing a shudder among criminals and less-conscientious colleagues alike. Only out of courtesy had the commissioner decided to attend the press conference herself.

***

The converted restaurant was filling up with excited journalists, whilst the serious-looking police officers were mostly at the rear, with their chief superintendent and inspector sitting at the front behind a table, preparing themselves for what would obviously be a barrage of questions. Inspector Harling used the opportunity to make a proposal, "Sir, something as dramatic as an explosion in the middle of Hatton Garden can't have been unnoticed by the scores of CCTV cameras around the area. Would an official requisition of all films taken on all local CCTV systems this morning be valuable to our inquiries, Sir?"

Chief Superintendent Price pondered, "That would probably require a judicial involvement from a magistrate, which would be much more difficult than just asking for a specific search warrant. I'm not sure about it Harling, but I'll think about it after the press conference." The eager journalists and media technicians crowded together among the plethora of cameras, sound booms, microphones and lights, clearly like fox hounds scenting their quarry and creating an ugly scene for the polite and professional police officers wanting only to do their duty. The Chief Superintendent stood up, "Ladies and gentlemen of the press. Thank you for responding so quickly to the Metropolitan Police's invitation. The press conference will begin with a brief situation report by Inspector

Harling of the Bomb Squad, who is the officer in charge of the investigation."

The horde of cynical news men and women made no attempt to hide how callous, unfeeling and disrespectful they had become, seeing Harling as the proverbial 'Stag at Bay' in that well-known painting. Dozens of journalists leapt to their feet and screamed questions at him as he stood, stern-faced and inwardly disgusted at the melee in front of him, without a compassionate face or voice amongst them. His hatred of crime gave him a distaste for all criminals, yet these media piranhas yelling for his answers, sickened him more than many of the criminals that he knew. The cacophony of sound made his spoken statement very difficult to hear, contributing to the alarmingly obtuse reporting. Factual or otherwise, it sufficed to fill insatiable TV time-slots and newspaper pages with as much horror and excitement that producers, directors and editors could glean from their reporters. Chief Superintendent Price remained seated, a fact registered by the unrecognised lady sitting at the back. "Tell us how many are dead!" shouted out a reporter. "Who was the suicide bomber? What was the value of the jewels? Were they mostly diamonds? Have they all been destroyed? The public deserves to know how much they were worth! Tell us!"

Inspector Harling restrained his emotions, "The casualties known so far include four males who perished, including the perpetrator of the crime, three others were seriously injured; one of whom is in a life-threatening situation. A number of other persons sustained lighter injuries."

A heavily made- up TV journalist yelled out, "Just tell us who is dead, Inspector!"

Harling parried her with, "Until next of kin have been advised, Madam, I cannot give you the names of the deceased."

She screamed her response, "Oh, come on now! We know that an important Arab was killed and also a British aristocrat and one of the owners of the shop. All we need is their names! Tell us!"

Harling, looking in vain for his boss's approval, replied, "At this early stage of the enquiry we have reason to believe that Mr Reuben Klein, part owner of Klein's Jewellers died, along with His Highness Crown Prince Sheikh Abdullah bin Rashid Al Nu'masiq of the

Federation of Non-aligned Arab Emirates. We have reason to believe, but await confirmation, that the third fatality was Lord Henry Walsham, a son of the Earl of Suffolk." The room exploded with noise at this information, with journalists wetting their lips at the news that a royal prince of an Arab monarchy had been killed, which should make international news for several days, plus a British aristocrat which would keep domestic sales high for a week.

The inspector remained standing after giving the bare bones of what had happened and was determined to turn this cynical circus to his own professional ends, "It is vitally important for the people who planned this act of terrorism to be traced. Therefore, I appeal for all public and privately-operated CCTV film recordings made this morning in and around Hatton Garden to be handed in to my officers here immediately. All of us must work together to apprehend the criminals behind these dreadful murders. With your help we will succeed. Thank you."

Knowing that their editors craved only instantaneous news, the assembled news-hounds rushed outside to give their pavement interviews, passing the quiet non-uniformed lady sitting unnoticed. She approached the front table and held out her hand, "Well done, Inspector!"

He shook hands before saluting her, "Thank you, Commissioner."

Once the incident room had been cleared, Harling convened a meeting of his team leaders, "We're not waiting for any magistrate's approval, just send your officers to every shop in Hatton Garden, fanning out from the Klein's. I want all of today's CCTV films commandeered from them."

Sergeant Baines responded, "Would it be a good idea to include transport and council cameras as well, Sir? The bomber must have travelled here from somewhere and he may have been filmed at stations or on the streets."

Harling agreed, "Excellent idea Baines! Get onto the local council and set that up with them, and have a word with the British Transport Police to do the same. It will be an immense task to scrutinise hundreds of films, but it should be well worth it. I'll arrange for a team at the Yard to be prepared to start work as soon as you begin to collect films. Now let's get on with it!"

***

By mid-afternoon Inspector Harling was back at UCLH, relieved to be with people he respected instead of the aptly described gutter press. Doctor Jemielity introduced him to a middle-aged lady and two teenagers who were consoling each other. "Please accept my commiserations, Mrs. Klein. This is a dreadful business, but I am sure that your husband died instantly and without any knowledge of what was happening."

Naomi Klein stumbled out some thanks then asked, "May I see my husband's brother now?"

The hesitation shown by the doctor and policeman caused a violent reaction in her son Isaac, "You mean that as well as my dad being blown to bits by some evil madman, my uncle's dying too don't you! Why does Britain let these evil creatures in, to plot their religious murders against innocent British citizens?"

Isaac's sister Ruth intervened tactfully, "Please understand, Inspector, that our family is horrified at what has happened to Daddy. Please can you tell us what has happened to my Uncle Aaron?"

It was the doctor who replied, "Your uncle has significant facial and upper body lacerations and dislocated shoulders. He is now undergoing X-rays, scans and other tests to discover whether or not he has internal injuries as well."

The teenaged Ruth responded calmly, "When will those results be known please, Doctor?"

Jemielity replied, "If the family will wait in this room, we will do all that we can to let you see Mr. Klein for a brief visit, hopefully within the hour."

Mrs. Klein mumbled the family's thanks.

The inspector was introduced next to the surgeon and head of department, Doctor Shuban Chaudhary, who went with him to formally notify the FNAE's ambassador of the death of Crown Prince Abdullah. Ignoring the Indian doctor, the ambassador addressed Inspector Harling, "I demand to see the crown prince's body immediately and to be told the name of the murderer!"

The policeman's reply that the body could not be viewed was not accepted, "That is vital political information which I insist on being given."

Inspector Harling replied politely, "Please understand, Sir, that Prince Abdullah's body is not intact. You will be advised once the remains have been collected and assembled, if that proves possible. With regard to the person who committed this morning's murder, we are seeking further evidence as it is not possible to identify his or her remains."

The ambassador scowled, "Your government's foreign secretary and your police commissioner will be told of your ineptitude."

The inspector replied, "Thank you, Sir, if you have nothing more to assist my enquiries, I must attend to my duties. However, I note, Sir, that you have not inquired about the surviving Prince Salim?"

The ambassador snarled, "That is correct officer! He is of no political consequence!"

As the inspector stepped into the corridor, his WPC Taylor spoke. "Excuse me Sir, but there's a woman waiting in another room to see you… actually, she's not exactly 'waiting' Sir, more like bouncing off the walls! Her name is Ms Susan Bambridge, a flat-mate of the young woman injured at the shop, Sir."

Harling thanked her, knocked and entered the room. "Just you look here, Officer," grimaced the woman. "I will not be fobbed off any longer. If you have any authority, get me permission to visit my friend Christine Templeton!"

He breathed in and said, "Excuse me, Ms Bambridge, but I must ask you to calm down. Please remember that you are in a hospital and not a police station. Miss Templeton has been badly injured and the doctors will certainly not allow any visitors to see her for some time."

Susan Bambridge fumed and selected another track, "You police allow hordes of disgusting Muslim refugees to infiltrate our cities and now they've murdered an innocent Christian man who had chosen foolishly to go into a Jewish shop with Miss Templeton. You failed to prevent it and now you're cow-towing to yet more Muslims: I've seen you! Why don't you do something to protect us British Christians!"

The inspector ignored her rhetoric, "Please tell me what Miss Templeton was doing in Klein's jewellers this morning and why was Lord Walsham with her?"

The reply came with a snarl, "Can't you see even something as obvious as that officer? They were there to buy wedding rings, although God has at least saved her from that future!"

Monique Taylor, who had been recently married, stood shocked at the callousness of this so-called friend of the injured woman, whilst Inspector Harling turned to leave the room, "Excuse me, Miss, but I have important duties. This officer will escort you outside. Please leave your full contact details with her. Goodbye."

***

Doctor Chaudhary was aware that Inspector Harling needed to investigate the bombing and that there were only two witnesses available to him. He intimated that as long as no internal injuries were discovered, Sheikh Salim had had a remarkable escape, probably because his Arab clothing had swathed and protected his head and body. Thus, the inspector went again to speak with this least injured victim, gaining his permission to record their conversation, "Please will you describe the moments either side of the explosion, Sir?"

Salim's ears were being bombarded by a cacophony of noises, his whole body was hurting and tiredness was sapping his energy, yet he desired to help this policeman and the young woman who he realised had saved his life. "I remember clearly that my brother and the older Mr. Klein were deep in conversation on the customer's side of the counter on the far right of the shop. The English couple were in the centre with the younger Mr. Klein assisting them from behind his counter. I was on the extreme left of the shop on my own. I heard the shop door open and glanced round to see that a young man with light brown skin not unlike my own had come in. He hesitated just inside the door, looked briefly at my brother to his right, then stared directly at myself on his left. His face was very perturbed. He took two or three steps forward and stood just behind and a little to the right of the tall Englishman, who along with my brother and Mr. Klein took no notice of him. The English lady, who was on her friend's left side, turned sharply to look at the strange young man who was dressed and acting very unlike customers of jewellery shops."

Harling asked the Sheikh to describe the man as accurately as possible. "He was aged about twenty, not very tall, maybe 5'6", not very big, perhaps ten stone or so. He was dressed poorly and looked unhealthy and very unhappy. He had a slight growth of stubble, but no beard or moustache. He had a dark coloured, woollen hat over black straggly hair, a short black padded coat, which I believe ironically is known as a 'bomber jacket', and faded dark blue-black trousers, not jeans. He was totally nondescript excepting that he wore noticeably expensive white trainers."

Harling asked very carefully, "Where were the young man's hands, Sir, and was his coat undone?"

Sheikh Salim remembered, "He was holding his right hand, half in and half out of the top of his jacket, which was unzipped about halfway down."

The inspector asked innocently, "Was he the only other person to enter the shop, Sir?"

Sheikh Salim recounted the events, "The young man had entered the shop very deliberately and had not closed the door. I noticed nobody in the doorway. He spoke clearly enough, but without any zeal considering his text: '*Death to all Jews and Christians.*'"

Harling picked up on that, "What made you use the word 'text', Sir?"

The sheikh explained, "Because the man's speech was unnatural, like an actor reciting words carefully learned and rehearsed."

The inspector suggested that such dramatic words must have been noticed by everyone in the shop, but the Sheikh was becoming very tired, "Perhaps so, Inspector, but only the young lady seemed to comprehend the words and the situation. She alone acted with her mind and body, stepping half back and to her right to be behind her friend, punching out her left hand towards the intruder's face and calling out '*No!*'"

Harling slowed down his questions, "What was the young man's reaction and what happened next, Sir? Please be very careful as you answer."

Sheikh Salim was nearing exhaustion, "He became hidden from my view by the young lady, just before the other man strode quickly through the open doorway and pushed himself deliberately between the young man and the woman." Inspector Harling did not believe the Sheikh and decided to ask Doctor Chaudhary about victims of explosions experiencing hallucinations among otherwise well-remembered facts.

He knew that he was pushing the witness, but continued probing, "Please will you describe this second man, sir?"

The answer came without any hesitation, "Medium height and build, aged thirty to forty, pale skinned, wearing a short brown overcoat. He appeared to know exactly what he was doing."

The inspector picked up on that, "Please excuse me, Sir, but your words 'appeared to know' are of doubtful evidence to a police officer. It's not that I disbelieve your very factual and accurate descriptions, but the rather incredible nature of this event troubles me."

The sheikh responded, "I take no offense, Inspector. I am often astounded at the complexities of design in plants and flowers, which might appear incredible."

Knowing that his witness must not be over-taxed, Inspector Harling asked a final question, "Although your view was obscured, Sir, what can you tell me about the explosion?"

The sheikh answered resolutely, overcoming his weakness, "The young man's right hand was hidden unnaturally half-inside his jacket. Immediately after the second man's intervention, the explosion occurred. I assume that the young man had been holding some sort of detonating device which he activated, blowing himself up and taking out of this life my brother and two other persons at the least. I thank my God that the immensely courageous actions of the young English lady and the second man saved my own life."

Inspector Harling stood up and thanked him, "You have been through a dreadful ordeal today, Sir. Please may I enquire about your family's plans resulting from this tragedy?"

The sheikh fell back exhausted, "I have spoken on the telephone to my father, the emir of my country, and briefly to our ambassador in London. I must leave them to their own intentions, but I do not anticipate seeing either of them at present."

Harling thanked him again, wished him well, and left the room.

***

Although the Inspector had learned a lot from the Arab Sheikh, who was clearly an intelligent and truthful man, the bomb-blast must have given him an hallucination about a second man. Harling's best way to check this would be to speak again to the Jewish man, before those two men could collaborate. Doctor Chaudhary confirmed that Klein was of sound mind and that his injuries would require him to remain at UCLH for about a week. Aaron Klein accepted the inspector's intrusion into his room and agreed to him using a recording device, "I'll try to be as descriptive and exact in what happened Inspector: Miss Templeton arrived first at exactly 11 o'clock, followed almost immediately by the two Arabs. Lord Walsham joined his fiancée five minutes later and they began looking at the trays of wedding rings that I had prepared for them to consider.

"My brother and I had decided that I should stay with them, whilst he dealt with the more demanding Arabian customers. We'd sent our staff to their work rooms behind the shop, then deliberately spread out to enable privacy. Reuben was on the right of the shop with the Crown Prince but the Arab's brother was not involved in buying jewels for royal wives so had moved to the opposite side of the shop to view our displays of less expensive but particularly attractive jewellery. I didn't have much to do myself, as Lord Walsham and his fiancée were happy to talk over their choices of rings between themselves, thus I hung back behind the counter just close enough to respond to any questions that they might wish to raise." Aaron Klein rested, surprised at how much his shoulders, back and upper body hurt. His ears and eyes felt awful and he was alarmed at the surprising amount of blood disgorging onto his dressings. Yet, he wanted to keep his mind active and was eager to answer the inspector's questions, "At about ten minutes past eleven, the shop door opened and a man came in, looking and acting very unlike a customer. He was only young — maybe late teenage or early twenties — poorly dressed in a cheap coat, grubby trousers and a woollen hat, but incongruously wore expensive white trainers. He was obviously very nervous. He looked around and noticed the two Arab gentlemen, one on either side, which seemed to perplex him. Then he moved quickly to stand immediately behind Lord Walsham. Although almost hidden from my view, I noticed that he was holding open the upper part of his zip-up jacket. Then he spoke out his prepared speech..."

Inspector Harling interrupted him, "Why did you say 'prepared speech', Sir? Can you recall his exact words and how he delivered them?"

Aaron Klein grimaced, "Those words will stay with me for the rest of my life, Inspector!"

Harling apologised as his witness looked away, "I'm very sorry, Sir. Please forgive me for concentrating on facts and not on what your family is going through today."

After composing himself, the Jewish jeweller continued his account. "He said, *'Death to all Jews and Christians.'* but not in a severe voice, more like a poor actor in an amateur dramatic performance. Only Miss Templeton reacted, but instead of trying to hide, she turned behind Lord Walsham and confronted the young man, crying out '*No!*' as she punched out at him with her left hand. I'm not sure if she made contact, because the other man rushing in up to them so suddenly further obscured my view."

The inspector showed no reaction as he asked, "Please can you describe this 'possible' other man, Sir?"

Aaron Klein prickled, "Why did you say 'possible' other man Inspector? I know what I saw! Without doubt, this other man rushed through the open door and pushed himself between Miss Templeton and the young man. He was quite ordinary, in his 30s, medium height, size, clothes: medium everything really. He didn't speak. I know it seems ridiculous but so has everything else been today Inspector!" Suddenly, Aaron Klein looked hurt and vulnerable, reminding the policeman that shock and trauma must be respected. As he had learned what he needed to, he made a polite departure.

***

The inspector spoke hurriedly to Doctor Chaudhary, who advised that Christine Templeton's situation was unchanged in the emergency operation unit and expected to be in intensive care for a very considerable time. Harling summoned Sergeant Dent to send his tape recorder straight to Tony Jenkinson's team of background boys at The Yard, with careful instructions about secrecy. His sergeant told him that the incident room was receiving CCTV films from many shop and other businesses in and around Hatton Garden, also that the British Transport Police were copying all films taken at main-line, commuter and underground train stations within two hours travel distance of the area between 9.00 and up to 12 noon. The inspector told Dent to take WPC Taylor with him to Jenkinson, to co-ordinate the anticipated huge numbers of CCTV films that required registering and examination. "Tell him to copy my own tape recordings then to concentrate his CCTV attention on absolutely all images recorded between 10.30 and 11.30 within fifty metre of the Klein's shop entrance. Then meet me back at the incident room as soon as you can!"

***

Inspector Harling arrived at the incident room balancing professional duties with his dilemma concerning the 'second man'. His officers respected and even liked their boss. As long as you obeyed AH's orders quickly and willingly, you knew where you were with him. Thus, his preoccupied look was noticeable, as he entered the partitioned off semi-private compartment prepared for his use at the rear of the restaurant, showing that something unusual was troubling their inspector. It took him very little time to re-arrange the furniture and fittings to his liking, before Sergeant Dent phoned to confirm that the CCTV arrangements at The Yard were going well. Sergeant Baines reported that the local council and several security contractors, along with very many businesses, were steadily bringing in their films, which were being logged, receipted, packaged and sent in batches to WPC Taylor and Jenkinson's team of background staff to examine.

When Dent arrived, the Inspector took his four team leaders to make a further visit to the Klein's shop, with the senior photographic officer accompanying them. The improved clarity of air enabled the officers to see the effect of the bomber in stark reality, with all surfaces of floor, walls and ceiling smothered in a hideous mixture of materials, including particles of human origin of less than limb size. All larger pieces had been photographed, referenced, placed carefully in plastic containers and taken to The Yard for initial scrutiny and later meticulous examination. Their feet crunched on unidentifiable debris, which they realised included a fortune of jewels. Harling instructed the photographer to take a new series of photos, at various focuses and directions, from each of four exactly recorded locations which he believed were the places where Salim, Aaron, Reuben and the shop door had been.

They paused in what had been the shop doorway, "Dent, concentrate CCTV analysis on those four or five shops on the opposite side of the street where cameras could see the Klein's entrance. The bomber must have entered The Garden on foot and probably from a bus or train before that. I want special attention on Farringdon mainline and tube stations, remembering that there are two entrances, and at local bus stops. Foster, we must clear up this floor, but very, very carefully. Make a one metre square grid from side to side and front to back. Take great care to photograph each square from above, and from each side. Then collect every item from each square into a separate plastic container — not a sack! Reference each one and send it off to The Yard. I want you to take responsibility, not Jenkinson, to catalogue each container as having estimated proportions of human remains, building materials and furnishings, supposed broken glass and supposed jewellery, remembering that those may not be easily differentiated as you're a policeman not a jeweller, right!" Returning to the incident room, he took a few minutes to update the chief superintendent with his actions, then phoned his wife, Mary, to say that he might be very late home that evening. Almost immediately, he received a surprising request from Doctor Chaudhary to accompany him quickly to Miss Templeton's bedside.

**

'AH', anticipating that an unexpected improvement in her condition would enable him to interview a third primary witness, entered UCLH's Gower Street A&E Dept. entrance with excitement. He was met by Doctor Chaudhary who quickly explained that the reason for the doctor's invitation was not Miss Templeton's improvement, but the very opposite. "Miss Templeton's life may be ending, inspector. She has several internal injuries and has had partial limb and facial amputations. Her loss of blood and the trauma typical of explosion injuries in each of the categories four to one are evident. I asked you to come because, if in fact she does not have long to live, it may be possible for you to learn something important from her."

Inspector Harling was puzzled, "But if she is gravely injured, Doctor, how could she give me any answers to questions, even if she was capable of hearing me and strong enough to want to respond?"

Doctor Shuban Chaudhary explained, "Look, Inspector, any doctor has to walk a fine line with helping his patients to recover. We do not profess to heal anyone, as that is something beyond natural man's ability, being in the realm of God. What doctors do is to search for the best treatments that could help their patients to be healed, including mental as well as physical opportunities. You told me that this young woman acted courageously, even maybe heroically, in an attempt to stop a suicide bomber destroying himself, together with her fiancé, other persons and herself. Such action surely shows that Miss Templeton has very strong moral reactions and a high regard for life including her own, if she is not thwarted by her severe injuries. It is my medical opinion that we should try to enable her to help you." Doctor Chaudhary commented on her being incapable of giving verbal answers, but explained that normal speech was not the only way that conscious communication was undertaken. "I propose that you formulate a few succinct and vital questions, Inspector, which she may be able to hear, understand and respond to by giving tactile answers. I would be present while you attempt to communicate with her, and retain the right to stop you if I believe it to be necessary." The doctor explained, "If you hold her undamaged right hand and speak your simple questions clearly to her, and if she has a strong wish to respond with yes/no answers, she could squeeze your hand in reply. Now, Inspector, we have already used much time and she may not have much longer. Shall we go to her?"

Harling was made ready and accompanied into the operating room where Christine Templeton was being kept alive. He quickly prepared a few simple questions and the code for answering them, showed them to the doctor and tried not to dwell on her horrendous appearance. He tenderly took Christine's right hand in his own left hand, leaving himself free to note down any responses. The doctor spoke to her first, "Miss Templeton. It is Doctor Chaudhary speaking to you. With me is Inspector Harling of Scotland Yard, who is holding your right hand. Please listen to his questions and if you wish to answer him, please do so. The inspector will speak to you now."

'AH', had no time to dwell on his barely alive witness' condition, "Miss Templeton, please will you confirm your answers by squeezing my hand with yours, giving one squeeze if you want to say 'no' and two squeezes if you want to say 'yes'. Do you confirm that your name is Christine Templeton?" For a moment, Inspector Harling thought that this exercise was futile, but then he felt a gentle but deliberate squeezing of his own hand twice. Keen to continue whilst this brave young woman was able to respond, he asked, "When you were in the Klein's jewellers shop earlier today, did you see or hear any person enter the shop who was not a customer?" There was no facial or bodily indication at all, but two squeezes followed directly. The inspector recorded 'Yes' on his pad and asked, "Was the person a woman?" One squeeze. "Was the man young?" gained two. "Did you try to hit him?" Two. "Did you shout at him?" Again, two squeezes. His own heart was pounding, "Was this young man the only other person who entered the shop?" One firm squeeze registered her 'No'.

"Was the newcomer a woman?" One. "Was he of an early middle age?" Two. "Did he stay near the door?" One. "Did he come near to you?" Two. 'AH', tried his best to keep calm, "Did he go behind the young man?" A hesitation was followed by one squeeze. "Did he come between you and the young man?" Two resolute squeezes made the Inspector's heart race.

The doctor signified that he should stop, but he asked a final question, "Have you answered my questions truthfully and with your own free will?" Two squeezes, but then a third followed, bringing unheralded tears to the eyes of the inspector. He sensed himself giving a short series of squeezes back to her, whilst he spoke in a faltering voice, "Thank you very much indeed, Miss Templeton, Christine. You are a brave and honourable lady. Now I will leave you in the good hands of Doctor Chaudhary. Please rest assured that I have accepted your answers to my questions and will do all that I can to discover the identity of the two persons who entered the shop. Thank you."

The inspector was immensely impressed with this young woman, who would probably die soon, yet had desired to help him in the only way that her tortured body would allow. He struggled to understand how she had described something so similar to the other two witnesses, but he trusted that his scientific mind would fathom it out somehow. He knew categorically that there was no such thing as miracles, which must only be some phenomenon that scientists hadn't quite identified yet. He composed himself, secretly annoyed that he'd allowed his emotions to cloud his habitually solid judgement, so why had he promised to seek this imaginary second man? He had no possible way of knowing that Christine Templeton was content in her anticipations of either a slow recovery, whilst undergoing operations and treatments, or of a peaceful submission to death and hence a welcome from her Saviour.

***

The inspector made one further visit to the incident room in Hatton Garden, receiving reports and briefing his various Officers. WPC Taylor phoned to tell him that some of Jenkinson's people, including her own husband Peter, would be working overnight viewing, analysing and reporting on the large number of CCTV films flowing in from many different sources, and that he should expect a phone call at 8.00 am with an initial synopsis. Suddenly, realising just how tired he was, Alan Harling headed for his home on the Ealing side of Gunnesbury.

He found the household much as anticipated: Pauline was already asleep in bed, Emily was systematically working through her physics homework, Brian was watching a football match on the TV, and Mary was ironing whilst listening to a talk on the tape-player. The familiar 'Hi Dad!' and 'Welcome home Darling!' warmed his heart as he sighed himself down into his favourite chair at the kitchen table and placed his briefcase carefully on the sideboard ready to be grabbed quickly if he was summoned away. Over his re-heated dinner, he shared some parts of his day's story with Mary, although other parts were kept resolutely to himself. His professional realm was fact and actuality: gathering, assessing and dealing with evidence, yet later, as he lay in bed trying to ease himself into much-needed sleep, the mysterious 'second man' would not leave his mind. He argued back and forth within himself, "How could three very different people, an Arab sheikh, a Jewish jeweller and an English rose, each give such detailed factual evidence of the drama that had occurred at 11.10 that morning, in absolute agreement and without each other's knowledge?" He concluded that each of them, being honest and sensible persons although of markedly different cultures and faiths, must actually believe the ridiculous incident of a 'second man', however crazy he knew that to be.

CHAPTER 3

The alarms rang far earlier than the Harling household wanted, encouraging the family to begin their days in an orderly way, except for Pauline who was, being a ballet dancer, tired out after yesterday evening's show. Alan was phoned at 7.15 by Sergeant Dent. "Morning, Sir. It might be good if you could drop in on Jenkinson at the Yard before anything else. He says he has some useful films ready to show you. I don't think his team went home last night, Sir."

Half an hour later a bleary eyed, bespectacled middle-aged man, looking very ordinary but revered by those who mattered at Scotland Yard, took the Inspector and Sergeant Dent into a faintly lit room with a large screen switched on ready for their attention. Tony Jenkinson directed his team of technical experts behind the police's public face. He was tired but excited, "Well, Inspector, your idea to gather CCTV films from around Hatton Garden is paying off! We're only at the start of examining them, but you'll be interested in this extract from what we've prepared from cameras in sight of the shop."

Jenkinson started the film running and added his comments, "You can have the detailed locations and times afterwards, but this compilation shows you all the persons entering the shop from 10.45 onwards, starting at 10.58 with a smartly dressed young woman, then two Arab men, and at 11.05 a tall military-looking man, after which there was nobody else for six minutes until another man entered."

Despite the obtuse angles, the inspector was amazed to be watching the customers and then the bomber entered the shop, including the drab clothes and incongruous ultra-white trainers that had been described to him. "Brilliant! Now we'll be able to search for other films to trace the bomber's movements back to where he'd come from! Well done Jenks! Just run the film on for the next few minutes please."

The boffin looked puzzled, "But, Inspector, nobody else entered the shop so the only other thing you'll see is the sudden flash of the explosion, followed later by the emergency services arriving."

The inspector was inwardly relieved that real facts, such as CCTV films, had proved categorically that professional police investigative work far exceeded any peculiarities in memory of otherwise reliable witnesses. With a lightened heart, he could begin his search into the hidden world of a fanatical suicide bomber. "Jenks. Could you print off some—"

The Inspector's sentence was interrupted by the clearly delighted technical master, "I anticipated your question Harling!" as he placed four A4 colour photos on the table, each showing a different view of the same young man. His face was not very clear but they showed him sufficiently well to reveal 'designer stubble', no beard or moustache and black hair beneath a dark woollen hat. His cheap 'bomber' jacket and 'lived-in' trousers were in marked contrast to his expensive white trainers, on which the fashion symbol could be easily seen.

"Dent, these will be fine for distribution. Thanks again Jenks!" 'AH' beamed with delight at police professionalism, after yesterday's mixture of fact and fable.

***

Once back at the incident room, 'AH' briefed his team, "The bomber may have been brought by car, but more probably came by public transport. There are several bus opportunities at either end of Hatton Garden, more at Holborn Circus junction than at Greys Inn Road or Clerkenwell Road, but look closely at all bus possibilities and check which bus-stops service which routes. It looks as if he was walking uphill to the shop, so maybe from Farringdon Station which is slightly lower down and easy access into Hatton Garden. My 'nose' says that he came by tube or main line train, so check the train options."

Sergeant Foster spoke up, "Sir, I've been down to Farringdon Station and confirmed that there are two entrances and exits, with Circle

Line passengers using Cowcross Street and Metropolitan line coming right next to the main line station. As several stations only allow either entry or exit depending on the time of day, to help control rush-hour traffic, our chap would have needed to know which gates would be open." The inspector told Foster to focus on Farringdon, with Sergeant Dent to get copies of the CCTV photos issued asap to British Transport Police and let them know where to concentrate on, while he went to check again on the surviving witnesses at UCLH.

***

Doctor Chaudhary greeted Inspector Harling and updated him, "The Arab sheikh is remarkably free of obvious bomb damage effects and he's responding well in preliminary tests. Although his surface wounds will take some days to heal and his ears have suffered quite a lot, his eyes appear remarkably undamaged due to his thick cloak. Mr. Klein is not quite as fortunate, with significant cuts and bruises on his upper body and we've needed to reset both his dislocated shoulders. It's too soon to be sure of his internal organs and eyes, and we're keeping a close check on his ears as we think he's suffered perforation of at least one ear drum and denudation of the tiny hairs that influence hearing so much. Once he begins to relax, instead of living in the horror of yesterday, he'll notice significant changes in his hearing, either being accentuated or the reverse and his balance and other effects of tinnitus may be become apparent. He must be made to rest his eyes and allow pressure-related problems to recede slowly, so he'll need a week's careful observation, but he's extraordinarily lucky to have escaped more severe results of bomb blast."

The inspector asked, "Does that mean that they must be kept very quiet and isolated?"

Doctor Chaudhary replied, "Actually, no! We need to keep each of them safe and well, but not too much alone because it's better for them to gradually focus on some other influences than their injuries. In fact, it would do them good to receive short visits by sympathetic and unemotional visitors."

Inspector Harling smiled, "Do you include me in that category, Doctor?"

The medical man was equally pleased to bring even a little humour into their ultra-serious daily duties, "Only in very small doses!"

When the inspector enquired about Christine Templeton, their smiles vanished, "Yesterday's experiment with hand squeezing doesn't appear to have had any bad effect, but she is gravely ill. The next three or four days will be critical to determine whether she will live or die, which may depend on her natural spirit, if she will unconsciously fight for her own survival, otherwise she may be lost. As yet, we cannot undertake all the tests and treatments that we would like to. She remains stable and is under constant monitoring and observation.

"Whatever the results are, Inspector, she will be permanently disabled. We needed to tidy up her left hand, which had lost two fingers, by amputating a third. Most of her hair was blown or burnt away, as were her eyebrows and about thirty per cent of the skin on her face and neck. Half of her left ear was blown away and our first attempts at sewing up the remainder has not gone well. Her eyes and other ear have been damaged permanently and she is on life support machines for significant loss of blood and damaged organs. It is too early to say how badly damaged she is inside. She needs us doctors but mostly her own spirit to stay alive."

The saddened inspector asked quietly, "Does that mean that further attempts at communicating are ruled out?"

Doctor Chaudhary replied, "Not necessarily, but not in the next day or two. The only external stimulation that I recommend is some positive encouragement from close family, together with some sympathetic words from the two male survivors, including about the explosion. I'm not a psychologist, Inspector, but I have learned that tremendous benefits can be brought about by enhancing a person's basic desire to survive."

Inspector Harling showed his surprise, "But surely, Doctor, such news must include the knowledge of the death of her fiancé?"

Again, the doctor explained the wisdom of his methods, "Yes, indeed, Inspector, but please remember that the sheikh and Mr. Klein also lost close relations. Often, there is a sharing of comfort for their grief between victims, thus we must allow the three of them to try to console each other."

Harling was beginning to admire this wise Indian man, "I really appreciate your approach to this, Doctor, and I will do my best not to mess up your methods. Just out of interest, Doctor, could I ask if persons might suffer hallucinating effects, added to their actual memories, if they had gone through the trauma of an explosion?"

Doctor Chaudhary half-realising what was behind the question responded emphatically, "Not in my experience, Inspector."

***

At about 11.00am, a nurse showed Esther Klein to her brother's room. Neither of them had really appreciated the loss of their elder brother, Reuben, until they grasped each other's hands without finding the words to say. Their long lonely cycles of winters into spring, then summers into autumns and relentlessly into winters again, dissolved away as they held each other and cried, soaking up the comfort of bodily contact that each had discarded so long ago. Eventually, Aaron assumed his new relationship of eldest and only brother to his sister who was four years junior to himself, "Now Esther, we must help each other and also Naomi and the children. Reuben has gone, so we must be him for them, at least for the first few months."

Esther hesitated, "I can see that, Aaron, but neither of us has been a parent or even married, which makes it more difficult for us all. Yesterday lunchtime, the police located Naomi whilst she was shopping in Oxford Street, took her to the children's school and helped her to tell the head teacher what had happened. Ruth and Isaac were collected and all three of them were driven up to me up in Golder's Green, where I'd been alerted half an hour before. Aaron, they absolutely mustn't be allowed to see their destroyed home and shop! They're consoling each other with a kind young policewoman standing by. We made up temporary beds for each other last night, although none of us slept."

Aaron held onto his sister, "What do you think we should all do now Esther? You've lived alone in that great big house for so many years."

Her answer was very practical, "Naomi and I must work out how to rearrange the bedrooms to make a sort of private sitting room for the three of them to use. I've enough spare clothes for Naomi and we'll just have to buy some basics for Ruth and Isaac for the time being, until the police allow someone to collect the family's belongings from their home. A young policewoman called Karen Francis has been delegated as our support manager, with authority to call up cars and vans and anything else the family may need. She seems very capable and sympathetic."

Aaron was relieved, "Good! This Inspector Harling seems to be an efficient man, really professional and compassionate. He'll wait until the building is declared safe, then I think that Mrs Mayer should go for them or with them, to make it less personal. They could take just what's necessary for the first few weeks."

Esther said very softly, "But what about you, Aaron? I could have lost both of you so easily. Are you going to be all right?"

Her brother spoke with a new authority, "Yes Esther, I've got my own bachelor flat and I'll be fine after the reverberations from the explosion stop going round and round inside my head. I'm rather sore, my eyes ache a lot and I'm a bit dizzy, but I don't feel bad inside."

Esther kissed his cheek, "Thank God! It's probably best if I go now, so that I don't tire you out Aaron." The two unmarried, unimportant, usually unnoticed ones, looked at each other with much greater understanding of true sibling love.

***

About half an hour later, Nurse Ryan asked if he was up to a visit from a Mr. Lemuel of the 'Reliant Bespoke Insurance Company Ltd.' Gaining his approval, she showed in a tidily dressed, middle-aged man. "Hello, Aaron, I'm dreadfully sorry about this awful business." They did not shake hands, but Natan Lemuel acted genuinely as he placed a friendly hand on Aaron's shoulder, "You know that I have to see you on business, but when I put the insurance papers away, please ask me to do anything else that I can to help you and Reuben's family."

The jeweller replied, "Thanks, Natan. Yes, I knew that you'd need to come soon to discuss the shop, so let's do that first whilst I'm not too tired please."

Lemuel took out some papers and explained the situation, "OK Aaron. I'm afraid that there's no way to read something into your insurance policy that just isn't there. As far as Reuben's three story property is concerned, all damage that has occurred is covered, which means that all costs involved in re-building the shop front, repairing any damaged walls, ceilings and the like, plus anything that needs doing out the back where your staff work, and on the two floors upstairs of his family's private flat: all the rebuilding, fitting out and decorating work is covered to a limit of ninety per cent of invoiced costs, which you'll realise is a most generous agreement."

Aaron responded, "That's about what I expected, Natan. Our family has paid in for so many years, but never anticipated the need to draw on the policy. But what about the stock?"

The insurance man looked serious, "I'm sorry, Aaron. Your father never wanted that covered, neither did Reuben. They were insistent, so there can be no reimbursement of any sort for what you've lost. I'm very sorry, but that's how it is. What do you think might have been the total value of the jewellery and gemstones that have been destroyed, and what do you want to do about the business?"

Aaron had already considered his reply, knowing that Naomi and the children would never return to live in The Garden, with daily memories that would tear their hearts out. He was equally certain that his career of smiling at well-off customers and selling diamonds in his own or any other jewellery shop was finished, "Look, Natan, with Reuben dead and the shop totally destroyed, what we had for sale is rather academic, but for the sake of The Garden as a whole, let's get the premises rebuilt. Obviously, Reuben's family couldn't return to live above the place where he was blown to bits, nor could I spend yet more years selling expensive trinkets to people."

Lemuel stood up, "I understand, Aaron. I'll sort out the paperwork for a re-build, and I'm sorry about the stock. Just let me know if there's anything else I can do." Aaron allowed the medical staff to deal with him, then rested for half an hour before asking Nurse Ryan for a phone call to be set up for him.

***

Mrs Mayer had anticipated a summons from her remaining boss. You don't work for a family of employers for twenty years without getting attached to them. She'd seen Reuben and Aaron mature and take over their parents' business, witnessed Esther's heartbreak as a young woman forbidden to follow love's path with a man of unacceptable status, watched Ruth and Isaac grow from babies to young people, and admired Naomi's dedicated life of subservience to the family. They met early in the afternoon, "Thanks for coming so quickly, Libbel. I'm so pleased that you and the others weren't hurt. When Reuben sent you out back to look for more items for that sheikh, he saved your lives you know."

Libbel Mayer whispered, "Yes, Mr. Aaron. What are we all going to do? I must see Naomi and the young ones. Are they at Miss Esther's? What shall we do…?"

Aaron comforted his trusted shop manager, "Yes, they're all safe up at Golder's Green and I'm sure if you ring Esther you can arrange to visit them. Now look, there's no point beating around the bush: the shop and the business are finished with. I'm sorry to be blunt, Libbel, but none of us could start up again after what's happened."

Mrs Mayer breathed a long sad sigh, "Yes, Mr. Aaron, I'm sure that all of us feel the same about it. We've had some good years but they're over and done with."

Aaron continued, "What I suggest Libbel is that each of you accepts a month's paid compassionate leave and goes away from The Garden to be with your own families. But before you do that, although I don't want to rush you, please let me ask an important question. All four of you are good jewellery people with whom we've been delighted. The Garden is a close network of more than a hundred jewellers, many of which would jump at the chance to get such experienced people as you. You're a mature shop manager, Yentel Hirsh is a great designer, Zoe Walker is a fine lapidorist and young Isabel is a competent sale's assistant. If you agreed, I'd like to talk to Arush Zingel, the chairman of the Hatton Garden Diamond Bourse, and ask him to talk discreetly with a few of the better shop owners, who you know yourselves and would trust. Then, but only if you wanted it to be arranged, let the Bourse help to transfer your employment within the network. Can you talk to the others Libbel, then let me know your views please?"

Mrs Mayer couldn't hide her tears as she left his bedside rather quickly, "You're being very wise and more than fair Mr. Aaron. I'll speak to the others and let you know what we think. Now, please get some rest Mr. Aaron. You're very precious you know."

***

The police's systematic work inside the Klein's shop was slow and revolting. Each square metre of the floor, wall and ceiling surfaces had been marked with tape, referenced and photographed before anything at all was removed. Then working in pairs, four officers crawled over the floor, noting down and then collecting every item big and small from the individual squares. After that, they examined the walls and ceiling, amazed with the amount of items that had lodged themselves into the surfaces. Each square's items were placed inside its own referenced plastic box. Inspector Harling watched a little of their meticulous work before returning to the incident room where Sergeant Noddy Foster approached him, "Sir, a Mr. Kravitz came in but didn't want to confide in me. He wants to tell you something that he believes is important, Sir."

'AH' was not really interested but asked, "Who is this chap?"

Foster replied, "He's the owner of another jewellery shop, just around the corner in Grenville Street, not far from the 'Bleeding Heart' pub, Sir."

The inspector's 'nose' twitched, "OK Noddy, if he really wants to see me, go and fetch him!"

A few minutes later, Sergeant Foster introduced the short, elderly Fishel Kravitz, then made a discreet exit from Harling's partitioned off section of the room. After shaking hands, the jeweller began, "All the talk in The Garden is about the disaster at the Klein's, Inspector, they were good men, good jewellers, good shop owners and good employers."

'AH' was impatient, "Yes, Mr Kravitz, so what did you want to tell me?"

The man continued, "We jewellers have tried hard to maintain security throughout The Garden, especially after the terrible heist in 2015. If four or five men even older than me could spend their Easter weekend calmly robbing our bank deposit boxes of many millions of pounds…"

'AH' was getting fidgety, "Yes. Sir, now what do you want to tell me?"

The reply came like a whiplash, "I think I might have seen the ring-leader of this dastardly crime!"

'AH' woke from a myriad of other thoughts, "What do you mean by 'ring-leader' and when did you see him?"

Fishel Kravitz started to explain, "We all know that the young bomber was nervous, but who wouldn't be if you were going to blow yourself to smithereens…!" 'AH's frown of annoyance hurried the man along, "Some of us think that the boy must have been brain-washed and trained to do his horrific job, probably by another coffee-coloured man, but one older and with really evil intentions. Well, Inspector, about ten days ago I saw someone poking about The Garden who obviously didn't want to buy or sell jewellery. You see, most of our customers follow a pattern. Although they may have different ages, nationalities and temperaments, they only come here to transact business, but this man seemed so different that a few of us noticed him and discussed it at lunchtime over at The Heart."

'AH' began to pay serious attention and yelled for Sergeant Foster to come and take down what Mr Kravitz was saying, "You mean, 'The Bleeding Heart' pub, do you Sir? Can you describe this character and say exactly when it was that you saw him?"

The elderly man was pleased to be taken seriously, "He was Middle-Eastern, aged about forty, wearing a black coat, blue jeans, brown trainers, had swarthy skin, black slimy hair and no hat. He was overweight, about 11.5 stone, approx. 5' 8" and nasty looking. He stopped outside several shops, entered a few furtively but stayed only for a minute or two, looking around but speaking to nobody. It was on Saturday 14th April in the late morning, say about twelve noon."

Inspector Harling stood over the seated man in amazement, "Now, listen, Mr Kravitz, if this is true, and I say carefully 'if' it's true, you must withhold nothing. Giving false evidence is a serious crime!" The rather shocked elderly jeweller swallowed hard and repeated his account meticulously whilst it was written down.

The inspector spent only a few seconds thanking and ushering Fishel Kravitz out before he summoned his team leaders together. "Heavens on our side chaps! This talkative little chap has just come in here and told us that him and his Hatton Garden mates saw the bomber's master-mind who organised the whole show! He's described him and his movements in phenomenal detail! This is just the lead we needed! I'm going to divide you up to find this evil bomb-master. It's urgent, but take great care, we mustn't foul up on this! Foster, take the description down to Farringdon Tube, see the station master and get the CCTV films for Saturday 14th 10am to 3pm and rush them to Jenkinson. Baines, check the possible tube routes to there, specially from the East End or North London. List all stations within an hour's journey, then contact each one and get any CCTV films of from 9am to 4pm on the same day. Dent, prepare Jenkinson to receive lots more films and get his artist chap to do a mock-up of our man. OK chaps, let's move!"

***

Later that afternoon at UCLH, having received encouragement from Dr. Chaudhary, Sheikh Salim knocked at the door of Aaron Klein's nearby room. He was welcomed warmly, "Please come in, Sheikh. It will be good to have your company. I can't really move much since the doctors put my shoulders back into place. I'm rather sore all over and my head's not so good, but how are you?"

Salim sat down, "It's good to see you looking positive, Mr. Klein. Please call me Salim. I'm in much the best shape of the three of us survivors. I believe that we were put into this terrible ordeal together, to co-operate and help each other. I'm very sorry to hear that Miss Templeton may not even survive, after saving our lives."

The jeweller replied, "You probably know that my name is Aaron. I'm very sorry about Sheikh Abdullah, your brother. He and my brother Reuben didn't stand a chance. Miss Templeton, whose first name is Christine, was incredibly brave to turn straight towards the bomber and attack him. Her intervention alone would have saved us, even without that other man who rushed in and got between her and the bomber."

Salim smiled, "I'm pleased to hear you recall that incident exactly as I remember it Aaron, especially as the police inspector didn't really want to believe me when I told him."

Aaron responded, "Me too. Whoever that man was, he was a real hero to give up his life to save us Salim."

The Sheikh quietened, "You don't look as healthy as you sound Aaron. Both of us need peace and time to recover now. I'll drop by again in the early evening if that's OK?" Aaron thanked him and laid back to rest.

***

Dr. Chaudhary didn't like the look of Roland Templeton, who demonstrated his arrogance and lack of consideration immediately, "You've done a decent initial job, but Miss Templeton needs the most efficient treatment. I'm making arrangements to transfer her to a private hospital as soon as possible."

The doctor replied politely, "Please excuse me, Mr. Templeton, but University College London Hospital is known to be one of the leading teaching hospitals in the world. You may have no fears for your sister's treatment here."

The man's body language showed his annoyance, "That's not the point, Doctor. This busy hospital may be suitable for the rush and bustle of central London, but my sister needs the best environment in which to recover."

Doctor Chaudhary withstood the bullying, "I appreciate your concern for your sister Mr. Templeton, but there is no possibility of Miss Templeton being moved. Her life was nearly taken from her and she may not survive. As her next of kin, we will keep you advised of major changes in her condition. If you wish to see her very briefly, it would do her good to know that a family member is visiting." No answer was given as the man strode contemptuously from the room, ignoring his son and the doctor.

Peter Templeton spoke, "I apologise for my father, Doctor. He's a busy man. I would love to see my Aunt Christine for a moment please." Doctor Chaudhary gave permission, noting the marked differences between people from this family.

***

Early on that Wednesday evening a sad family meeting took place in Aaron Klein's room. Naomi's haggard features showed a refusal to accept the situation, akin to senility. The shock of her husband's death and how it had occurred was too much for her to comprehend. She sat meekly on the indicated chair staring silently at the floor, while her fifteen-year-old, Isaac, looked similarly stone-like, although for different reasons. As soon as he had learned of how his father had been so viciously murdered, he had resolved hatred and retaliation to all Muslims. His sister, Ruth, bore no such primitive responses, but a mature resolve to step into the obvious vacuum that her mother was creating. Ruth knew that she must see to the daily requirements of her mother, brother and herself. She must also act like father, recognising the concentrated anger in Isaac's face, but wisely not arguing against it for now. Ruth saw also that she must be the ever-supportive and helpful presence for her Aunt Esther, who after her solitary lifestyle was suddenly to share her home with others. For her mother and brother, she would demonstrate a compassionate life; whilst for her beloved Uncle Aaron, she would be the younger sister, always looking up to him for advice and leadership, whilst loving him back to full health.

Esther broke the silence with a positive statement, "Since Granddad and Grandma retired from business and bought a house at Golder's Green to enjoy their retirement years, I have lived with them, although their plans were thwarted by ill health and early deaths, since when I have rattled around the big house on my own. Its size and location are suitable for the whole family to live in, unless Uncle Aaron wishes to stay at his own flat in The Garden. Public transport at Golder's Green is adequate and before long Ruth and Isaac will be considering their higher education. Thus, with Ruth's practical assistance, I propose that the contents of the flat above the shop, be professionally packed up, transported and unpacked at Golder's Green early next week, for you all to have your own clothes and belongings available." Aaron and Ruth gave their immediate thanks and consent, whilst Naomi and Isaac remained oblivious to such practicalities. Esther continued, "Uncle Aaron has advised me that the shop and flat are to be restored physically under the terms of the insurance policy, although it is presumed that the family will have no further interest in living or working there."

Aaron replied, "Thank you dear Esther for your unselfish proposal, which must be the best way for us all to support each other as family. Although I will continue to live at my flat, I intend to be as much help to you all as I can be."

Whilst tears were very close to each of them, Ruth managed to respond, "Thank you, Aunt Esther and Uncle Aaron. We will do as you say and make the necessary arrangements straight away. Now, Uncle Aaron, please tell us how you are?"

Ruth succeeded in diverting the distraught family's thoughts to the situation of her Uncle Aaron. "Thanks Ruth, although I'm not yet hearing or seeing too well, and obviously I'm uncomfortable and sore, the doctor seems pleased with my insides. Probably they'll keep me here for about a week, to make sure that nothing nasty develops, then I intend to get back to health as quickly as possible."

Esther responded enthusiastically, "That is good, Aaron! Rest assured that a room will always be kept available for you up at the family home in Golder's Green."

Aaron then explained his proposals for the shop staff, "I shall wait for Libbel Mayer to tell me what they think of my plan." Since the immediate family and business situations had been discussed adequately, and with Nurse Ryan hovering meaningfully; kisses and smiles were exchanged between Esther, Aaron and Ruth, whilst Naomi and Isaac maintained their numb expressions.

***

Towards the end of the afternoon, Inspector Harling was phoned by Chief Superintendent Price, calling him to meet immediately with Associate Commissioner Laurence Williams. 'AH' marched briskly to the A/C's outer office, where George Price was waiting for him. "Come in gentlemen!" began Williams. "The Commissioner is being pressured by the Prime Minister for some positive police results concerning yesterday's shock terrorism in central London. Do you have something worthwhile for me to tell her?"

Chief Superintendent Price nodded to the Inspector who remained stiffly at attention to make his report, "Yes Sir! It is now thirty hours since a currently unidentified suicide bomber blew himself and three other persons up in a jewellery shop in the Hatton Garden district of Central London..."

The A/C broke in and smiled, "Please relax a little, Inspector!"

'AH' continued, without much obvious change in style, "Sorry Sir! All three primary survivors who were in the shop when the explosion occurred have given useful and confirmatory statements. Major research into local CCTV cameras has been instigated, resulting in positive recordings of the culprit entering the shop. His detailed description is being used to ascertain his identity and movements prior to the incident, Sir. In addition, we have interviewed witnesses of a visit made ten days previously by a person suspected of master-minding this act of terrorism, whose description is being used with discretion in order to discover and apprehend the perpetrators of the crime, Sir!"

A/C Williams thanked the inspector, "Good work, Harling! That should be enough to keep the PM happy for now." Turning to the chief superintendent, he added, "Be careful with your investigations up the chain beyond the bomber, Price. Terrorism must be handled with extreme care. Is that understood?"

The Chief Superintendent answered, "Certainly Sir!" and the meeting concluded.

***

'AH' returned to the incident room, where he learned that a café manageress clearly remembered seeing the 'swarthy man' and had verified his description. His delight was tempered by the phone ringing, "Hello Harling, its Pigott here at the morgue. I wonder if you could drop in on me on your way home this evening?"

Inspector Harling had great respect for Simon Pigott, Scotland Yard's senior pathologist, "Certainly, Doctor, I'll be there in about half an hour, if that's OK?" The meeting was anticipated by 'AH' as having no real significance, but at 6pm that all changed.

"Thanks for coming, Harling! I've concluded my initial investigations into the various bodies and partials that you sent me yesterday from Hatton Garden."

The pathologist indicated his draft report but did not hand it to the inspector. "OK Doctor, you're a particularly thorough chap and I can see that something's bugging you."

Pigott replied, "Look, we've known each other for many years and admire the professionalism of each other's work. That's why I wanted to have a private chat with you about something that I'm choosing not to include in my draft report."

'AH' picked up the single sheet of paper, listing well-referenced bodies and major parts of bodies, by identifying and describing them succinctly. Nothing seemed unusual. "We're on our own here Harling, just come over to this cabinet and have a look at something."

The pathologist pulled open a drawer and took out an item about ten inches long, handing it to the policeman, "Tell me what you think of this please?"

'AH' donned rubber gloves, "It's a human hand and wrist, presumably from one of the victims at the Klein's shop, but what's the significance, Doctor?"

The pathologist asked, "What side hand is it, Inspector?"

'AH' checked the fingers and thumb and replied, "It's a left hand, but I still don't see what the mystery is."

Pigott asked him to read the draft report again. Harling obeyed, "You'll have to explain, Doctor. I can't see anything funny here."

The pathologist spoke seriously, "How many persons died in the shop Inspector and what is the condition of the survivors in hospital?"

Suddenly intrigued, 'AH' reported carefully that four men had died in the shop and that two male and one female survivors were at UCLH.

Pigott asked, "Do any of the survivors have limbs missing?"

'AH' confirmed that the female had had some fingers amputated, but no-one had missing limbs.

"Are you certain of that, Inspector?"

'AH' was becoming prickly, "Of course I'm sure! What's going on doctor?"

The pathologist continued unemotionally, "My list is thorough and describes the intact or amputated limbs of four persons, Inspector. It excludes the hand that you have just seen for yourself. We appear to have an extra hand."

AH' was lost for words, knowing Pigott far too well to suspect a mistake. "Look, Harling, I'm giving you my official draft report now, but tomorrow I will make meticulous examinations of that extra hand and won't report on it until I have definite better information. Is that understood and agreed?"

The perplexed police officer swallowed hard, "Certainly, Doctor."

It was a long time since Alan Harling had had a proper holiday. He lived under constant stress and managed to keep his scientific mind clear of superfluous or superstitious obstructions. Despite allowing his wife and children to enjoy their 'comfort zone' of so-called faith, he considered his confirmed atheism to be intellectually far above such nonsense. Of course, he would mention this apparently extra hand in his own professional police report, but without highlighting any link to the witness' claims that a second man had entered the shop. 'AH' sighed with frustration at this further peculiarity to resolve, as he began his journey home.

***

Aaron was pleased when Salim visited him early that evening, grateful for the chance to chat with someone not connected with the Klein family, for whom life was not going to be easy from now onwards. Knowing that their paths would diverge on leaving UCLH, Aaron didn't hesitate to disclose his family's relationships and situation with this polite man from a faraway country with its rather closed culture. "My sister, Esther, is going to experience huge changes, Salim. It was fifteen years ago when our parents bought a big old house in Golder's Green, near Hampstead in a well-off part of North London. They intended to semi-retire, leaving my brother Reuben and I to manage the day-to-day running of the business, whilst our father would keep a watching brief on it; but things didn't work out to plan. After coming to Britain as war-torn refugees, needing to struggle just to survive, it wasn't easy for our parents to simply stop working. They didn't know the people or the area that they had moved to, and discovered that driving or using public transport between Golder's Green and Central London was uncomfortable, inconvenient and slow. They missed the daily life of Hatton Garden, which is very much a world within a world, with constant repartee between a hundred or so jewellery businesses, mostly with Jewish owners exercising our rather specific humour."

Salim respected these confidences, "All this is very interesting to me, Aaron. It is like trying to transplant an unknown species amongst plants that are familiar and supportive of each other. It is the same with your English ways being as different to Middle Eastern life as Venus is from Mars. When you talk about close family relationships, supportive local businesses, the bustle of a century's old city: all such aspects are alien to life in the Federation of Non-aligned Arab Emirates or indeed any Arab country."

Aaron commented, "Yet Salim, we are all people made in God's image, learning about and then struggling through our short lives. Each generation believes it has the answers to the problems of its predecessors; yet what has modern progress really achieved?"

Salim answered, "Compared to nature, not very much! If you look at a beautiful flower, or even rather a plain one, you realise that it has been designed amazingly well to fit it for its life."

Noticing Salim's enthusiasm for nature, Aaron asked him tentatively, "Do Muslims believe in evolution, Salim?"

The sheikh replied earnestly, "Our faith reveres the one and only Almighty God, whom we call Allah, who is the supreme creator and sustainer of all life and does not make mistakes. Hence any requirement for developing life by evolution, through ever improving variations, does not fit well as a concept with our faith. But what about you Jews, Aaron? However, seeing that you are in pain and I am feeling somewhat tired myself, let us postpone your answer to our next meeting."

***

Alan Harling was welcomed home by his family just after 7.00pm, realising immediately that they had been awaiting him for a special purpose. Brian looked very uncomfortable wearing indoor clothes beneath a wintry dressing gown and with a tea towel attached to his head by his school tie. Emily, looking as pretty as always, was dressed in her mother's very special, long blue dress. Pauline, wearing a dance skirt, frilly pink top and a large pair of feathery angel wings, was containing her excitement with immense difficulty. Mary quickly explained that their father's presence had been awaited eagerly and that, even before he enjoyed his evening meal, he must don his dressing gown and another tea towel to be the local shepherd, whereas Brian was the representative of the three wise men. "It's no good complaining that it's now after Easter and that the time for Nativity plays is Christmas, Darling."

When Pauline was in an imaginary situation, the family just had to comply with her wishes. "OK! Let's get on with it then!" said a rather grumpy, hungry shepherd.

"Action!" called Mary the narrator and Pauline stepped forward with dignified authority, "My name is the Angel Gabriel and I bring you shepherds good news. In Bethlehem, over there..." she said pointing to the kitchen, "a baby has been born tonight, whose name is Jesus, and you'll find him in a manger. He will be the Saviour of the world."

The wise man whispered to his father, "Come on, Dad! You've actually got to get up and walk over the hills to find us here in this smelly stable!" Alan stood up reluctantly, dislodging the tea towel from his head in the process, and ambled over to join his children. Noticing one of Pauline's obviously 'girl' dolls laying awkwardly in a bread basket on the floor, he attempted a cry of excitement and rapture, but it was such a miserable failure that he was reprimanded officially by Angel Gabriel, "Look, shepherds! How dare you react like that! When I announce 'Good News', Almighty God is eminently displeased if you exhibit facial expressions and stammer out interjections more obviously associated with 'Bad News'!" Her father stared in disbelief at the seven-year-old Angel Gabriel, who had just told him off using words that his older children might not know themselves.

He looked intently at Pauline, but her eyes weren't right. Instead of a gentle blue, set in an innocent freckled face, he was looking into jet black orbs that seemed to see right through his own. Mary, seeing that something untoward was going on and being a very experienced and wise mother and wife, applauded the actors, congratulated Pauline on remembering her lines, manoeuvred her husband to the table and fetched his dinner.

For maybe five minutes, Alan didn't eat, looking dreadful with an ashen face and slumped body. Mary realised that her husband had not spoken since the reprimand of Angel Gabriel, "Eat up, Dear, you look tired. I'll put Pauline to bed while Brian and Emily finish their homework, then I'll come and hear about your day." He picked up his knife and fork and ate mechanically. Mary brought her husband a small glass of brandy. "Drink this, Dear, it will do you good after a hard day at work." Alan sipped the brandy without comment or expression.

At 11.00pm Mary joined her husband in bed, where he was sitting up and staring straight ahead. She dimmed the bright lights and climbed in beside him, "Look, Alan, I can see that you're tired. Let's just turn out the light and have a good night's sleep." Two hours later, she awoke suddenly to find him still in the same position.

At last he spoke, muttering, "It was the Angel Gabriel, Mary. Good night." Then Detective Inspector Harling, Head of Scotland Yard's Bomb Squad, lay down his head and fell asleep. At 06.00am the alarm woke them as usual. No mention was made by Alan or Mary of the peculiarities of the previous evening.

CHAPTER 4

The Inspector was at the incident room by 07.30 on Thursday, to be updated by the night staff. Sergeant Foster reported that Jenkinson's team had located a CCTV film from Harrow & Wealdstone's 'Over ground' railway station, automatically timed at 09.28 on Tuesday 24th, almost certainly showing the young bomber walking away from their station, accompanied by another man. Noddy Foster gave his boss some copies of a printout, "Here's our chap leaving the station, Sir!"

'AH's' adrenaline was pumping, "Baines, get two chaps up to Harrow & Wealdstone to check how someone could get from that station at 09.28 to arrive at Farringdon shortly before 11.00 o'clock. Tell them to make the journey themselves and note all relevant timings. Now, let's find out where he travelled from! There aren't many stops on the 'Over ground' heading up to Watford, so where did he start from? Dent, tell Jenkinson to check all CCTV films from northern stations from 08.30, Baines, send two officers to Watford station with the photo and check if anyone there recognises these two youngsters. Foster, concentrate on the other chap in the photo and find out if he came all the way to The Garden with the bomber. Do the rounds of Farringdon Station, shops and cafes again, showing the photo of the two young men together."

Within three hours, several reports had been received of possible sightings of both men, some together and others of each of them alone. 'AH' began building a picture of their two sets of movements, believing that the accomplice's job was to ensure that the bomber completed the mission, which meant that he too was an actual or potential terrorist. 'AH' was firmly on the scent now, unconcerned that he was investigating acts of terrorism rather beyond his commissioned brief.

In mid-morning, 'AH' received a phone call from Station Sergeant Jordan at Watford's Central Police HQ, who had 'used his loaf' when a middle-aged, local Asian man had come to report that his son might be missing. The sergeant had provided the requisite forms and taken careful note of the name and address of the visitor, but wisely had given him no hint of a possible connection with the Hatton Garden bombing. 'AH' spoke to Watford's Police Commander Cricksure, who agreed for Sergeant Jordan to be told to wait until mid-afternoon before phoning the man surreptitiously, asking him to let the station know by 08.00am tomorrow whether or not his son had returned home.

At 11.20pm, a rather breathless member of Baines' team, PC Hippy Ipperstaff, phoned in, "Sir, this is important! I was dropped off at Harrow and Wealdstone Station and the staff there recognised our first young man's photo. They told me that as Farringdon is not on the 'Overground' anyone wanting to travel there would need to catch a Metropolitan Line tube from Harrow Station about a mile away. I've just walked along 'Station Road' that connects the two stations, Sir. The shops and businesses along the road are mainly Asian, especially on the Harrow side of the mosque, Sir. When I reached Harrow Station, they thought I'd been sent in response to something they'd reported this morning."

The Inspector was on his feet willing his man to give the whole story, "Come on Ipperstaff, spit it out!"

The PC took a breath, "A manager from Watford Council's technical department was here at the station, with one of his workmen. They've given me something, Sir."

'AH' shouted, "What? What is it Ipperstaff?"

The PC continued, "Well, it looks like any old jacket or fleece Sir, but it's got an assortment of nails and screws sewn into it..."

'AH' yelled at his PC, "Commandeer a local police car, bring it and both men to me immediately. Keep it clean and ready to be finger printed. Well done man! Hurry up!"

Less than an hour later, PC Ipperstaff and two men rushed into the incident room and straight up to the inspector. "Sir, this is Mr. Jones, manager of Watford council's works department and this is Bill Lucas one of his street sweepers."

'AH' shook hands, took the fleece carefully from them and asked

Lucas to explain where he had found it.

"Well, Sir, I was cleaning up outside the station like I do every evening, well apart from Sundays, and I'd finished sweeping all along from the big shops up the ramp to the station. So I took my trolley down to empty the bins outside the station and I found it, Sir."

'AH' spoke officiously, "Exactly which litter bin was it in? Was it on top, or was there stuff covering it?"

Lucas told him, "It was about three down from the station entrance, Sir..."

His boss interrupted, "That's about forty metres, Inspector," then prompted his cleaner to continue. "Funny thing is, I didn't notice it yesterday morning, but then I remembered that I couldn't empty that bin because of the painters..."

Harling's tolerance disappeared, "Go on man!"

Bill Lucas obeyed instantly, "You see, Sir, I emptied it on Tuesday at about 8 o'clock, but yesterday morning those painters had stacked their ladders, tools and stuff all around the bin, cos it's outside the shop they were going to paint. I didn't see much point in moving their stuff just to empty that one bin when there's plenty of others for the public to use like. But them painters must have worked hard so I emptied it this morning; full up with their empty tins, old rags and stuff! That's not right, Sir, cos it's 'Trade Waste'. Shouldn't be put in our bins, right Mr. Jones?"

His boss agreed, but hurried him on to describe what he did when he emptied it today. "I was loading up my trolley and when I reached into the bottom of the bin; there it was, Sir. I didn't like the look of it, what with nails and screws sticking out of it. I was suspicious so I asked the chap at the station to call Mr. Jones and he come down, Sir."

Back in control of himself, Inspector Harling thanked and congratulated the two council men, waited until they had been sent away, before proclaiming, "This was the bomber's nail-bomb coat chaps! Why did he dump it? Good job he did though, or we'd have had seven corpses not four!"

***

Towards the middle of Thursday morning, Aaron Klein was visited again by Libbel Mayer who came quickly to the point, "It didn't take the staff long to decide Mr. Aaron. Young Isabel says she's had enough of jewellery shops and The Garden, so she'll look for a different sort of job in Stepney nearer to her mum and dad. The rest of us accept your kind offer for the Bourse to find new jobs for us in The Garden, please Mr. Aaron." Thus, an hour later, Nurse Ryan showed Arush Zingel, Chairman of Hatton Garden's Diamond Bourse into Aaron's room.

"This is a dreadful thing Aaron. The entire Garden is devastated about your brother's tragic death and your business being destroyed. Now tell me what I can do for you."

Aaron explained that the Kleins would not be returning to live or work at their premises, also that the staff had been given a month's leave. "As active members of the Bourse, Arush, we wish to enable fresh employment in The Garden for three of our staff. We would be delighted if you could act as broker to find suitable posts, with your usual discretion please."

The dignified jeweller replied, "Yes, Aaron, that is the right thing to do. We must pull together when something catastrophic happens, like we did in 2015 after that gang of monsters broke into our strong room. I know your people would be assets to other jewellers. Let's call it redeployment rather than new jobs. It shall be accomplished very discretely!"

Soon after Mr. Zingel had departed, Nurse Ryan asked if he was up to receiving another visitor with the name of Julian Steinburg. "Certainly, Nurse, please show my friend in."

Julian entered quietly and formally, following hospital visiting etiquette, "Hello Aaron. I'm terribly sorry about all this. I was out of the country when it happened." After ten minutes of fragmented discussion, mainly concerning the police investigation rather than Aaron's health, Julian made a suitable excuse to take his leave. Aaron was a little surprised, but put his friend's lack of personal concern, down to the unfamiliarity of their surroundings.

Doctor Chaudhary also had a surprise when he received a phone call from Dr Martyn Evans, Director of The Heath Private Hospital, Hampstead, "You may remember we had a good chat last year at Barts, after Sir Martin Bachelor's lecture on the association between surgery and trauma? I'm calling about one of your patients, a Ms Christine Templeton. Her brother is a bigwig up here and he's trying to push me to get her transferred from UCLH to us. Could you tell me her situation please?" Shuban Chaudhary described his patient's critical symptoms and uncertainties, keeping carefully to medical facts rather than opinions. "Just as I expected, Chaudhary. I'll tell Templeton to cool off. It's out of the question to move a patient in her condition, exactly as old Bachelor concluded! Well done with your work at UCLH! It doesn't go unnoticed you know. Hope to bump into you somewhere soon. Bye!"

***

Towards the end of the afternoon, Sergeant Jordan from Watford advised Inspector Harling that the young Asian man's father had let him know that his son had not yet returned home. 'AH' decided on prompt action and arranged with Commander Cricksure for a joint operation tomorrow morning, with the local force liaising with his own teams for an unannounced visit to the father's home in Cromer Road. At exactly 08.00am squad cars with backup teams were to be in place, surrounding that part of North Watford. 'AH' attempted to advise his boss of his plans, but failed to reach Chief Superintendent Price who was said to be in conference with top brass.

"Look, Price!" began Associate Commissioner Williams, "I'm responsible for Special Branch and the Commissioner is angry! It seems to have become a nurse-maid service for foreign governments, instead of focusing on preventing major crime! Its budget is spent mostly on officers standing outside embassies with machine guns, just in case a passing terrorist decides to break in! It's more interested in satisfying embassy officials than chasing criminals! I've been instructed to bring in major changes very quickly."

Price asked his boss discretely why he was being told about this. The A/C explained, "I'm considering splitting SB into a diplomatic division, headed by the current old fogy superintendent until he retires two years from now, and creating a new division led by an experienced investigative detective from outside, with a good track record of achieving results. I'm looking for a policeman's policeman, Price, and between me and you only, I've got my eye on 'AH'. It would mean his promotion to chief inspector and he would have to come in 'clean', so I don't want him having any involvement with SB affairs for the time being, understood?"

The Chief Superintendent replied, "Certainly, Sir. His investigations into the Hatton Garden bombing can be restricted to discovering who the bomber was. I'll keep him away from higher matters concerning who was behind the terrorism, Sir."

***

At 05.15 on Thursday Sheikh Salim was amazed when Nurse Ryan brought him important news, "The hospital's chief executive has just been told that an emir of the Federation of Non-aligned Arab Emirates and their ambassador will be here in ten minutes! They're coming to see you, Sir!"

Salim was mystified, "But why would my father come all this way to visit me, Nurse?" They had no time to reflect on such questions before UCLH's officials began arriving at Salim's room, followed shortly by the CX who knocked and entered, ushering in the emir, HRH Sheikh Rashid bin Hamad Al Nu'masiq and the FNAE's ambassador. Salim bowed to his father from his bed, making as much of a salaam as possible.

The emir smiled, grasped his son's hands and put him at his ease. "Please excuse the abruptness of this visit Salim, but I wanted to see you and to understand the situation here for myself. I can see that you are not uninjured my son."

The emir turned to the hospital's CX, "Perhaps, Sir, you would like to give our ambassador a tour of your splendid hospital, whilst the sheikh and I confer?"

The ambassador accepted reluctantly and the room emptied, leaving theemir and his son alone. "Father, it is very good of you to come, as I do not deserve your attention. Father, I must tell you that I am alive only because of the heroic actions of a young English woman, who attacked the bomber, saving my own life and that of the younger Jewish jeweller, yet now her own life hangs in the balance."

The emir frowned, "Whilst applauding her selfless bravery that has ensured your survival Salim, do not forget the historic and hateful religious crusades made against us Muslims, by Christians who also showed real action in their faith. I was not made aware of this English lady and her actions. We must honour her, Salim. You must understand, my son, that the effects of this outrage on our own country and the entire FNAE are serious. When Crown Prince Abdullah, your brother, was killed it left a political vacuum. My visit is not only to ascertain your health and talk with you Salim, but also to meet with British diplomats and satisfy them that there will be no diminution in the FNAE's position of influence within the Arab world, or with themselves. In just three days' time, on Sunday 29th April, the emirs hold their monthly council, at which I must advise them of the name of the succeeding crown prince."

Salim reflected, "Father, surely my elder brother Hamad bin Rashid has been well-prepared and held available for such a situation?"

The emir replied, "That is true, my son, but only in the context of Abdullah, who was acknowledged by the Council of Emirs and the Council of Crown Princes to be a strong and forceful man. He was respected for what he was, a military-minded leader, who would ensure that our role for the FNAE would remain powerful if I left the scene. The relationship between Abdullah and Hamad may have served us well for some years. However, time moves on and international situations change. Now our nation needs to achieve greater recognition and understanding in the wider world, Salim."

With his painful ears, eyes and body, Salim had difficulty in comprehending his father's reasoning, which was noticed by the observant emir, "Listen carefully, Salim. Our own country is safe, well and very prosperous, but it must introduce certain internationally recognised reforms, with which Abdullah had no interest. Also, the FNAE is a strong confederation, accepted by other Arab states, but the emirs recognise some brittleness in how it is perceived on the world stage. It may appear as an increasingly arrogant nation, worthy of notice solely for its oil and money. The emirs have begun to see the need to moderate that image, and portray the FNAE as a conciliatory voice in the Middle East and of notice globally. However, with Abdullah as their leading voice, the Council of Crown Princes has not grasped our vision.

If a bomb should remove myself, or another of the emirs, the FNAE could turn increasingly inwards: more proud, belligerent and isolated in the eyes of world leaders. That must not happen. Our ambassador in London is in Abdullah's mould, with no respect for any Arab leader who does not tote a big gun. British diplomats dislike his one-track mind and disrespect him." Salim recognised that his father was seriously concerned as he continued. "The abruptness of my arrival was not an accident, my son. I needed to gauge for myself what calibre of person you really are Salim. When do you expect to be discharged from hospital? It must not be too late, nor too soon. Could you be ready to fly home next Tuesday?

The perplexed Salim replied, "Father, Doctor Chaudhary decrees that I expect to be here for one week, mainly to ascertain that typical latent explosion injuries do not materialise internally. But Father, what are you suggesting?"

His father smiled astutely, "Salim! Emirs and crown princes are not in the habit of 'suggesting'. We dictate! Your character illustrates the difference between most of us and yourself. The fact that your life has been hidden from political and monarchical intrigues is not a bad thing. Effective leaders sometimes emerge from the wilderness, perhaps through a good education in technology and business, which our country should not be too proud to acknowledge. You have lived mostly in London for eight years, acclimatised to the culture and language of others. Salim, on Sunday, I intend to advise the Council of Emirs that you are to be my next crown prince. They will understand my motivation for bringing changes to the Federation. I believe that they will be very pleased with my decision. There is to be a Council of the FNAE's crown princes on Sunday 13th May. Will you be there Salim?"

The respectful son forbade false modesty to arise, "Father, you do me great and undeserved honour. This was never anticipated, but neither was the bomb that killed Abdullah. I defer to your decision and to the unseen world that moves our spirits. Yes, Father, I will fly home to you next Tuesday and will fulfil your desire for me to take my place on 13th May. Thank you, Father."

***

Late that afternoon 'AH' visited Simon Pigott again. "Come in old chap!" called Scotland Yard's pathologist jovially, "I've sent my people off early so we can talk in peace! Have you been thinking about the extra hand?"

'AH' answered conservatively, "I admit that there is no obvious solution, but thorough police work will reveal the answer."

"Maybe, Inspector! Now have another look at this hand. Does it belong to a man or a woman, young or old, healthy or frail, rich or poor, etc. etc. Come on detective, tell me what you think!"

'AH' donned rubber gloves and examined the hand and wrist carefully, "Well, Doctor, it's obviously a left hand and was severed with great force. The skin is smooth but not effeminate, light brown and unmarked. The nails are not painted or manicured. It's not a woman's hand, but the size and shape are not of a strong man." 'AH' turned it over, "I can't make out the typical creases, lines and finger prints. Possibly they softened and faded after the amputation?"

Simon Pigott exclaimed, "Well done, Inspector, apart from your final point! Once a limb is separated from a body, it tends to harden rather than become softer. So why can't you see the usual creases, lines and fingerprints?"

'AH' professed that he couldn't answer that question. The pathologist responded eagerly, "But I can Alan!" The inspector was amazed at the use of his first name, something unheard of between such professionals. "You can't see them because they're not there! I've had time to examine it very carefully. This extra hand comes without finger prints or natural blemishes. It's just a perfect hand!"

'AH' stared at the doctor, "You'll keep it very safe and private won't you doctor?"

The pathologist assured him, "Absolutely under my personal lock and key and properly preserved until it's needed to be shown to a disbelieving world!" They parted without further words.

On his way home, the inspector pondered over the recent strange happenings: witnesses describing a 'second man' although not recorded by CCTV, Pauline's eyes and words whilst acting as Angel Gabriel, his boss's apparent lack of enthusiasm at a vital stage of the bombing inquiry, and now this unidentifiable 'extra hand'. If there was any significance to these mysterious things, he'd have to discover it by solid, methodical police work.

***

Sheikh Salim went along to Aaron Klein's nearby room at about 7pm and found him eager to relieve hospital boredom by continuing their discussions. Salim spoke first, explaining that because he had foreseen no significant role for himself in the FNAE's affairs, he had interested himself in far wider matters, including the life of the great Biblical King Solomon from whose name his own derived. Aaron was amazed that Salim had not hesitated to read those books of the Judean/Christian Bible that concerned a person's inner seeking of God's righteousness and justice, however that might be described. Salim said he had sympathised with King Solomon's frustrations, recorded in the book of Ecclesiastes, at the futility of political, military, academic or social exploits to lead a person into any acceptance of righteousness from divine eyes. Thus, he had sincere respect for Solomon's conclusion that, *'Everything is meaningless apart from the necessity to fear God and keep His commandments.'* seeing no problem with balancing a universal view of that conviction alongside his assured Muslim faith. "In my examination of flowers, Aaron, I recognise God as the creator and sustainer of the immeasurable universe, which includes gigantic stars as well as delicate and inconsequential plants. Without such recognition, what use are religious doctrines and regulations? Now friend, what about you Jews: do you believe in evolution?"

Aaron smiled, "I cannot answer for my entire race, Salim, but our Torah describes creation in such detail that a hypothesis such as evolution is unnecessary! I have heard that all Muslims believe the Hebrew Bible to be untrue, for example with the account of the Jews' patriarch, Abraham, preparing to sacrifice his son, Isaac, whereas I understand that Muslims say that it was his other son Ishmael? We Jews would ask why Almighty God would require that son of the slave woman Hagar, rather than Abraham's promised son and heir Isaac, who was conceived after so many years of patient waiting by his wife Sarah?"

Salim phrased his answer astutely, "Perhaps a more important consideration Aaron, is Abraham's willingness to sacrifice his precious son, whichever of them it was, in absolute obedience to God's command? As so many different Jewish and early Christian men composed the books of the Bible, would it not be easy for errors to have crept in?"

Aaron recognised this common-sense argument, "Yet as you know, Salim, both Arabs and itinerant Jews dwelling in desert lands, placed immense importance on handing down meticulous verbal records from their forebears. That is one reason why countless generations of Jews, so familiar with the 2,500 years old record of Abraham's life, find it impossible to believe your prophet Mohamed's account of his vision nearly 1,000 years later."

After half an hour of stimulating discussion, the long day of medical attention, re-dressings of wounds, X-rays and examinations, plus their meetings with people, had been very tiring.

They both puzzled over the peculiarities in their hearing and bodily balance that was so aggravating, with incessant noises of electric motors, low scale drumming and high-pitched bells. Doctors and specialist ear technicians had undertaken several tests, but had not yet confirmed that a common result of explosions was the condition of tinnitus. Aaron and Salim agreed that quietness and sleep were necessary, thus wishing each other 'Goodnight', they separated again.

***

Alan Harling and his family had an uneventful evening and night. He woke refreshed on Friday morning and phoned the incident room at 06.40, discovering that Watford police's Sergeant Jordan had just phoned the boy's father who confirmed that his son had not come home. "Phone Watford and tell them the plan's on and to bring a WPC. We'll rendezvous on the High Street and drive together to be at Matey's at exactly 8.00am. It must be absolutely unannounced! Get Sergeant Atkinson to collect me from home and drive me up there straight away." Promptly at 07.59 the local police car stopped outside the small terraced house in Watford's rather squalid Cromer Road. The inspector hung back to allow the Sergeant Jordan to speak to the man, who invited the officers in and shut the door. Harling saw that he did not have swarthy skin or slimy hair, wore no fancy ring and clearly was not the man he had half-hoped would be the bomb master. Changing to 'Plan B' the inspector took firm control, "Are you Mr. Ibrahim Halleem and do you reside here in Cromer Road, Watford?"

The man answered, "Yes of course, but why are you all here? I've only reported that my son is missing."

Harling showed him an A4 photograph and pointed to one of the two young men shown leaving Harrow & Wealdstone Station, "Is this your son, Sir?"

The puzzled man answered, "Certainly, Officer, but what is this photo? Where is he? Tell me if you know!"

Seeing that a woman and young man had joined them, Inspector Harling introduced himself formally, glanced at the WPC, then spoke resolutely, "I am very sorry, Mr Halleem, but we have reason to believe that your son, as identified in this photo, entered a jewellery shop in Central London on Tuesday morning and blew himself up."

The woman shrieked and fell into her younger son's arms. Her husband stared blankly, then whispered, "Our fears were right. We saw about the bombing in London on the TV. Was it really our Khaled who did that?"

Alan Harling felt like any other father would do, but continued, "We believe so, Sir. I'm very sorry. Please can you identify the other person in the photo?"

The young man looked, "Yes. It's Khaled's friend Ammar from Yarmouth Road."

The Inspector asked to be shown Khaled's room and noticing two beds, he asked the seventeen-year-old Rashid, "Do you share this room with your brother?"

Rashid confirmed that he did then said, "Please, Sir, Khaled would never have done something like this on his own. He must have been made to do it."

After asking to take a few items belonging to Khaled, Harling showed the photo of the 'swarthy man' to the family, none of whom recognised him. The inspector explained that the police woman would stay with them and that they must be prepared to answer many further questions. He shook hands with Mr Halleem, "I'm very sorry, Sir. I'm a dad too."

Turning to young Rashid, Inspector Harling said, "Look son, your mum and dad are going to need you to be strong, OK? I've got to find out who's behind what your brother did. Call me anytime you want."

Taking the inspector's proffered official card, Rashid Halleem replied, "Yes, Sir!"

The police reconvened back at the High Street, sent squad cars to block off Yarmouth Road then drove to the terraced house said to be the address of the bomber's friend Ammar Sharmu. Sergeant Jordan knocked loudly on the door which was eventually opened by a man aged about thirty. The police gained permission to enter and confirmed that Ammar Sharmu was not there, discovering that he was one of five housemates, but had not been seen since Tuesday morning. The man told them that the manager of the High Street hardware emporium had also been inquiring about the whereabouts of his two regular assistants.

Inspector Harling returned to the Hatton Garden Incident Room, from where he put out a blanket CCTV search for Ammar Sharmu at major transport points exiting London, but saw no urgent necessity for advising Chief Superintendent Price of his efficient actions.

***

Overnight, Aaron had finally allowed his mind to dwell on the loss of his only brother Reuben as a person, rather than business colleague. Incongruously, although spending their lives in such close daily contact, they had never really been friends. Now that was too late. His older brother was no more. He was on his own. After their morning's various medical examinations, treatments and exercises had been completed, Aaron was pleased to have a further visit from Sheikh Salim, who deferred mentioning his father's auspicious visit until Aaron had spoken first. "Look Salim, what are we doing? We didn't know each other before this tragedy, now here we are discussing intensely private things. Muslims and Jews, not to mention Christians, are entirely different people groups, from cultures and religions that mostly fail to understand each other, or even want to do so. A knife or a gun is far easier to wield than kindly spoken words. I'm sorry about that, because all my life I've avoided extremists who advocate power and force as the way to win arguments, especially when they talk about my race as being inferior, and that the 'Jewish situation' needs 'addressing'!"

The sheikh was surprised at the sensitivity shown by Aaron, "Is that a reason for us to desist, Aaron?" They looked at each other with respect. "Please remember, Aaron, that very many Jewish persons have excelled in all aspects of life; for example, in achieving Nobel prizes for all manner of subjects."

Salim widened the discussion astutely, "We Muslims consider that Christians worship their Jesus Christ rather than Almighty God, who they say was his Father, whereas we esteem Allah as the one and only, infinitely perfect God, who cannot be divided or share his glory with another, including such an impossibility as a 'son'. Please tell me your Jewish opinion Aaron?"

Never having discussed his faith with a gentile before, but appreciating the openness and toleration of this considerate sheikh, Aaron responded, "We Jews too believe that Christians worship their Jesus, whilst claiming him very ironically to be our Jewish Messiah, rather than Almighty God. However, to their credit, they also believe the Jewish Torah, prophets and writings of our Hebrew Bible, referring to those as their Old Testament. In those books are many pointers to our coming Messiah, whom we Jews await. We differ radically concerning God's Spirit, whom Jews know was sent to certain individuals for specific reasons, but whom Christians somehow believe is universally available, of course only to followers of their Jesus!"

Salim responded, "Look, Aaron, Muslims share in the belief of our, and your, patriarch Abraham, and my creation views concur with yours; also, many Christians hold those very same beliefs. Perhaps the spurious connections between ourselves as believers, are more important than the denials of persons of nominal belief and the very many who are secular in all but the actual title of their faith? It may not be easy to reconcile such large differences between the understandings of these three faiths Aaron, yet shouldn't we all delight in reverencing this same Almighty God as creator and sustainer of the universe?"

Sensing the fatigue in Aaron and not wanting their conversation to become doctrinal, Salim requested that their discussion be postponed, as a matter of great personal impact had occurred. "Last evening, I received a very unexpected visit from my father, one of the five emirs of the FNAE. Whilst each country is an absolute legal monarchy, several years ago they decided for strategic reasons that they could achieve more standing in the world by forming the FNAE in a similar way to the larger UAE. Each country is ruled by a king, called the emir, whilst the FNAE is governed by the council of the five emirs. Each emir appoints a son to be crown prince, being destined to become emir on his father's death. You know that my eldest brother, Abdullah, held that title, but you may not be aware of his deliberate choice for me to accompany him on many visits and functions. That was due to my lifelong position as a 'lesser son' of the emir, hence not one to be considered as a rival or threat. That situation was acceptable to me, permitting my freedom to follow fewer stern disciplines. Whilst Abdullah was the aggressive fighter epitomising the Arabian desert hawk, I was allowed to be its opposite, the placid dove."

Aaron interrupted the sheikh briefly to explain the similarity with his role as 'assistant' to his only brother Reuben, the first born of their father, Abraham Klein. "Then yes, Aaron, we can understand the situations which each of us has followed until now. After Abdullah's murder, my elder brother Hamad wrongly assumed a swift appointment as the new crown prince, but please be advised, friend Aaron, that my father has decreed myself to become crown prince, anticipating my character to be more acceptable to world leaders who may not enjoy the antagonism that a desert hawk cannot hide."

Aaron was amazed and asked, "Have you accepted this high honour, Salim?"

The sheikh smiled, "The decisions of an Emir are not proposals, Aaron, but a sovereign desire. I must return to my home country early next week to be formally bestowed as crown prince."

Aaron gave his sincere congratulations, commenting that they came from a 'mere Jew', but was instantly admonished. "Not so, friend! Yours is a conciliatory voice that I am learning to respect, especially with your similar understanding as a lesser son. I relish your non-Muslim, non-Middle Eastern Arabic viewpoint and I sincerely request your independent voice in my ear in the future." Aaron Klein, displaced from his business and livelihood, shook hands warmly with His Highness and designated Crown Prince Sheikh Salim bin Rashid Al Nu'masiq, as they wished each other 'Goodbye for now'.

***

After a very productive Friday, 'AH's afternoon was drawing to a close as he reviewed the last four days. His interviews with the main witnesses had gone well, despite their puzzling assertions of an unknown man. He'd identified the bomber and circulated a photo of his accomplice to transport connections far and wide. He had witnesses and a photo of a swarthy man who might be the bomb master. The doctor at UCLH was being very co-operative and the police pathologist had done his gruesome work very professionally, although the extra hand without usual markings was a mystery. His bosses seemed equally satisfied with his work as he did himself. Next, he could search into why a young man from Watford should have walked into a Hatton Garden jewellers to blow himself and others into smithereens. 'AH's reverie was interrupted shortly before 6.00pm when Chief Superintendent Price walked into the incident room, "I've just called in to congratulate you, Inspector! You've done a sterling job this week. It's only three days since the bombing and you've identified the murderer. Well done! Everything's tidy and on Monday we'll disclose the bomber's name to the press. Now, go on home and do some gardening!"

Surprised at his joviality, 'AH' replied, "Thank you, Sir, I'd like to do that, but I'm following up a few useful leads right now, backtracking to discover who set up this terrorism..."

His boss interrupted, "I understand what you're saying Harling, but Rome wasn't built in a day was it? Just put further inquiries on hold for now."

'AH' tried to explain, "But, Sir, the trail is hot and we're gathering good evidence..."

Price jumped in, "Professional policemen should keep their eyes down, not gazing for a wider picture. Mr Williams and the commissioner see things differently to us 'coppers', so just hold the ship steady and don't rock the boat, Inspector!" 'AH's feint 'Yes Sir' could in no way conceal his displeasure.

He arrived home at about 7.00pm looking forward to the weekend, "Hello, Alan, darling!" called Mary.

"Daddy, daddy, guess what Ayesha did at school today?" burst out Pauline.

"Hi Dad!" called out Emily and Brian. Alan congratulated himself at raising such a contented and well-behaved family as a welcome foil to his onerous police work. After an uninterrupted evening, Alan and Mary went to bed contentedly, but just after midnight, a noise of breaking glass woke him suddenly. It wasn't quite like a window being broken and he was unsure where the sound had come from. He crept out of bed without disturbing Mary, put on slippers and dressing gown and picked up the heavy flash-light that stayed at his bedside. Creeping onto the landing, he saw a light coming from the kitchen. He went down the stairs very cautiously and quietly pushed the kitchen door open.

"Oh, hello, Dad!" called Brian cheerily from the middle of the floor, on his hands and knees wielding a dustpan and brush.

"Brian, what's happened?" asked his dad, relieved that no intruder had broken in.

"I'm sorry, Dad, but after the football finished on the telly, I came to get a drink of water and the glass slipped right out of my hand and smashed. I'm very sorry and I'll clear it up quickly. Sorry, Dad."

Alan ushered Brian out of the kitchen, "OK, Son, don't worry. You go up to bed and I'll finish it." He wanted to collect every fragment of broken glass, not leaving even a splinter for Pauline to tread on. It took him a few minutes to carefully wrap the fragments of one of their best wine glasses inside last week's local newspaper and put them safely in the bin. Climbing the stairs, relieved to be returning to his warm bed, he pondered, 'Why on earth didn't he use an everyday glass to get himself a drink of water?'

***

On Friday evening, Aaron repeated his shoulder exercises once again, trusting the medical advice of how important this was for his future health. Nurse Ryan gave him his tablets, commenting cheerfully, "They should help you to have a good night's sleep, Mr Klein!" He sat up in bed reflecting on Salim's momentous news, agreeing that the emir's decision was far wiser than appointing another firebrand like the obnoxious Abdullah. With his mind locked onto Middle-Eastern politics, Aaron was too awake to simply fall asleep, tablets or not. As he had no books or magazines to read and hated the TV's crass materialism, he rummaged in the drawer of his bedside cupboard for anything stimulating. Finding something hard stuffed behind his few personal items, he pulled out a book with the words 'Holy Bible' on its plain brown cover, and a sticker explaining that Bibles were placed in hospital wards by an organisation called 'Gideons International'. Gid'on was a favourite hero of Aaron's, who had led ancient Israel to victory over their Philistine enemies. He recognized the Gideons' emblem of a man blowing a trumpet from the story he had heard so many times at synagogue.

    Deciding to check if it would be told similarly in this Christian book, Aaron turned to the table of contents and searched for 'Shof'tim'. Unable to find that Hebrew title, he noticed that the book before Samuel was called Ruth and the one before that was Judges. It was easy to recognise that these English names were the Hebrew's Rut and Sh'mu'el; therefore, he deduced that Judges must be the English name for Shof'tim. Testing his theory, he looked up Judges and began reading familiar accounts until reaching chapter six where the familiar Jewish story of Gid'on, was recorded. Aaron was amazed that the text of this Christian Bible seemed identical to synagogue readings from the Hebrew Bible. He remembered how ADONAI, the Jewish name for Almighty God, had told Gid'on to send home all but 300 of the 32,000 strong army, on purpose, to demonstrate that He would defeat the foe without the people's arrogant belief in their own military strength. He was pondering if Sheikh Salim's quiet trust in Almighty God would make him a far better representative for his country than the proud Abdullah, when with eyes and ears hurting and various wounds feeling sore, Aaron turned out his light and fell asleep.

    Abruptly at 11.00pm, the night duty nurse switched on the lights to give Aaron his next regular checks, after which, sleep eluded him. He reached again for the Christian Bible and decided to check their first book Genesis, known in Hebrew as B'resheer meaning 'In the beginning'. The familiarity relaxed him as he read of the creation of the universe, Adam and Havah, or Eve as this book called her, and on and on, up to and past the catastrophic flood that wiped out all but Noah's family and the animals saved from death in the Ark. In the quiet solitude of his room, Aaron read further, through the accounts of Avraham, Sarah, Yishma'el, Yitz'ak, Esar, Ya'akov and Yosef, names that were easy to recognize in their English translations. He skipped through Genesis and read on into Exodus, which he recognised as Sh'mot meaning 'Names'. He loved the stories of Moshe and his brother Aharon, after whom he had been named, relishing the familiar accounts until arriving at chapter twenty-five. Here, he began what he knew as 'Section 19: T-rumah' meaning 'Contribution', continuing through chapters twenty-six and twenty-seven describing the tabernacle with its glorious golden ark. He turned the page into chapter twenty-eight where the High Priest's garments were detailed, including the fabulous jewels sewn into the precious breastpiece. Such exact descriptions had always impressed his jeweller's knowledge, but now he puzzled over the names given to the individual jewels in this English Bible, knowing that the translations were far too shallow. Suddenly, at 02.30 on this entirely silent and very early Saturday morning in the middle of Shabbat, his attention was drawn to a piece of card falling out of the Bible. It was a ticket to a horticultural show in somewhere called Gunnesbury, an area of West London with which Aaron was unfamiliar.

Looking back at the Bible page, he was greatly surprised to find some words written in pencil on the margin: *"You must find these jewels."* Why had someone written that note? Who did the '*You*' refer to? Why had a horticultural show's card been used as a bookmark? Aaron closed the Bible, turned out the light and fell soundly asleep.

CHAPTER 5

'AH''s phone woke him callously at 06.15 on Saturday morning, "Yes, what is it?" he asked sourly.

Sergeant Foster explained, "Sorry it's so early, Sir, but I thought you'd like some news about the bomber's accomplice. He was spotted on two CCTV cameras on Tuesday afternoon: firstly, at Paddington around midday and then in Devon a few hours later, Sir."

AH was instantly on duty, "Send a car for me straight away, Noddy, then get hold of Paddington Station's police. Tell them to meet us at 7 o'clock. We're going to Devon, Noddy!" Although Mary wasn't at all pleased, she knew how vigilantly Alan viewed his work. The lawn and garden shed could wait even if her husband was out all day. If he was happy, then she was happy.

"Good morning, Inspector Harling," said the keen young British Transport Police Constable Trent, "Your Sergeant Foster is in our office just along the platform."

AH was escorted there and the three men talked over large mugs of railway tea. "The person whose photo we received from your team yesterday was definitely here at on Tuesday in the middle of the day, Sir. Here's a shot of him coming up from the Circle Line tube at 12.08, Sir." 'AH' compared it with the issued picture, which clearly showed the same man. "Then, Sir," continued the excited PC Trent. "We got him on the Platform three entrance camera at 12.20 catching the 12.25 to Penzance!"

'AH' remembered the keenness of his own first years in 'The Force', "Well done, constable!" Sergeant Foster added, "As soon as I was alerted at about 4.00 a.m. I asked Constable Trent to check with all stations where that train was scheduled to stop, Sir. There weren't too many because it was an express train to Cornwall. We struck gold with a station in Devon where the local BTP night staff ran through their CCTV films for Tuesday afternoon. They've faxed us this picture about an hour ago Sir, showing our man walking out of Newton Abbot Station at 14.56, Sir!"

Full of zeal and enthusiasm 'AH' asked, "How quickly can we get down to Newton Abbot today, Constable?"

PC Trent consulted his timetable, "There's a slow train leaving at 07.50, Sir, but a faster one goes at 08.25, getting to Newton Abbot at 11.15."

'AH' asked the officer to phone the Devon station staff to let them know they were coming. "Tell them it's a Scotland Yard inquiry so I want no idle talking. I'll speak to the Devon police myself once we've sorted out a plan."

PC Trent snapped out his "Yes Sir!" whilst 'AH' turned to Sergeant Foster, "We've got less than an hour to wait and we need to handle this right, without alerting the media. We'll have a quick breakfast here at the station before we catch the train."

Courtesy of their police travel passes, Inspector Harling and Sergeant Foster were shown to an empty table in the first-class coach H, where they couldn't be overheard and had a good view down the central corridor. As their train pulled out of platform three, 'AH' reviewed what they knew about Matey, not using his real name in case other ears picked it up. "On Tuesday morning, he and his chum travelled from Harrow-on-the-Hill by Metropolitan Line tube to Farringdon Station, walked up Gresham Street, past the new Cross Rail complex and 'The Bleeding Heart' pub and into Hatton Garden. At 11.10, Chummy walked into Klein's to do his business, but what did Matey do and how did he get to Paddington?"

Noddy Foster suggested, "I think Matey's job was to make sure that Chummy got to the shop, and then he'd scarper quickly, but not too fast to arouse suspicion. Probably, he'd leave Hatton Garden by a different route than Gresham Street, Sir."

'AH' agreed that was plausible, "But what was the overall plan? If the two boys were being directed by 'Swarthy', who'd cased the joint ten days beforehand, what had he told Matey to do after the job was done?"

Foster considered, "Well, Sir, he wouldn't want Matey to head back to Watford, if that's where he hails from too..."

'AH' jumped in, "But if Swarthy comes from Watford, why did the boys travel first to Harrow & Wealdstone on the overground, then walk nearly a mile to Harrow-on-the-Hill to catch the tube to Farringdon? It wouldn't make sense for ordinary people, let alone one dressed up in a cumbersome bomb jacket!"

Foster asked, "What about that fleece sown with nails that was found in a bin outside Harrow Station, Sir?"

'AH' suggested, "They probably dumped it because they were scared to go through the barriers with one of them wearing enough metal to trigger any security devices!"

Sergeant Foster asked, "So where did they get the bomb jacket and the nail fleece from? I don't think they travelled from Watford Junction carrying them, Sir!

'AH' thought about that, "It had been planned very carefully by Swarthy, who wanted the boys to leave Watford looking innocent, then afterwards to have a journey of only about half an hour on the tube to Farringdon…"

Foster jumped in with, "That means that they collected their equipment somewhere along Station Road, Sir, between the two Harrow stations!"

'AH' beamed, "Exactly! We need to look for Swarthy in Harrow not Watford! Somewhere along Station Road he was waiting for them. It must have been inside somewhere, but probably not his home; so maybe in a shop?"

Foster asked, "What about the preparations for this mission, Sir? The boys must have been trained up to know where to go. They must have been to Swarthy's at least once before. What sort of shop would it be and is Swarthy still there, Sir?"

'AH' thought that it wouldn't be a grocer's or a shop where the public wander in and out all the time, "It must be some sort of a business open to the public, but not in constant use. Probably with a back room with the shop being just a 'front'!"

They both felt that they were achieving something important so Foster asked, "Do you think we should send some of the lads to scout it out Sir?"

His boss shook his head, "Certainly not at the moment, or we'd alert Swarthy. Let's concentrate on Matey: how did he get from Hatton Garden to Paddington?"

Noddy Foster reviewed what they knew, "CCTV cameras picked up Matey at 11.00 at Farringdon and 12.20 at Paddington. The bomb exploded at 11.10 so Matey had about seventy minutes until being filmed coming off the tube at Paddington..."

'AH' showed his excitement, "He would have half an hour to walk nonchalantly up the Greys Inn Road to get a tube to Paddington! It was the Circle Line so he probably got on at King's Cross! We'll check their cameras. Yes! It all fits!"

As their train pulled into Reading Station, its first stop on the six-hour journey south-westerly to Penzance, 'AH' noticed that his fellow officer was yawning and clearly very tired. "Were you at Hatton Garden all night, Noddy?"

His faithful sergeant replied, "Actually yes, Sir. I'd volunteered for the night shift."

TheInspector sat up, "Right! That's enough of our chatter. I'll need you fresh when we get down to Devon. Go and sit over there and get some shut-eye." As they sped onwards through Berkshire, Wiltshire and eventually into Devonshire, 'AH' was working things out in his mind. As it was Saturday, there was no need to let his boss know what he was doing until he'd found something more tangible down at Newton Abbot. Why had Matey run off to Devon immediately after he knew Chummy had done his job?

Perhaps Matey had been told to get a long way away from London and hide out for a bit. Probably, he'd got relatives in this quiet old railway town that the inspector had heard of but never been to before.

'AH' woke his sergeant when the train reached Exeter. They both sat enthralled at the spectacular journey down the River Exe to the estuary opposite the seaside town Exmouth. There were boats of all shapes and sizes and flocks of sea birds, geese and ducks. They passed a tiny station called Star Cross, then passed huge empty beaches at Dawlish Warren giving a glorious view of the sea. It was so beautiful to the tired and unaccustomed eyes of Metropolitan Police officers. The train snaked in and out of tunnels through the red sandstone cliffs, then right alongside the sea wall at Teignmouth, where strollers waved at the passengers on the train. 'AH' thought it was idyllic, as the announcement came that they would arrive shortly at Newton Abbot. As they were leaving the train, 'AH' spoke, "Listen, Noddy, don't use titles. I'm Geoff and you're Tony. We're on holiday looking round a town we don't know, OK!"

The sergeant grinned "Yes, S... Geoff," as they strolled out of the station, ignored the hovering taxis and walked towards some shops and a pub.

"We'll have a quick half here, Tony, and get our bearings before going in to town. It's only four days since Matey walked along here and he may be somewhere close!" 'AH' ordered some cheese sandwiches and found the barman happy to chat with holiday-makers from 'up country', being anywhere east of Devon! After munching their sandwiches, with free pickled onions, they strolled towards the town centre through 'Asian Alley', as locals called the quarter mile stretch of Asian restaurants. Turning around, 'AH' whispered, "He could be hiding around here, Geoff!"

Noddy Foster corrected him, "Excuse me, Sir, but I'm Tony. You're Geoff!"

His boss continued, "Oh yes! We'll start at this end of the restaurants and walk back towards the station, checking them for Matey."

The sergeant answered, "I'm sorry Geoff, but this isn't London. They don't open until 5.30 p.m.!"

As it was only 2.40 p.m., 'AH' decided, "OK, Tony, you wander into town and see what you can find out, while I phone the chief. Bet he'll be surprised that we're down here!" 'AH' found a bench to sit on and phoned his boss.

"Harling...! Why on Earth are you calling me on a Saturday afternoon...? You're where...! Chasing up a new lead...! What did I tell you last evening?!"

'AH' tried to explain, "But, Sir, early this morning we discovered that the bomber's accomplice..."

Chief Superintendent Price's voice was unaccountably angry, "Inspector Harling, this is an order! Get back to London immediately! Don't talk to anyone! Do nothing in Devon! Report to me at The Yard on Monday at 9.00 a.m.! I hope that you haven't messed up something important!" Amazed at being told off for his zeal, 'AH' called Sergeant Foster and the pair of them returned morosely to the railway station. They had a slow disconsolate journey back to London, taking no pleasure in the majestic scenery, they passed through.

***

During that quiet Saturday morning, Christine Templeton began to emerge from the last four days, rather like an animal sniffing the air after months of hibernation. Very slowly, her memory recalled her inability to respond to a meaningless jumble of unknown events and persons, sounds and smells. Conscious that a life-changing event had occurred and combined itself with significant physical injuries, she began to take authority over her thoughts. She realised that she could not see at all, although she sensed that she was not blind, could not move from wherever she was, could not hear but could speak. She wanted to communicate.

"Ag..." coming from her scarred lips was sufficient for the attendant nurse to send for Doctor Chaudhary.

He bent near to her remaining ear and spoke calmly and authoritatively, "Miss Templeton, you may speak to me now if you wish to."

Blood flowed, at least metaphorically, through her veins as in a clear, loud voice, Christine said, "Where am I please and who are you?"

Hearing this only as a faint breathing out of air, the doctor was jubilant that her will-power had combined with his professional attention, to enable her to speak, "You are in safe surroundings at the University College of London Hospital. You are recovering slowly from several injuries. My name is Doctor Chaudhary. Nurse Peterson is at your bedside constantly. If I ask you some medical questions, please will you give me some short answers?"

Christine struggled to stay alert, "Yes." The doctor chose his questions very carefully, knowing their impact on patients re-emerging into life.

Dialogue was more important than exact answers, so he did not rush her and tried not to worry her. As her answers followed, providing the 'inside view' that sophisticated technical machines could never match, he was alerted by Nurse Peterson to the blood pressure monitor. "Thank you, Miss Templeton, you have been very helpful. Now you must rest."

As he raised himself upright from above his patient, he heard her ask, "Doctor Chaudhary, is my fiancé dead?" Years of experience may help doctors, but cannot exclude all, natural emotions.

He answered, "Yes Miss Templeton, I am very sorry to tell you that Lord Walsham died."

Back inside her own self, Christine began to think. She was satisfied that she could not see because of the copious bandages surrounding her, but what was the horrendous cacophony of noises inside her head? She tried delicately to move her limbs, hoping to discover if they were there and available for her to use. She sensed that she must have been visited by somebody and vaguely recalled her hand being held purposefully. Christine determined to pray; firstly, with thanks that she was alive and belonged to Jesus Christ; secondly, that her life would fulfil the purposes that Almighty God had ordained for it, despite her situation.

***

Aaron had slept very little overnight, but was pleased when Salim visited him on Saturday afternoon, with news that Doctor Chaudhary had consented to him flying home next Tuesday, unless his condition worsened. "Is your journey home so soon really necessary, Salim?" asked Aaron.

"Yes, my friend. Tomorrow, the five emirs will meet in council, needing among other matters to support my father's designation for me as his crown prince. As monarchical states must ensure that their populations receive information about their royal families, the public announcement that I have succeeded Abdullah is to be made on Tuesday evening."

Aaron asked, "Will your population be pleased, Salim?"

The sheikh replied, "Those who think that our region can survive on oil and military fire-power will hate it, but others inside my country, the FNAE and perhaps throughout the Middle East will recognise my father's change of political emphasis to one of toleration for other points of view." Aaron showed his concern, "Salim, you have been thrust so unexpectedly into these matters of state. Will you cope with the huge changes to your situation?"

The sheikh considered, "My future direction concerns the FNAE, not solely the decisions of the ruling emirs, but also on how my fellow crown princes will respond to my joining their ranks. Arab princes behave differently from western politicians and rulers, who may need to placate the opposition and carry the media with them. My prayer is that the crown princes will accept me as a positive step towards an improved relationship with the outside world."

Aaron wanted to broadened the issue, "Last Tuesday, Salim, our personal worlds were blown apart literally by an immature young man, who had been trained to believe that intolerance of other persons and their faiths, gave legitimate permission to murder indiscriminately. Your own years of training may have fitted you for a life of wise leadership and advice far beyond your own desert affairs. When someone is elevated astronomically, not by his own prowess, there may be a phenomenal purpose behind it. Let me give you a true example from more than 3,000 years ago, when the Jewish nation had been overrun by the Midianites, who lived in the region that your FNAE occupies today. This arrogant people devised particularly horrible and effective ways to persecute Jews, by allowing them to sow crops necessary for their survival, but then to invade them annually to plunder their harvests for themselves. They destroyed what they didn't take, thus without resorting to weapons of warfare they were annihilating the Jewish nation. An unassuming young man called Gideon was affronted, not only with the Midianites, but the fact that his nation had turned away from worshipping God. The account can be read both in our Hebrew Bible and the Christian Holy Bible, in the book they call Judges. Gideon was untrained in warfare and leadership, yet God's angel visited him and appointed him to defeat the Midianites. He raised an army of 32,000 but God told Gideon to send home all but 300 men, who were simply to follow God's wisdom and strategy to defeat the enormous host of enemy soldiers. Their obedience made the enemy force turn inwards and destroy itself, giving Israel peace for the next twenty years under Gideon as their leader. Could Almighty

God be bequeathing such a role to you now Salim, not for personal gain or valediction, but for the sake of righteousness, however, a person chooses to define that word?"

The Sheikh spoke graciously, "You educate and flatter me, Aaron. Our Muslim faith tends to begin its direction from the time of our prophet Mohamed in the year 600 thereabouts, whilst also adhering to Abraham being our father who pro-generated Ishmael as his first-born son. "He was our patriarch and I am unaware of this Gideon. Please let me tell you something about the young bomber, of which you may be unaware my friend? When he strode into your shop, he hesitated, looked straight at my brother Abdullah and then myself, as we were on his extreme right and left sides, whereas you and the others were in front of him. He looked at us with such a perplexed expression because he had not expected to find fellow Muslims there! Although he managed to state his business by calling out '*Death to all Jews and Christians.*', that was a few seconds after he had been made to consider the most important question of his short life: '*I know that I must kill these infidel Christians and the accursed Jews, but... should I also kill my brothers in the faith?*' He chose to fulfil his designated mission, but my question is: '*At what point does nationality or faith become so overtaken by proud intolerance of another person's right to exist*?' That young man decided to kill and maim because of his devout training in intolerance. Perhaps your and my futures may be involved in doing the very opposite my friend?"

Aaron responded, "I can see your auspicious opportunities, Salim, but there are no possibilities for my own unnoticeable life."

HH Sheikh Salim smiled at his Jewish friend's belittling of himself, "Let us postpone the discussion of that most intriguing opinion Aaron, at least until our ears and blood pressures have calmed themselves!"

***

Alan Harling arrived home on Saturday evening after his apparently fruitless day's travelling to and from the West Country, with his face showing the family that he was in no jovial mood. Mary called, "I've saved some dinner for you, Darling, just in case you didn't have any on your journeys."

He grunted, "All I've had are cheese sandwiches at a pub and ridiculously expensive fruit cake on the train!"

His wife held him, "I can see that it hasn't been a good day for you, Darling. Do you want to tell me about it?"

He tried to relax, "Probably best not to, Mary, in case I burst a blood vessel all over the kitchen floor. Talking of which, I'm very disappointed that Brian managed to break one of Aunt Dorothy's wedding present glasses last night! I don't know what made the boy choose one of our expensive wine glasses to get himself a drink of water! Why couldn't he use a 'free with petrol' tumbler like usual?"

Mary frowned. "Oh, Alan, I don't think Brian would do that."

He was getting worked up again, "We'll just ask him then shall we! The evidence is in the bin unless you've chucked it out already! Fetch him in!"

Naturally, when Mary called Brian, his supportive sisters came too, "What's up, Dad? I'm sorry I broke a glass, but this isn't a court case. It was only a cheap one."

Alan exploded, "What do you mean 'cheap'? I know I'm only a police officer, but our family needs to recognise an expensive wine glass when they see one!"

Brian was annoyed, "But, Dad, it really was just a cheap one!"

His father yelled, "I know what I saw! I know what I spent ten minutes on my hands and knees for, in the middle of the night, clearing up after you kids again!"

With his hostile tone upsetting the entire family, Emily spoke in a conciliatory voice just like her mother's, "Look, Dad, if you and Brian both saw a broken glass, even if you each thought it was a different one, then it's not really something to argue over, is it?"

He shouted, "So it's a conspiracy is it? Four against one! If Brian wants to lie to his father to hide what he's done, it's a bad show! I know when I'm right!"

Mary intervened, "Alan! This has gone far enough. Brian doesn't tell lies because you and me have brought him up right. There's obviously a mistake been made somewhere."

He sprang from his chair, "Too right! We'll examine the evidence shall we? You can't go against solid factual evidence, even if my boss thinks he can! Mary, empty out the rubbish bin!"

His wife obeyed. "Just realise, Alan, that I've been putting stuff in it all day so it's full up and messy now."

Alan grabbed the next week's local paper that had just been delivered, "Never mind that! It's evidence we want!" He spread pages of it on the floor and up-turned the bin onto it. All the family gasped, not only at the smelly mess, but also at their hero's loss of temper. "Right, here it is! I wrapped this bundle up myself, using last week's paper! Watch this!" Alan ripped open the newspaper parcel exposing the remains of a cheap tumbler. The dramatic silence was broken only when Alan had had time to think things out in his logical mind, "So now we really do have a conspiracy! How can you go and smash another glass just to conceal the crime? That's interfering with evidence, that is!"

Emily comforted Pauline who had started to cry, Brian's face was white as he tried to decide whether to shout back at his father or not, but their mother went into the sitting room and called the whole family to join her, "Alan! Please count how many of Aunt Dorothy's wedding present wine glasses are in the cabinet." All five of them took meticulous care to count the slender-stalked glasses… one… two… three… four… five… six!

"Children," instructed Mary. "Please leave us alone for a few minutes. Your dad and I need to talk." Emily, Brian and Pauline were very pleased to escape upstairs to their bedrooms. "Now look, Darling, my own dear, darling husband. This has been a very hard week for you. It's not unnatural for things like this to happen, so don't be worried. We're going into the kitchen to clear up the mess, then we'll have a strong cup of tea and some of my delicious and very inexpensive home-made cherry cake." Alan followed Mary meekly into the kitchen.

Shortly after 10.00 p.m., Detective Inspector Harling of Her Majesty's Metropolitan Police's Bomb Squad knocked at his son's door. Receiving permission, he went in and spoke in a serious but humble tone, "Brian, I apologise to you. You're a fine young man who I admire very much. I was totally in the wrong. I am very sorry that I doubted your word. I love you, Son."

As they hugged, Alan heard his son's quiet voice, "I love you too, Dad."

***

It was already hot when the five emirs of the FNAE convened their monthly Sunday meeting. They quickly settled their business and financial issues, mostly concerning their enormous oil revenues and how best to increase these to even further benefit their royal accounts. Officials followed the hand instructions of their masters politely and silently before withdrawing, allowing coffee and sweet meats to be consumed in private. With quiet dignity, Emir Sheikh Rashid bin Hamad Al Nu'masiq reported on the murder of his crown prince son, Abdullah, in a terrorist attack in London five days before. He listened politely until the anticipated suggestions of revenge attacks and statements vilifying Israel and those Arab enemy states with which they disagreed, had subsided. Once this rhetoric had achieved its purpose of showing strength, he continued, "Crown Prince Abdullah was well-known for his military prowess and helped to show our strength of force to the world. Now we may wish to consider whether our political abilities and standing would be better acknowledged under a different approach? Would our Federation be more noticeable and acceptable in the Middle East, Europe and America, if an equally strong successor should have a different character and background, with a voice that would be listened to for its wisdom and humility rather than belligerence? Would the wider world, and particularly those nations including our own, which aspire to join the leading players, have greater respect for an approach not portrayed by an Arab soldier, but by an experienced royal sheikh accustomed to dealing with persons of other cultures and languages, such as my son, Salim?"

The other four emirs indicated their unanimous support without resorting to words or emotion, as by monarchical movement of hands and eyes they endorsed HH Sheikh Salim bin Rashid Al Nu'masiq as the emir's successor crown prince. Bows of satisfaction concluded the meeting.

***

A rather subdued Alan Harling prepared Sunday morning tea for his wife and himself according to their weekly ritual. He understood the importance that Mary and the children saw in being properly prepared and able to get to their church before the service started at 10.30 a.m., thus he willingly helped to ensure that his family had a comfortable departure from home. He further contributed by clearing up the breakfast things and tidying their home for the family's return from church, along with any additional stray persons that they occasionally brought with them.

At about 11.00 a.m. he made a fresh cup of coffee, sat down at the kitchen table and spread out paper and pens in preparation for writing a report. He'd always been a meticulous man, at work and at home, careful not to make mistakes and mostly being correct in his assumptions and decisions. The peculiarities of the last few days made no sense at all. What was going wrong with himself and why was his beloved police work being hampered by his boss? Why wasn't he being encouraged to get after the evil people who had trained an ordinary young man from Watford to become a terrorist? What could be more important than finding out who was behind it and stopping them before the next bomb exploded? He'd respected George Price for a long time as a good 'copper', not afraid of going out on a limb in the course of duty, so why had he stamped so hard on his investigations? He was not superstitious and had no belief in any inward or outward forces that could interfere with scientific normality. He was happy that his wife and children believed in their God, but he didn't. Yet could he, when he spent his working life amongst the horrors of reality? How could any 'god' be involved in this sordid world, where evil could be kept at bay only by good people's determined efforts?

Then how could a highly professional pathologist have found an 'extra hand' in the bits and pieces of bodies from the Klein's shop? Even worse: how could it have no finger prints, lines or the normal wear and tear of a person's hand and not even be recognisable as male or female? Also, how could three honest and sensible witnesses be so adamant that they'd seen a nondescript man rush into the shop and push himself between the bomber and the brave young woman? Now he was being hurt by his family's silly peculiarities, instead of providing their usual solace and reassurance during his time at home. It had started when young Pauline told him off in a voice that was definitely not her own, which if he believed in angels, which he didn't, sounded to him just like the Archangel Gabriel would sound! Then that broken cheap glass definitely seen in the kitchen bin, whilst the entire family had counted all six fancy wine glasses still in their cabinet, when he knew for certain that he'd swept up the remains of one of them in the night?

Alan dragged his mind away from all this nonsense and reached for his pen. He was a police officer with knowledge and responsibilities, whose allegiance was to queen and country, rather than to superior officers. As the officer-in-charge, his duty was to record everything that he knew about the Hatton Garden bombing in an official report. He began writing in his usual methodical and efficient style by setting down some basic information about the Klein's shop and the persons inside it at 11.00 last Tuesday morning. He gave their brief biographies, a summary of their injuries being careful to emphasise their soundness of mind, then their statements. The report's second section described his police-work following the explosion: setting up an incident room, the assistance of Hatton Garden people, researching CCTV footage for the bomber and his accomplice, then for the reportedly 'swarthy' man behind it all.

At that point, his phone rang, annoyingly interrupting his train of thought, "Yes, what is it!?"

His faithful Sergeant Foster explained "Very sorry to disturb you on Sunday morning, Sir, especially after yesterday, but one of Jenkinson's boys just phoned me. They've located three separate films showing Swarthy: one walking up Grenville Street, one in a café in Hatton Garden, and a third going into Farringdon Station, Sir."

'AH''s mind leapt, "Brilliant! I've got to meet Price at The Yard tomorrow morning before we tell the press the name of the bomber. This new evidence will change his mind and let us get after the bosses who set up this murder. Well done for letting me know, Noddy!" He was even more certain that it was right to have gone to Devon. Knowing he must be careful, he began what he thought was a diplomatic way of telling his bosses what they must allow him to do next: 'Recommendations for immediate identification and apprehension of culprits managing this act of terrorism.' The title pleased him as that alone would surely give him permission and encouragement to go after them. His first recommendation concerned the bomber's accomplice, believed to be in hiding in Devon, whilst the second was to search for and find Swarthy, believed to be in the Harrow area.

Time had passed too quickly whilst he'd been writing and he heard Mary unlocking the front door, followed by the children bursting in to tell him about their morning at church. He knew that they liked to do this each Sunday, in the hope that their father would be convinced by their sound spiritual examples and arguments. "Wow we're hungry, are you, Dad? It was great this morning! You should have heard the worship, it was awesome! Then the visiting preacher spoke brilliantly: just what we needed to inspire us, Dad!" Alan made appreciative gestures and responses, designed to please them all. "Oh, and Dad, this is for you," said Emily holding out a small brown envelope. It had his name on it in handwriting.

"Who gave you this, Em? Why would anyone at your church send me a letter?" He guessed that it would be yet another invitation to an evangelical event, especially designed for unbelieving friends and families of the initiated. He opened the envelope honourably, whilst already considering which excuse he could use, but it wasn't an invitation.

He pulled out a small folded piece of paper with a hand-written note, which took very little reading: *'Alan, why are you ignoring the signs that I am sending you? It is hard for you to kick against the pricks.'* The words meant nothing to him, so he folded up the note and was putting it back into the envelope when Emily asked, "What is it Dad? The man said that I must be sure to give it to you. He was really nice and friendly!"

Her father replied haughtily, "So he might have been Emily, but he wasn't brave enough to sign his own name! Just a clever Dick trying to persuade me about something, but to do it anonymously shows how little it's worth! Who was the chap who gave it to you? Is he a regular at your church?"

Emily replied cautiously, "Actually no, Dad. I'd never seen him before. He was in the queue for tea, after the service, and when I passed him the mug, he gave me the envelope, smiled, and said I was to be certain to give it to you. Then he went off with his tea to speak to the visiting preacher. Maybe they came together?"

Her father shouted, "So he didn't even say who he was! Fine! Just a crank messing around!" The rest of the family stopped what they were doing and looked at their normally polite and respectful leader. Surely, he wasn't going to get angry again, so soon after last night's episode?

"Come on Emily, describe him! I'm a police officer, you know! Strangers giving girls anonymous notes for their fathers might not be as nice as they appear! What did he look like?" Mary nodded to Emily, who was clearly hurt by her father's manner and was trying not to get upset.

"Well, Dad, I'll try and give you the best description I can: he was middle-aged or a bit younger, maybe forty or fifty. He wasn't very tall or fat, perhaps 5'7" and maybe less than eleven stone, had respectable clothes, not flashy or expensive, was clean and tidy without a beard or moustache, had medium length middle-brown hair; in fact, quite ordinary really, Dad."

Her father refused to stop, "That's not much help to me, Em. There must have been something else about him!"

Emily pondered, then said, "We're not supposed to emphasise these things, but... well, he was disabled, Dad."

Alan grinned nastily, "Disabled! How disabled? Wooden leg or only one eye, or what?"

Mary moved closer to her husband, concerned at the upsetting way he was acting. Emily burst out her answer, "He only had one arm Dad! Actually, he had a left arm but the sleeve was tied up. He didn't have a left hand, Dad!" Detective Inspector Alan Harling of the Metropolitan Police Force tried unsuccessfully to look composed, but his staring eyes and ashen face showed otherwise as he slumped heavily onto his kitchen floor.

***

Mary phoned a work colleague whose daughter was in Pauline's class at school. Emily took Pauline round to this friend's house to play, then decided to visit some other girls from church. Brian expressed great interest at going to watch a local football match at Ealing Broadway. The house was very quiet as Mary and Alan sat hand-in-hand on the sitting room settee, but the tea cups and cherry cake were left untouched on the coffee table. "Alan, you need a break. This is not like you and I'm concerned. You don't need to tell me anything that you don't want to, but you can if you want. I've nothing planned for the afternoon and evening, the children are all right, we're here in the safety and comfort of our own home, so there's nothing to worry about, Darling. I do love you, Alan."

Holding his wife's hand tightly whilst looking vacantly straight ahead, he heard himself telling his beloved wife some of the unexplained things that he knew were affecting his mind. "Mary, I knew the man who gave Emily the envelope had only one arm. I've examined his missing hand at Scotland Yard. It got blown off last Tuesday when the bomb went off in Klein's Jeweller's in Hatton Garden. He rushed into the shop to save Christine Templeton's life! The three witnesses who were in the shop gave me the identical description as Emily." Mary listened dutifully, but her husband's words only added to her confusion and alarm. She knew about intelligent and sensible men of his age going round the bend. Surely this couldn't be happening to her own husband? Whilst Mary had been listening, she'd also been sending up prayers for help for them both. Remembered the note in the envelope, she suggested that Alan put his feet up on the settee and have a sleep if he wanted to, whilst she read in the armchair. She helped him take off his shoes, and made sure he was comfortable and went upstairs to collect her mum's old 'King James Bible', which was an old-fashioned translation, not as modern as her 'New International Version'. Mary knew exactly where to look in the Acts of the Apostles, chapter nine. The dramatic words described how an ultra-intelligent and very zealous religious professional had been searching to arrest other Jews who'd chosen to believe in Jesus Christ as being their Messiah. This man, Saul, was extremely keen on his detective work, but was suddenly and forcefully spoken to by Jesus, using the same words as were in the note. The absolute surprise of his voice and a dazzling light had been enough to make Saul fall off his donkey and remain blinded for the next three days.

Ever since that event of 2000 years ago, the phrase *'He's seen the light'* had been used to describe persons coming to believe in Jesus Christ. Mary had learned that *'kicking against the pricks'* referred to oxen pulling heavy carts and instead of doing their work contentedly, struggled to avoid it by kicking backwards towards their human master on the cart, but wounding themselves against sharp pointed sticks that had been fixed to protrude forwards to just behind the animal's legs. Thus, these 'pricks' were a reminder for the animals to keep their heads down and stick to their job, rather than rebelling. Mary closed her Bible and devoted the rest of the day to loving and encouraging her husband in his obvious struggles.

***

Saturday and Sunday passed extremely slowly for Christine, but she did not mind. Further short daily visits from her nephew Peter had stimulated her, especially with the knowledge that he had shared his aunt's faith, following her encouragement a few years previously. Now, if she was to have a future, although doctors and other people might be able to help her, it was her own responsibility to try to build a new life. Whether as a horribly disabled invalid, confined to technical medical contraptions for a few painful years, or a person with a partially repaired body managing to survive, she would do her best. She decided rationally that her status was now a 'bereaved widow', in all but legal terms. She had loved Henry sincerely and was truly thankful for their short courtship, but that portion of her life was finished with. She would lock away her memories of him as something from a past experience that would not be repeated. She would look forwards and not backwards, not stealing tomorrow out of God's hands, but giving him time to reveal his purposes for her.

Soon, she would ask the gently spoken doctor to give her a summary of her condition and future opportunities, concentrating on abilities rather than disabilities. Obviously, her bodily sensations were being numbed by drugs, but she could sense little movement on her left side. She longed to be able to open her eyes, even if it showed her to be sightless. The insistent head pains were dreadful, but in what condition were her internal organs? For now, she would enjoy the wonderful peace of her prayer life, which could never be extinguished whilst she lived.

It was early on Sunday evening that Christine sensed the presence of someone new standing near her, "If somebody is here, please tell me who you are?"

Despite her pains and the muffling of anti-infection masks, she heard two voices, "Good evening, Miss Templeton, I am Aaron Klein from the jewellery shop."

"And I am Sheikh Salim, Miss Templeton. We have permission to visit and talk with you for a short while, if that would be your own desire."

Deciding that her new life could begin straight-away, by helping these two vaguely remembered men who were being sent to her now, Christine responded, "My name is Christine and I shall be delighted with your company Aaron and Salim."

It was the Sheikh who spoke for them both, "Christine, firstly, we thank you most humbly and sincerely for saving our lives at Mr Klein's shop." They spoke on very gently for another ten minutes until exhaustion caused Christine to wish the two men 'Goodnight'.

***

After leaving Christine Templeton, Aaron and Salim realised that their hopeful discharge from hospital within days would part their company, maybe for all time. Thus, they relished the opportunity of discovering more of each other's cultures, "You always seem to avoid answering my questions Aaron, when they touch on yourself or your Jewish faith!"

The jeweller apologised, "Sorry Salim! Perhaps it's because your potential is headed upwards, whereas mine is stuck firmly in obscurity."

The sheikh responded, "Be careful friend Aaron, or I shall summon Doctor Chaudhary to check if your mind is deranged as much as your ears!"

Aaron acknowledged the gentle rebuke with a smile, "Jews are used to being downtrodden. We're not desert sheikhs ruling their tribesmen. Many of us have a less ambitious station in life."

Salim settled himself into the bedside chair and asked, "So what is your station, Aaron? Never mind philosophy and high-minded thoughts, just tell me about yourself, please. What has been on your mind during our time here in hospital and what will you be involved in next?"

Aaron stretched out on his functional hospital bed to begin his repartee, "After our chat on Friday evening, I couldn't sleep and was so bored that I tidied my bedside locker. I discovered that a book had been pushed to the back, presumably when I arrived and my stuff was just packed into the locker in front of it. I pulled out the book, finding that it was what Christians call the Holy Bible, with an emblem and explanation showing that it was donated by the 'Gideons International' organisation. Apparently, they focus on gaining permission from hospitals, prisons and colleges to place their books in inmate's rooms, for bored people to read if they want to. It seems like a clever ploy! Anyway, I began to skim through it rather distrustfully, as it is a thoroughly Christian book and I'm assuredly Jewish!"

Salim smiled as Aaron took a breath. "I soon realised that they'd copied and anglicised our Hebrew Bible before adding their own new text onto the end! It's a confounded cheek, Salim, to take someone's book of faith and use it, together with your own ideas, to construct your own holy book! Feeling safe as long as I stuck to 'our part', I began to read from the beginning, describing how ADONAI created the universe, placed mankind there and then watched them make their mistakes over and over again, lurching from one catastrophe to another with occasional and wonderful divine interventions when necessary."

Salim added, "Yes, Aaron. We Muslims don't disagree with much of the early parts of the Christian Bible; in fact, we endorse a lot of it, especially giving honour to our Abraham and your Moses and other prophets."

Aaron picked up the book, "I read quite a long way on Friday night, all through what Christians call Genesis, describing our patriarch's lives, and into Exodus when Moses was sent to rescue the Israelites from Egyptian slavery. I just couldn't sleep so continued reading on and on until at 02.30 a.m. something very strange happened. As I turned the page into chapter twenty-eight, this piece of card fell out."

He passed it to Salim, who smiled with delight, "It's a ticket for a horticultural show, but not one that I know of. Is Gunnersbury in London, Aaron?"

The two friends were becoming intrigued, "Yes, but it's a part of West London that I don't know, I think near Ealing. Their show can't be prestigious like Chelsea's. It's probably just a local society's own event for local gardeners and enthusiasts."

Salim asked, "Could there be any significance in this ticket Aaron?"

The answer was hesitant, "Maybe? I think it was being used as a bookmark by a former occupant of the bed I'm lying on. The significance, if it exists, may be in what was written in pencil on that page of the Bible. Look here, I'll show you." He explained first about Israel's original high priest Aaron, after whom he'd been named, then pointed out the pages describing the Tabernacle with its furniture and the high priest's clothes, "Look! Exactly where the text describes the 'breast piece', with names of individual jewels representing our Hebrew tribes, somebody has written, *'You must find these jewels'.*"

Salim was perplexed as he inspected the Bible text, the pencilled note and the ticket to a horticultural show which had marked the place. "Did you read beyond this, my friend?"

Aaron frowned, "Somehow I didn't want to, Salim. I'm a jeweller and I know all about precious stones. Why would some person reading this Bible be so bold or offensive to deface it by writing such a note?"

Salim commented, "This has been written carefully in pencil, with some meaning to it Aaron, but why and who could the word '*You*' refer to? It could mean that the person writing it meant '*You*' referring to himself or herself, or it could mean that some person in general should look for these jewels."

Aaron answered, "There is a third interpretation that I am rather nervous about mentioning to you Salim."

Seeing the serious look on his Jewish friend's face, Salim asked him politely to go on, but only if he wished to. "From a grammatical point of view, the word could also mean, '*You*', the person reading this note!"

Aaron paused to let his interpretation sink in. Salim asked, "But how could a person sometime in the past, write a note intended for somebody else to read in the future?"

Aaron responded, "That's what I've been pondering ever since! In the natural way of course, it's impossible and ridiculous, but not everything in this world is natural Salim, some things are justly called 'supernatural'. Without wanting to be disrespectful, wasn't your prophet Mohamed given the words of your Holy Book, the Koran, supernaturally?"

Salim answered carefully, "It was our God, Allah, who gave his prophet the words to speak out. Other persons present wrote them down and many persons memorized them. Yes, Aaron, our Koran was given 'supernaturally', but you and I are intelligent men content in our own faiths, who would never expect to receive a message written in a book belonging to a different faith, for us to read sometime in the future!"

Aaron leaned forward, "One week ago, Salim, did you expect that your father would fly to London to ask you to become crown prince of your country, in place of a murdered brother?"

A knock heralded a nurse to check their temperatures, blood pressures and general demeanour. Once she had left them, Salim responded, "Let's keep our rationality, Aaron. Surely, no items of jewellery could remain in existence since the time of Moses, but even if preserved, how could anyone find them buried under layers of debris from countless past civilisations? Also, what could be the reason for finding them? Surely, this is too irrational… isn't it?"

Aaron answered Salim's points objectively, "I'm certain that any fabric from about 3,500 years ago would have disintegrated long ago, so the garment described as a 'breastplate' surely cannot have survived. I'm no archaeologist or historian, but as a jeweller I believe that the actual gemstones attached to it, could still exist. If they were thrown away or hidden indiscriminately then they would probably have been broken and destroyed hundreds of years ago. But please realise that these garments were most holy to my Jewish ancestors and in all civilisations, people take great care in preserving relics. As for reasons to find any of the jewels which remain intact, there would be great historical interest, corroboration for ancient texts, professional jewellery attention, plus financial gain because they would have immense value. However, Salim, there could be another reason, concerning any original artefacts still in existence which show the glory of God, whether Jewish, Muslim, Christian or of any other faith. There are copious ancient holy relics of doubtful integrity, but nothing that could compare physically to what is described here in this holy book. The religious significance would be immense!"

Salim responded, "I just don't understand how such tiny items could be discovered under vast amounts of debris, in totally unknown locations."

Aaron replied, "Indeed, it might be utterly impossible, unless their hiding places were very well disguised. We can't answer such huge questions Salim: we are not detectives!"

CHAPTER 6

'AH' was sitting at his office desk at Scotland Yard by 7.00 a.m. on Monday morning. He didn't like typing, but he knew he had to prepare his report professionally, so he began formalising his hand-written draft using the heading *'Recommendations for immediate discovery and apprehensions of culprits managing the act of terrorism committed at Hatton Garden, London on Tuesday 24 April'*. After stating the relevant facts, police-work undertaken and conclusions reached, he gave his own recommendations, clearly requesting sanction from his superiors to go after the people who directed the bombing. He left space for signing his report, but realising that he had filled only one and a half sheets of typing, and being a tidy man, he wanted to use up the remaining space. That was when he decided to write an 'Addendum Report' below his signature. It was a big decision, but 'AH' concluded that it might be better if he disclosed something of the recent peculiarities, using the following words:

'In order to provide the fullest information concerning the bombing described in the main report, I include the following notes of an acknowledgeable strange nature.

(1) All 3 survivors who witnessed the bombing inside the Klein's shop were interviewed as soon as doctors permitted me to do so on the Tuesday 24th afternoon. I ensured that none of them had had opportunity to communicate with each other before my interviews. I concluded that they were all intelligent, rational and honest persons. Each of their clear and unbiased factual accounts of what had happened, agreed with the other's statements. Additionally, each one of them added the following identical and most peculiar account: "After the young man entered the

shop, he hesitated and then strode up to stand behind Lord Walsham. Miss Templeton turned and thrust out her hand, attacking the assailant's face and called out 'No!' At the same time, another man entered the shop through the open door and rushed to stand completely between the bomber and Miss Templeton." Each of the three persons then described this man, in exact agreement.

(2) The police pathologist Dr Simon Pigott received all the bodies and body parts from the shop, referencing and examining these in his normal methodical style. However, on Wednesday 25th, he asked me to visit him and showed me that he had identified an 'extra left hand'. This was further examined with close scrutiny and was found to have an absence of normal fingerprints and lines. It was also not clear if it belonged to a male or female person.

(3) On Sunday 29th, I received a note through a third party, that was given for my personal attention by a man exactly fitting the description given in Item 1 above, excepting that this man now had a missing left hand.

I cannot and will not try to explain the above three points, but include them here as they appear to be material facts concerning the bombing.'

The inspector checked through his complete report, took two copies and at 8.30 a.m. handed one, plus the original, to Chief Superintendent Price's administration officer for his boss' immediate attention. 'AH' called in his team leaders to brief them about his anticipated events of the day. At the same time, Associate Commissioner Laurence Williams attended his pre-arranged meeting in Chief Superintendent Price's office, intending to have a quiet talk before 'AH' was due to arrive in twenty minutes' time. However, given that the inspector's report had just been handed in, they each read it through. Then they re-read it and sighed. "Look Price, I don't know what's going on with Harling, but he's certainly living up to his nickname! It isn't only his junior officers who call him 'AH' behind his back! His bosses share the same sentiments! He just makes you sigh! He's such an excellent professional policeman but he's also so aggravating! What do you make of this one-handed man nonsense?"

The chief superintendent answered solemnly, "I sent for him today

to reprimand him for charging off down to the West Country the day after I warned him not to do anything 'extra', just as you had instructed me, Sir. The man seems to think that he can disobey orders whenever he believes that they get in the way of his own investigations! He's a firebrand, Sir!"

Williams grimaced, "Although I agree, Price, please recall our conversation of last week. I'm seriously worried that my Special Branch has become weak. I've got to inject some oomph into it and maybe a firebrand is what it needs! Let's bring him in now, sound him out a bit and then put him out to grass for a couple of weeks. We'll see if some time away from The Yard will settle him down without quenching his spirit! You play it hard Price, because he disobeyed orders, while I play it soft because of his obvious zeal. Then we'll discuss what he should he do with us later on at the press briefing, before closing down the official investigation." Price agreed with his boss and the inspector was summoned to come in.

They received two immediate surprises: 'AH' was wearing full uniform rather than normal CID clothes, also he looked like 'death warmed up'! His eyes told the story of lack of sleep and his stony face portrayed anger and frustration. "Good morning, Inspector!" said the A/C "Thank you for your report. That was good thinking. Sit down and help us to understand things better."

His obviously soft approach had no impact as 'AH' replied, "I'd prefer to stand, thank you, Sir".

Price interjected angrily, "Very well, but 'at ease' man. You're not on parade!" The inspector answered their questions woodenly, clearly being unable to relax. The serious reminder that all police officers, including himself, must obey orders was received and acknowledged curtly.

The senior officers outlined the arrangements for the 11.00 press briefing, and then the A/C smiled and spoke less officially, "Inspector Harling, we've all known each other for donkey's years so let's not beat about the bush. You have an excellent professional record and now you've done another fine piece of police work in identifying the bomber. After the press briefing, we want you to go down to Hatton Garden, see our chaps and some local people, close down the incident room, and then come back to The Yard to clear up your desk. It appears to us that you'd benefit from a short break, so we're giving you a fortnight's gratuitous paid leave."

Chief Superintendent Price instructed, "Go home and do some of your neglected gardening, Inspector!"

The A/C lent forward meaningfully, "In addition to that Harling, why don't you take your wife down to the coast for a week, somewhere with bracing winds and rough seas coming off the Atlantic. Potter about on your own, and whatever you do don't start making contact with local police officers! Just chat to the locals and enjoy doing what you like to do best. Afterwards, I want you to report here to me on Tuesday 15th May at 11.00. Is that all understood?"

'AH' managed to answer, "Certainly, Sir, but what about the recommendations in my report, Sir?"

The A/C replied, "We'll discuss those on the 15th, Inspector. You can go now." The meeting ended with only A/C Williams sure of what he had been saying. Back in his own office, 'AH' made a few phone calls. He made sure that a Watford police officer would be with be with the young bomber's family to watch the televised press briefing at 11.00. Then he asked Doctor Chaudhary to let the witnesses watch in their rooms at UCLH. He told Sergeant Foster to prepare for his visit to the incident room after the broadcast, then to expect to clear up in Hatton Garden and return the teams to their normal duties awaiting another incident.

***

Doctor Chaudhary's rounds on Monday morning encouraged all three of his explosion patients. Sheikh Salim would be discharged early tomorrow morning, being sufficiently well to fly to the Middle East although needing to return to UCLH for weekly check-ups for latent internal problems. Aaron Klein must stay for at least another day before possible discharge. Christine Templeton asked to be told more of her injuries and advised of her likely medical future. Doctor Chaudhary arranged for further tests and examinations to be undertaken, including by specialist eye and ear staff, to enable him to report the results to her tomorrow afternoon.

***

The police press briefing went quietly and efficiently with the A/C referring to the Chief Superintendent by rank and name, but making no reference at all to Inspector Harling. The atmosphere in the nondescript terraced house in Cromer Road, north Watford was tense, with father, younger brother, mother and little sister staring transformed as their Khaled was named as the terrorist bomber who killed himself and three other persons in central London six days ago. His photo filling the screen was a hideous testimony that this quiet first-born son had been turned into a radical Muslim suicide-bomber, to hate and kill any who disagreed with his own religion. With his name now public knowledge, neighbours, wider family, friends, employers, school teachers and fellow pupils — indeed, all who knew any of this quiet and thought-to-be respectable family from Watford — would be shocked and forced to react themselves. The young policewoman sitting behind the distraught family, knew herself to be an intruder into their lives, whilst wanting honestly to show compassion and support for them. The short news item concluded and was followed without a break by hyped-up football heroes celebrating a goal, bored politicians shaking each other's hands in some place somewhere, and lurid pictures of violence in central Asia. Every image was carefully designed to entertain the insatiable appetites of avid viewers who hadn't had their own broken family's innermost secrets shown publicly around the world.

Inspector Harling made an uneventful last official visit to Hatton Garden, acknowledging and thanking his teams and those members of the public pointed out to him, especially the owner of the cafe that his men had already started clearing of their incident room equipment. After a short visit to his own office to tidy up, he selected a few items for his briefcase and left Scotland Yard. He went next to UCLH, thanked Doctor Chaudhary and the staff for their co-operation with his enquiries, and then called briefly to see Sheikh Salim and Aaron Klein. He made a point of giving them his card with official contact details and his private phone number. Then with a last "Goodbye!" 'AH' went home.

***

After the Inspector had left them, Aaron and Salim reviewed their arrangements. Salim sent for new clothes from his embassy and arranged transport for him to be taken directly from UCLH to Heathrow Airport on Tuesday morning for the flight to Dubai, from where he would be met and taken to his father that evening. Aaron phoned Esther asking her to visit his flat tomorrow morning to fetch him some clothes to exchange for the hospital's emergency store reserved for accident victims. Now, on this last private afternoon that they foresaw, Aaron and Salim wanted to discuss the question that remained hanging unanswered in the air: "Who did the '*you*' mean in the pencilled note '*You must find these jewels*'?" They decided that whoever had written the note in the Bible must be found, but how to trace him or her from the bookmark was an unanswered dilemma. Salim considered that whoever wrote it was a seriously-minded person, maybe with an obsession, healthy or otherwise.

Aaron had been using his jeweller's mind, with questions concerning the varieties, shapes, sizes and degrees of purity of the jewels going round and round in his head. Where they were was a complete mystery, as was their condition, possibly so damaged to be of no use or value. Aaron had tried to identify which particular gems were worn by his ancient namesake on the high priest's garments. Although the Christian Bible at his bedside was helpful, he didn't think the names used for the individual gems was necessarily correct. How indeed could Moses in the Sinai Desert know what names applied to gemstones, which must have been included in untold treasure showered on the Israelite slaves to persuade them to get out of Egypt before any more catastrophes took place? After every Egyptian family experienced the sudden death of their firstborn child, the Israelites must have loaded up their belongings in chaotic circumstances to escape for their very lives! Then some months later Almighty God had instructed that twelve gemstones of different specified varieties should be collected and attached to the breastpiece, plus two more jewels to be placed on the shoulders of the high priest. Thus, it was the fourteen fabulous jewels that the unknown pencil-writer felt were so important to find. Aaron knew that in his flat, he had his Hebrew Bible and many specialist books to help his investigations into which each gem had been, and maybe still was. He was anxious to try to do this for the rather obvious reason that he had little else in his life to do.

***

Aaron was visited that early Monday evening by Joshua Shulz, who had stayed only five minutes on the previous Thursday finding his old employer in no state to talk so soon after the explosion. "It is so good to see you looking much improved, Mr Aaron, after last week's dreadful experience. How are Mrs Naomi and the dear children taking their terrible loss? What will you do with the shop? I hear that it was totally destroyed! Will you ever work there again, Mr Aaron?"

Aaron recognised that old Joshua was used to keeping his own company and not conversation with others, so he began to answer the stream of questions kindly. "Thank you so much for coming to see me again, Joshua. Mr Reuben's wife and young Isaac are keeping their emotions to themselves for now. Dear Ruth is being a brilliant help to her Aunt Esther, who immediately took them all into her own home, where she's lived alone since Mr Abraham and my mother passed away. There's plenty of room for the whole family for the time being, and Golder's Green is not too far away. It's too early for decisions about the shop, but it will definitely be rebuilt under the insurance agreement. After that, we will think what to do, but I can't imagine ever working there again and Mrs Naomi will probably never want to return to live above the shop. Those days are ended Joshua, but what about you? It must be about seven years since you retired. Are you still living up at Kilburn?"

"Yes, Mr Aaron, I don't think that I shall ever leave my home in Brondesbury Road, after things have worked out so badly for me. It was twenty years ago when I moved there, when everything was going so well for Mr Abraham. You and Mr Reuben were just young men then, of course. I rented a top floor flat, which was quite enough for me, but three years later the owner decided to sell the whole house. I didn't want to move and have to start up again somewhere else, so when I asked if he would like to avoid estate agent's fees and sell it directly to myself, he was most agreeable! I managed to obtain a bank loan to add to my savings and I purchased the whole house and its small garden. It has three liveable floors each with two bedrooms, living room, kitchen and bathroom, plus a large basement partly underground. I believed that I would make sufficient money by renting out the two lower flats to working couples to enable me to pay all the bills and make a good profit. For the first several years my plan worked very well, but as soon as I retired from the shop, everything changed. First, the ground floor tenants left on one Sabbath night — knowing, of course, that I couldn't take any action. They already owed me two months' rent, having made such plausible excuses that I'd been happy to wait for them to pay. But Mr Aaron, they stole all of the smaller fittings that they could take: kettle, electric fires, toaster and even the cutlery and crockery! They must have loaded everything into their van and then disappeared from the neighbourhood. But just a year later, something even worse happened."

Aaron decided to let old Joshua talk on and on, even though it was hurting his ears. "The first-floor tenants served a writ on me for failing to keep their flat in line with building regulations and sanitary laws. They'd never complained at all to me, but tried to use the law to have their flat made into a palace. The local council took their side and threatened me with the police if I didn't comply with their thick rulebook. Of course, the council wasn't satisfied with me renovating only one flat; it had to be the whole house! I can tell you, Mr Aaron, that it took all my savings and gave me sleepless nights for months. Then, suddenly, those wicked tenants left without paying me their last month's rent! I decided to give up having tenants, because of the stress, so I try to manage on my national pension and the one that you and Mr Reuben allowed me so I manage to pay my bills. My savings have all disappeared and I've only the bare minimum of possessions. The rest needed to go to the second-hand furniture shop on the High Street. I've had a dreadful time since I retired, Mr Aaron."

Naturally, Aaron was saddened to hear Joshua's tale of woe, but the details were tiring him and making Joshua rather red in the face. Deciding to change the subject and give the elderly Jew something positive to think about, Aaron asked, "Joshua, I wonder if you would be interested in something very unexpected that has happened to me here in hospital?"

He agreed willingly, "Oh, please excuse me Mr Aaron for talking so much. I don't have anyone to talk to nowadays. Please tell me what has happened, especially if it is good news!"

Aaron reached into his locker and took out the Gideons' Bible. "Mr Aaron, whatever are you doing?" exclaimed Joshua jumping up in high alarm.

"Hold on Joshua, I haven't done anything silly. This Christian Bible is just the same as our Hebrew Bible, at least in what they call the 'Old Testament' although they've muddled up the order of our holy books. Just listen to what I'm going to tell you and you'll see that there is no alarm. The other night when I couldn't sleep and had nothing to read, I found this book in the back of my locker. I started reading and discovered that the start was identical to our Torah. Very early on Saturday morning, I reached what they call Exodus, all about our ancestors being slaves in Egypt and how ADONAI brought them out at PESACH, which they call Passover. Then in their chapter twenty-eight, I read about the High Priest Aaron's garments. Do you recall what he wore, Joshua?"

The old man's face was extremely serious, "The High Priest had special underclothes and an ephod, a sash, a breastplate to enclose the Umin and Thumin, and a mitre." As Joshua was looking more relaxed now, Aaron asked if he remembered what was on the breastplate. "Naturally, Mr Aaron. There were wonderful jewels attached to it, each one with the name of a tribe of Israel engraved on it." With barely contained excitement, Aaron turned to chapter twenty-eight and showed the old man the pencilled note *'You must find these jewels'*. "Well, Joshua, I think that this hand-written note was intended for me and that I must find those jewels, wherever they are!"

Instead of showing genuine interest, or polite surprise, old Joshua's face had turned from its previous high colour to an alarming white. Aaron wondered if the involvement of the Christian Bible had been too much for the devout elderly Jew, so he changed the subject to something less thought-provoking. After making sure that Joshua's face was gaining a little of its colour, Aaron suggested that it was time for him to rest and that Joshua might like to return on another day. Very seriously, Joshua made restrained farewells and quietly left the hospital room to return to his solitary home in Kilburn.

***

Mary was very pleased to see Alan home early, or at least not late, for once. They sat at the kitchen table enjoying a cup of strong tea with Mary's new coffee sponge cake still warm from the oven. It was after dinner that evening that he began to relax and disclosed to his family that he was actually on official leave and would not be going into The Yard for two weeks. "Wow, Dad, what on earth will you do…? Won't all the criminals in London be extra active with you out of their way? Surely you won't take two weeks to clean out the garden shed will you?" He was delighted that he had a loving family, and had a real desire to deepen his relationships with each of them.

Once the children had left them, Mary asked very gently, "What would you really like to do during your leave, Darling, and what did the A/C actually tell you to do?"

Alan repeated Price's order to '*Go home and do some of your neglected gardening.*' then tried to explain the A/C's additional words, "It seemed that he wasn't disagreeing with the chief's orders, but was telling me something more confidential.

"His words were, '*I recommend something additional to that, why don't you take your wife down to the coast for a week, somewhere with bracing winds and rough seas coming off the Atlantic. Potter about on your own, and whatever you do don't start making contact with local police officers! Just chat to the locals and enjoy doing what you like to do best. Then I want you to report here to me on Tuesday 15th May at 11.00. Is that all understood?*'"

Mary frowned in puzzlement, "That sounds rather unusual Alan, almost as if he was giving you a secret message that he didn't want Mr Price to understand. But that's silly! Have you remembered it properly, Darling?"

Alan explained, "I'm sure that it was on purpose and something much more than trying to be nice. I've never really had much to do with him because he's far too senior for that. He's a clever chap so he must have intended something. The way he handled the press briefing was really good, letting those piranhas know that the Met was in control and that Fleet Street were on-lookers and not directors."

Mary decided to play detective, "Well, he was recommending something additional to gardening, not instead of it. He clearly proposed that you and I go away for a holiday by the sea and not just any old seaside place either, somewhere with strong winds and rough seas."

Alan began to understand, "You're right Mary! It has to be the Atlantic coastline, not Yarmouth or Margate, but why was he so specific?"

Mary asked, "Alan, did he say all that to you before or after he'd read that report you were scribbling out yesterday?"

He answered, "He'd just read my nicely typed version of it before I was called in."

Mary asked eagerly, "Was it exactly the same, just typed up, Darling?" Alan hesitated not wanting to hide things from his wife, but now that the bombing investigation had been officially closed, perhaps it was safe for him to tell Mary about last week's peculiarities? Very shyly, he told her about Sheikh Salim, Aaron Klein and even using a hand squeezing system with Christine Templeton, all of whom gave exactly the same testimony and description of the 'second man' entering the shop. Then he disclosed the pathologist showing him the 'extra left hand'. "So that's why Emily's note had such a huge effect on you yesterday, Alan! Why hadn't you told me before?"

He smiled at her, "Well, for one thing it was confidential police business, but the main reason was I thought that you'd think I'd flipped!"

Mary hugged him, "Come on, Darling, let's try to work out whatever it was your A/C was trying to get through to you. I'll cut another slice of cake whilst you pour out another cuppa each…! So your A/C knows what you've just told me and he knows you're not a nutter! He must trust you and want you to do something for him, Alan! I think you already know what he meant, don't you?"

Alan said very sheepishly, "I think he was telling me to go back to Devon, but to make my enquiries down there unofficially without involving the local police." They stopped to consider the impact of the hidden proposal, which couldn't be called an order.

"Somehow, your A/C is doing something that you don't know about,

Alan. He told you to do what you like doing best and we both know what that is don't we, Darling: your beloved police work! Some sort of holiday this is going to be!" Mary was overjoyed that a very senior police officer believed in her husband and appreciated his skills.

"Well, Mary, I wouldn't have to work all of the time would I?" he grinned.

***

Alan Harling had rarely watched his children go off to their schools, or his wife to her work at Pauline's school where she was a volunteer teacher's assistant. This Tuesday morning, he did the washing up, tidied the kitchen and put on his favourite old outdoor clothes that he forbade Mary to throw away. He strolled around his entire estate, noting that the front lawn and flower beds were just about up to the standard of his neighbours' along Princes Avenue in Gunnesbury. The semi-detached house with mock Tudor painted beams looked as tidy from the outside as Mary kept it on the inside. Alan decided to delay cutting the lawns to the afternoon once the sun had dried the grass. He walked round to his much preferred back garden with its smallish timber shed and tiny greenhouse. He set to work immediately, emptying them both out and laying the contents in meticulous rows on the back lawn. Alan spent ten minutes searching in vain for extraneous items to throw away or give to less well-off neighbours. He dared not dispose of anything belonging to Mary's jurisdiction, or to any of Pauline's vast collection of scooters, skipping ropes, hoops and pushchairs for her dolls. He took out his Suffolk Punch petrol lawnmower that he half-loved and half-hated. It had been a wedding present from his parents nearly twenty years ago and when it went well it was brilliant, taking him only half an hour to cut both lawns. However, there was the all-too-frequent two hours work of cleaning and sharpening the blades and attending to carburettor and spark plug. He decided to postpone those frustrating maintenance jobs and opened the side door into the garage.

The children's bikes leant annoyingly against one wall, whilst his and Mary's were placed perfectly opposite them, next to Mary's number two freezer full of food in case of a Siberian winter in West London. His hand-built bench, racks and shelves were at the back of the garage, never dared to be touched by another member of the family, who knew that the master recollected the exact location of every box of tools and containers of specific sizes of screws and nails. Alan spent a lovely hour and a half tipping them out and reorganising them to perfection, when there was a knock on the garage door. "I knew where to look for you didn't I, Darling! I expect that you've prepared some lunch for us?"

Mary teased. "Oh! Do you usually have lunch? I always eat my sandwiches whilst I'm working." Mary called him indoors ten minutes later for a delicious lunch of cold cuts and pickles, after which they sat at their computer and searched the internet. They found a holiday flat at Teignmouth available from the coming Saturday, aptly named 'The Atlantic Spray' being right on Den Crescent, overlooking the old-fashioned sea-side resort's village green with the sea in front of it.

"It's on the top floor with a brilliant sea view and the price includes full English breakfast downstairs!" enthused Alan. Mary was over-joyed to see her husband so enthusiastic about this very surprising opportunity to get away entirely on their own, without the children for the very first time.

"OK, Darling, let's book it up quickly before somebody else does!" Click, click, click...

"Done!" exclaimed Alan. He was soon sent out to collect Pauline from Berrymede Junior, after which the lawns couldn't be put off any longer. By the time that Brian and Emily had come home from Acton High School and the family had shared all the day's news, enjoyed a delicious hot dinner and separated to their various private places, Alan was beginning to enjoy this unexpected time away from his beloved work.

***

HH Sheikh Salim bin Rashid Al Nu'masiq's flight landed on time at Dubai International airport to be met by servants of his father in a commodious black Mercedes that purred sedately up to the aircraft's steps. The other passengers were asked politely but firmly to wait whilst a VIP disembarked. The car glided out of the airport's private exit and straight onto the motorway. Four hours later, he was escorted into a vast anti-room and asked respectfully if he would follow the servant into the interior of his father's palace. Salim was ushered reverentially into a sound-proofed inner sanctuary, lined with gorgeous tapestries and furnished with a mixture of Arabian desert couches, Western settees and huge coffee tables. His father was standing waiting for him. Salim made a courteous salaam to the emir who grasped his hands and took his son to a pair of Parisian sofas either side of a low table displaying bowls of Middle Eastern cooked and cold dishes. Water and hot towels were brought for their hands, and with due deference to their emir, no orders were necessary as the palace servants silently closed the doors and left their Majesty alone with his son. Palace rumour had advised them that he was to become next-in-line to the royal throne and good servants are always zealous to respect a future master.

"Now, my son, you must be tired and hungry after your gruelling flight from London. Please, eat and drink whilst I explain today's arrangements. At 18.00, we will make a televised address to our nation, which naturally will be viewed with great interest throughout the Middle East. Many countries around the world will show excerpts of your formal bestowing as Crown Prince on their international news programmes. This means that ill-advised or ignorant political commentators will be struggling to think of something to say. Their editors will demand something tangible and interesting, preferable including a mixture of good and bad news with consequences that could affect their own part of the world."

"What do you have in mind, Father?" asked Salim respectfully.

"I shall be pleased to introduce you to the world as a mature sheikh who has been well-trained in international affairs, whose knowledge of Western cultures and languages will assist inter-continental understanding, particularly concerning important Middle Eastern issues." Salim congratulated his father on a suitably wide-ranging introduction, which should not cause offense in many quarters. "That is all very well for politically correct nothingness Salim, but you will need to say certain things of far greater relevance which leaders can recognise. I trust that you have prepared something suitable?"

"Father, your decision to bestow the honour of becoming crown prince on myself, rather than on my older brother, needs to be recognised as being wise and meaningful. Would it be fitting for you to comment on Hamad bin Rashid's abilities as making him your choice for a newly established role that will be of surprise and relevance whilst not being greatly strategic?"

The emir smiled, "Already I see the benefit of choosing you my son. Although you did not say 'exiled from court', perhaps something distanced from real decision-making was in your mind?"

Salim continued, "To some degree yes, Father, but also to give what the West calls 'added value' to your main decision. The crown prince holds many responsibilities in his hands, predominantly that of preparation for succeeding his father in the very far distant future."

The emir gave a courteous bow, "Very graciously said Salim. I am eager to know what device you have in mind!"

His son continued, "Would it be good, Father, to allow Hamad bin Rashid certain freedoms whilst channelling him into a useful enterprise? Our Federation is small in terms of geography and population giving us some similarities with less important countries, but we may not desire close involvement with those. However, there are several larger countries which comprise major regions which are economically viable yet thwarted in strategic issues by needing to remain good 'team players' within their nation. Such significant regions that aspire to higher status internationally, whilst remaining politically firm within their respective nations, may see benefits in forming ties with our Federation."

The emir understood only partially, "I follow your train of thought Salim, but what do you have in mind for your brother sheikh?"

Salim continued, "Father, if he were able to 'scout ahead' for us in his royal role, but not as an official, he would be able to undertake discussions at an initial level, with you alone, Father, directing his specific involvements."

The emir began to understand, "Yes and for you to manage them Salim! What title did you have in mind for your brother?"

Salim answered, "Perhaps, 'Prince of Exploratory Negotiations with Strategic Partners', Father? It is rather a mouthful, but may it be suitably innocuous for our purposes?"

The emir was pleased at his excellent choice in selecting his eventual successor, "Now, my son, you must tell me of your own speech."

Salim waited purposefully for a moment, to allow his next words to hold their own importance in his father's eyes. "I should want to use the events of a week ago to prompt responses in the hearts and minds of senior world leaders, but also in people in general, Father. I propose to describe the suicide-bomber's motives and actions, with the repercussions for those very different persons inside the jewellery shop, and within our own nation, Father. I should ask peoples around the world to reflect on 'How should we recognise, understand and learn to tolerate each other, as coming from different cultures and faiths?'" The emir was silent. Was his son's far-reaching statement too close to major cultural, religious and social issues, indeed straying into areas that were best left untouched?

He sighed deeply, but not sadly, "My son, I had not appreciated your bravery and determination alongside your wisdom. Your proposed speech would have significant implications for yourself, our Federation and indeed throughout the world. Your words are those of a fearless desert sheikh, Salim, and I approve of them."

Thus, it was that the entire ruling family of their country, together with fellow emirs and crown princes from within the Federation of Non-aligned Arab Emirates, gathered together in state, with TV cameras deferentially recording the event for the Middle Eastern and world's attention. The emir spoke briefly of Crown Prince Abdullah, a soldier in true Arabian style, whose life had been snatched away so viciously. He then announced that his eldest son Hamad bin Rashid was to become 'Prince of Exploratory Negotiations with Strategic Partners' commissioned to research closer economic ties with viable regions around the world. Finally, the emir announced his choice of the succeeding crown prince as HRH Sheikh Salim bin Rashid Al Nu'masiq, describing him as a mature sheikh, well-trained in international affairs, whose knowledge of Western cultures and languages would assist inter-continental understanding, particularly concerning important Middle Eastern and global issues. The emir than invited Salim to speak, focusing all attention on this unknown 'lesser son', so different from his belligerent predecessor.

Salim spoke clearly and confidently, "One week ago, the motives and actions of an immature young Englishman of Eastern origin, resulted in life-changing repercussions for a small group of very different people. They had gathered for innocent business in a jewellery shop in central London. What this man thought and did has impacted our own country and the Federation as a whole. May I ask all those who will listen to my brief account, please to consider honestly their own reactions? The young man had prepared himself to be a suicide-bomber, ready to attack whoever would be in a small Jewish business on a quiet Tuesday morning. He entered the shop and in reviewing his targets, his eyes met with mine. Totally surprised at finding my brother the Crown Prince and myself in the shop, he had a tiny moment in which to make his immense decision. Should he continue with his plan to kill and maim innocent persons because of their culture and religion, or should he reconsider because now that would include fellow Muslims? His decision led to a short prepared speech: *'Death to all Jews and Christians!'*. He had chosen to go ahead and murder because his intolerance of persons who held values other than his own was greater than his recognition, understanding and respect for them. As he reached for the detonator to kill us all, the actions of one person alone interfered with his results. A young English Christian woman, realising what the young man was about to do, had to make her own immediate decision. Shouting out an impassioned *'No!'* she acted with self-sacrificial bravery in an attempt to stop him.

"Stepping right up to the man, she punched out at his face. He detonated his bomb, killing himself along with Crown Prince Abdullah, one of the Jewish owners of the shop, and the fiancé of that young Christian woman. Her actions saved the lives of the Jewish owner of the shop and myself; yet, this heroic woman has been terribly injured, disfigured for life and been denied her husband-to-be.

"Please reflect on the two persons that I have just described and consider my question to myself, and also to all of you who are listening today. *'What would each one of us have chosen to do? Would we have followed the young man, allowing our intolerances to drive us relentlessly to kill innocent people simply because of our different cultures and beliefs? Or would we have risked our very lives like the young woman, to try to stop religious hatred achieving its evil aim?'*

"Within my role as crown prince of my country, I shall be seeking opportunities to restore or create relationships throughout the world which will support the divinely-inspired human motivation to recognise, understand and tolerate each other's differences. Will you support me in this? Thank you for listening."

***

Aaron Klein had been disappointed not to have been allowed to leave hospital on that Tuesday morning, but Dr Chaudhary needed further tests on his internal organs undertaken. Knowing that the doctor was to explain Christine Templeton's condition to her that afternoon, Aaron went to encourage her beforehand, "Whatever the doctor says, Christine, I can see an amazing improvement in your health. Once you have lost some of the dressings, you'll be able to help yourself get on."

She was pleased with his positiveness, "Thanks, Aaron. People can get all sorts of help for minor disabilities nowadays. I know that my left hand took a bashing, but my right one feels fine. But when my eyes start to work again, please don't show me a mirror!" Aaron promised to visit her again later on.

***

Doctor Chaudhary began, "You are a brave woman, Miss Templeton, so we can talk honestly together. Nobody comes away from an explosion right in front of them without sustaining serious injuries. Although the visual effects may appear dreadful, it is internal injuries that will really influence your future. Blast injuries are a complex set of traumas, which medics usually divide into four classes, the first of which is primary injuries caused by intense shock waves. Ears are far too sensitive to cope with such over-pressure, so you lost most of the left outer ear, which eventually can be hidden by your regrown hair, as it was mostly burnt away. However, the workings of the inner ear are what matters most. Your left eardrum was badly perforated, the hair cells within the cochlea have virtually all been destroyed and the blood vessels and neural pathways within your auditory system were significantly damaged. Your hearing has been seriously impaired, probably losing you 75% of hearing in your left ear, and about 50% in the right. That can be mitigated by modern appliances, but you will probably suffer an unpleasant condition called tinnitus, rather a horrible continuous orchestra of noises at differing pitches, often low drumming and motor-type noises intermingled with high-pitched school bells, resulting in a disconcerting cacophony of sounds. There is no known cure for tinnitus, but in time people learn simply to put up with it and its nauseous day and night feelings. The likely effects of primary blast injuries on internal organs and systems frequently include severe damage to lungs, blood vessels and other vital working parts. However, Miss Templeton, I am pleased to report that you do not appear to have suffered as badly as may have been expected, nor significantly from blast-induced traumatic brain injuries, as evidenced by us having this conversation.

"What we call secondary blast injuries include amputations and partial destruction of mostly visible parts. In addition to your left ear, you have lost part of your left hand. On admission, your smallest finger was missing and during the first operation it was necessary to remove the damaged second and third fingers as well. Your pointing finger and thumb should be able to operate well together hereafter. Given your immediate proximity to the suicide-bomber, it is amazing that you have not received many of the common tertiary blast injuries, often referred to as 'blunt instrument' types, probably because other persons involved who did not survive the explosion took the fullest force of such impacts, saving you from broken limbs and further amputations. The last category is quaternary blast injuries from which you have sustained severe flash burns predominantly on your face, neck, upper chest and shoulders. These are beyond the scope of natural healing and must fall into the realm of skin grafting and cosmetic surgery, requiring much time for nature and the skills of specialist surgeons to do their best for you. I am sorry Miss Templeton to have needed to describe such a catalogue of injuries, yet I am very pleased that you have survived this violent explosion so well. Given the great spirit I see in you, I believe that you will live a proper life — once various treatments have been undertaken. You must remain at UCLH for at least two or three months in order for you to receive close attention, including smaller operations. Additionally, it is so that I can be sure that you have escaped further blast-induced damage to your internal workings. This will be scrupulously monitored here for the next month, where emergency treatment is available to give any suddenly required assistance. Tomorrow morning, we will begin to leave parts of your body relativity free of dressings to enable natural healing processes to accelerate. Please, try hard not to let the sight of your injuries perturb you too much. Thank you for listening so calmly, Miss Templeton. Do you have any questions that you wish to have answered?"

Christine spoke without emotion, "Thank you very much, Doctor Chaudhary, for being so honest with me. I will do my best not to hamper the work of the wonderful doctors, nurses and therapists attending to me. My faith and spirit are strong and I am determined to do more than simply overcome my injuries. I aim to have a good future life, if rather different to that anticipated."

***

A little later, Christine's nurse admitted Aaron into her room, where he listened attentively to her summary of the medical prognosis that she had received. Not wanting to dwell on that, Christine asked him to tell her any news. Thus, Aaron related his adventure of the previous Friday night, then the subsequent discussions he had had with Sheikh Salim concerning the pencilled note '*You must find these jewels*'? that he had found written in his hospital room's Gideons Bible. When he described the horticultural show bookmark and the mystery of who had placed it in the Bible, and written the note, Christine became most interested. "Surely such a quandary requires professional help, Aaron? We've had so much contact with a stalwart detective recently, why don't you simply ask him for assistance?"

Aaron was startled, "You mean Inspector Harling from Scotland Yard? Surely, he would be far too busy and uninterested in such a petty thing?" Christine would have liked to smile, "I'm not so sure, Aaron! He was keen for us to approach him if we needed something and now we do!"

Aaron told Christine Salim's conclusion that the note writer was a seriously-minded person, who may have had an obsession with jewels.

After explaining that he had been considering what varieties, shapes and sizes were the 3,500 years old gemstones; Aaron asked Christine, with some hesitancy, if she was familiar with the Christian Bible's description of his ancient namesake's high priestly garments, on which the fabulous jewels were attached. "Yes, Aaron, the Bible's wonderfully detailed description of the tabernacle that Moses was told by God to make in the Sinai desert is a favourite study of mine! It would give me much joy to join your research about these precious jewels, Aaron." He felt humbled to hear this courageous disfigured woman apply the word 'joy' to herself. "It would be wonderful if you could help me please, Christine, but I really mustn't tire you."

Christine persisted, "The nurse or I will tell you when to stop, Aaron. How would Moses have known what name applied to the specific stones and how to sort them out from the horde of valuables that the Israelites were given to persuade them to leave Egypt as quickly as possible? How could they fashion the fourteen specific jewels that were needed by Adonai, including the two to be placed on the high priest's shoulders, into the exact design described by Adonai to Moses?" Hearing Christine use the Jewish name for God '*Adonai*' made his pulse race. Could this Christian lady's Bible knowledge, allied to his jewellery skills, co-operate in an attempt to discover the details of the gems?

Returning to his own room with excitement stirring in his veins, Aaron began to think that he may have a purpose in life after all. He decided to act immediately on Christine's suggestion to contact Inspector Harling, "Good evening, Inspector. Please excuse me for phoning you after work like this, but I wonder if you have five minutes to talk please?"

Alan Harling was on duty even in his armchair, "Certainly, Mr Klein! I was just thinking about you and the others up at UCLH" Aaron explained that Sheikh Salim was discharged that morning and had flown straight home as he had important state business with his father, the emir, and that Miss Templeton was stable, although terribly injured after her immense bravery in attacking the bomber.

"Doctor Chaudhary may discharge me tomorrow morning and I was wondering if you and I could meet somehow please? It's not really about the bombing, but Miss Templeton and I wondered if you could spare a little time to show us how to track down someone whose name we don't know, please?"

The inspector, beginning to think that his fortnight's leave was not going to be all relaxation, asked Aaron to explain, especially as he much preferred having things to investigate and problems to solve, rather than sitting around at home. "Well, Inspector, a very surprising thing happened here in my hospital room, which I would like to consult you about, concerning something which may be important."

Alan Harling sat up, "Actually, I'm having a spot of leave away from Scotland Yard. I may be busy tomorrow morning, but if you do get released, I mean discharged, would you like to call round and have a few minutes with me at home? I live in a place called Gunnesbury, just a short walk from Acton Town tube station… Hello… Hello… Mr Klein… are you still on the line?"

Aaron shivered, "Err, yes… I'm here, Inspector, but did you say 'Gunnesbury'?"

Alan Harling frowned, "Yes, that's right. It's not a bad place to live. It's right at the beginning of the M4 and there are several train and tube routes, so it's easy to get in and out of. My wife and I like it here because it's got a big park and an enthusiastic gardening club which we enjoy." He gave the shaken Aaron Klein his address and walking directions from the tube, arranging to meet at 7.00 p.m. next evening. "We can enjoy a cup of tea and I expect my wife will have some home-made cake on the go whilst I listen to whatever it is you want to talk about."

CHAPTER 7

It was nearly 9.00 a.m. on Wednesday when Alan's phone rang, "Good morning, Inspector Harling? This is Rashid Halleem, Khaled's brother, speaking on behalf of our father." Quickly composing himself, the inspector asked him to proceed. "Please Mr Inspector; we don't know what to do. Since Monday's TV broadcast, we have been receiving hate mail and horrible messages..."

'AH' interrupted as kindly as he could, "I'm sorry Rashid, but that is to be expected after such a violent hate crime. I can't do anything about that."

The young man continued, "We expected that, Sir, but also we are receiving messages of congratulations." 'AH' thought carefully. Was this young man really saying that people were congratulating the family on what Khaled had done? That was deplorable! Was there something here that concerned his work? Could such despicable persons be so like-minded that they too might attempt racial murders? "Listen, Rashid, it's not good to talk about such things over the telephone. I could meet with you and your father, to see what you have received, but it would need to be tomorrow morning and not at Watford." Rashid quickly gained his father's approval. "Okay, Rashid. We can meet at 10.00 am tomorrow at the coffee shop opposite Golder's Green Station, on the corner. That's about half way for both of us to travel. Is that OK for your father?" The invitation was willingly accepted and the meeting set.

***

Sheikh Salim met privately with his father, the emir, on Wednesday morning. "Your inaugural speech as crown prince yesterday has had great effect, my son. What you spoke into the wind has been carried far across the deserts of Arabia and many sheikhs will be sitting as we are now, considering what their own reactions are to be. Already, the UAE's chairman of emirs has phoned me saying that he has been aroused as from a dream. He believes that your speech and the challenge that you threw down will have far greater effect than the bomb that blew Abdullah apart last week. He says that you have stirred up a wild creature's nest; yet, you will have made many more friends than enemies. His advice, with which I concur, is that you act quickly and decisively. Words are easy to say but become forgotten Salim, but a statesman uses them to introduce determined actions."

Salim bowed, "Thank you, Father. My first responsibility is to you as mye, and our own nation, and then my second is to the FNAE as a whole. After those primary affiliations, may I be led into the will of God." His father pushed him to go further. "Father, Abdullah was a soldier building up his own stronghold from which he attacked opponents at will. I have no desire to live in Abdullah's exotic palace epitomising an empire within an empire. I assure you that I will not be weak, but if you permit me, I request that I live and operate from your palace, showing daily allegiance to you, and keeping you as much involved as you choose to be. I would like to help our Federation illustrate to the world that our nation is ruled by a team of emirs overseeing their crown princes, who show deference to them.

"I will build a small strategic personal team sufficient to help exercise my responsibilities, including a mixture of persons chosen for their ability and enterprise. A priority will be to encourage and enable our own population to become more involved in the Federation's affairs. It is not democracy that I propose, Father, but an opportunity for our talented people to have a role in life, rather than sitting in comfort enjoying our oil revenue whilst watching foreign experts do everything. We should respect our invited foreigners, but not abdicate all activities to them. I aim to bring our own university and college graduates, who demonstrate ability and aspiration, into greater involvement in our Federation's life. Father, we must not blame leading nations if they prefer not to welcome desert kingdoms, ruled by monarchical hierarchies, to sit at their dinner tables where strategic issues are discussed."

The emir enquired, "I follow your proposals, Salim, to maintain our ancient rights but enable fresh blood to flow in our veins, but how do you propose to influence our Federation's rulers to approve your strategy?"

Salim pondered, "Father, I am like a new boy at school with few credentials or talents to offer to my fellow crown princes. Do you have advice for me in this matter?"

His father spoke, "Salim, another voice spoke seriously into my ear last night, whilst the stars shone clearly and brightly over the desert. The chairman of the Council of Crown Princes was much affected by your speech. He has been disappointed with our foreign relationships in recent years, especially at the lack of invitations for involvement in Middle Eastern and wider discussions. He believes that our reputation has become stagnant and needs an injection of new life. You are aware that our crown princes and other royal princes exercise the highest roles in our political life. The current crown prince who acts as our Foreign Minister is struggling. He does not enjoy good health and hates long-distance travelling. He has a fine mind, but privately has made it clear that he would appreciate some strategic assistance, but not from an employee. If you were willing to help him in some way, would you drive over to visit him, my son?"

***

Doctor Chaudhary shook hands warmly with Aaron, "I am very pleased to allow you to be discharged as soon as you can be collected Mr Klein. You have responded well to our attentions and may progress even better in a non-hospital environment. You must continue your exercises and please visit me once a week for regular check-ups." Aaron thanked the doctor and phoned his sister, Esther, who was parked nearby. He called in on Christine and told her about the very strange 'Gunnesbury connection' and his meeting to be held that evening with Inspector Harling. She asked to be kept in touch and wished him well, believing in her heart that his steps were being well-directed.

Aaron's niece, Ruth, carried his bag and Esther held his arm as they descended the hospital's wide steps, walked round the corner of the constantly busy Euston Road into Gower Street where the car was parked nearby. They drove first to Aaron's flat in a relatively secluded part of Hatton Garden, where he looked around his bachelor home with great pleasure. Esther and Ruth made coffee to go with UCLH's excellent cafeteria's cake which they had purchased earlier. Aaron packed an old briefcase with a few items and after the celebration snack, Esther drove cautiously up the busy Gray's Inn Road, skirted round the back of King's Cross and St Pancras stations, then north-west through Camden and up to Hampstead, before turning downhill towards Golder's Green. Esther's — and, currently, the family's — home was near the bottom end of Heath Road West, nearly opposite the pond in Golder's Green park. She drew into the short drive of the large detached house and parked the car, relieved to have negotiated the London traffic without mishap.

Ruth shepherded her beloved uncle indoors and sat him down in a comfortable arm-chair. She fetched her brother Isaac, who had a frequent fifteen-year-old's sullen expression and soon made an excuse to disappear. Aaron detected something extra, knowing that he followed similar traits to Julian Steinburg's, concerning Jewish persecution at the hand of gentiles. Aaron's sister-in-law, Naomi, was not to be seen. Noticing the cold atmosphere, he asked after her mother. "She's taking this very badly, Uncle Aaron. It's not just that she's lost Dad. She knows that her home and reason for living — everything she valued — has been snatched violently from her. She simply doesn't know what to do. Aunt Esther is being brilliant, not rushing Mum into anything and keeping Isaac and me healthy. We're not going to school for a while, so Aunt Esther is encouraging us to be a part of the new family situation. At present, Mum is withdrawn deeply inside herself and Isaac isn't helping anyone by his belligerent attitude. You probably know that he didn't get on tremendously well with Dad and I'm afraid that he too is living inside his head just now."

Lunch was not a joyous meal. Isaac ate but didn't speak and Naomi didn't appear. Esther, Ruth and Aaron tried keeping up a friendly and supportive dialogue, but it was very difficult. Afterwards, Aaron took Esther aside and thanked her sincerely for stepping into the family's breach so magnanimously. She seemed to have come alive, just as much as others had done the reverse. He wondered if, much as with himself, she had begun to see purpose to her previously routine and unexciting life. By helping other people, through service to the bereaved Naomi, the angry and bitter Isaac, and to her fast maturing niece, Esther was helping herself. She and Aaron perceived that they could come closer together now, as two single people who had apparently preferred independence to sharing life with another person.

Aaron explained that he must make some visits that afternoon and evening; firstly, to old Joshua Shulz who had given so many years of good service to the Kleins — being their lapidorist for twenty-five years before retiring seven years ago. He had phoned Aaron at UCLH early this Wednesday morning to say that he felt too unwell to travel to central London. Because Aaron had some hours free before travelling to Gunnersbury to meet Inspector Harling, he'd decided to reverse the compliments by making a surprise visit to see Joshua at his home in Kilburn. Ruth asked to walk the ten minutes down to Golder's Green centre with her uncle, mentioning fresh air and exercise, but really to talk and encourage each other. Seeing her uncle off at the bus-stop outside the tube station, Ruth felt stronger and less alone, determined to do her very best to help her aunt and uncle to keep the family going forwards, rather than allowing the bomber to claim more victims.

***

Before the bomb, Christine Templeton's dress design business in Hampstead had been blossoming. She loved her work producing modern reserved styles that were becoming highly esteemed in the fashion business. Her customers were not necessarily rich, although that helped, but ladies and their menfolk who wanted discretion, attention to detail and something not to be found in High Street chain shops. Now that she felt strong enough herself, even if she might look terrible to people unused to meeting explosion victims, she had arranged for her staff to visit her. The nurse showed in Hilda Prentice her efficient and businesslike shop manageress, her prized assistant dress designer Belinda Wallace, Melissa Townsend the artistic accessories designer and young Rose Theobald their shop assistant. The four ladies sat down trying not to look closely at their enshrouded employer, holding back their tears with great difficulty. They loved their work at the Hampstead High Street shop and they loved Christine. She had always encouraged and supported them, yet now their elegant mistress was a disfigured shape in a hospital bed, attempting to speak whilst clearly in great pain.

"You will realise that I won't be able to work alongside you for a few months, so let us consider what is to be done. Belinda, please can you continue designing along similar lines to those that we have developed over the last eighteen months, but bringing in your own distinctive styles? Melissa, please build up the lovely ranges of accessories that have become so popular with our customers, particularly further bags, shoes and items that complement our dresses so well? Hilda, I would love you to continue managing the shop and keeping a watching brief over the whole business for me please, whilst I would like Rose to become increasingly responsible 'front-of-house' please. Is that satisfactory for you all, my dears?" Christine's ladies quietly affirmed their willingness and personal determination to keep the business going, leaving the room resolved to keep their promises and support their courageous employer in her battle for life. Once in the corridor, they found it impossible to restrain their emotions any longer.

***

Aaron's bus went on its convoluted route from Golder's Green, down the busy Finchley Road, passing the Hendon Way junction, down Fortune Green Road and West End Lane, past West Hampstead Thameslink station and into Quex Road in Kilburn. Aaron left his top deck front seat, thanked the bored looking driver and jumped off the bus outside Kilburn High Road tube station. He remembered the location just well enough to cross over the busy road and walk past the bus stops, over the railway bridge and in front of several ugly food outlets and phone shops. Aaron turned into the second street on his left, the even less attractive Brondesbury Road. He noticed a new development on his right-hand side where a housing association was developing a new rabbit warren of homes, walked on down the street of tired looking four storey terraced houses fronted by phalanxes of wheeled rubbish and recycling bins, builder's skips, old motor bikes, prams and small front yards affording steps up to the front doors and down into dismal basements. About half way down the street, Aaron recognised Joshua's home, pushed the top bell and waited.

It was a few minutes before the door opened slightly, revealing a dishevelled old man wearing a dressing gown and slippers. "Hello Joshua!" said Aaron brightly. "I hope it's not inconvenient, but I thought that I'd call and see you at home. Is that okay?"

The old man opened the door a little wider and answered in a very quiet voice, "Come in, Mr Aaron. I was not prepared for a visit, but if you don't mind seeing me in my squalor, please come upstairs." He led the way up dark stairways, where occasional light-bulbs shone faintly over dirty steps. They reached the top floor and Joshua opened a door. Aaron was shocked by the coldness of Joshua's living room, with its scanty furniture, threadbare carpet, dirty wallpaper and musty smells. He was becoming alarmed for his faithful old lapidorist, who had obviously gone far down-hill since his tenants left. "Please, sit here, Mr Aaron," said Joshua shepherding him to one of two small armchairs.

"Look Joshua," Aaron started. "If it's not convenient right now, I could come back another time."

The reply was chilling, "All times are the same to me Mr Aaron. Now is as good or bad as any other."

Alarmed at Joshua's depressed words, Aaron resolved to try cheering up the old man. "It was so good of you to travel all the way down to the hospital to visit me. Let's have a short time catching up on each other's news, shall we?" Joshua went through a curtained doorway into his large bare kitchen to boil a kettle for tea.

The picture of abject poverty was clear to Aaron. He was so glad that he had come, and decided immediately that he must do something for this faithful servant who had given twenty-five years of honest service to his employers. He must not be allowed to fade further into nothingness. The tea came in mugs and without biscuits or cake. Aaron took the lead, "When you visited me on Monday, Joshua, I think I tired you out — sorry! Just tell me when you've had enough conversation and I'll leave you in peace."

The response showed alarming sadness, "If you mean '*Shalom*' Mr

Aaron that is only in the past for me. Your visit here today was unexpected, but not a surprise. Adonai has been leading me on a downwards slope for the last six years. When you spoke to me about the Aaronic breastplate and its jewels, you could not know the terrible effect on me. Please listen to my confession, Mr Aaron."

The perplexed jeweller responded, "But Joshua, how can you use such a word as 'confession'?"

The old man began, "It is seven years since I retired. In my last month, Mr Reuben asked me to undertake less lapidary work and help him with some small errands and services. One day, a middle-aged gentile blustered his way into the shop and thrust a linen bag on the counter. He said that his elderly parents had died, leaving their belongings to him, amongst which were some unwanted items of antique jewellery which he wished to sell. Mr Reuben emptied the bag and told the gentile that although a few items looked interesting, there was nothing of more than sentimental value. The man was annoyed as Klein's had been recommended to him as a fair business and he expected to get a fair price. Mr Reuben made a very quick assessment, then explained that Klein's did not sell such antique items themselves, but could buy them for a fair price to sell on to a specialist shop. The figure of £5,500 was mentioned as an estimate and accepted. The bag of jewellery was receipted and left with Mr Reuben, who promised a more exact price in two days' time. The gentile left the shop and Mr Reuben called me over, 'Here is a job for you, Joshua. Make a detailed list of the items showing their descriptions and weights, then take them with your list to our friends round the corner in Kirby Street. Ask them to have a look and if they are interested in buying them from us for at least £7,000 in cash, they can take them there and then. Do you understand Joshua?'

"I examined the items and wrote my list, but before I went to see Simeon with the jewels, I asked Mr Reuben to type it out so that it looked more professional, 'That way, he will offer you a better price I, think.' Well, Mr Aaron that is exactly what happened. I made two copies on the shop's duplicating machine and went round to old Simeon. He emptied out the bag, sorted through the items, wrote a few notes, added up some figures and offered me £6,300. We'd known each other for many years. He always started his pricing like that and then wouldn't haggle, but respected a proper argument. I asked him to consider a particular sapphire brooch that looked as if it should fetch over £4,000 on its own. He inspected it, agreed that perhaps it may be valuable, made a big play of re-calculating his figures and offered me £7,200. I played along with him until we agreed on £7,350 for all the listed items. I gave him the typed list and he carefully replaced all the items except one into the bag, and went to his back room safe and brought out the money for me. He counted it out very carefully and smiled, suggesting that I should definitely retire after making such a silly mistake. He handed me a single stone that he had saved from the bag because it was not included on the typed list. He was pleased to have acquired all the items for the agreed sum so, not wanting to offend him, I put the odd stone in my pocket and took the money back to Mr Reuben. When I gave him the £7,350 in cash, his face beamed and he gave me £50 as a reward. I did not want to make any fuss so I simply left the odd stone in my pocket. The following day, the blustery man came and was delighted when Mr Reuben gave him £5,800. He was not interested in any list of what he had sold to us, so I simply kept his typed copy. After a day or two, I became bothered at not disclosing the error, but as no-one was concerned apart from myself, it seemed ungracious to spoil what all the parties had been happy with. That is why I have kept that stone to this day, Mr Aaron. Please look at these two lists that I have kept carefully. On my handwritten list, the stone is listed, just here, but Mr Reuben was busy and somehow omitted it on his typed version. Now, Mr Aaron please recollect the book of my name 'Y'hoshua' in our Hebrew Bible, and in particular the battle of Jericho."

Aaron sat intrigued, "Well, Joshua, the Israelites followed Adonai's exact instructions, walked around the walls seven times on the seventh day shouting and blowing their trumpets, after which the city's walls simply fell down flat. It was a glorious victory."

Old Joshua became animated, "But what happened thereafter?" Aaron recounted that the next battle Israel fought was lost because a man named Akhan had disobeyed Adonai's strict instructions by taking and hiding some of the Jericho treasure for himself. "Yes, Mr Aaron! So Akhan with all his family and possessions were ordered to be destroyed by Adonai. Now I know why my retirement has seen only deep disappointment and trouble, because I too kept and hid some treasure that was not mine. That stone has done me great harm, but I have been too ashamed and fearful to do anything about it. Since you told me that you will search for the original Aaron's jewels, I am confessing my sin and returning that jewel to Klein's Jewellers because it is not mine." Old Joshua reached into his pocket, took out a small purse and handed Aaron a beautifully clear red gemstone. "Now let my sin be quenched Mr Aaron! This stone is yours!"

Aaron held up the almost scarlet jewel and noticed something. "Joshua, what is this writing engraved on it in Hebrew?"

Old Joshua smiled for the first time in months, "I always knew it was there, but I was too scared to realise its significance until your words last Friday Mr Aaron! It is the Hebrew word 'Naftali' which means 'my wrestling'! What gemstone do you believe it to be?"

The two men sat together, each using his jeweller's eye-glass, turning the cabochon shaped jewel over and peering at its format. "I am sure that you examined it properly when it came into your possession Joshua. What can you tell me of its technical attributes?"

The lapidorist was quickly back in his element. "At first, by its vitreous colour I thought that it might be coral, but it scratched glass too easily with a hardness factor of about 7 on Mohs scale. I checked its specific gravity to be 2.65 and refractive index to be just over 1.54, suggesting a variety of chalcedony. Then I checked in the Torah Mr Aaron and read that the jewel for Naftali was jasper, but this stone is not mottled."

Aaron considered, "Very rarely jasper is found in a perfectly clear format Joshua. What did you make of the strange mark on the reverse?"

Joshua explained, "It is not the name of the craftsman B'tzal'el, who Adonai chose to prepare the High Priest's garments, so I assumed it to be a jeweller's mark made to identify the stone for some reason."

After taking the stone to the window, Aaron showed the backside of the gemstone to Joshua, "That mark looks more like an emblem than a name Joshua. Does it resemble anything to you?"

The old man examined it carefully, "Something like a stretched-out eye Mr Aaron."

The jeweller exclaimed, "Exactly, Joshua! When Moses led the Israelite slaves out of Egypt, those proud masters who had ill-treated them for hundreds of years begged the Hebrews to leave their country before Adonai ruined their nation even more. They heaped valuable treasures of all sorts onto their departing slaves, including fabulous jewellery. I recognise that emblem as what is called a 'wedjat', the symbolic eye of the Egyptian's god 'Horos'. This stone came out of Egypt, Joshua!" With absolute awe, Aaron held up the superb jewel — aged 3,500 years or more — that would start him on his mission.

***

Leaving Joshua in far better shape than he had found him earlier that Wednesday afternoon, Aaron walked buoyantly back to Kilburn High Road Station. He travelled down to Kings Cross and St. Pancras and changed onto the Piccadilly Line heading south-westerly towards Richmond. It took less than half an hour to reach Acton Town station, where a local pointed out the way, just a two minutes' walk along the always busy Gunnersbury Avenue and into the much quieter Princes Avenue. He rang Inspector Harling's door bell and wondered what would happen next on this most auspicious day.

"Good afternoon, Mr Klein! Please, come in! Welcome to our home!"

Aaron was very surprised at such a friendly welcome from someone he had thought was a most serious professional and unsocial police officer, "Thank you so much for agreeing to my visit, Inspector. I promise not to interrupt your well-earned leave for any longer than is necessary…" began Aaron.

"Oh, don't worry about that, Mr Klein. Come and meet the wife. I'm Alan and she's Mary." Aaron was ushered into the homely sitting room, introduced to the inspector's wife and offered a comfortable armchair. He realised immediately that these people were not proud or pompous, but genuinely pleased to see him. Once furnished with a cup of tea and Mary's cherry cake served on proper china-ware, Aaron explained the reason for requesting his visit. He described being bored and unable to sleep in his hospital room then finding a Gideons' Bible pushed to the back of his bedside locker. When Aaron introduced some gentle humour, by exaggerating his fear as a devout Jew of opening the pages of a

Christian's Holy Bible, Mary smiled whilst Alan remained straight-faced. Explaining his surprise at finding obvious agreement between the beginnings of the Hebrew and Christian Bibles; he described reading on late into the night until reaching the twenty-eighth chapter of Exodus. Whilst Alan's face did not relax, Mary was becoming very interested.

Aaron produced the Gunnersbury Horticultural Show ticket that had been used as a bookmark and showed them a photocopy of the Bible page that Nurse Ryan had made for him. The Harlings looked them over, "I remember going to that Garden Show, Mary. It was last autumn and it was cold enough to snow!" His wife agreed with Alan's recollection and asked Aaron what it was he wanted them to do.

He replied cautiously, "Because I appear to be being led into finding the ancient jewels described in the Bible, through what may be described as 'an instruction' from a previous occupant of my hospital room, I hoped that the inspector might point me in the right direction for discovering who wrote it, please."

Alan meant to be friendly, but spoke in his normal semi-official voice, "Well Aaron, I understand that the person who wrote that note in the Bible was keen on somebody looking for the jewels, but naturally he could have no idea who would find what he had written." Mary smiled demurely at Aaron but did not speak, allowing her husband to continue. "The freedom of information laws would not allow the hospital to tell you who had been in your room before you. It's probable that the person went to the show himself or herself and being a keen gardener, simply kept the ticket as a souvenir. There must have been hundreds of visitors at that show, so how could anyone discover which one of them it might have been? Sorry Aaron!"

Mary Harling suggested very modestly, "Excuse me, Dear. Do you think we could ask the Horticultural Society's Chairman Norman Evans if he knows any members who love jewellery?" Alan was a little put out by his wife's clever idea, but could only agree to her doing so. Mary phoned Mr Evans whilst the men watched her face. "Oh yes, Mr Evans… I think I might know Mr and Mrs Glover a little… I bump into her at the shops sometimes… Oh yes, I believe that I've walked past their home occasionally and noticed what you say in their garden... Oh, I'm so sorry to hear that the husband died… When was that did you say…? Thank you so much, Mr Evans... yes, my husband and I will certainly be at this year's show! Goodbye for now and thank you again."

Alan looked at his wife with real admiration, feeling that her conversation was worthy to be used on police training courses. Mary disclosed her information with pleasure and without pride, "Mr and Mrs Glover live in Bollo Lane, the other side of the railway, not far from the tube station. He was well-known for being rather fanatical about jewellery to the extent that he made a flower bed in their front garden into a shape of a necklace and earrings. Most unusual! Apparently, Mr Glover, Colin was his name, died in hospital about two months ago. Is that useful for you, Aaron?"

Not to be outdone on discrete detection work, Alan decided to make his own suggestion, "If we had more than one possible name, there may be a legal way to allow the hospital to let us know the room's occupant without them actually stating his name."

Mary remarked coyly, "Oh, I'm so glad that the law can be bent a little sometimes, Dear." Alan took the phone from his wife and dialled the number for UCLH, asking to be put through to Dr Chaudhary's department.

Once connected, Aaron and Mary heard him ask, "If you could assist my enquiries, please, by saying if the previous occupant of Mr Klein's room was not one of these three names that would be most helpful: Brian Lockhart, Colin Glover or George Henderson... Not the first or the last... I see... Thank you so much, Nurse... Please will you give my regards to Miss Templeton... Thank you very much... Goodbye." Alan beamed a wide smile of success at the others. After further tea and cherry cake, the Inspector decided to walk with Aaron Klein back to Acton Town tube station, but to go a little further into Bollo Lane. It was not difficult to spot the house with such an unusual flower bed, shaped as a diamond necklace, in the front garden! The two men stopped for some moments, surprised at the unkempt condition of the garden and the entire semi-detached house, but neither of them saw the sad face observing them from behind the curtains in the unlit sitting room.

***

After her shop staff had left her, Christine fell to contemplating her own future. It was all very well to encourage her employees, but how could she ever encourage herself? What really could she do with her shattered life? She made herself turn from selfish thoughts into prayers, not of despair calling out in anguish to her God, but of praise for who he was and for the immense love that he had for her. She perceived that his love would be more noticeable, since her natural affections with her fiancé had been dispatched. Her musings were interrupted when her nephew Peter made a further visit. Approaching respectfully to her bedside he began, "Aunt Christine! It's so good to see you looking better once again!"

His delighted aunt replied, "Oh Peter, it's wonderful that such a handsome young man like you would want to come and visit such an old wreck as me!"

She detected his disapproval, "Now then, Aunt Christine, that's enough of that sort of talk, if you please! Anyway, I'm looking at you with my spiritual eyes, rather than my natural handsome eyes!" They held each other's hands very gently, with Peter showing common-sense and compassion far beyond most eighteen-year-olds. His sincere faith in Christ and total lack of embarrassment at seeing his aunt in such awful physical condition was an immense tonic to Christine. They talked a little then, very willingly, she accepted his offer to pray for her. His straightforward words were very bold as he called on their Almighty God to strengthen and fully heal his beloved aunt, to which she added her own '*Amen!*'

***

On Thursday morning, Aaron walked up to Natan Lemuel of Reliant Bespoke Insurance who stood waiting for him outside the remains of Kleins Jewellers. He was introduced to the manager of Central Refurbishment Contractors, who were assigned to carry out the repairs.

"Before we go inside together," asked Aaron with a serious expression on his face. "Please allow me a few minutes in there alone." Understanding that a little 'private time' was deserved before discussions on building issues, the two men walked a discrete distance away along Hatton Garden.

"Just call us when you're ready Aaron." Going through the door in the solid wooden hoarding, Aaron entered what had been the shop, took a few moments to reflect on what had happened only nine days ago, then strode purposefully to the far-left corner. He bent down and used a brush from his briefcase to clean the light debris that had settled on the floor, used a small hexagonal head spanner to unscrew four retaining bolts and removed a metal plate. It was six months since he and Reuben had performed their occasional ritual, instigated many years ago by their father Abraham. Aaron transferred the black material bag from the recess into his briefcase, replaced the cover, tightened the bolts and strewed a little debris over their secret depositary.

Stepping outside, he beckoned to the two men waiting for him. They entered the shop for their site meeting, agreed that the contractor would thoroughly clean all surfaces, to ensure that nothing of value had been missed by the police, re-plaster the ceiling and walls, and then lay a new thin but strong floor over the existing one. After that preparatory work, they would meet again to decide how best to continue the refurbishment. The two visitors shook hands and went to their cars, whilst Aaron walked the short distance to Hatton Garden's Bourse, that had become famous in 2015 for Britain's biggest ever robbery.

Showing his security pass to the guard, he entered the anti-room, used the touch-screen to enter his details then faced the opposite wall. Placing his right hand on another screen, he read the day's questions and typed in the technical answers which would be known only by professional jewellers. A door opened by itself, letting him enter a hallway where he punched in another code to open the door into the strong room. Aaron unlocked his private strong box and placed the cloth bag inside, after selecting a single piece of jewellery which he put nonchalantly in his trousers pocket. He returned to the pavement, walked thirty yards towards Holborn Circus, crossed the road and entered a jewellery emporium. Passing the phalanx of traders, Aaron went to the rear and wished, "Good morning, Greta." to a lady standing behind her display cases.

"Good morning, Aaron. I am very sorry."

He took the sapphire bracelet from his pocket and placed it between them. Greta examined it meticulously, replaced it and said, "Two thousand eight hundred."

Aaron moved the bracelet towards his side of the cabinet, causing Greta to hesitate then say, "Including the garnet embellishments, three thousand one hundred."

He answered, "And...?"

"Fifty," Was her response.

Aaron pushed it towards her and waited whilst she opened the safe behind her, turned back and counted out three thousand, one hundred and fifty pounds in banknotes. The exchange being completed, they wished each 'Goodbye!" and Aaron went outside.

***

Shortly after 10.00am, Inspector Harling watched the two men enter the crowded coffee shop, and beckoned them to join him at the quieter table in a back corner. He came straight to the point, "It is very irregular for me to be meeting unofficially with persons connected with a major crime. It's only because I'm on leave that I have agreed to listen to what you want to tell me. I'll just fetch you both a drink, then you can explain about these contemptible congratulations you've received."

Ibrahim Halleem asked that his son should speak for him, being more articulate than himself.

Rashid began, "The family expected to receive hate mail, but have been disgusted at how vitriolic some letters have been. We'd not anticipated the filth that's been thrown all over the front of our house and garden, nor the fence broken down and things stolen from our shed. Now we realise that we must learn to live with the consequences of my brother's crime, but we have asked to meet with you, Sir, because of these letters." Rashid placed three envelopes on the table, "The first to arrive was this one."

The inspector took the proffered envelope and opened it with his fingertips, "Don't you realise that if these letters have any significance, the police must consider finger prints and any forensic evidence with them! This envelope has not been through the post and does not have your address on it, so how did you receive it?" Rashid replied, "It was put through our letter box on Tuesday morning before any of us was awake, Sir. The letter inside shocked us." The inspector removed the single sheet of cheap paper, using a clean handkerchief. He read the letter out loud quietly, '*I want to thank you Mr Halleem for what your wonderful son Khaled has done. Not many of us get the opportunity to assassinate enemies of our faith. He is now in Heaven receiving his well-earned reward. If I am given the opportunity, I will certainly follow his example, being ready to die in pursuit of our holy goal against all infidels.*' The letter was unsigned and bore no obvious signs of identification. The inspector dismissed it as coming from an outspoken crank with 'more mouth than trousers'.

He was handed the second envelope, postmarked Eastbourne on Monday evening, soon after the televised disclosure of Khaled's name. "How did they know our address Inspector?" asked Rashid. The inspector did not reply, but extracted the two sheets of writing paper with great care and read the neatly written words, '*Dear Mr Halleem. The sadness that you must feel at the loss of your eldest son cannot be compared with the joy of being the proud parents of such an hero. Clearly you brought up Khaled in ways of truth and honour, rather than the insipid and cowardly ways of our blinded society. Thank you on behalf of the enlightened minority who are prepared to take action to cleanse our nation. The time is ripe for others to follow your wonderful son's example to rid us of Jews and pathetic Christians sitting on Sunday morning listening to religious tripe. Those lily-livered vicars, in tow with rich owners of anti-British businesses, use their disgusting methods to attract silly women and spine-less men, leading our proud nation to drift into pointless nonsense! Where are our heroes? Where is another Nelson, or Drake? Where are the new exponents of vigilance and force that our country needs? Where are persons with the assured convictions and determination of Hitler or Stalin? Britain cries out for leadership and direction, not liberality! We have the pride and ability to re-conquer the world! We must fight against the screen of whitewash and those fat smiling diplomats...*' The inspector read the rest of the diatribe through to himself, "This is obviously from some crank who is against just about everything and everybody but themselves. They don't have the guts to give their name and address! The only signature is 'SL'! It's worthless!

What's in the third envelope?" He was becoming very disappointed at spending his holiday reading such tripe. The last envelope, postmarked 'Birmingham North' late on Monday afternoon, was addressed absolutely correctly and contained a single sheet of paper with words typed only in capital letters. It gave no address or indication of who had sent it. The Inspector read it out, '*Mr Halleem. Your son Khaled died with honour, acting for our beleaguered brothers living in this nation of hypocrites. His heroism exclaims the message that all infidels must die. There are many of us prepared, as Khaled was, ready to kill as many of them as we can. Please use the enclosed £200.00 to meet unexpected expenses, or to set up a memorial to your esteemed son.*'

The inspector re-read the letter. Was it from another crank, or could it have come from someone involved? Being careful not to disclose his thoughts, he remarked, "Look, Mr Halleem… and you too Rashid, we often receive crank letters after a major crime has been committed. Sometimes people with twisted minds want to join in anonymously by writing such nonsense. You can't take them seriously. May I take these away for further examination please?"

Ibrahim Halleem decided to speak himself, "I respect your professionalism and opinions, Inspector, yet I see that the writers of these letters have more than just audacity to support murder for that is what my son committed. They have the stated impassioned desire and perhaps ability to follow his example. You must help to stop other families being bereaved like ours has been!"

Alan Harling realised that his reserved professional approach had ignored the emotionalism felt by the bomber's family and their sincere desire to help stop further such heinous crimes of terrorism. "I am sorry Mr Halleem. You are right in that Scotland Yard needs to take these letters seriously. I promise you that we will use all of our technical resources to identify the writers and investigate their motives. If evil is intended, we will expose it. Thank you sincerely for bringing these letters to my attention. Here is the £200.00, but may I keep the letters and envelopes for the time being, please?"

Again, Ibrahim Halleem surprised the inspector, "That is blood money and unworthy of any use except the alleviation of further hate crime! It is abhorrent to us! Take it away from us! Please give it to a charity of your choosing. Now we must ask your indulgence to listen to something further, Inspector."

He looked at Rashid who remained silent now that his father had found the spirit to speak for himself. "Our situation is intolerable, Inspector, being either hated by normal British people in our part of Watford, or congratulated by persons with evil minds. We cannot stay in our home and must move away to begin life again somewhere else. As we have no ability to do that ourselves, please will the Metropolitan Police help us?"

Alan Harling was amazed. Was a murderer's family actually asking the police for financial help in moving away to protect them from hate mail? He responded seriously, "Her Majesty's Police Force could not be expected to assist non-involved persons to escape the consequences of their family's crimes. It is very improper of you to even ask such a question, Sir."

Ibrahim Halleem was not perturbed at the response, "Quite so, Inspector, which is why we are simply telling you, as a man as deeply involved in this terrible affair as ourselves, that we wish to move away to begin life more honourably somewhere else. Our predicament needs assistance in a human way, rather than by institutional means. Thank you, Inspector Harling." He stood up, shook hands, summoned Rashid and walked from the coffee shop with solemn distinction.

***

During her lunch break, Mary Harling walked from the school round the corner into Bollo Lane and rang Mrs Glover's doorbell. The front door was opened cautiously and once Mary had explained the reason for her unannounced visit; Alice Glover asked her inside, "Come in, my dear. I thought of you only last evening after noticing your husband and another man looking at our, I mean my, garden. She turned away but could not stop Mary noticing that her change of language had been yet another constant reminder of her bereavement.

Mary put her arm round her shoulders and waited whilst tears came and then stopped. "Oh, I'm such a silly woman! Please excuse me, Mrs Harling." During the next half an hour, they shared a pot of tea, some rather stale biscuits and opened their hearts to each other. More tears flowed before Mary hugged Alice and returned, rather hungrily, to her school duties. Before leaving, she had obtained Mrs Glover's permission for her husband and herself to bring Aaron Klein to see her that late afternoon.

A few hours later, Alice Glover believed that she had composed herself sufficiently enough to receive her visitors. Mary made the introductions and explained that Mr Klein had recently been discharged from the very same room at UCLH that had been occupied by Alice's late husband Colin. That information, although she had already received it at lunchtime from Mary, was too much for Alice who clutched at Mary and dissolved into body-wrenching sobs. Mary shooed the men outside, suggesting that they look for something that needed doing in the garden, which was not difficult as the whole front and back gardens were in a state of wilderness. They surveyed the scene with apprehension, not knowing where to start. Realising than any tools would be in the garage or garden shed, Alan looked cautiously through the living room window, where Mary spotted his signal of turning his hand as if to unlock something. A few minutes later, the back door opened and shut very briefly with Aaron finding a bunch of keys and two mugs of tea deposited on the doorstep. Now that they could get at some tools, albeit not in good condition, they set to work. The practical policeman was determined not to let a soft-handed jeweller outdo him, which aim was reciprocated by Aaron. Soon with two sweaty bodies and four blistered hands, they stopped to drink their tea in the shade and discuss the situation. "Look, Aaron, you've just come out of hospital and I'm going away on holiday on Saturday morning. We can't do more than play at what's required here. We need significant help."

Aaron summed up the situation, "This lady is distraught over the death of her husband; they can't have close family or friends otherwise the garden could never have got into this state; perhaps we should scratch around our own families and friends and see if we could organise something practical and achievable." They agreed that their time would be better spent in measuring areas, sorting and cleaning tools and making tentative plans for the necessary work.

When Mary opened the back door and called them, they were in a more positive frame of mind. "Come and wash your hands then have a little time with Mrs Glover."

They all sat uneasily at the kitchen table, afraid to state the truth that the house and garden were simply too much for the widowed lady. She thanked them profusely as they outlined their plan to form a working party of volunteers to attack the garden as a first job, but surprised them as she said determinedly, "What I want most is to move from this home of thirty-five years, away from the drudgery and bitter memories. I want to go somewhere else, make a simple new home and perhaps find a purpose to go on living!" They asked her a few pertinent questions, ventured that the house might have a value of about £220,000 pounds and the car perhaps £3,000 pounds, although in their present condition they would never attract any buyers. As they were exchanging proper names, addresses and phone numbers, Alice asked Aaron, "Excuse me Mr Klein, but are you Jewish? I'd like to know because my husband hated Jews and would never have allowed you onto his property. As for me, I can only say that you have already been very kind to me and I am very sorry for your own bereavement. You will always be welcome here, thank you."

That brave speech was enough for her and tears swept over her face as deep throbbing sobs wretched her body and her three visitors departed reverently back to Princes Avenue.

As they sat in the Harling's kitchen, they realised that the purpose of their visit to Alice Glover had not been fulfilled at all. They had failed to discuss the Gideons Bible with its hand-written message of '*You must find these jewels*' now believed to have been written by her husband, although Mary had mentioned that at lunchtime as the reason for them visiting her. As both of the men were prepared to begin tidying up Alice's garden next day, Aaron thought that if she was amenable, he would show her the Bible and its note then. Mary phoned Alice to ask if she would like Alan and Aaron to come, receiving a thankful 'Yes please!'

Soon after Aaron had left them to return to his own flat, their phone rang, "Hello, Inspector Harling, this is Rashid. My father wants to thank you for meeting with him this morning and to ask your forgiveness for thinking that the police force could help him to move home. He did not mean to burden you with our family's difficulties, which we have brought on ourselves. We are sorry, Sir."

Rashid's voice was so courteous and considerate that Alan Harling made an impromptu and surprising decision, "Thank you Rashid, please tell your dad not to worry. May I ask you, Rashid, if you might be free tomorrow morning to help someone in need of some gardening help?" Even as he heard himself asking the question, Alan realised that he was mixing his sober police work with something else that was going on inside him.

He actually wanted to help the Jewish Aaron Klein and the little old lady Alice Glover, and now he even wanted to help a Muslim bomber's family! "Well yes, Sir, Mr Inspector, I should be very pleased to do some gardening. I am fit and strong but I don't know much about plants." To that humble apology, Alan declared to Rashid that he didn't either. They made arrangements to meet at Acton Town tube station at 9.30 a.m..

Mary smiled and thanked her husband, keeping her quiet thoughts to herself. "I just don't understand, Mary, how a son of such a respectable and honest family could have become a terrorist. He must have been seriously got at by someone very evil and I want to find out who!"

***

Salim was shown into the private quarters of Crown Prince Sheikh Sultan bin Zayed Al Sharyan, Foreign Minister of the Federation of Non-aligned Arab Emirates, where two men awaited him. Although they were of similar age, Prince Sultan looked twice as old as the other, aged not by years but by ill-health. He did not rise in response to Salim's salaam but smiled from his couch, "Salim, how good of you to come! Welcome! You know Sheikh Khalifa of course, who is joining us for our discussions."

He indicated Crown Prince Khalifa bin Mohammed Al Mu'alla, Chairman of FNAE's Council of Crown Princes. Salim's shocked expression at Sheikh Sultan's appearance, prompted an explanation, "Salim, my condition has been kept private for diplomatic reasons, not wanting any weakness to be shown in our Federation's abilities, but you are seeing the effects of severe vertigo which has removed my good health. Doctors can do nothing for me, thus I simply suffer when its cruel ravages occur. Whilst remaining in one position I am nearly as strong and able as yourself, but my slightest change of position, especially sitting down, standing up and lying down, causes God's entire environment to be wrenched from my sight as it spins helplessly away in the opinion of my brain. It is nauseating and incapacitating with the results that I can move only with assistance and any travelling is catastrophic for me — hence, our meeting today Salim!"

Sheikh Khalifa joined the explanations, "Salim, our brother has the brain and heart of a desert lion, but he and our Federation need support. A nation's foreign minister who cannot travel anywhere is shunned by other statesmen who spend so much time flying around the world on their nation's missions. Both of us appreciated your fine speech, which is reverberating around the globe, challenging leaders to revisit their policy decisions. Now the FNAE and yourself must be ready to respond in compassionate strength to what will be said in reply, but our brother can speak only from his couch. We wish to ask you to accept a title of Deputy Foreign Minister, but in reality, to be the envoy of our Federation, using your own heart and mind as God continues to fill them, whilst leaning on Sultan's wisdom and experience in Foreign Affairs. By acting in that way, I believe that our Council of Emirs will show solidarity and resolve, which will open new prospects abroad for our nation. What do you say, our brother?"

Salim made a simple and sincere salaam to each of the others, "May God's will be done."

***

Just as Mary and the children were about to leave home for their schools, Rashid phoned Inspector Harling yet again, requesting that his father might be an additional worker today at Mrs Glovers, enabling them to drive there instead of using the tube. Thus, at 9.30 on this Friday morning, their modest car drew up outside Acton Town station shortly before Aaron emerged from the exit and walked towards the inspector standing nearby. He made the introductions, causing great surprise, but no alarm at the unique connections between these four men: the detective investigating a terrorist bomb explosion, a victim and bereaved innocent persons caught up in the hate crime that had so dramatically impacted their families and themselves. They recognised that their joint involvement was innocent and that they must pick up the broken pieces of what others had done, to go forwards in life. The inspector, usually the dispassionate professional observer in such circumstances, surprised himself by sharing in these strange thoughts as they all drove together down to Bollo Lane. At the agreed time of 10.00 they shook hands with Alice Glover, who was naturally surprised to see two men with coloured skin with the others, but she was not perturbed. Never would her husband have shaken hands with a Jew or a Muslim, yet this morning Alice felt strangely better than during the past nightmare months. Doors were opened, tools taken out and jobs apportioned between the men while Alice busied herself making tea, interrupted less often today by spells of crying.

Although she'd gone out earlier to buy sticky buns for her workers, at lunchtime Aaron and Rashid were despatched to the shops to find something hot. They returned from the chip shop with an assortment of food, reasonably acceptable for their various faiths and cultures. The inspector had asked Ibrahim Halleem to explain why he wasn't at work again today. "At 6.00 p.m. yesterday, my manager at the building maintenance firm where I have worked for fifteen years came to our house. He told me that my services were no longer acceptable to his reputable business, handed me my employment payments and two weeks' pay, then walked quickly away." During the afternoon, the five people so very different from each other had begun to relax in each other's company, looking for small ways to co-operate and help. It was natural for each of them to talk about their families and daily lives, just like any people getting to know each other from being strangers. The intensity of recent happenings did not form huge barriers, simply because each of them wanted to try to recognise and understand what the others were going though, and to sympathise with them. Even the occasions when father and son Halleem knelt discreetly on a corner of the lawn to pray, was not a concern of the observers. The actual gardening went quite well, although it was soon obvious that today would need to be the first of several days. It became evident that it was better for Aaron to be pruning plants than doing heavier work and that Alan was best at collecting and sorting heaps of garden arisings, and that Ibrahim had several broken items to repair whilst Rashid concentrated on mechanical things. He had cleaned the lawn mower and adjusted its workings into better condition than it had ever been. Slowly, their individual and team efforts became settled and they began planning the next stages of work, even leaving Alan a little disappointed that he wouldn't be working with them because of his holiday in Devon.

After receiving a phone call from The Yard, Alan asked Aaron what he should do with the thirty-three large plastic boxes of shattered materials that had been so carefully gathered from the Klein's shop by the police. It would need somewhere with lots of space to sort meticulously through all the rubbish that probably included fragments of jewellery with some value. Aaron saw no obvious solution, but promised to think about where they could be taken to as soon as possible. During a rest in their afternoon's work, Aaron showed the photocopy of the Gideons Bible page with its note in the margin, which Alice declared instantly not to be her husband's handwriting. When Aaron exultantly produced the first discovered jewel, the other men's eyes opened wide in excitement at its beauty and antiquity whilst Alice merely glanced at it without comment. The inspector's recognition that the Halleems were intelligent, hard-working and willing people, decided him to make an extremely unofficial approach. Firstly, he told them that Khaled and Ammar were known to have walked from Harrow and Wealdstone station along Station Road all the way to Harrow-on-The-Hill station, probably stopping at a small business where the bomb equipment was fitted. "If I sent policemen searching along that road to find possible places, they'd be spotted easily, but if a young Asian man sauntered along in an apparently aimless manner, it might be possible to find out where Khaled stopped. Rashid, would you be willing to do that for me early next week?" His father nodded and Rashid assented readily as a way of clawing back some of the family honour that had been destroyed. "Be tremendously careful Rashid. Whoever persuaded your brother to do what he did is a ruthless man who wouldn't hesitate to kill you if he thought you were helping the police."

It was approaching 6.00 p.m. when a tired but happy Aaron arrived at

Golder's Green tube station, being met unexpectedly by Ruth. "Uncle Aaron, you look so suntanned! Where have you been? Are you OK?"

He grinned, "Yes, Ruth, I'm fine thank you. Actually, I'm extra fine!" As there was still sufficient time of daylight and sunshine left to them before Shabbat would start, they walked slowly up to the family home. He brought Ruth up-to-date with most of the recent happenings to which she was very attentive and secretly delighted that her beloved uncle had had more than one new venture fall into his lap. Their obvious joy was noticed by Esther as they entered the house, but Naomi and Isaac could not be persuaded to enter anything pleasurable. Very soon, the Shabbat meal and evening began in rather a gloomy atmosphere.

CHAPTER 8

As their car pulled out of Gunnersbury and started on its long journey down the M4 motorway to Bristol, and then the M5 down into Devon, Mary and Alan Harling breathed deep sighs of relief. Brian and Emily had been left in charge of Pauline and the home for the first time in their lives, thus this week's holiday would be important for the whole family thought their parents, as the pressures of constant responsibilities fell gradually from their shoulders. They made only 'small talk' until they had stopped briefly at Swindon Services.

Regaining the road after enjoying a takeaway coffee and Mary's sandwiches in the car, they began rather shyly to share some of the things that had been building up in their minds. "We both really need this break don't we, Alan?" started Mary. "You've been worrying me lately, what with this bombing in Hatton Garden, but that isn't all is it, Darling? I think you realise that something's going on inside of you."

After a long pause, Alan responded, "Look Mary, a detective works on rationality, logic and clear evidence. I've never been much good at philosophical stuff. I just don't understand it, or maybe I've just blocked it out? You know me: I don't even like films that don't add up!"

His smiling wife added, "Or has a happy ending!"

Alan agreed, "That's right! What's the point of films that end sadly? I see plenty enough of that in my job! Sergeant Dent showed me the cover photo of a fashion magazine that, for some reason, his wife likes. It showed a handsome aristocrat and a beautiful young woman announcing their engagement. I never met that man before he was blown to bits, but I've spent time interviewing the young woman. She looks absolutely hideous after that evil bomber's work! She should be crying out 'blue murder' against swine like him, but she's not! It's ridiculous Mary, but Christine Templeton is reacting so calmly and kindly! She should be full of anger and bitterness, but she shows only the opposite! What's she got that I haven't Mary!? No, don't answer that please, or at least not yet!"

Reaching the interchange near Bristol, they turned happily onto the M5 following the signs to 'The South West'. It seemed like driving downhill as they rolled joyously past Bridgwater, Taunton and Exeter. Driving now through some of Devon's delightful gorse-covered hills, they followed the signs towards the sea and their so-suddenly-arranged holiday at Teignmouth. Alan didn't mention its proximity to Newton Abbot as they peered for their first glimpse of the sea. They drove past Teignmouth's busy docks and some shops, and then came out at the theatre on the edge of 'The Den', this gentle seaside town's village green. They spotted the 'Atlantic Spray Hotel', which was really a Victorian terraced house converted into a B&B, justifying its name by its wonderful situation overlooking the pier and the flower-bedecked promenade.

Alan sat on the bed whilst Mary unpacked their suitcases and set up home for the week. "Shall we go and find some fish and chips, Darling?" she asked.

"Maybe let's just have a stroll along the sea front first shall we Mary?" replied her husband in an innocent voice. They strolled arm-in arm along the long promenade, admiring the sea as its waves washed relentlessly up the sandy beach. Reaching the railway line, reputed to be one of the finest and most picturesque stretches of rail travel in the world, they walked on and on, with long trains sweeping past them either 'up country' towards London, or down to Cornwall's final station at Penzance.

Alan and Mary decided to save the further walk to the tunnel mouth at the 'Parson and Clerk' and on towards Dawlish for another day. They turned round at 'The Point' and retraced their steps slowly along the promenade to their hotel. "I'm pretty hungry, Mary, let's take a short drive along to Newton Abbot and have a good curry!"

She accepted that this week would not be totally separated from Alan's unofficial duties, so mysteriously hinted at by A/C Williams, "As long as it's not too spicy please!" Much relieved at getting over the first hurdle so easily, Alan smiled back and squeezed his wife's hand.

They parked at the railway station and walked past the pub, of recent cheese sandwiches and picked onions memory, and towards the town centre. "But there's a whole row of Asian restaurants here Alan!" He selected a smallish one in which to begin his investigations and chose a quiet table at the rear which gave him a good view of the staff's activity. They quite enjoyed their meal but concluded that his quarry was not to be found at this particular venue, so after an exotic ice cream each, they returned in the dusk to their Teignmouth hotel.

On Sunday morning, Mary went to the local evangelical church whilst Alan opted for a walk round the harbour entrance and on to Back Beach. They relaxed through the afternoon until at 7.00 pm Alan and Mary entered their second restaurant in Newton Abbot's Asian Alley. It was more 'classy' than Saturdays, with several staff milling about. One middle-aged man appeared to be the manager, not approaching the diners himself, but delegating that to lesser staff. It didn't take long for Alan to spot a very unskilled waiter, in his early twenties, who fumbled the plates and dishes and kept a tremulous expression on his face. In the dim light, Alan surreptitiously took a photo from his coat pocket and nudged Mary. The amateur waiter under so much scrutiny did not approach their own table, but Alan found an opportunity to speak with him when a near collision took place at the kitchen doorway. An older waiter said something with real anger, enough for the manager to notice and summon the young man to one side for a lecture. Alan waited a few minutes for the dust to settle then chose a moment whilst the senior waiters were very occupied and beckoned to the youngster, asking for the bill. Looking bewildered as he had not served these customers himself, he stammered an apology. "Look here son," Alan quickly began, "I can see that you're finding your work difficult as you certainly don't look like a professional waiter to me. I might be able to help, if you'd like to have a chat after work tonight?"

The young man hesitated, but then said very quietly that he finished work at 11.30 and could walk to the railway station entrance. Alan smiled and agreed to meet him there then, taking no notice of the manager's look of disapproval at their conversation, he summoned another waiter, paid the bill without leaving a tip, took Mary by the arm and walked out of the restaurant whispering, "Mary! I think it's our man!"

***

At 10.30 p.m. Alan left his rather disgruntled wife in their bedroom and drove back to Newton Abbot Railway Station. He spotted the young man soon afterwards and made himself obvious, "Jump in young man and let's have a chat, shall we? My name's Geoff and I'm here on holiday. What about you?" Receiving no reply, Alan continued. "Look, I don't want to pry into your affairs, but you look like a fish out of water in that restaurant. Do you want to talk about it? I promise not to get angry."

Eventually, the youngster dared to open his mouth, but remained looking resolutely at the floor of the car. "I'm not from round here and I'm not a waiter!"

The inspector continued his paternal approach, "That's very obvious son, even to a Londoner like me! I couldn't be a waiter for love nor money, so why are you doing it?"

Very slowly the words came out, "I'm from London too, but I had to get away for a while and my second-cousin who works in that horrible restaurant got me a stand-in job there, which I'll probably lose soon if I make many more mistakes."

Quietly probing, and following his 'copper's nose' resolutely in search of his quarry, the inspector offered him a boiled sweet and said, "My name's Geoff and I'm from west London. Whereabouts are you from… and what did you say your name was?"

A sigh heralded the answer, "My name's Tashir and I'm from north of London, but I can't go back there for a while."

The inspector carefully changed his questioning, "Life can be very difficult sometimes. It's always good to get away for a while, but not to get into more trouble than you were already in at home."

For the first time he looked up, "I don't have a home or family, Geoff. I had a friend, but he died. Now I'm alone and aren't sure what to do next."

The Inspector asked, "Well, Tashir, if you could do anything at all, what would you choose to do… anything at all?"

The young man began to relax, "That's easy: go fishing! I love fishing!"

Following this lead cautiously, the inspector lied, "I like fishing too, so I've come to do some mackerel fishing at sea. What about coming with me one day? I've seen it advertised where I'm staying with my wife in Teignmouth. We could go out in a small boat for an hour or so if you'd like to."

The bait was taken eagerly, "Yes I'd like that very much Geoff, but I only get Tuesday and Thursday mornings off work."

With just the right degree of enthusiasm, the detective smiled, "Great stuff, Tashir! Let's say Tuesday morning. I'll book us both in for a two-hour fishing boat trip and I'll meet you at Teignmouth Railway Station at 10 o'clock!" They parted company with very mixed feelings. The young man felt just a little less like a refugee from society, whilst the police officer felt as if he was floating on elevated constabulary air.

***

On Sunday morning, Aaron Klein had phoned Alice Glover to invite her to accompany him when visiting Christine Templeton in hospital that afternoon. Alice had gleaned quite a lot of information from her volunteer workers and knew about Christine's horrific injuries and bereavement from her fiancé. Thus, at 2 p.m., she found herself once again at UCLH — very close to the room where she had visited her husband so many times. By way of a chaperone, Aaron took Ruth with him, firstly to Alice's Gunnersbury home then back up to UCLH, during which Alice and Ruth did not stop chatting despite their significant age differences. He supposed that women were better than men at sharing personal things with each other, thus once the pair of them had settled at Christine's bedside, Aaron was beginning to feel rather unnecessary. Hence, when his phone rang, he was happy to escape to the corridor to take Joshua's call, during which a bold idea occurred to him. "Joshua, this is a big thing to ask you, but could it be possible for the boxes of materials collected from the shop to be stored in your basement, please? Maybe I could come this afternoon to talk about it, and if it's OK, please could I bring Ruth and another lady with me?" The idea of women visiting his grubby and untidy home scared Joshua, but he agreed willingly, as long as Aaron brought some cakes.

They stayed for half an hour with Christine, before another visitor arrived. Introductions were made with Peter Templeton, before the nurse suggested politely that her patient may have too many people at her bedside and sufficient excitement. Aaron was amazed when Alice asked Christine if she could visit her again in a few days' time. Christine responded with delight and Alice needed no persuasion to continue her afternoon's outing by visiting an elderly man in Kilburn. She advised that good home-made cakes were sold at her well-remembered UCLH cafeteria, taking Aaron to buy half each of a coffee and a chocolate sponge cakes. Ruth took hold of Alice's arm as they crossed Euston Road and caught the tube up to Kilburn. Aaron had puzzled over several things recently, as he watched an apparently relaxed relationship developing between his delightful niece Ruth and an elderly lady full of heartaches with seemingly nothing to live for. He decided to say nothing and let them get on with it, but he feared how Alice and the very Jewish bachelor Joshua might get on!

The door in Brondesbury Road was opened by a respectably-dressed, clean-shaven and smiling gentleman. "Hello dear Aaron and ladies! Please come in! It's lovely to see you on this quiet Sunday afternoon! I'm sorry that there are so many stairs to reach my third floor flat. Please follow me!" Aaron kept his immense surprise at Joshua's appearance and behaviour to himself as Joshua shepherded his guests into his sitting room, "Please, sit down, ladies! It is so wonderful to see you again dear Ruth after too many years. I'm so sorry about your father's tragic passing."

Ruth kissed him tenderly, "Dear faithful Uncle Joshua, it's been far too long, but perhaps now that circumstances have changed; we'll be able to get back together."

The elderly Jew held out his hand and gave a small bow, "Mrs Glover, you are most welcome to my untidy old home. May I offer you some tea, either Earl Grey or perhaps a green tea?" Aaron was astounded! What was going on here? Joshua had only known of this visit for about an hour! Why and how could he have prepared himself and his home to be so much more clean, tidy and welcoming than it had been? The two old people chatted happily about their preferences of tea and cake, making Aaron feel again that his presence was not too essential. He placed the cake boxes on the table, Joshua fetched pretty china plates, a silver knife and rather antique cake forks, then went to make tea. Alice jumped up and began sorting out the plates and cutlery. "Oh, thank you for helping Mrs Glover, please would you cut the cakes and serve whichever people prefer, or maybe a piece of each, whichever you think best!"

Ruth smiled at her Uncle Aaron, as they watched the elderly lady and gentleman pottering about like old friends instead of new acquaintances. Joshua brought the teas, "It's such a long time since I entertained guests Mrs Glover. Somehow when you're on your own there doesn't seem much point in using nice plates and things."

Alice agreed, "Have you lived alone for very long Mr Shulz? It's only three months since my husband was taken into hospital and died there soon afterwards."

Joshua sipped his tea, "I'm very sorry to hear that. It must be very hard for you. As for myself, I never married and have always lived alone."

Eventually, Aaron broached the subject of thrity-three large plastic boxes of the shop's shattered remains and if Joshua had space to store them. As they discussed how the tremendous work of sorting might be accomplished, it was Alice Glover who proposed that they all go and look around. Aaron and Ruth deliberately held back as the two elderly people inspected available rooms and discussed possibilities. Alice disclosed that she had been a book-keeper and would be pleased to help with making necessary records. Joshua spoke joyously, "In that case, Mr Aaron, if Mrs Glover would be so kind as to undertake the paperwork, I suggest that the police deliver the boxes to the basement and that we bring them one at a time to the second floor flat, just below my own, to be sorted."

Alice joined in, "Oh yes, Mr Shulz, I do agree with those arrangements. It will be a long difficult job and we would need assistance from some younger persons. Mr Klein, could that nice young coloured man Rashid be invited, and what about you Ruth, dear, if your school work permitted?" Aaron was amazed at how this desolate bereaved lady and an impoverished old man were simply proposing to undertake and manage a major work for him!

***

After acquainting his father, the emir, regarding his meeting with the foreign minister, Sheikh Sultan bin Zayed, Salim set about creating a small personal team of staff to assist his new career. He moved quietly around the Federation's middle ranking servants, seeking men who would be capable and very willing to help his endeavours. His selection comprised: Hasan bin Rahma Al Ghazarian to become his private secretary and number 1 aide, Faisal bin Abdullah Al Humaidi as chief of staff dealing with all administrative business, Rashid bin Mohammed Al Raminan to become liaison secretary charged with communications and personal visits on behalf of Salim. For the vital position of head of security, he made a bold decision to create a link with his predecessor, Crown Prince Abdullah by appointing Ahmed bin Sultan Al Hilali who had fulfilled that role for his brother. Salim reasoned that Ahmed, who had been very surprised at the invitation to continue in his role for this so-different crown prince, had been into all but the very inner sanctuaries of meetings accompanying Abdullah; hence, was acquainted with very useful information about external situations as well as the inner whisperings of servants.

On Sunday morning, Salim took his place at the regular meeting of the Council of Crown Princes, being introduced by its chairman, Prince Khalifa to those he had not previously met: Mohammed bin Humaid Al Mak'qi and Hamdan bin Hamad Al Nahimi. The foreign minister, Prince Sultan sat very still and yet spoke with vibrancy in his voice, "Brothers, you are all aware of my medical difficulty, which makes any travel impossible for me. Hence, it is my pleasure to formally propose Prince Salim as my deputy and envoy for our Federation." The chairman looked from face to face, acknowledging each tiny bow of approval, some more truthful than others, before confirming Salim in his role and welcoming him to their council.

On returning to his own offices, newly established in his father's palace, Hasan bin Rahma updated him with further responses to his recent speech, requesting visits with a variety of persons and organisations around the world. One such caught Salim's eye, coming from a respected mosque in the town of Walsall, near Birmingham in Great Britain's Midlands. It was an invitation for him to speak at the dedication of an extension to the mosque, in the presence of guests invited from open-hearted establishments of Muslim and other faiths. "Let us consider this request Hasan. Please ask Rashid bin Mohammed to make contact with them."

***

After a great full English breakfast at the Atlantic Spray Hotel, Alan and Mary strolled along the promenade along with joggers, dog-walkers and day-trippers of all sorts. Mary began very slowly, "You haven't asked me about the church I went to yesterday Alan."

Her husband responded cautiously, "Well, I'm just enjoying the peace and quiet here in Devon, Darling. I suppose it must have been all right?"

Mary replied, "Yes it was actually very good, but I was sorry that you didn't come with me Alan."

He stopped to throw a pebble into the sea, "It's been several years since you started going to church; Mary and you know that I've never tried to interfere, even when you started taking the kids along with you. In fact, I'm quite pleased that you all enjoy going. It's just that I've never wanted anything like that for myself."

She squeezed his arm and spoke very gently, "Anything like what, Alan?"

He hesitated then said, "Why do such ill-matched groups of people want to spend Sunday mornings together when they have nothing in common with each other? I've seen young people going in with pensioners, busy young mums with other people's babies, well-off business people mixing it with out-of-work bums! It just doesn't make common sense to me Mary! I'm sorry."

They were walking arm in arm along the narrow and precipitous wall, with the sea nearly thirty feet below them. As the tide was out, the water exposed the glorious sandy beach, already occupied by excited children and delinquent dogs rushing everywhere without a care in the world. "Look down there, Mary, that's like church: people with or without dogs, just enjoying their freedom to do their own thing. I'm happy to be up here and not playing around down there with them. Don't push me off the wall, Darling: it's a long way back up." They walked on as far as the tunnel, crossed under the railway tracks and found the tucked-away cafe straight away.

"You can't be hungry again already, Alan?"

He grinned, "Well as we've come this far, we might as well have a sit down, especially if it had one of those Devon cream teas attached to it!"

A train roared by, but Alan just heard his phone ringing. "Hello! Sorry, I can't hear who it is calling me!" The train disappeared into the tunnel and quiet resumed.

"Good morning, Alan! It's Aaron Klein here. I didn't want to interrupt your holiday, but just to let you know that the plastic boxes can be taken to Joshua Shulz's big old house in Kilburn please. He's agreed that they can be stored in his basement, before a start can be made on sorting through them." Alan and Aaron quickly agreed the arrangements, then the inspector phoned Sergeant Dent and asked him to sort out the details. Mary watched her husband, as he instantly fell back into his police role. She admired him for that, but also longed for him to have something else in his life, especially in the spiritual realm that she believed to be so much more important than everyday work issues. Mary prayed quietly and waited for guidance.

***

Rashid strolled slowly away from Harrow and Wealdstone Station, passing the empty car park of the unoccupied council offices on this quiet Bank Holiday morning. He walked past the large Mosque and Islamic centre on the opposite side and towards Harrow town centre, remembering that he absolutely must not make anyone take notice of him. Most of the shops and businesses along Station Road were closed, which helped his surreptitious duties as he stopped briefly to look in shop windows. He came to an Indian buffet-style restaurant, opened the door and stepped inside to be greeted by a middle-aged woman in a sari, who led him to an empty table. Rashid helped himself modestly from the various exotic dishes of Asian food and got into conversation with some of the younger waitresses. He told them that he was a stranger to Harrow, and wondered if there were any shops or small businesses run by Middle-Eastern people. The ladies discussed his surprising question then said, "There's a grocer's shop quite close to Harrow-on-the-Hill Railway Station, although it may not be open today as the owner is quite elderly and frail. Other than that, there's a fairly new dry-cleaners where a Middle-Eastern man seems to be the owner or manager, although he isn't there every day. There's usually a 'large' lady who does most of the work there. It's on the opposite side of the road, half way towards the station."

Rashid thanked the waitresses, finished his meal and left the restaurant. He continued ambling along on the same side of the street, passing two dry-cleaners which were clearly Chinese or Far-Eastern. Occasionally, he glanced over the road and soon spotted another cleaners', but he strolled on to some traffic lights, where he crossed over and walked casually back the other way. There was a hand-written notice taped to the door, below the dry-cleaners' opening times, stating that it would be closed for a few days due to family illness. Rashid walked a few paces, took out his phone to feign a call then turned around to take two general photos plus a close-up of the notice, before strolling nonchalantly on his way. At midday, he phoned the inspector to say that he thought that he may have found Swarthy's place. "Very well done, son! Now get right away from Harrow! I'll arrange for plain clothed police to investigate further. Well done, Rashid!" Straight after that conversation, the holidaying inspector phoned Sergeant Dent again, telling him to send two officers shopping along Station Road, Harrow tomorrow morning.

***

Both Alice Glover and Joshua Shulz found this particular Bank Holiday Monday especially sad and difficult. Although they had only made each other's acquaintance on the previous day, it had been a happy introduction in the company of enthusiastic and agreeable people. Now on this supposedly joyful holiday, they found their loneliness hard to bear. Alice was coming to like the courteous Jewish man Aaron Klein and felt rather grandmotherly towards the lovely young woman Ruth. Although Alice had never been a mum, she sympathised maternally and deeply for Christine Templeton, whose life had been all but destroyed. Then she had been taken to meet an elderly Jewish bachelor, pre-warned that he may be rather lacking in social skills, yet when the opposite became evident, it had given Alice a very surprising and happy day.

Now that was gone as instantly as a balloon being burst. She had woken to the usual tomb-like silence in the home which she had begun to hate. As her husband's widow, the sole ownership of the house had passed to her, yet she had no money in the bank and only the state pension to survive on. Alice re-read the recent letter from a firm of solicitors for the twentieth time. It was couched in polite language, but made it perfectly clear that their client's demands for instant repayment of a debt of ten thousand pounds must be met. She had not known of this particular loan, but supposed that her husband had once again borrowed a large sum of money, without her consent or even knowledge, simply to foster his absurd scheme of buying jewels as an investment for their old age. Despite searching the house thoroughly, Alice had never found any of these expensive jewels that her husband had been buying on and off for so many years. The solicitor's letter was like the proverbial millstone tied around her neck. She stood on the brink of a cliff top, not knowing what to do. Miss Templeton would be praying to her God in faith, but Alice had never moved from a childhood's simple belief in his existence. She found no comfort and her heart pounded within her as she allowed bitter remorse to overcome her, crying more on this day than when her husband had died, who truthfully, she had utterly disliked for most of their forty years marriage. Colin had been an unpleasant man, with a temperament so arrogant and selfish that people avoided him. At home he had spoken and acted howsoever he wished, with no regard for his wife, whilst at work he was shunned as the disgruntled store-man throughout the factory. Alice hated the constant reminders of him that her home threw up. 'How can I be so horrible and wicked to feel like this?' was her increasingly bitter entreaty to herself. Yet she did! The last few days had begun to warm her heart, yet now bitter tears filled the day for Alice.

Being alone for Joshua was natural for him, giving the freedoms that bachelorhood allowed. Yet the last seven years of retirement had been a constant struggle for Joshua, who had loved his work and deep involvement with the Klein family. It had been good to be able to buy the whole of his large house; yet, the years since had been swamped by the constant frustrations and responsibilities of making decisions and living with their consequences, entirely alone. He had not wanted to admit it, but he felt truly unwanted by anybody at all. Yesterday had been more than just a bright interval. The new involvement with Mr Aaron, young Ruth and even the surprisingly pleasant Mrs Glover had hidden his constant worry of how to repay his latest bank loan of twelve thousand pounds. He had been forced to borrow it through the demands of his tenants and the local authority's regulations, but what good was it to be the owner of a valuable property, yet have no savings and ever-increasing debts? Although his Jewishness was an integral part of him, in reality his faith in his God was purely nominal, never emulating King David's acknowledgement of his ever-present Lord and God. Now on this supposedly joyful Bank Holiday, despite his best avowed bachelor efforts, and with or without the distant God of his ancestors, Joshua could not dispel the surging waves of depression and a hopeless dread of his remaining years.

***

Sheikh Salim had flown back to Britain on Monday morning and was taken straight to the Federation's embassy, where he presented their ambassador with a formal letter from the chairman of emirs, Salim's father. In it, the ambassador was charged to comply fully with all instructions from the Federation's deputy foreign minister, HRH Prince Salim. At the ensuing meeting with the Embassy's entire operational staff, Salim outlined the changes in policy and procedures which were to be implemented, not by hard arrogant demands made on British officials, but by methods involving recognition and respect for the host nation and its capital city, London. The prince then interviewed the senior staff individually to ascertain their agreement with the new regime; also, to offer opportunities for each of them to aspire into wider spheres of operation. Salim found two of the staff to be very co-operative, whilst others showed a lack of enthusiasm. The only one who refused to comply was ordered back to the desert kingdom within three days. During further and more informal meetings that evening, the prince began to soften the attitudes of some of the staff, who recognised that their new master aimed to foster improved international views of the Federation, and that this was to be obtained by understanding and tolerance rather than domineering.

On Tuesday morning, Sheikh Salim kept his medical appointment with Doctor Chaudhary at UCLH, who was more than satisfied with his condition. He then had great pleasure in catching up with Aaron Klein and Christine Templeton, listening to their news whilst making little of his own recent affairs. The sight of the first recovered Aaronic jewel added a further fillip to the sheikh's resolve to go forwards with his own bold plans.

***

Mary was pleased to see her husband looking much more relaxed than he had been, but she was very disappointed that he was ignoring the spiritual influences that were producing conflicts inside him. She was praying for these to be resolved during their week away, but already she sensed that Alan had returned into his 'outer shell' of professional self-confidence. They went down to breakfast, which Alan ate as if he hadn't eaten for days. "Where do you put it all Alan?" asked Mary.

"Well, Darling, as I'm having a voyage to sea today, I must have a proper start, in case we drift over to France and I have only frog's legs to eat tonight! I've asked the hotel lady to cook the fresh mackerel that I catch for supper this evening. I can almost smell them frying in the pan already! Are you sure that you'll be all right while I'm out fishing this morning?" At 9.45, Mary walked with her husband to the railway station, being careful to keep out of sight. The local train pulled in on time at 9.52 and Alan watched the young man stroll over the footbridge, through the barrier and onto the forecourt. Mary saw them greet each other and walk away to the Back Beach fishing boats, before she went off to the shops.

Alan and Ammar, masquerading as Geoff and Tashir, climbed carefully into the boat, following the weather-beaten skipper's instructions. "Make sure your life-jackets are tightened up, don't move around in the boat, always let me know what's going on with your rods, haul in the fish smoothly and put the line back quickly to catch another. We'll be in a nice shoal of them today, so you'll all take some home for supper!" The five hopeful fishermen grinned at each other, looking confident of their morning's adventure.

"Good luck with the fishing, Geoff! Thanks for inviting me!" said Tashir. The skipper opened up the engine and steered straight out to the harbour entrance. They left the shelter of the River Teign estuary and manoeuvred over the sand bar that guarded it, encountering their first real waves.

"Hold on tight boys while I take her out about a mile," called the skipper as the engine roared into full power. The fishermen were soon covered with salty spray as they clung obediently to the boat's gunwale. Geoff felt his confidence dissolving as his legs became weak and he began struggling to keep his composure. He checked once again that the small tape-recorder inside his sweater was working properly, and spoke loudly with false confidence for the benefit of the recording, "Bit of a swell out here, isn't there Tashir!" The young man nodded his agreement.

After fifteen minutes, Geoff's legs and stomach had stopped co-operating. The boat hove too and the skipper told the fishermen to prepare their rods and lines. Now that the boat had stopped travelling forwards, it rose up and down and twisted round in all directions. He leaned forwards to capture Tashir's voice on the recorder, "Have you been sea-fishing before, Tashir?"

He replied, "No! This is my first time Geoff!" They'd been in the boat for half an hour, with a further hour and a half for Geoff to endure, before the situation changed when the man opposite him pulled in his rod and line, turned around and retched violently over the side. He became an unwanted catalyst for Geoff, whose tormented stomach finally overcame his mental efforts, heaved a few times and convulsed. He tried to face over the side of the tossing boat, but did not allow for the wind as he disgorged his full English breakfast all down his clothes. Tashir looked on helplessly whilst the experienced skipper showed no surprise, simply throwing old cloths to the victims before passing them an opened bottle of brandy, "Take a swig of this boys. You're not the first or the last to find out that it's better to leave sea-going to the likes of me!" The sight of the others hauling in mackerel in quick succession did not make the two sufferers feel any better, as they took turns in retching time after time, oblivious to the constraints of politeness. The following hour or so felt like a lifetime sentence to them both. After Tashir had caught eight fat glistening mackerel, he put down his fishing gear to try and comfort Geoff, "Please don't worry about being sick. It's just how it is for some people. It won't be long before we're heading back to Teignmouth. You'll be OK when we're safely back on land Geoff."

The honest sympathy and kind words affected the inspector's composure, "Thanks, Ammar, I'll be OK when we're back safely."

The young man's face lost all of its colour, "What did you call me, Geoff?"

The awful realisation that he had forgotten to use their pseudonyms hit the inspector, "Look son, it's no good us trying to be too clever. Shall we be honest with each other now?"

Ammar's face hardened as he shouted, "Who are you and how do you know my name's Ammar?"

'AH' began to come back to life, "What you told me about your friend dying recently was true, Ammar. I know all about it. My job was to clear up the stupid mess that you caused in Hatton Garden."

Ammar was petrified, "Are you a policeman? How did you know about me? How did you know where to look?"

His years of training and experience helped him at last, "My name is Detective Inspector Alan Harling of the Metropolitan Police's Bomb Squad. Now let's get down to business. Your friend was Khaled Halleem and last week I was with his mum and dad in their home in Cromer Road. I'm not here officially because I'm on holiday with my wife. You know that being an accessory to a murderer makes you almost the same under the law. I could have you arrested as soon as we get back to the harbour, but I don't have to do that. It depends on you, son." He reached out a hand to Ammar's arm and continued. "What's been done is done. What matters now is what you and I are going to do next. If you want to play at being a proud young terrorist, I'll have to arrest you, despite feeling terrible and being covered in my own vomit."

The worried young man pondered the inspector's words, "And what if I don't? What chance could there ever be for me? Khaled was scared stiff. I didn't know if he'd dare go through with it until I heard the explosion. At least I'd stopped him from wearing the nail-coat, but I was just as scared as him. Now I'm done for until it's my turn to blow myself up. Where can I run to if the police know about me and…?"

'AH' responded to the sudden hesitation by taking a photograph out of his soiled pocket. "…And who? This man also knows all about you, doesn't he?" Ammar looked at the creased photo of the swarthy man with real fear. He couldn't speak. He thought about jumping overboard and drowning himself, but realised that he would be rescued by the skipper. What could he do? His only options were prison, or to run for the rest of his life, or to follow Khaled's example. Alan followed the unspoken thoughts, knowing what he must say, "As well as being a policeman Ammar, I'm a dad. You're not much older than my own son. The real culprits are the evil people who persuade young people like Khaled and you to murder innocent people for the sake of their twisted religious ideals. Try to understand that you've been recognised and are trapped just as surely as we're trapped in this boat. Whatever we want to do, we simply can't escape the truth of it. The only person alive who can help you is me. You can run away as soon as we get to the beach, or you can come quietly with me to my hotel and we'll work out a sensible solution. The choice is yours Ammar."

He found his voice at last, "You're lying, just like you were in that restaurant. Why should you want to help me? You're a policeman, worse than an ordinary enemy. You're tricking me deeper into jail, or worse!" The chance for further conversation was over as the boat's engine roared into life. The inspector and his discovered quarry could only contemplate what would happen back on the beach. They had about fifteen minutes to decide.

***

Mary Harling looked idly around Teignmouth's shops and decided to return to the railway station where earlier that morning she'd seen a sign in the cafe window adverting 'home-made bread pudding'. As that was one of Alan's favourite foods, she would buy some to go after his mackerel. Whilst the lady was wrapping two big slices in grease-proof paper, they were both disturbed by a young man running very fast across the station car park and straight up to the platform barrier. They watched him jump straight over it and rush up the nearside platform.

Mary recognised the young waiter, who had met with her husband that morning right here. Why had he rushed back so quickly? Where was Alan? Why weren't they together? Unable to answer any of those questions, Mary acted spontaneously by running in the same direction as he had, but was separated by the platform fence. She and Ammar looked straight at each other with sure recognition, as a train pulled into the station, "Ammar! Ammar! It's no good running away again! My husband's a good man! He'll do his very best to help you! Stay here and talk! It's your only chance! Wait until he comes! Wait Ammar! Wait!" His eyes were wild and he looked just like one of the frightened schoolboys she saw being bullied in the playground at school. Again, she called to him as any wise mother would, "Ammar! Stop! It will be all right!" She knew that he would jump on to the train that was waiting to depart for Newton Abbot, yet her instinct told her to help this frightened young man. Her purse was still in her hand, ready to buy the bread pudding. Quickly, she took out all the notes it contained and held them over the fence, "Ammar! You'll need money! It's all I've got with me! Take it quickly!" She scribbled her name and phone number on a piece of paper in her purse and reached out as far as she could.

He ran towards her, snatched the money and the piece of paper, turned and leapt onto the train, "Thank you, Mrs Harling!" he mouthed to her through the window as the train accelerated away.

Mary returned quickly to the hotel, without the bread pudding, to find her forlorn husband sitting outside looking and smelling terrible. She could see what had happened and took firm control, "So the fishing trip was not too much fun, Darling. Come on up to our room and let's get you cleaned up a bit, shall we?" Alan followed her with an ashamed look on his ashen face, passively responding to his wife's authority. Sometime later, he told his beloved wife of the morning's exploits, stressing the inadequacies of local fishermen to operate sea-worthy boats. He explained that his error had changed the undercover police approach into a semi-official situation.

He'd correctly given the suspect the opportunity to 'come quietly to the police station', but the culprit had literally 'jumped ship' as soon as they reached Back Beach and had run off at top speed. "I've blown it, Mary! He's run off and will easily get into hiding! It was bad police work! I moved too quickly and now I've lost him forever!"

Mary spoke quietly and without any pride, recounting what had happened at the railway station. "You've not lost touch with him, Alan. My God will honour my faith in Him. Ammar will make contact when the time is right. Now, stop feeling sorry for yourself and have a shower! You smell like a dead fish! I'll make us a cup of tea, then we're going to start a real sea-side holiday!"

Alan replied meekly, "Yes, Dear."

***

Ibrahim and Rashid Halleem shook hands with Mrs Glover, "Please accept these small items that my wife prepared for you this morning. They are savoury delicacies which she made without many spices for yourself, expecting that you might not appreciate fiery food as much as my sons. I mean my son, and myself." Ibrahim bowed and placed the sizeable package into her hands, then opened up the garage to prepare for work in her garden. Alice took mugs of tea to them whilst they worked steadily and at mid-morning Ibrahim asked permission to inspect the car lying unused in the garage. Alice fetched the car keys and watched as he drove the car onto the short drive and began to check it. When she undid the intriguing parcel, she discovered a selection of unidentifiable pastries which she knew that she would never eat on her own. At lunchtime, she took them with a simple salad for them all to share at the garden table. Rashid had just finished cutting the lawns and during their lunchtime Alice admired the respect and deference that he showed to his father. Talk flowed without difficulty until Mr Halleem proposed that work should re-commence.

By mid-afternoon, Mr Halleem had confirmed that the car was in reasonable condition and asked Mrs Glover if she would like to drive it out somewhere whilst the men continued gardening. "Oh Mr Halleem, I have never driven a car in all my life!" Unperturbed, he proposed that as a road test would be very good for the car, Mrs Glover might allow him to drive it a short distance away, naturally with herself accompanying him. They drove slowly down Bollo Lane, talking only a little until he parked carefully and peered beneath the bonnet and under the car. Alice Glover and Ibrahim Halleem sat in the parked car, discovering that they could speak quite comfortably with each other, despite their very different backgrounds. After a while their bereavements were discussed, with Alice not trying to hide her negative feelings about her late husband, and Ibrahim not trying to cover up what his son Khaled had done to dishonour his family and ruin several others. The two beleaguered persons continued their test drive very sedately, with increasingly open discussions on the subjects of homes and occupations, declaring to each other their urgent needs to move away, but that an absolute lack of necessary finances made that appear to be impossible. Mr Halleem asked if Mrs Glover if she had any thoughts about the car, being herself unable to drive it. When she suggested that she might like to sell it, they stopped at a newsagent's and bought a local paper displaying many car advertisements. Back at her home, they scrutinised these and concluded that the car might be sell-able for between £2,500 and £3,000. After a final cup of tea, Alice thanked them both for all of their days' work and assistance, agreeing most happily that they could return the next day.

***

Alice slept much better that night and woke happily on Wednesday morning. The men arrived and continued working systematically amongst the hedges, shrub beds, lawns, trees and paved areas. They cleaned and tidied the garage, without in any way interfering with the abundant contents. They emptied the shed, swept it out, washed the windows and replaced its contents neatly. Alice was delighted with their quiet and efficient workmanship, which was making her garden look as nice as most others in that part of Gunnersbury.

At break times, they pored over the local paper together, selecting two local car dealers as being perhaps slightly less dishonest than the others. Rashid washed and polished the car until it gleamed, whilst his father and Alice sat in quiet contemplation of their earnest desires to leave their homes and areas, to set up somewhere new with at least the chance of a new life. Despite their aspirations, they concluded that the financial hurdles were far too high for either of them, leaving them very disappointed with their situations. Their rather morbid conversation was interrupted by Alice receiving a phone call from Joshua Shulz, advising her that the thirty three plastic boxes were to be delivered by the police tomorrow morning. Alice looked meaningfully at Ibrahim Halleem, who registered her action and half-listened as she told Joshua of the great help given to her recently by Rashid and his father. Making a quick decision, Alice asked Joshua if the Halleems would be permitted to help searching through the boxes. The elderly Jewish man knew of the strange connections between Aaron Klein, Mr and then Mrs Glover and the police inspector, all through the catastrophe of the Hatton Garden terrorism; yet, now Joshua amazed himself as he agreed willingly for these two so sadly connected Muslim men to take part in the work at his home, realising that the gruesome probing might perhaps mitigate their own grief.

Early that afternoon, Ibrahim drove with Alice to the first of their selected local car dealers. She stood watching from the small office as the proprietor walked round the car with Ibrahim, but was very surprised when the two men walked back to her so soon. "Well Mrs Glover, I'll offer you £2,650 in cash. That's my offer, take it or leave it." The man's abrupt manner and Mr Halleem's face said enough to Alice who answered, "No thank you. Goodbye."

She walked almost regally to her car and was driven not far away to their second choice of dealer. Almost before Ibrahim had stopped the engine, a young woman came smilingly to his door and waited whilst he and Alice got out before asking them if they were interested in selling their car. As they had arranged, Ibrahim spoke for them both, saying that they might be interested. "Please can our Mr Holmes take a look right now, Sir? I believe that he's available. Perhaps you would like to look around some of our newer models for sale on the forecourt?" They strolled together amongst the freshly-washed vehicles, trying hard to look like prospective purchasers.

Mr Holmes came over, shook hands with them, gained their approval to make a short test drive, called a mechanic to join him and began his inspection. Ibrahim steered Alice away from the more expensive cars being displayed and towards a few older cars and commercial vans which he found more to his liking. Twenty minutes later, Mr Holmes returned and invited them to discuss matters in his office, offering them a cup of coffee. "Please understand that our business is based more on selling newer vehicles than purchasing older models. The best price for your car would be obtained as a sort of discount from the price of a replacement vehicle which you might like to purchase." Ibrahim told him that they preferred not to buy a replacement car at present, but that they may have an interest in a commercial van that he had noticed in the near future.

Mr Holmes responded, "We would be pleased to have you as our customers, whenever the occasion was right for you, Sir. Therefore, I must lower my valuation for your vehicle to that for a one-off sale. Would an offer of £2,750 be of interest to you?"

Alice signalled to Ibrahim who answered, "We had hoped to obtain £3,000 Mr Holmes, as the car has such a low mileage and is in excellent running order."

The dealer consulted some papers on his desk and spoke again, "I am very sorry, but that price is not possible. However, in recognition of your future interest in a commercial van, I could offer you a special slightly higher price, with no strings attached of course. Would you accept a cash offer of £2,850?"

Alice gave a small smile to Ibrahim who replied, "We would be pleased to accept that figure Mr Holmes. Thank you." The keys and car documents were handed over and the cash counted out carefully to Mr Halleem. They all stood up, shook hands and smiled, leaving Ibrahim to escort Alice to his own car, where Rashid who had driven behind them, opened the doors, settled them together in the back seat, and drove away as smartly as any professional chauffeur would have done.

Once back at Alice's home, they enjoyed a victorious cup of tea with Asian pastries. She had just phoned Joshua Shulz to agree the next day's arrangements, when the doorbell rang. Alice found the young woman from the car dealers waiting on her door step, still smiling as she explained, "Please excuse me, Madam, but just after you and your husband had driven away from our forecourt, Mr Holmes realised that he had not asked you to remove all personal items from your car. He apologises and has sent me very quickly to follow you home with the contents of your car's boot and interior. Please tell your husband that we were very sorry. Goodbye!"

Alice looked at the items returned to her, and smiled back, "Thank you very much, my dear. Please thank Mr Holmes and tell him that we are very pleased to be dealing with your firm. Goodbye!"

Back in her kitchen, Alice told the Halleems about her visitor without mentioning the married title that had been bestowed mistakenly on Ibrahim. She asked the men to bring the returned items indoors, and made another decision. "Instead of taking them to the garage, as I certainly do not want to keep my husband's heavy tool box, grubby clothes, two cardboard boxes and an out-of-date road atlas, which would be of no use whatsoever to me, please can I ask you to take them away? You have been so very kind to me, so please keep anything at all that might be of some small use for yourselves and just dispose of anything that you don't want." Ibrahim thanked her and he and Rashid took the items to his own car, together with some things that Alice had collected together as being of possible use in the search through boxes at Joshua's.

***

Aaron and Ruth Klein were the first to arrive at Joshua's house on that Thursday morning 10th May, followed shortly by Ibrahim Halleem who had dropped Rashid at Kilburn High Road to escort Alice from the tube station. Thus, by 10.00 a.m., the six-strong party of volunteers had assembled and was making its plans. At 10.30, precisely as arranged, they watched a large unmarked white van arrive outside the house. Aaron and Joshua stood waiting at the door as Sergeant Dent approached, "Good morning, Mr Klein and Mr Shulz! I have the special delivery for you as arranged by Inspector Harling." They showed the sergeant down the stairs to the large room in the basement, which had been emptied and cleaned in readiness.

Two officers assisted by the Halleems transferred all thirty-three large plastic boxes from the van down to the basement. Sergeant Dent thanked Joshua for relieving the police of the boxes and gave Aaron a copy of the floor grid reference chart of the shop, which numbers were written clearly on each box. Aaron and Joshua both signed the receipt form and the police van drove away.

Joshua showed the team to the first-floor flat's sitting room, where they moved the furniture aside to create a large open space in the middle for working. They walked downstairs, looked in at the ground floor flat, which was still fully equipped and furnished since the days of its last tenants, before descending the last flights of stairs to the basement. Aaron showed them the reference chart and explained that the shop measured approximately seven metres wide by six metres deep. The police had referenced each square moving from left to right simply as columns one to seven, at right angles to rows designated A to F moving from front to back. There were additional very short rows G and H entering the rear passage leading to the work rooms behind the shop. The doorway entrance was square A4. Aaron decided not to start with the square marked A1, but to begin furthest away from the point of the explosion and work around the inside perimeter towards the centre. Thus, they expected to be working with the easier least destroyed material before coming to the completely shattered central area. He pencilled in the positions of the shop fittings and the persons who had been in the shop as far as he could recall them. The rear counter, behind which he had stood on that fateful morning, was marked as being from E2 to E4/E5, with the only other counter which was along the right-hand side being from C6/7 to E6/7. It was separated by a narrow gap for staff to pass between the two counters into the customer area. Reuben had been standing in that gap E6 advising Sheikh Abdullah in D6. Salim had been on the left rear side of the shop, at about D2. Miss Templeton and her fiancé had been together in front of the main counter at D4/D5. The bomber had approached them somewhere near C4.

Aaron, Rashid and his father carried up one box each at a time until boxes A1, B1, C1, D1, E1 and F1 had been placed in sequence ready to be emptied. The lid of box A1 was removed, revealing a hideous mixture of fragmented materials, twisted jewellery parts, congealed blood, but mostly unidentifiable things. At that point, the real poignancy of this volunteer working team began to be recognised by each other. How could the bereaved Jewish victims Aaron and Ruth Klein and the equally bereaved Muslim father and brother of the bomber be co-operating with each other, in the bachelor home of the elderly Jew Joshua Shulz who had worked for nearly thirty years in that shop? It was only Mrs Alice Glover who had no logical connection here.

In that brief emotion-packed atmosphere, it was Ibrahim who asked to speak first, "Please listen to something of tremendous importance that my son and I have to disclose to you. Yesterday, Mrs Glover sold her husband's car and afterwards gave us the unwanted contents of its boot. Rashid will fetch them in now." The others waited in anticipation until a large heavy tool box and two cardboard boxes had been placed on the floor in front of them.

Ibrahim opened the boxes and took out a magazine from each of them. "There are many of these magazines that Mr Glover must have been storing, all entitled '*Jewels Worldwide*'. Last night, we skimmed through a few of them, discovering that they advertise items of jewellery and precious stones for sale or purchase by collectors around the world, but in a strange almost illicit way. Now Rashid will open the tool box." He took out an assortment of hammers, pliers and other tools, then waited. "Now Rashid, please lift out what was beneath the tools."

Mrs Glover gasped in amazement at two shallow blue plastic boxes, "But they're my Tupperware boxes that I lost about ten years ago!"

Ibrahim beamed at her, "Yes, dear madam, your husband needed them and forgot to ask your permission." Ibrahim placed the boxes side by side on a stool and with as much drama as a magician uses to enthral his audience, he very carefully removed their lids. No-one could speak for several seconds as they gazed disbelievingly at two boxes of gleaming jewels.

Eventually, Ibrahim turned to Alice, "Dear Mrs Glover, yesterday you gave us some very ordinary things, but that came from your pure and thankful heart. Now, I can return to your gracious person what your husband strived for over many years. His worthy intentions were unknown to you, but on his demise, he has provided a glorious blessing for his wife." Although Alice did not agree with Ibrahim's poetic words about her husband, it appeared that indeed he had been acquiring jewels then storing them away as a squirrel does nuts for a time of future need. Now here they were in front of her, assuredly in her own time of desperate need, but also to be gazed upon by new and friendly faces which her unpleasant husband would never have acknowledged, respected or dared to look into.

The volunteers picked up jewels delicately with shear admiration, whilst Aaron and Joshua were more selective. Their eyes met as they isolated two gemstones from the collection, turned them over and drew their breath. Aaron's face had become rather solemn and the emotion building up in him made it difficult for him to speak, "Please friends, my words will not express what is in my heart, but please forgive me. Something awesome is happening and somehow each of us is involved. We are of a variety of faiths and backgrounds, but if any of us has a trusting relationship with Almighty God, it may be proper for us to thank him, before we look more closely at these jewels which he has surely chosen to reveal to us today." A short time of silent contemplation ensued, with each of the six persons obeying Aaron's words respectfully, in simple personal ways not of any religious doctrine nor from holy books of prayers, but from their individual hearts. They silently acknowledged their own and each other's grief and gave grateful thanks for each other and for the amazing discovery of these glorious jewels. Awareness of something more than just respectful tolerance for each other was growing, as desires emerged within themselves to help and support one-another truly in their present difficulties.

Aaron spoke again, "You know of the message that I found written in the hospital's Gideons Bible, *'You must find those jewels'* which I believe was intended for me to find and obey. I presumed that it was written by her late husband, yet Mrs Glover assures us that the handwriting was not his! Then who did write it and for what overall purpose? Surely the magnificent jewels of God's glory, worn first by the original High Priest Aaron 3,500 years ago, really do exist and are to be discovered and shown to the world's mostly unbelieving and incredulous eyes! Already I have recovered one jewel, a beautifully clear red jasper, inscribed with the tribal name Naphtali. Now I can see two further inscribed gems, which were simply waiting to be discovered in one of Mrs Glover's humble plastic boxes." Slowly, the beautiful jewels were replaced and the team turned their thoughts to starting work, soon realising that sorting the gooey mess inside the plastic boxes was not an indoors job. Somehow, the materials had to be clean enough to allow systematic examination to begin. The Halleems asked to look round Joshua's back garden, whilst Alice asked him if she could go and lie down for a while in the quiet ground floor flat, and Ruth offered to go and buy fish and chips, buns and cake for lunch. Aaron and Joshua were left alone to inspect the two inscribed jewels.

The jeweller and the lapidorist turned the two beautiful gemstones over and over in their hands, Aaron taking the one cut in emerald format, whilst Joshua inspected the banded reddish-brown-pale jewel. "I have never seen such evenly spaced concentric bands in an agate before, Mr Aaron. As it moves in the light, I can understand our Hebrew meaning for agate as 'sub-divided into striking streams of fire'! This ancient gemstone has consistently vitreous lustre and the word M'nasheh is inscribed on it."

Aaron described the jewel that he was holding, "This almost orange stone is surely a zircon, rarer than the dazzling blue variety, and with a lustre more of a brilliant sheen than the common vitreous!" Joshua fetched some simple jeweller's equipment and the examination continued for a few minutes. "Yes, that is definitely a zircon Mr Aaron as its hardness is about 7 and refractive index nearly 2. Its specific gravity is so high, about 4.6 and look: it shows us its double refraction! The tribal name of Efrayim is engraved upon it!"

Aaron passed the other jewel to Joshua, who took only a few minutes to report. "The agate's specific gravity is just 2.6 although its hardness is also 7 on Mohs scale. It has a refractive index of about 1.53 and both jewels show their streak on unglazed porcelain as white. The inscription is M'nasheh, sister tribe and always together with Efrayim as being the two sons of Joseph. Both gems have the 'wedjat' emblem of an eye representing the Egyptian god 'Horos', as you explained on the jasper. The identification of both is quite clear Mr Aaron!"

They all met up for their impromptu lunch and reviewed the situation. The existing furniture was inadequate and the floor would not be a good place to work on, so they would need work benches of some sort then containers of various types into which items could be stored for further detailed inspection. The Halleems had found Joshua's back garden sizeable enough, with an outdoor tap and hose, various old tables and containers for them to establish a 'first stage' cleaning area. However, they proposed that a number of strong sieves be purchased to allow the materials to be thoroughly screened and separated. Alice spoke about the necessity for exact written records which would require various books and a systematic filing system. The contents of each referenced box needed proper recording for two reasons: firstly, in case the police required forensic evidence; secondly, to help Aaron identify the likely items of jewellery that had been blown apart. They must be certain that nothing of value or interest was disposed of, amongst the resulting rubbish from the boxes. Aaron proposed that the categories of items found should include: wood, metal, plastic, glass, paper, building rubble, jewellery and human remains. Where to put the sorted items needed to be thought through, with such a range of values from gold, silver, gemstones right down to those materials to be thrown away.

After lunch, Joshua and Alice walked to the High Road shops to consider their requirements, with Alice having cash available from the sale of the car. They visited a second-hand furniture shop, spotting a huge oak table with extending leaves which once must have graced a mansion. Six cheap but large coffee tables painted in gaudy colours were pulled out for them, as was an old architect's plan chest with fourteen large shallow drawers. They paid in cash and the shop keeper agreed to have them delivered in about two hours' time. Next, they went to a 'Pound Shop' where they bought twenty clear stackable plastic boxes with lids, several rolls of plastic bin bags in different colours and sizes, plastic food bags with ties, some remnant rolls of plain wallpaper and one hundred pairs of thin plastic gloves. The shop manager agreed to take them up the street to the furniture shop for them, while Joshua took Alice to the local stationery shop where she purchased A4 lined pads, lever-arch files with indexes and an expensive A3 hard-back accounts book. She bought tea cakes from a bakery and fruit from a grocer's before strolling back to Joshua's big sparsely-occupied house, being delighted with such a good variety of independent shops in close walking distance. Ibrahim and Ruth had followed their shopping example, finding a hardware shop in which they bought a two way tap adaptor, sieves, watering cans, buckets and a coil of hosepipe.

It wasn't long before the furniture and other items were delivered and carried up to the first-floor workroom. The team went further upstairs to Joshua's flat to enjoy tea and cakes, after which Alice asked Ibrahim to show her round the garden. She noticed the large shed and ancient greenhouse, surprised at the garden's size, privacy and sunny position, although it looked just as untidy and unloved as her own had a few days ago.

At 4pm a visitor called to see them all, leaving Ahmed bin Sultan his concerned chief of security and other staff outside while Prince Salim went inside alone. Aaron introduced him to everyone and showed him the two latest Aaronic jewels to have been discovered so miraculously. Salim was amazed at the jewels and equally impressed at how this multi-cultural team of volunteers was co-operating. Whilst preparing to search painstakingly amongst the hideous remains of the Klein's shop, they appeared to be relaxed and happy in each other's presence. Aaron and Salim took some tea into one of the bedrooms and closed the door. "Look Salim, I might like to ask for some help please, which I believe is in line with your principles. These people are becoming more than just tolerant of each other's vastly different backgrounds. They are actually overcoming the crazy relationships between the bomber and themselves."

Salim asked, "Then my friend, how could I further assist what is already taking place?" Aaron described the hatred shown to the Halleem family in their Watford locality, creating the obvious necessity for them to move away. He went on to explain Joshua's impoverished state with a large bank loan dragging him down and Alice's needing to repay her late husband's large loan, plus her despondency of being alone and her longing to move to another locality.

"It seems to me Salim that with their capital tied up in their homes, and without any available finance, they are trapped for ever unless some catalyst was applied. It's rather like a row of dominoes standing on end, unable to fall until someone knocks the first one down and they cascade into each other."

The sheikh considered a moment, "Perhaps, my friend, some judicious use of a rich Arab nation's prolific finances could form such a catalyst?" The two friends smiled and agreed to keep in touch over that matter. They returned to the work room, where Salim noted the team's enthusiasm about the long, onerous, even disgusting work ahead of them, which they were undertaking with such willingness.

Before the team broke up that afternoon, Ibrahim Halleem asked with due deference, "Mr Klein, can we ask about the situation concerning the other jewels in Mrs Glover's boxes?"

Aaron began to explain, "Look friends, those are not insignificant gemstones, but are very specific jewels. They may have a high value, yet, a cloud could hang over them. Many jewels have had colourful histories, and matters of identification and ownership may need to be investigated. Beautiful jewellery has a nasty habit of being connected with trouble, death and crime. We must all take great care about this matter. I will be pleased if Joshua would assist me in trying to identify each stone before any decisions could be contemplated. I would be surprised if the nine additional beautiful jewels together would fetch less than twenty thousand pounds, if their sale was legally possible. Mrs Glover, now that we have all looked at them, please will you permit me to take these jewels into safe keeping and to research their identities and origins?"

Alice replied, "Most certainly Mr Aaron! Please do so!" She admired that the question had been asked of herself, not being used to such honesty and respect. She glanced at Aaron, Ruth and Joshua, Ibrahim and Rashid, whose differences of skin colour, age, faith and social situations were no hindrance to her or each other.

Joshua and Aaron decided that several photographs should be taken, before the jewels were listed by probable type with some brief descriptive notes on each, after which they would need specialist jewellers equipment to make a detailed examination. Aaron asked if Joshua would visit the rear workrooms of his shop tomorrow, to collect whatever of his old instruments and tools remained there. He would begin research into the likely past histories of the gems. Together, they would compose a comprehensive list of this amazing find to assist Alice in her decisions of what to do with the gems.

***

On Friday morning, Alice went by tube to Euston Square and walked resolutely up the steps into UCLH, where at 11.30 she was permitted to visit Christine Templeton. "My dear Mrs Glover! Thank you for visiting me again. It gives me so very much pleasure!" Alice pulled up a chair very close to Christine's bedside and instinctively grasped her right hand.

"Miss Templeton you are an inspiration to me, as you must be to many people. You have every right to be a bitter person, but on the contrary, you show nothing but love and kindness to people, including a silly old woman like me." Alice burst into tears, whilst Christine said nothing and prayed silently. When she had composed herself, Alice described her long marriage of discontent where her husband showed no interest in his wife, leading her to reciprocate with him. She spoke about his obsessive interest in jewellery, for which he squandered their savings and borrowed more money to buy gemstones supposedly for their retirement years. They became two separate people living in a shared house which was certainly not a home.

Alice changed tack and described the days since the bombing, mentioning Inspector and Mrs Harling, Mr Aaron Klein and his lovely niece Ruth, Rashid and his father Mr Ibrahim Halleem, Mr Shulz and Christine herself. "Oh, I've been such a terrible woman Miss Templeton! Only yesterday, when we were all together, dear Mr Halleem brought me a treasure horde of jewels that he found by accident, hidden carefully away in the toolbox of my husband's car. You see he had been saving up for our retirement years after all, but in the only way that he knew of, by buying expensive jewels! Mr Klein spoke seriously to us about this discovery, as being something very special, then asked any of us who had a relationship with God to silently give him thanks. Everybody responded to Mr Klein's request, even though we have different faiths and I'm not at all sure about what we're supposed to agree or disagree about. We all bowed our heads and prayed however we wanted, but how can I dare to talk about prayer when God could never forgive me for how I treated my husband for all those long lonely years when all the time he was…" Christine remained silent as Alice's tears flowed, unable to hug her, yet bringing immeasurable comfort.

Alice breathed a deep sigh and explained how it was not only herself who was in deep financial trouble, but also the elderly Jewish gentleman Mr Shulz and the gentle family of the Muslim bomber. "Oh Miss Templeton, they're being so kind to me and my heart wants so much to help them, but how can I when I have no savings just large debts, even though I own a house? Mr Shulz is in the same situation and the Halleems are desperate to move home! Miss Templeton, I have a plan, but am terribly afraid. Please tell me if I am being ridiculous. If Mr Halleem could buy my house, his family could begin a new life, but would it be wicked of me to ask to rent one floor of Mr Shulz's house which would be perfectly big enough for me? Oh, Miss Templeton, could those lovely things ever happen when none of us has any money?"

Christine suggested that they pray. After a while, she explained, "Dear Mrs Glover, faith is not about rules and regulations, but a personal relationship with God. Please take the Bible from my locker and find Psalm 23. A simple shepherd boy trusted God so much that he became the King of Israel, so your difficulties can surely be resolved. You have confessed: now God has forgiven you for your years of bitterness. Please follow the words, but learn to follow my example by speaking them out personally like this *'The Lord Jesus is my shepherd, I Christine shall not be in want.*

Jesus makes me, Christine, lie down in green pastures', and so on. Now, please borrow my Bible…" At that moment, a knock was followed by the entry of Peter Templeton. Alice was introduced and learnt that his exams had finished, prompting her to invite him to join the team of volunteers sorting through the boxes. He expressed willingness, and then noticing the heavy Gideons Bible in her hand as she stood to take her leave, offered, "Mrs Glover, please accept this pocket version of the New Testament and Psalms as a gift! It is much easier to carry with you!"

***

Once outside, Alice made her decision. She caught a bus up to Kilburn, sitting on the top deck to get a better look at that unfamiliar part of London. Taking out her gift, she turned to Psalm twenty-three and followed Christine's advice, speaking very quietly so that the few other passengers wouldn't hear her, *'The Lord Jesus is my shepherd, I Alice shall not be in want. Jesus makes me lie down in green pastures. Jesus leads me, Alice, beside quiet waters. Jesus restores my soul. Jesus guides me, Alice, in paths of righteousness for his name's sake.…'* She read on until she recognised Kilburn High Road, stood up and made her way to the stairs. A woman sitting a few rows in front turned and spoke to her, "Thank you, my dear, for reading those words to me. They were just what I needed!"

Alice walked around the area, popping into shops and walking some way down each turning off the High Road, learning more and more of the locality. She passed the police station, looked into the library and had a cup of a tea in a cafe. Down a side street she came across an old factory building which had a bright sign outside proclaiming 'Harvest Church'. On their poster, Alice read the words 'Why don't you… come and join the Harvest?' The space left in that sentence confirmed her course of action, leading her straight to Brondesbury Road and Joshua's front door. "Dear Mrs Glover, please come in. What a lovely surprise!"

Alice and Joshua chatted easily, getting to know and trust each other, wanting to lessen their aloneness whilst retaining independence. She told him that she really liked the ground floor flat, with its large front room with two bay windows allowing views in both directions up and down the quiet street. She had noticed such ordinary life outside: young mums pushing children in buggies, tradesmen calling at the rows of terraced houses, school children running and shouting with their friends on their way back home, and older people carrying their bags of shopping back from the High Road. The flat's kitchen was more modern and far better equipped than her own and the bathroom was clean and bright with a modern shower over the low-sided bath. She liked both back bedrooms which overlooked the currently unkempt garden, especially the larger room with its practical built-in cupboards and pretty features including a padded window seat and an original Victorian washbasin set into a marble-topped dressing table. All the rooms had high ceilings and were much bigger and lighter than in her own home in Gunnersbury. She could visualise herself here, being totally independent, but knowing that there was a kind gentleman of an age similar to her own not very far away in the same big and nicely modernised old house.

"Mr Shulz, let us not beat about the bush after sharing our problems and disappointments with each other. I have decided that now is the time for me to go forwards, having spent far too long in the doldrums!"

The elderly Jew agreed wholeheartedly! "But what is on your mind to have brought you back here so unexpectedly today? I am very intrigued."

Alice decided not to hesitate in case her determination faltered. "I have made a plan that is radical, but which does not frighten me, although you may think that it is just a dream from a silly old... No!" She forced herself not to say anything negative and against her new resolve. "Mr Shulz, I am determined to move from my unhappy home in Gunnersbury and would like to ask you if I could become your tenant for the ground floor flat?"

Joshua's heart returned to normal as the anticipated dreaded words of romance towards himself failed to appear. "The Halleems are desperate to move away from Watford, so what would be against them buying my own house, which is big enough and far enough away for them to start afresh in life? As all of us have the same problems of an absence of any ready money, plus heavy debts, I have decided to pray for a solution."

Joshua's face was solemn as he walked up and down in his sitting room for what seemed like an age before he answered in a subdued voice, "Mrs Glover, I am very sorry, but I do not wish to rent you the flat. During the last few years of letting out the two flats, I should have received an income and security, but instead I have had nothing but trouble and financial ruin. Therefore, I have resolved never to let either flat to a tenant ever again. I am very sorry." Alice was so shocked at the firmness and finality of his decision that she was almost ready to show her deep chagrin. Yet, she didn't want to reveal her great disappointment which would hurt him just as surely as his words had hurt her. She forced herself to remember Christine and called out desperately to God for his help, almost missing Joshua's further words. "I absolutely cannot rent the flat to you, Mrs Glover; yet, it would give me great pleasure if you were living in my house. May I make you a bold proposal in return?"

Alice's heart turned over at his particular choice of words. "If you were to sell your house to Mr Halleem, would you be willing to lease the ground floor flat from me?"

Suddenly, the picture emerged for them both, each desiring the same thing! It took very little time, over further cups of tea, for these two determined and independent persons to discuss the good and not-so-good points, legalities and financial issues concerning his proposal. They concluded that a lease of twenty-five years should see them both to the end of their days whilst allowing them ample funds to pay off their debts. At their ages, they were more than happy to put things into rapid motion and let the formalities catch up later. Alice was invited by Joshua to move into the ground floor flat as soon as possible, regardless of the actual sale of her house. "Mr Shulz, now that we have agreed what our hearts want to do, we must resolve the financial issues properly. Although there is a total lack of available money between us all, Miss Templeton has shown me how to overcome such a dilemma. Do you have a Bible please?"

Once again Joshua was shocked at what was happening in his well-ordered Jewish life. "Well yes, Mrs Glover, I have my revered Hebrew Bible, but it must be very different from your own Christian book."

Undaunted, Alice asked him to fetch it and read aloud the Second Book of Chronicles, chapter 7, verse 14. Joshua, knowing that book as Divrei-Hayamim Bet spoke tremulously, "*If my people, who bear my name, will humble themselves, pray, seek my face and turn from their evil ways, I will hear from heaven, forgive their sin and heal their land.*" Alice astounded Joshua by suggesting that the word '*land*' could be personalised to mean the various issues concerning their sales, purchases and leasing of properties. "Mr Shulz, why should we not pray right now that the Almighty God of Abraham will heal our problems, if only we decide to humble ourselves and seek his face?"

Although he was very impressed with Alice's business-like yet sincere way of interpolating holy scripture, without any hypercritical religiosity, he baulked at her suggestion, "But dear Mrs Glover, you are a Christian and I am a Jew! How could we seek God's face and pray together? Surely that cannot be done?"

Alice answered with surprising determination. "Why not, Mr Shulz? Isn't Abraham's God the same Almighty God of Jews and Christians alike?" Finding no fault with her simple logic and overcoming his natural reserve, he sat quietly opposite her as each of them spoke silently and sincerely to God about their problems and desires. Soon afterwards, Alice returned joyously to Gunnersbury whilst Joshua prepared happily for Shabbat to begin.

CHAPTER 9

Aaron enjoyed the peace and solitude of this Sabbath in his own Hatton Garden bachelor flat. He had selected a dozen of the nearly four years' worth of the '*Jewels Worldwide*' magazines to bring with him, leaving the bulk of them in the boxes at Joshua's. Altogether they spanned the period between April 2014 and October 2017, each one filled with basic quality printing in black and white, mostly privately-placed advertisements without any names or addresses other than post office box numbers spread around the world. Some were offering items of jewellery or individual jewels for sale, whilst others were seeking to purchase specific types of the same. The magazines were not attractive and appeared to have a global clientele of unidentified jewellery collectors. Aaron had certainly never heard of this magazine within the Hatton Garden jewellery empire. He selected one or more advert from each of his sample magazines and was able to trace some patterns of specific items being traded back and forth around the world. Only the name of the city was given, but without access to the buyers' or sellers' post office boxes, there was no way of identifying who had placed the advertisements. Some of the descriptions of items were obscure, such as '*medieval necklaces*' whilst others were very specific, including '*famous European aristocrat's eighteenth-century emerald brooch set in surrounding ring of alternating topaz and beryl auxiliaries*. For a jeweller like Aaron, such a description would tend to identify any well-known pieces from the plethora of items available to the market. There were enough suspicions of illicit or even illegal trading going on, that Aaron was alarmed sufficiently to phone Inspector Harling that evening, asking for a meeting the next day. Alan invited Aaron to visit him at home tomorrow morning, whilst the family would be out at church, bringing some example magazines with him.

***

On Friday afternoon, seven years old Fatima Halleem was attacked by other children in her school playground. Rashid had great respect for his father and knew that the murderous suicide of his elder brother Khaled had blown away all happiness and optimism from him. The sudden dismissal from his job had really hurt his father, and then Rashid's college principal had suggested that he postpone further studies until after the summer holidays. His mother had hardly ventured outdoors since Khaled's fateful day, but now Rashid was becoming scared for the whole family. He decided to speak, "Father, you know that Mrs Glover is very unhappy in her home in West London and wants urgently to move home. We have noticed that no modernisation has been done and she has no money or strength to think about central heating, double glazing, kitchen and bathroom improvements which would make it more attractive to purchasers."

Ibrahim responded quietly, "Yes my son, but how could we help Mrs Glover when our own situation is so difficult?"

Rashid answered, "Father, we must move far away from Watford, but what could you afford to buy even if anyone would consider purchasing our house from such a repugnant family? Father, if Mrs Glover would allow us to stay with her and we ourselves carried out the necessary improvements free of charge, if she could purchase the materials, perhaps it would enable Mrs Glover to sell her home?"

Ibrahim responded, "Son, I like your idea and I honour your compassionate heart, but we must earn money to live and Mrs Glover has her husband's large debt to repay. None of us has any significant money. God alone can provide the solutions, by his own methods and only if indeed it fits his purposes. We will both ask him during our times of prayers my son, and he will answer us when he is ready to."

That evening, back home from Kilburn, Alice had decided to make an immediate start with sorting and packing up what she intended to take with her to a much smaller home. She had no need or desire to take furniture, just some crockery, kitchen equipment, clothes and personal items, so had stopped at a shop near the tube station where the owner promised to flat-pack and save a dozen clean largish cardboard boxes for her that evening. Now, on this sunny Saturday morning, Alice made two trips to collect the boxes, ate a small breakfast and feeling settled in her mind, phoned Ibrahim Halleem. He listened attentively as she told him of her and Joshua's agreement for her to move into his ground floor flat. Alice then proposed that he bring all of his family to visit her today to give them a break away from Watford.

Ibrahim agreed willingly and said that his wife would bring enough for all of them to eat. Being a book-keeper, Alice spent all morning making detailed lists as she went methodically through her rooms, noting down the contents as being either 'fixtures' or 'removable' then allocating each of those to one of three columns headed 'To take with me', 'To leave behind' and 'To be discussed'.

When Rashid rang her door bell, Alice shook hands with the three adults and smiled at their darling little girl Fatima clinging nervously to her mother's hand. Alice was not put off when Mrs Halleem and Fatima sat silently in the sitting room whilst Ibrahim and Rashid went with her into the garden to consider what further work they should do that afternoon. Alice returned indoors to find her visitors looking very pale and worried. She shepherded them into the kitchen and sat them down at the table with glasses of water. Slowly and very, very quietly, Mrs Halleem mouthed the words, then dared at last to utter them very gently, "Khaled! Oh, my Khaled! My boy Khaled! Oh Khaled! My son Khaled!" Her tears came slowly at first, then engulfed her whole body, which heaved and shook uncontrollably.

Fatima followed her mother's actions identically, thus soon Alice had both of her arms around them and wept her own heart out with them. Half an hour later, Alice took Fatima's hand and led her uncomplainingly outside into the garden where she calling to Rashid to come and play with her. Returning to her kitchen, Alice sat down opposite Mrs Halleem with another box of tissues and waited. Gradually the bereaved mother shared her heartache of seeing her adored first-born son named as an evil terrorist murderer. Alice thought of no suitable words to say, but her simple presence with the distraught mother had similar effects to that of

Christine Templeton with herself. Tears, great sobbing tears and indescribable remorse, poured out in repeated swathes of agony.

At long last, the pangs of hunger prompted the ladies to remember their responsibilities to the menfolk and children. Mrs Halleem simply stopped her crying, stood up and collected the bags of food that had been left unattended in the hall. Together, they put the cold pastries onto trays and took them to the back garden. Rashid and Fatima helped to arrange chairs and spread plates of food around the table, before Mr Halleem was called to join them for lunch. He was carrying a large brown envelope marked '*Good quality paper to be kept*'. He handed it to Alice and asked her to look inside it, "I had been tidying the boxes beneath your husband's workbench and opened one labelled '*Old newspapers*' but I found this clean envelope amongst them." Alice took out a collection of detailed invoices, receipts and post office paperwork, all concerning the purchasing of jewels through the magazines '*Jewels Worldwide*' that had been stored in boxes in the boot of her husband's car. She surprised the Halleems by putting it down on the ground as almost unwanted.

Ibrahim decided to reveal his son's idea, "Mrs Glover, I have an important question for you to consider please." He explained Rashid's thoughts of the family staying with her here for some time and undertaking modernisation of the house freely, if she could pay for materials.

Alice listened politely then answered, "I am sorry, but that kind idea is unnecessary thank you Mr Halleem." She told them of her agreement with Joshua Shulz to move to his ground floor flat virtually straight away. "As this house will be empty, which might attract squatters, I would be very much obliged if your family would come to live here until it is sold, please. Of course, none of us has any available money, but I am praying that the Almighty God of Abraham will undertake the financial arrangements for selling my home, most preferably to yourself Mr Halleem. Now, after lunch, please can Fatima help her mother by taping up the big cardboard boxes for me, as I wish to start packing my things?"

Ibrahim's bow and simple words were sufficient to show his deepest appreciation, "It is a palace Mrs Glover. Thank you for your angelic generosity to our family."

Discussions of the practicalities of moving and how to save money took place, concluding that as no large items of furniture needed transporting, the best way would be to do things themselves, even if it took several car journeys. Ibrahim and Rashid considered that it would be better to leave their own home partially furnished and equipped, in the hope of gaining a slightly better sale price, particularly as Alice would be leaving so much behind. As their thoughts turned to hiring a van for the moves, they remembered the kindness shown by Mr Holmes during the sale of Mr Glover's car. They wondered if the van that Ibrahim had liked the look of would be available for hire. Alice went upstairs and fetched her coat, whilst the others cleared away the lunch things, before they left Mrs Halleem and Fatima in the garden and drove away.

Parking on the sales forecourt, they spotted the large Mercedes van still for sale at £4,250.00. The nice young woman came to them, then took their message of wanting to hire the van to Mr Holmes in the office. He soon walked over and shook hands, "How good to see you back here so soon! I moved your old car on very quickly thank you. However, I'm sorry that we never hire out our sale vehicles, but why don't you consider buying it?"

Ibrahim frowned, "We are not able to afford such an expensive van Mr Holmes."

He smiled, "Please don't say that until you know the actual prices! Why shouldn't you take it for a test drive while I do the same with your car?"

Ibrahim looked shocked, "But I don't want to sell my car Mr Holmes."

The smiling salesman owner continued unabated, "This is a brilliant van, typical Mercedes quality with air-condition, GPS, two rows of front seats enough for six burly workmen and a carrying capacity of two and half tons. It has so many extra features and is perfect for a business man like yourself." They exchanged keys and began their test drives with Alice Glover feeling like the queen sitting up high on the back row of comfortable seats, Rashid next to his father who drove cautiously around the local streets. They parked and Rashid crawled beneath the van, then checked under the bonnet amazed at the cleanliness and size of the engine.

"It looks like an excellent van, Father, but could we really afford to buy it?"

Back on the forecourt Mr Holmes was waiting for them. "Your car is not in bad condition for its age, but its steering and brakes need attention so I cannot offer you the book price. However, I could give you £2,850.00 in part exchange for the Mercedes van, meaning a net purchase price of £1,425.00. What do you think?"

Ibrahim shook his head, "I am sorry Mr Holmes, but I do not have such money; therefore…"

He broke off as Alice spoke up, "Ibrahim, let us talk in Mr Holmes' office to see if there is a solution."

They accepted a coffee each and the salesman made a suggestion, "We give all our existing customers a 7.5% discount off further purchases, so if you bought the van in Mrs Glover's name, that would reduce the differential to only £1,104.00, say a round £1,000.00 for immediate cash purchase. Also, I could offer you two years guarantee, a year's free servicing and fill it up with diesel. Now what do you think?"

Alice opened her handbag and took out exactly a thousand pounds, "That is a fair offer, Mr Holmes. Ibrahim, let us accept it." The gentle Muslim man was equally astounded at Mrs Glover using his first name, as much as producing £1,000 from her handbag.

Thus, Mrs Halleem and Fatima were soon taken for a drive around Gunnersbury, feeling like princesses along with Queen Alice in the back and Ibrahim and Rashid looking very professional in the front seats. Back in Bollo Lane, they celebrated with more tea, samosas and bhajis before agreeing the next two days arrangements. On Sunday, Alice would pack her belongings whilst the Halleems would do the same in Watford. On Monday morning, the family would drive down to Gunnersbury very early and move in, after which their men would take Alice and her dozen boxes up to Kilburn to start her new life in Joshua's ground floor flat.

***

Alan and Mary Harling had enjoyed the last four days immensely, having had at last some real time to breath in the pure sea air and enjoy walking along Teignmouth's sea wall. They had spent only three hours apart, whilst Alan had visited a certain restaurant in Newton Abbot, spoken to an older waiter and discovered that his inept younger colleague had announced his sudden departure last Tuesday afternoon and had headed reportedly to The Midlands. Now, on Saturday morning, the Harlings drove home contentedly from the West Country to find the loving arms of their three children.

***

Before Aaron left his flat that Sunday morning, he was phoned by Sheikh Salim, "Friend Aaron! Let us begin your suggested game of dominoes straight away. Please contact each of the individuals today, requesting that when they gather at Joshua Shulz's house tomorrow morning, they take with them any official documents that might assist dominoes to fall over: such things as property title deeds, birth or death certificates, mortgage and loan documents, bank account passbooks, plus a spare set of house keys for each domino! A lady will be calling on you all to explain the rules of the game and get the match in progress! The game should not take too long to play, as long as each contestant obeys the rules! Goodbye, my friend!"

***

The inspector welcomed Aaron Klein into his home that Sunday morning and sat him down at the kitchen table. Together, they turned the pages of several of the '*Jewels Worldwide*' magazines with puzzled looks, "Do you really think there is something fishy with these, Aaron?"

The jeweller pointed out to the detective, "See how the adverts are worded in such mundane and seemingly innocuous language! They just don't seem designed to attract ordinary people who want to buy or sell jewellery, who would expect better details with proper descriptions and prices, plus some brief history of previous ownership."

Alan nodded, "Yes! My 'Copper's nose' is beginning to twitch! Each text uses a similar format and the details have been carefully hidden. What information is given by the editors?" They read the instructions for potential subscribers and advertisers, noting that no identification other than post office box numbers must appear in the adverts. All communication with the editors had to be via their own box number based in Lille. Alan concluded, "It seems that these magazines are designed for a very particular clientele, which may well be buying and selling stolen goods!" It was agreed that he would take all but one of the sample magazines to Scotland Yard for detailed examination, whilst Aaron would concentrate on the remaining edition. He added an extra point, "I've noticed that the most recent magazine was published six months ago and that Mr Glover had been receiving it for three and half years. This is his last edition." Aaron extracted an unsealed A5 envelope from inside its back cover, and took out several small pieces of paper. Their eyes boggled as it became clear that the nondescript slips were receipts for jewels that Mr Glover had bought, totaling an astonishing £38,000. "I wonder if the next six month's issues were sent to him, but never collected because he became ill and went into hospital?"

Alan congratulated the jeweller, "Yes Aaron! That means that somewhere nearby there may be half a dozen uncollected magazines: probably at the local post office! Although Mrs Glover didn't know about them, now that her husband has died, she could probably retrieve them, which might help our investigations! I think we should go round to Bollo Lane and talk with her right now!" Shortly afterwards, they shared their considerations with an amazed Alice, who quickly agreed to the plan for both of them to accompany her to their local post office the next morning.

Aaron was in a jubilant mood that evening, until Julian beat him quite easily at chess.

***

The inspector, Aaron Klein and Alice Glover achieved great success at Acton Town post office, where the manager agreed willingly for Alice to take over her deceased husband's box number (Acton 273). He retrieved the last six months of uncollected magazines for her and even provided a copy of the account holder's entire record of sent and received faxes.

When advised that Mrs Glover would be moving to Kilburn, he recommended that she should authorise Inspector Harling and Mr Klein to collect or send further faxes for her. That action set up, they escorted

Alice home, to find that the Halleem family had arrived with most of their belongings in the big van. "What a beauty!" commented the inspector. "But you won't catch many cows in Gunnersbury with that 'outback style' cow-catcher!" He left them all to unload and then pack up Alice's boxes to be taken straight up to Kilburn, whilst he returned home, cleared the kitchen table and began writing his report by hand. He kept it as short as possible, knowing that busy senior policemen shuddered to receive lengthy essays to study, addressing it only to Associate Commissioner Williams, who he believed had covertly suggested a seaside holiday and with whom he was to meet at 11 am the next day. 'AH' concentrated on two main points: firstly, his investigations into the Hatton Garden bombing; secondly, his considerations concerning worldwide jewellery crime.

The actual bombing was condensed into two paragraphs, before he described his 'accidental' meeting with 'Suspect X', considered as a possible accomplice of the bomber, with various leads concerning 'Suspect Y', who was thought to have managed this act of terrorism. He explained simply about Aaron Klein's involvement in locating Biblical jewels, achieving phenomenally quick success in obtaining three of the ancient gemstones, which in turn had led into the discovery of a covert magazine *Jewels Worldwide*. The inspector gave his professional opinion that this publication hid the criminal activity of buying and selling jewellery which may well have been stolen. He explained that his personal involvement was primarily in support of one of the bomb victim's own researches and actions. After tidying up the grammar and spelling, he went outside to mow the lawns before going buoyantly to Scotland Yard to type out his report. However, 'AH' learnt much more from his Bomb Squad officers', enabling him to update his report significantly before leaving copies, together with suitably disinfected tape recordings of his short sea voyage, for A/C Williams and Chief Superintendent Price, marked 'private and urgent'.

***

Peter Templeton arrived at Joshua Shulz's house before midday to join the assembling team of volunteers. They unloaded Alice's boxes into her flat then donned protective gloves and began pulling out some of the revoltingly messy material from 'Box A1' onto the big table. It was quite easy to disentangle larger bits of wood and plaster from the mass, but finer articles proved much more difficult to identify, with glass and jewels looking very similar to untrained eyes. Fabric materials were easy to recognise but the remaining items were just too difficult. They tried sorting a further six helpings before realising the impossibilities caused by the contents being gelled together by blood and other liquids into a disgustingly coagulated mass. It was obvious that the contents of the boxes must be thoroughly washed and screened out of doors, then dried, before any inside work of separation could begin.

Rashid and his father volunteered to establish an amateur processing system in the garden, before the others could begin seriously detailed work indoors.

At 1.30 p.m., the volunteers were halted by the arrival of the awaited 'lady' in an expensive car. Joshua brought her up to the first floor flat where she introduced herself as Penelope Roberts of 'Peacock and Wright' a firm of Chartered Surveyors based in Mayfair. He asked her to sit down and Alice fetched her a cup of tea. Ms Roberts waited while Ruth, Peter and Rashid went outside and Aaron took the opportunity to sit alone in an empty room and scan through the latest few *'Jewels Worldwide'* magazines. She opened her briefcase and took out three envelopes, handing one each to Joshua, Alice and Ibrahim. They read their letters, which were addressed very formally, beginning, *'In accordance with my firm's instructions from the Crown Prince and Deputy Foreign Minister of the Federation of Non-aligned Arab Emirates Sheikh Salim bin Rashid Al Nu'masiq...'* The lady smiled and explained, "We're sorry to need to use such official jargon, but I can assure you that we have a friendly face as well as a business approach! Firstly, may I thank all of you for gathering together this afternoon. Our firm is used to dealing with illustrious clients and huge business enterprises, but we are delighted to be dealing with private persons who demonstrate so much recognition, understanding and support for each other's difficult situations. We are well aware of the incident which resulted in you coming together and are greatly impressed at how you are overcoming and tolerating your differences. Indeed, it is because of your resolve to co-operate with each other that our client and our firm are more than happy to take rather unusually prompt actions on your behalf." The listeners more or less understood her words, and asked her to continue in the hope of understanding more of what she was getting at.

"You are all invited to attend a formal meeting at our offices on this Thursday 17th May at 11.00 a.m.. Please feel free to bring your own solicitors if you wish to, although we recommend that you rely upon the services of our firm's in-house solicitor who will attend this formal meeting. We will propose and assist the explanations, acceptances and signing of several legal documents, together with the transfers of bank drafts for large sums of money. Subject to your agreement, the meeting will conclude with your signatures confirming several transactions including: the sale of Mr Halleem's house to the Federation of Non-aligned Arab Emirates, the sale of Mrs Glover's house to Mr Halleem, the establishment of a lease for the purchase by Mrs Glover of a flat and constituent parts of the property where we are meeting at this moment belonging to Mr Shulz, the repayment of an outstanding bank loan taken out by Mr Colin Glover, the repayment of two outstanding bank loans and the mortgage on this property taken out by Mr Shulz, the purchase of several jewels by Sheikh Salim bin Rashid Al Nu'masiq from Mrs Glover, the establishment of a private business by Mr Halleem and finally the transfers of various sums of money between the parties with residues being paid by cheques on behalf of the Federation of Non-aligned Arab Emirates."

Ms Roberts apologised for the long-winded statement she had just made, before putting into plain English, "The sheikh wishes to assist your desires and make all the transactions and payments between yourselves and himself as easy as is legally possible. Hence, our firm is drawing up all the necessary documents and preparing the money transfers in record speed, only requiring you to understand, agree the net results and sign your names. That's it in a nutshell! Now if you can give me the legal documents and house keys that were requested for our appraisal please, we will make a succinct survey of each of your homes, review your various documents and look forward to seeing you all again on Thursday. Thank you for the tea! Goodbye!" Joshua escorted her downstairs whilst the others regathered in the first-floor flat to discuss the amazing repercussions of Sheikh Salim's actions.

***

Aaron had noted several new advertisements in the latest few '*Jewels Worldwide*' magazines, being struck particularly by two recent offers from Montevideo and Sydney which included 'inscribed jewels'. The latter puzzled Aaron as he recalled reading an advert of half a year previously, emanating from Tel Aviv and offering an engraved golden yellow topaz. Could it be the same gemstone, sold then from Israel and purchased in Australia, but now advertised for sale again to give someone a quick profit? Aaron studied the scant details carefully before turning to the Uruguayan advert, which was offering a small collection of expensive jewellery including two inscribed gems: a diamond and an emerald. His attention was also aroused by 'an eighteenth-century diamond tiara with alternating sapphires in attendance'.

That description would surely be recognised by older knowledgeable jewellers as a famous item missing from the world scene for eighty years. Aaron remembered his father's sadness when recounting the story of a family of Polish Jewish jewellers which succumbed amongst many others to the Gestapo in Warsaw in the late 1930s. They had been the last known owners of the Gulchow Tiara, which had been designed specifically for the Countess of Gulchow in the 1780s. Aaron pondered hard about these particular items, which had assuredly 'dubious' histories. He realised excitedly that, with the most recent magazines offering possible Aaronic breastplate jewels, he could respond quickly to them using Mr Glover's post office box number.

***

Ibrahim and Rashid Halleem drove from Kilburn up to Watford to visit their old home for the last time, simply to collect their remaining larger items. It was nearing 10.00 p.m. when they finished loading up the van. "Rashid, please go and fill up with diesel whilst I have a last few minutes indoors." The young man expected that his father wanted to say 'Goodbye' to Khaled, before they drove all the way down to Gunnersbury where his mother and little Fatima were waiting for them in their new home. He drove onto the filling station forecourt and pulled up at the pumps. There was only one other vehicle there, next to the air compressor, with three men gathered round its back wheels. After filling up, Rashid locked the van and went into the shop to pay. As soon as he had returned and sat down in the driver's seat, a man holding a large knife yanked open his door and shouted at him to move over.

Shocked and alarmed, Rashid hesitated as the knife was pushed menacingly towards him. Then, the other front door was pulled open to enable a second man to jump in, trapping Rashid between them as the van was hijacked and driven off with great efficiency. He managed to get his phone out of his pocket, but before Rashid could use it the second man snatched it from him, opened the window and threw it away. The driver turned into the High Street and drove past a terrace of shops, accelerated and turned the steering wheel viciously to mount the wide pavement and drive straight into the front of a household electrical goods shop. The impact was dramatic and broken glass filled the air, yet none of the three men was badly injured. The two robbers jumped out and the low-slung black car from the filling station reversed onto the pavement. All three crooks worked fast to transfer the most expensive TVs and radios from the shop into their car. Rashid had hit his head on the windscreen and just sat there, utterly confused. As shop alarms shrieked out, he watched the men complete their raid, leap into their car and race off down the street. Within seconds, two police cars arrived with screeching tyres, Rashid was dragged from the van and bundled into the back of a police car. Handcuffs were forced viciously onto his wrists and the car was driven off with its siren screaming.

Ibrahim Halleem waited patiently for his son to return, but at 11.00 p.m., he began to think that a problem may have occurred. He locked the house door and walked along the dirty street towards the filling station. As he turned into the High Street, he noticed a great kerfuffle taking place on the other side of the road outside some shops. With a horrified feeling he saw the back of his wonderful van on the pavement surrounded by police. He ran over to them calling, "What has happened? Where is my son?" Two police officers rushed up to him and started questioning him in angry voices. They demanded his identification papers and he managed to tell them that all his documents were inside the van. As soon as he mentioned that his name was Halleem, the policemen pushed him into their car and they drove away from the scene dangerously fast to arrive shortly afterwards at Alpha Road satellite police station which Ibrahim remembered from only recently reporting Khaled as missing.

As he was dragged inside, the building, a grinning police inspector called out, "Well done, lads!

We've got the younger one too, so you've done pretty well. The getaway car hasn't been spotted yet but these two will soon tell us who their accomplices are, if we lean hard enough on them, eh!"

"Officer!" started Ibrahim, "Please let me speak... I don't know what is going on... Why have you brought me here? Where is my son...?"

The inspector stopped him. "Shut up, you scum! We'll ask the questions, not you!"

Ibrahim tried again, "But my wife and child they are waiting for me at home. I must go to them…"

The vicious reply was hurled at him, "What did I tell you… keep your evil Halleem mouth shut!"

He was dragged into a small room and pushed down onto a chair. "I must phone my son, Rashid, officer! Where is he? Why was my van smashed into that shop?"

The inspector put his face right in front of him, "Shut up! That's the last I want to hear from you until you're spoken to, right!"

Somehow, the cacophony of doors banging and police officers shouting aroused Rashid in a nearby room to his senses, "Father… Father… is that you? Have they got you too, Father?"

He had spoken automatically in Farsi language and Ibrahim managed to respond hastily, "Rashid… Rashid are you all right, my son? I am here near you… Be brave!"

Inspector Tome grabbed Ibrahim's hair and stuck his own hand violently across his mouth, "Shut up, you scum! First the bomber and now his family showing off their filthy colours! Your whole black family is wicked, but we're going to get all of you, just wait and see!" The night-duty desk sergeant was shocked at his boss' actions and words. He waited until the inspector strode up to him and demanded some charge forms, "Hurry up, Patel! We're going to nail these wicked cousins of yours to the wall! Quick… give me some forms!" Left alone again, Sergeant Waseem Patel made up his mind. He had had two years observing and suffering this racial hatred, but what could he do? Enough was enough. Quietly, he went into another room, consulted his pocket book and dialled a number.

Soon after getting into bed, Inspector Harling's phone ruined his relatively early night. "Please excuse me, Inspector, but I must let you know what is going on up here in my police station in North Watford." As quietly and politely as possible, Sergeant Patel explained the situation and described how the two men had been arrested after their van had been used to carry out a smash and grab robbery. "It's only because I speak Farsi myself that I understand what has happened, Sir. My inspector goes off duty at midnight, both men are now locked up separately, but I am concerned about what will happen tomorrow morning, Sir." 'AH' thanked the sergeant and asked to be kept in touch. He told Mary about the phone call, they got up, dressed and walked together to Bollo Road, where they explained to a worried Mrs Halleem that a 'mix-up' in north Watford meant that her husband and son would not be joining her in their new home until the next day.

***

Inspector Tome did not like daytime work, preferring to deal with the sinister situations that hours of darkness often enclosed. He also hated the boredom of minor crime work, checking names and addresses of arrested persons, interviewing them in expectation of their obvious lies, persuading greedy shop owners to prepare non-inflated lists of stolen goods, getting beaten-up break-in vehicles brought in for examination. All those duties might be necessary, but they were an unwanted routine for him. He had no concern for the actual persons involved in such sordid crimes, either the innocent victims or the arrested perpetrators. He usually went through the motions of his job, but now at last something unusual was involved: the name of Halleem stunk in his nostrils and he'd got two more of them locked up ready for interrogation when he went back on duty at 9.00 a.m..

Arriving unusually on time for work, Inspector Tome realised that something unexpected was going on. Several Scotland Yard cars were parked outside and detectives were clearly there in force. A nervous

North Watford constable met him and showed him where Detective Inspector Harling was waiting for him in an interview room at the end of a dirty corridor. "What's going on here? Why are you ponced up Scotland Yard people filling up my station? You have no authority…"

He was interrupted politely but firmly by Detective Inspector Harling, "Why have you not allowed Ibrahim Halleem and his son Rashid to see each other? What have you charged them with? Why haven't you given them access to telephones, first aid and a solicitor? What sort of police work are you doing up here Inspector Tome?" A knock at the door enabled Tome to slump down into a chair and try to think, whilst WPC Monique Taylor reported to her boss, "The Halleems are calming down now, Sir, but they've been in shock all night. Rashid wasn't badly injured and a doctor has been called to patch him up. Mrs Halleem and her young daughter are very relieved to be back together with her husband again, Sir. Mr Halleem is not making a fuss about the local police's mishandling of the situation, or being locked up all night, apart from his son being handcuffed, Sir. He's also concerned about what is going to happen to his crashed van, which the local police have commandeered for inspection, Sir."

Harling acknowledged his WPC's report then re-opened the door to let air into the musty room. "I'm asking you again, Inspector Tome, on what charges did you arrest Rashid Halleem and then his father Ibrahim Halleem last night?"

The sullen local inspector leant back, placed his feet arrogantly on the desk and snarled out his reply, "Suspected theft of a vehicle, dangerous driving likely to cause death, violent breaking and entry to a shop, resisting arrest, failure to disclose material information concerning terrorist activities and further suspected terrorist-linked crimes. That should do for a start, eh! You of all people should know what sort of a family they are, yet you come prancing up here interfering in affairs that don't concern your fancy Scotland Yard duties, messing up my official duties dealing with disgusting people who should be locked up to safeguard the public…"

'AH' interrupted him, "That's enough! Stop your ridiculous, biased banter Tome and stand up when speaking to me!"

Inspector Tome pushed back his chair, scraping it across the floor and letting it smash into the wall with a crash. "Listen to me, Harling… you have no… rights here at all. This is my patch and I'll… well, do things my way! Just … off back to your namby-pamby Scotland Yard!"

Harling crossed the room, opened the door and called to his own Sergeant Foster, "Fetch Sergeant Patel and both of you come in here. I want you to witness something." He waited until the two sergeants had entered the room. "Foster and you too Patel, take down in writing every word that is spoken by myself and Inspector Tome, starting from now: 'Inspector Tome, do you acknowledge your words and adhere to them, as spoken to me two minutes ago, I quote you as follows: *'I arrested Rashid Halleem and Ibrahim Halleem on charges of suspected theft of a vehicle, dangerous driving likely to cause death, violent breaking and entry to a shop, resisting arrest, failure to disclose material information concerning terrorist activities and further suspected terrorist-linked crimes. That should do for a start, eh! You of all people should know what sort of a family they are, yet you come prancing up here interfering in affairs that don't concern your fancy Scotland Yard duties, messing up my official duties dealing with disgusting people who should be locked up to safeguard the public. Listen to me Harling…. you have no rights here at all. This is my patch and I'll… well, do things my way! Just… off back to your namby-pamby Scotland Yard!'*"

The man glared like a caged wild animal as he spat out, "How dare you come here insinuating anything against my methods against these evil-hearted, black-skinned scum!"

Harling would not let him go: "Inspector Tome, do you deny your words that I have just quoted?"

In answer, he spun round, picked up the chair and smashed it into fragments over the desk. "All Pakistanis should be sent back to their own filthy country in chains! Evil terrorists, all of them, including you Patel! I'll do my best to get all these evil Muslims thrown out of England that I will…!"

'AH' stood upright, and spoke resolutely, "Both of you sergeants are to write those words down very accurately please, together with my response: 'Inspector Tome, in the name of Her Majesty's Police Force, I arrest you on charges of inciting religious violence and gross distortion of police procedures. Further charges will follow. Anything you say further will be taken down and may be used in evidence against you. You are relieved of your authority in this police station and will be taken under close arrest to Scotland Yard for further interrogation. Do you have anything further to say to me?' Thank you, sergeants. Please write down all of the exact words of Inspector Tome, including the expletives, in full. Have them typed and put on my desk by 09.00 tomorrow, ready for my report to the Watford commander. Sergeant Foster, take this arrested person to Scotland Yard straight-away, under guard and in handcuffs in order that he does no further damage to police property. Sergeant Patel, I authorise you to take immediate temporary charge of this police station until a replacement commanding officer be appointed by your local commander. Dismissed."

Two crisp replies of '*Yes Sir*' rang out boldly.

Detective Constable Jacobs reported that the Halleem's van was not badly damaged, but could not be driven. "I've arranged for it to be dusted for prints, Sir, and the locals have photographed it thoroughly. I can't see why it needs to be kept by the local police, Sir."

Harling agreed and told him to contact the Ealing car dealers. "Ask them to fetch the van and get it repaired. Get our people together, take the Halleems down to Gunnersbury and lets all get out of North Watford. Get me to The Yard quickly please and let's get back to some proper police work!" An hour later, Detective Inspector Harling was waiting outside the office of Associate Commissioner Laurence Williams.

***

Doctor Chaudhary satisfied himself with the medical progress of Prince Salim and Aaron Klein, acknowledging that, whilst they were probably doing far too much in their daily activities, the positive stimulus that this brought to them was far more effective than medicines. The two friends went together to visit Christine Templeton, but kept this brief after noticing that she looked physically very tired, despite appearing fine in her spirit. They chatted about recent events, many of which were happening at enormous speed and seemingly along designed paths, whilst this disfigured lady simply laid immobile and without apparent purpose. Once alone again, Aaron shared his thoughts with Salim about the magazine adverts from Montevideo and Sydney, "Most interesting friend Aaron, especially as my mind is on the southern hemisphere right now! Soon I must report again to our foreign minister with some proposals for taking the FNAE flag far overseas. I am concentrating on places that have little knowledge even of our existence, yet could become of joint interest with our small state. South America is a vast continent with one or two main players, but much untapped involvement for a rich Arab country like ours. Maybe Uruguay is suitable in size and location for an exploratory visit? However, Sydney is probably far too metropolitan and involved in world affairs to bother with the FNAE. Instead, I may think about some of Australia's less-affluent states. Perhaps we could combine your interests in searching out Aaronic jewels there with my own diplomatic investigations? Please leave this thought with me for a short while Aaron."

***

When 'AH' entered Associate Commissioner William's office, he found Chief Superintendent Price already there. The A/C opened the meeting in a buoyant manner, "Many thanks for your unexpected and succinct report, Inspector. That was good thinking! You appear to have had a good period of leave, apart from your maritime adventures! Am I correct that the possible 'Suspects X and Y' are not currently under observation?" On receiving the inspector's assurance of that, he continued, "Very good! Such investigations are not to be undertaken by Bomb Squad inspectors. Such major issues should be handled solely by Special Branch. Do you understand that Harling?"

'AH' stood stiffly at attention whilst replying, "Yes, Sir. I understand and will obey your instructions. However, with great respect, Sir, may I suggest that investigating officers of any rank or department should be encouraged to 'follow their noses' in accordance with Her Majesty's police instruction manual?"

Price looked horrified but the A/C merely gave a glimmer of a smile at Harling's response, before continuing, "Quite so, Inspector, in many circumstances. Now turning to your second point, it is most intriguing that you have been locating missing jewels of great value. Does my

interest surprise you Harling?" 'AH' was thrown off guard and did not reply. "How long have you headed up the Bomb Squad, Inspector? Possibly long enough, eh Price? Please explain," Chief Superintendent Price disclosed that there was a young inspector in the Essex Police, who could benefit by a spell at Scotland Yard and would bring fresh blood into that department. 'AH's composure just held, but he was clearly shaken at what almost appeared to be a reprimand. What had he done so badly that could have influenced his senior officers to decide to replace him? Being horrified and a little afraid, he maintained his silence, whilst the A/C turned to the Chief Superintendent and suggested that his business elsewhere may need his attention. Price left the room promptly, without looking at the inspector.

Once the door closed, there was an immediate change in the atmosphere. The A/C moved from behind his desk to a coffee table and two chairs under a window. He smiled and asked the inspector to join him there, "Look here Harling, I'm sorry to have been so pompous and stuffy with you, which is the last impression that I wanted to give, but there was a reason for it. Now that we're on our own, I have a lot to tell you. If you can trust me, please relax and join me in a cup of coffee. Let's move forward together, shall we?" 'AH' sat down, utterly mystified at what was going on. The A/C asked him a very direct and pointed question, "You've been around The Yard for a long time Harling. I want you to draw on your experience and give me your candid opinion of Special Branch. Just tell me what an anonymous, trustworthy, middle-ranking professional policeman might say, if I asked that question."

'AH' began to think that he might soon be forcibly retired, as being of no further service to Her Majesty's Metropolitan Police, so saw little purpose in 'pulling his punches'. He spoke with a straight face and without emotion, "They probably do a very decent job, Sir, standing around with machine guns on embassy doorsteps, but Bloggs Security Limited might do that better and cheaper. Other than that, they might occasionally do some proper police work, Sir, but not very effectively."

Laurence Williams smiled and invited Harling to take one of his favourite custard cream biscuits, "That's exactly the opinion of the commissioner and myself, Inspector! Thus, we're proposing to divide Special Branch into two functional divisions. One of them would continue to be headed by its superintendent, who is contemplating retirement within a year. He would remain responsible for all diplomatic work, whilst the other division needs an entirely new broom to sweep out all the clutter and recreate the specialist police department for investigating and solving major crimes. It would draw on The Yard's background resources as necessary, but would have a smallish staff of officers acting entirely on their own initiative. Liaison with government agencies and departments outside of the police network would take place when required, but it would demonstrate very practically that it was a policing unit and not yet another batch of spies. Certain recognition of and occasional co-operation with foreign police forces and agencies would be involved. These significant changes will be noticed in many places, including the criminal fraternity. This new venture needs a steady hand with sufficient authority and power to lead it and bring in the necessary changes, thus the commissioner and I are looking for a professional and capable policeman who we can trust. It's a serious job and we think that you are exactly the right chap for it; otherwise, I wouldn't be telling you all this!

"You'd report directly to me, whilst planning and undertaking significant actions on your own initiative. There are two main initial areas of activity: to go after the evil masterminds of the Hatton Garden bombing, in order to show the public and politicians that the Metropolitan Police is not insipid, pandering to over-liberal niceties. Secondly to counter the recent spate of jewellery crimes in Europe, which the Frenchies and Italians just don't seem to be able to solve themselves. You know that the Hatton Garden heist of 2015 was a big embarrassment to the Met, but you may not be aware that many of the stolen items were never recovered when the geriatric burglars were convicted? Perhaps now you will understand my surprise at your recent involvement in jewel hunting! I don't discount what amateur sleuths can do, Inspector, and neither should you. Their knowledge and contacts may be much more useful than police forces would like to admit. To head up this new division is a mighty job, Harling. Would you have a shot at it for us?"

'AH's emotions were all over the place. His mind was reeling, but he recognised that he was being honoured rather than reprimanded, "Thank you, Sir. It would be a very big task but it needs to be done, Sir.

Solid police work is exactly my cup of tea, but this new division's leader would require much more clout than could be given at inspector level, Sir."

Williams smiled again, "We recognise that ourselves Harling. If you agree to take this on, it would require you to accept immediate promotion to chief inspector, although authority obviously could be better exercised at superintendent's rank. Therefore, our proposal would be to appoint you as acting superintendent with all of that higher rank's status, pay and benefits, but strictly dependent on achieving significant successes during the first six months. If the idea, or you, failed to achieve results, you'd be farmed out to some provincial backwater as a chief inspector, but if you were as successful as we anticipate, you'd become a full superintendent twelve months after starting this new job. Do you need time to think it over, or shall we get straight on with the job, Harling?"

'AH' wondered if this was really happening! He sipped his coffee thoughtfully, analysing and assessing what he was being asked to do, recognising the enormous challenges, yet convinced that he was capable to take it on. He put down his coffee cup, stood up and spoke rather formally, "If you have sufficient trust in me, Sir, I thank you for the honour and assure you that I am prepared to give it my very best shot, Sir."

The A/C got to his own feet and held out his hand, "Good man, Harling!" He reached for a folder, "I've prepared some information for you to review and think about. Take it away, go home, live with it, then be ready to talk to me about it on Thursday morning here at 10.00am. But firstly, for Heaven's sake relax and smile a bit!"

CHAPTER 10

The Halleems joined the rest of the team rather later on Wednesday than planned and told them of the nightmare happenings at North Watford. During the afternoon, the first positively exciting discovery from Box A1 was made. Alice and Joshua had been sorting the partially cleaned materials rather mechanically, whilst chatting about all sorts of things, when Joshua suddenly exclaimed, "Mrs Glover! Look at this! It isn't just another piece of twisted steel, it's good quality gold! Although it's filthy, dirty and broken, you can see that it had been a ring. We must expect to find many such fragments which could have some value."

An hour later, Rashid brought in another container of washed and dried items. "Mr Shulz, Father and I think that box A4 on which we are working has some more interesting things in it, such as these." It had been decided from the beginning that Alice would extract fragments of glass, wood and plaster, whilst Joshua would make piles of metal, skin, bone and unrecognisable items.

Therefore, it was Alice who called out, "Mr Shulz, please take a look at this piece of glass, at least I think it is glass, but what do you think?" She handed him an oval shaped piece of material with a bluish tinge to its otherwise clear colour.

Joshua cleaned it further and held it up to her, "Mrs Glover! You have found a diamond and not a small one! This is a magnificent and undamaged jewel, despite its gold setting being mostly removed. It is rather too large for a ring, so probably came from a necklace. Would you permit me, dear Mrs Glover, to look again through the piles of glass that you have been separating?" Alice consulted her notes and the accounts book that she was using to record every single item that they were finding. She selected a packet of glass from box A3, tipped it out onto the table and looked in surprise as Joshua began dividing it into two heaps. Slowly and meticulously, often using his jeweller's eye-glass, he moved small fragments from one pile to another, smiling like a schoolboy.

***

In mid-afternoon, the inspector received a called from Sergeant Waseem Patel. "I'm sorry that I couldn't phone you before now, Sir, but the dust hasn't settled here yet and I don't seem to be too popular anymore."

'AH' thought quickly and asked a direct question, "How well do you know Harrow and do many people there know you, Sergeant?"

The reply pleased him very much, "My parents came over from Pakistan after the war and I was born near Stanmore, Sir. They moved to Harrow because the schools were better there for my brother and me. I went to college there, applied to join the force, got accepted and sent up to Watford, Sir. I've served in several Hertfordshire stations since then, but it's a few years since I spent much time in Harrow. I don't suppose many people there would remember me now, Sir."

Discovering that the sergeant would be taking a day's leave tomorrow away from his difficult involvement in Watford, Harling asked if he would like to visit him at The Yard for a chat. "Well yes, Sir, I would like that, but I must tell you that I'm rather fed up with north London. I'm sorry, but I'd rather not come if you want me to do something long term in Harrow, Sir." 'AH' reassured him and they arranged to meet at 10.00, not at Scotland Yard but near St Pancras Station.

The inspector reached for the thick envelope he had received from Peter Taylor of The Yard's forensic department. Inside were several papers, including significant enlargements from the handwritten letters received by Ibrahim Halleem after the bombing, the hand written notice explaining to customers that Swarthy's dry cleaning shop would be closed for a while, also of Emily's delivered note. A typed letter of explanation discussed the features of the various documents, giving clear conclusions, '*Despite the fact that only capital letters had been used on the poster, whereas the letter posted in Birmingham contained mostly small letters, there is such an obvious degree of similarity to suggest that the writer was one and the same person. Your personal note and the words written in the Gideons' Bible are most unusual in that I cannot say if they were written by a male or female.'* 'AH's heart raced as he considered that if Swarthy had indeed written the letter from somewhere in or near Birmingham, enclosing a cash 'reward' for Khaled Halleem's family, he may have made a fatal mistake.

The inspector sent for Sergeant Dent and told him to set up searches for a man aged about forty of Middle Eastern origin with connections in Harrow and Birmingham, checking discretely with the Passport Office, DVLA in Swansea, the Royal Mail's sorting offices, and the government's secret intelligence services. Harling dictated a memorandum, which the sergeant wrote out, then realising the impact of his new rank, he signed it off with his future credentials.

***

At the end of that afternoon, 'AH' visited the team working up at Kilburn and asked Aaron to go for a quiet walk with him along Brondesbury Road. They were coming to like and trust each other as men, also appreciating their respective talents. Alan explained a little about his new job and how it would include investigating jewellery crime in Europe, whilst Aaron updated him about the *'Jewels Worldwide'* magazine adverts. It was a staggering conclusion that secretive men and women around the world were spending large sums of money buying and selling jewellery between each other, obtained maybe from dubious sources. Who were these people that preferred not to use reliable shops or dealers? Were they looking at some sort of criminal or at least unsavoury network of jewellery activity? The benefits of a collaborative working relationship were obvious to the two men, so they agreed to maintain proper degrees of secrecy, but determined to assist and co-operate as far as possible. Alan encouraged Aaron in his plan to send faxes to Uruguay and Australia and asked to be kept advised of anything 'smelling criminal', whilst Aaron would talk to Joshua Shulz about the possibility for each of them to have a very private working base in his house.

***

At home that evening, Alan showed Mary some of the *'Jewels Worldwide'* magazines that were at the centre of his jewellery crime thoughts. She quickly declared that they were far too dry and boring to interest any casual reader or ordinary jewel collectors, "Why on Earth would anyone subscribe to such a dull magazine, unless they could gain something from it?"

Her husband agreed, "Look at this one: *'Available: separate pendant and bracelet rubies, sapphire necklace and diamond cluster brooch. Box 1764 Nairobi, Kenya.'* then another: *'Three antique diamond tiaras, two flower-design emerald brooches for sale; Wanted small beryl and jasper gems. Box 822 Zurich, Switzerland.'*

"But Alan, boxes can't write to each other, obviously there's human involvement, but why is everything so secretive?"

He turned to the inside front page, "This editorial note says: *'Correspondence is only to be carried out between Box Numbers and their city locations. Absolutely no names, addresses, telephone numbers or e-mail addresses will be accepted for publication. Box 1373 Lille, France.'* "So why is an English language magazine being published from a French post office box number?"

His wife smiled, "Very fishy indeed, exactly up your street, Dear

***

Sergeant Waseem Patel was waiting in subdued excitement at a quiet table in the bustling railway cafe, "Good morning, Sir, I've only just arrived myself."

'AH' shook hands and sat at the corner table, "I wanted us to meet here even though it's a very public place. We'll go up the road to the hospital, where there's a big cafeteria to talk in." They walked briskly along the Euston Road, with Harling assessing his man in a different context to Tuesday's in North Watford. He looked fit and ready to get on with things, without being in any way brash.

'AH' probed into his police experience and aspirations, then with coffee in front of them at the empty end table in UCLH's cafeteria, he outlined his plan, "I'm looking for some new people to join me at The Yard. How would you like a break from routine police work and get some opportunities for bigger stuff? It would be all plain clothes, involving travel and often in difficult situations. You impressed me up at Watford and I'm interested in your natural abilities to move around the country in Muslim circles. What do you think, Sergeant?"

Patel relaxed, "Thank you very much for thinking of me, Sir. I've had more than enough of sorting out people's sordid domestic problems and dealing with petty crime. What I love doing most is investigating crime, Sir."

Harling shook hands in confirmation of the appointment, leaving the paperwork to catch up once the real work had started, "Take an immediate week's leave, which I'll get sanctioned from your commander, then start revisiting your old haunts in Harrow. I'll get you copies of photos and information about a man code-named 'Swarthy'. He's highly dangerous and has bolted up north into hiding. Your first job is to discover his previous activities in Harrow, everything you can get hold of: where he lived, what car he drove, what happened at his dry cleaning shop, where he worshipped, who his contacts were, everything. Be extremely careful because this man set up a killer and may be one himself. This is serious stuff so keep very discrete from now onwards and report back to me in about a week, OK?" Patel acknowledged his instructions and they left separately shortly afterwards, walking in different directions.

***

It is always difficult to introduce significant changes to an organisation whilst its existing boss remains in place. 'AH' was as keen as mustard to exercise his new responsibilities in a professional way, but the current chief of Special Branch could hardly be expected to give his willing co-operation. Thus their introduction by A/C Williams was not easy, with his intended informal approach thwarted by two men standing at attention facing the wall with stony faces. "Now listen to me chaps, we each have ranks and roles to maintain, but you need to relax. It's clear to our bosses that a division of responsibilities in Special Branch is necessary and long-awaited. Superintendent Stewart will have greater time to devote to the diplomatic side of the work, dealing with embassies and VIPs from many nations. Detective Chief Inspector Harling, at acting superintendent rank, will concentrate on investigating and solving major crime. The two of you must learn to work together personally and help your staff to move into their separated duties effectively. Is that understood?"

Two instant 'Yes, Sir,' replies sung out.

"Good! Now we'll discuss staffing arrangements. What is Special Branch's current overall compliment Stewart?" Naturally, the A/C knew that answer already, but he wished to draw out the obvious point of over-staffing.

Stewart replied formally, "We have a hundred and eighty-four officers at a variety of ranks, including four Inspectors and eight sergeants, Sir. Our work is divided between time-based teams enabling constant cover for our responsibilities, Sir."

The A/C turned to 'AH', "What about The Yard's Bomb Squad Harling?"

The reply came, "We have twelve officers Sir, with four existing sergeants under an incoming new inspector, Sir." Having illustrated that point of differential, the Associate Commissioner continued, "Is that compliment satisfactory Harling?" 'AH' confirmed that it was, enabling the same question to be put to Superintendent Stewart?

The older man replied stiffly, "Mostly, Sir, although we are occasionally unable to fulfil all the requests of foreign embassies to give them their necessary front-of-house security, Sir."

His boss responded, "That refers to crime prevention Stewart, but how many of your hundred and eighty-four officers are engaged on crime detection on a regular basis? What's the split between prevention and detection?"

Superintendent Stewart saw the trap in front of him, "That's difficult to say, Sir, without thorough analysis and consideration of our necessary current responses to embassies, Sir."

Williams stood up, "Thank you, Superintendent. Now to make it evident to your staff that some changes are to be made, we will go together on an unannounced visit, after which each of you is to prepare an independent report with future staffing recommendations of your divisions, to be on my desk by 09.00 next Monday morning. We'll reconvene in my office at 10.00 on Tuesday to consider your reports and for me to authorise those changes that I deem to be necessary. Now let's go!" The two junior officers left the room with their boss, each wondering how they could ever attempt joint working in the best interests of the Metropolitan Police and Britain's public.

Superintendent Stewart's cherished empire was taken aback seeing Associate Commissioner Williams and his entourage stride in purposefully. Small groups of policemen and women, sitting relaxed and talking over ample supplies of tea and biscuits, were bemused. Some stood quickly to attention whilst others tried to hide their attempts to do up buttons, smarten their uniforms and look busy. Williams went through the entire complex of offices, meeting rooms, mess rooms and even the male toilets, speaking to no-one, with Stewart and Harling trailing behind him. Returning abruptly to the main entrance, he said, "You have my instructions. Each of you has until 09.00 on Monday to submit your reports. Dismissed!"

Once left alone, Superintendent Stewart invited 'AH' into his office, unlocked a filing cabinet and took out several folders of staffing information. Choosing one marked 'PRIVATE FOR HEAD OF DIVISION ONLY' he began his defence strategy, "Look here Harling, I don't know what's so upset our chiefs, probably those lazy bureaucrats in Whitehall or their political masters interfering as usual. I'm going to do a damage limitation exercise using these papers, simply to help Williams understand my position in heading up our diplomatic work. As you don't know any of my staff, or much about our operations, I suggest that you go back to your Bomb Squad office and do the same there." 'AH' showed proper respect to the senior officer, but managed to obtain some copies of anonymous staffing structures and non-personal details of some of the officers, before leaving the reluctant superintendent. On the way back to his own department, he called at The Yard's staff canteen and bought some cheese and pickle sandwiches. Over the sparse lunch in his office, he reviewed the meagre papers that he'd obtained from Special Branch, plus his own staff and personnel files, acknowledging his distinct advantage over Superintendent Stewart because he did not need to be defensive. He knew that he must be respectful, yet give some clear options to rebuild what Williams and his other Chief Officers had become fed up with, which was why he was being brought in to smarten up Special Branch.

He worked steadily on, gradually forming and reshaping his ideas and making tentative plans. Occasionally, he called in various members of his own staff, to discuss their own abilities, preferences and aspirations. The information went via his analytical mind onto scrap paper and hence into a progression of several drafts. Although he didn't know his chosen successor, he considered which of his sergeants would be the most helpful to that new inspector. Well aware that George Price had been contemplating retirement from his long and moderately successful career for several years, 'AH' took an adventurous step. He proposed an option for a brand new overall structure, that included himself as an intermediary, whilst giving the new inspector full authority for responding to hopefully infrequent bombings. That thought led him on to wonder if the Bomb Squad's mainly responsive role couldn't be widened into a professional police rapid response team for all terrorist activity. 'AH' thought that this approach would sit happily with those of the other emergency services, whilst giving himself flexibility to utilise the talents of his ex-staff in wider responsibilities. Finally, he proposed two new teams of (1) an Emergency Response Team and (2) a Major Crimes Team, both under his own authority. 'AH' thought that this would encourage those of the current Special Branch officers who wanted to be true detectives. In order not to be recommending a new empire for himself, he proposed that The Yard's central service divisions be held in readiness to assist or be seconded to his new division only in emergency situations. 'AH' believed that with two inspectors and eight sergeants he could operate his new combined division effectively with an overall compliment of sixty-seven officers, including himself. From the current one hundred and ninety-six officers, that would leave Stewart one hundred and twenty-nine for diplomatic protection duties. Desiring a trusted deputy at inspector level in the new Major Crimes Team, he recommended the promotion of one of his own Bomb Squad's sergeants, leaving three specialist sergeants for the incoming inspector and five sergeants operating under his own promoted man as snspector of the Major Crimes Team, thus enabling his two teams great scope for covering and supporting each other as needs arose and periods of leave required.

***

Rashid acted as chauffeur on Thursday morning, driving the temporary replacement van courtesy of Mr Holmes' car dealers. He collected Alice and Joshua from Kilburn and drove them and his father, all dressed in their smartest clothes, to the offices of 'Peacock and Wright — Chartered Surveyors' in Mayfair. He parked exactly as instructed by the uniformed attendant, before walking away to find an internet coffee shop. The guests were shown through the expensive glass doors into the atrium, where Penelope Roberts was waiting for them, "Hello again!" she beamed, shaking hands and escorting them to a lift.

They wooshed silently to the top floor where she led them through the picture gallery to the office of Sir Reginald Wright. He welcomed them in, "Oh a very 'Good Morning' to each of you! Please come in and make your selves comfortable over here!" He ushered them to a large round mahogany conference table with six solid upholstered chairs perfectly arranged with writing materials and bottles of mineral water at each place setting.

Sir Reginald asked Miss Roberts to open the proceedings by reading through the formal list of transactions that were to be undertaken that morning. "Does each of you understand and accept the expedient of dealing with all of these complexities in one hit, as it were?" asked the firm's chairman.

They all murmured a 'Yes thank you' although none of them knew what an 'expedient' was.

He smiled and continued, "As long we have your agreement, we'll go through each item sequentially before having a grand signing session at the end shall we?" Their nervousness was assuaged when two young ladies brought each of them their selections of coffee, tea, juice, biscuits and an aperitif.

Penelope Roberts led the meeting efficiently through the following arrangements:

* Sale of Mr Halleem's house to the Federation of Non-aligned Arab Emirates (FNAE) for the sum of £160,000
* Sale of Mrs Glover's house to Mr Halleem for £210,000
* Establishment of a twenty-five year lease for the purchase of a flat and constituent parts of the property belonging to Mr Shulz by Mrs Glover for £170,000
* Repayment of an outstanding bank loan, taken out by her late husband, in the sum of £12,000 by Mrs Glover
* Repayment of two outstanding bank loans taken out by Mr Shulz totalling £10,000
* Repayment of a mortgage on his property taken out by Mr Shulz currently standing at £30,000
* Purchase of several jewels as listed and valued initially by Mr Aaron Klein, Jeweller, being the property of Mrs Glover by Sheikh Salim bin Rashid Al Nu'masiq for the sum of £20,000 or higher as to be determined
* Purchase of two ancient jewels being the property of Mrs Glover by Mr Aaron Klein for the sum of £10,000
* Establishment of a private business by Mr Halleem to be known as 'Gunnersbury A1 Maintenance Service' with an initial capital input, repayable without interest over a period of twenty-five years, from Sheikh Salim bin Rashid Al Nu'masiq in the sum of £20,000
* Capital payment to 'Gunnersbury A1 Maintenance Service' for costs in making future improvements, yet to be detailed, to her ex-dwelling by Mrs Glover to the value of and in the sum of £30,000
* Capital input to 'Gunnersbury A1 Maintenance Service' for costs involved in making future improvements, yet to be detailed, to his house and grounds by Mr Shulz to the value of and in the sum of £20,000

Therefore, the net financial transactions for each of the parties is as follows:

* Mrs Glover: Input £240,000 less Output £212,000 = Balance £28,000 gained
* Mr Halleem: Input £230,000 less Output £210,000 = Balance £20,000 gained

- Mr Shulz: Input £170,000 less Output £60,000 = Balance £110,000 gained
- Mr Klein: Output £10,000 less Acquisitions of Jewels (£10,000) = Balance Nil
- Sheikh Salim and FNAE: Output £200,000 less acquisitions of a house in Watford (£160,000 and Jewels (£20,000) = Balance £20,000 expended.

Our clients Sheikh Salim and the Federation of Non-aligned Arab Emirates confirm their gratitude for the parties' agreement in discharging the aforementioned arrangements and financial transactions, together their great pleasure in expending the modest net sum of £20,000 for the major gains associated with the onward dealings of the parties. They wish to acknowledge the important lessons being demonstrated by the parties in recognising, understanding and tolerating each other's differences of culture and faith whilst supporting themselves to move forwards in life. Thank you all very much.

Sir Reginald asked Miss Roberts to request the presence of Mr Keswick their in-house solicitor, who arrived immediately bearing the various documents and bank draughts that he had prepared for signature. During the next half an hour the bank loans and mortgages of Alice Glover and Joshua Shulz were paid to their creditor third parties, the deeds for the Watford house were transferred to the FNAE, the deeds for the Gunnersbury house were transferred to Mr Halleem, the deeds for the lease of part of the Kilburn house were transferred to Mrs Glover, the ownership certificates for certain gemstones were made out to Sheikh Salim and Mr Klein respectively, the establishment of 'Gunnersbury A1 Maintenance Service' was formalised, its contracts for refurbishment at houses owned by Mr Shulz and formerly by Mrs Glover were signed. The morning's business being concluded, Mrs Glover, Mr Shulz and Mr Halleem were escorted to the car park by Miss Roberts, who shook hands with Rashid and said 'Goodbye' for the last time before he drove them away from Mayfair to the more humble environment of Kilburn.

***

Aaron sat in one of the spare bedrooms in the first floor flat at Joshua's house, visualising it as the future base of his jewel-hunting operations. He hoped that the adjacent room, also allocated willingly by Joshua, would be adequate for Inspector Harling's discrete police work. Aaron was very pleased that the elderly lapidorist had determined to make the main bedroom his own future workroom, having already collected his old equipment from behind the Klein's shop, ready to be installed properly after the difficult searching though plastic boxes had been completed. Aaron reread the Uruguayan advert for the umpteenth time, '...*collection including two inscribed jewels: a diamond and an emerald, and an eighteenth-century diamond tiara with alternating sapphires in attendance...*' He formulated some text for what he hoped would be an equally innocuous response: '*To Montevideo Box No 759: Expressing interest in offered inscribed diamond and emerald, also diamond tiara. Request details and availability. Box Number Acton 273.*' He referred to the Australian advert and drafted his reply, '*To Sydney Box No 2650: Expressing interest in offered engraved golden yellow topaz. Request details and availability. Offering sapphire and beryl cabochons. Box number: Acton 273.*' That Thursday afternoon, Aaron travelled down to Acton before the post office closed and sent off his two prepared faxes.

***

Alan Harling had discussed his future work situation fully with Mary during the previous evening, appreciating her wisdom and gentleness as such valuable attributes when he needed to make big decisions, also as excellent antidotes to his own single-mindedness. He woke refreshed and excited on Friday morning, enjoyed a good breakfast and went happily to Scotland Yard, where he reviewed and polished his draft report from yesterday. After some personal unofficial chats with his key staff, he signed and copied his report and took it along to the Associate Commissioner's office. Whether his new boss would read it over the weekend or not was not AH's responsibility, but he was fully satisfied that he had done his best and could enjoy the coming weekend.

***

Doctor Chaudhary's nature was to speak professionally and politely to all of his patients, but visiting Christine Templeton in Room 604 that morning he smiled with real pleasure, "I want to give you good news from recent tests Miss Templeton. I am very pleased to tell you that your external injuries are responding magnificently to the various surgical and medical treatments that you have received. That has been a great encouragement to our staff, as no doubt it will be to yourself. Thus next week, we will begin to concentrate more on internal matters, with yet more tests I'm afraid."

***

Alice Glover walked up the steps into UCLH and went straight up to Room 604. "How lovely to see you again Mrs Glover!" said Christine Templeton, "Have you called to see me today for a particular reason?"

Alice tried to stay composed, with proper elderly-English-lady reserve, but found it to be impossible as she burst out, "Oh Miss Templeton I just had to come and tell you the good news! Three days ago in my lovely new home at Mr Shulz's house, I took out my old school Bible which I hadn't touched for years. I saw my maiden name signed inside the cover, next to the Sunday School's certificate of attendance. It horrified me that I'd taken no interest in my Bible for so many years. I decided to look up a verse that you told me about, in the Second Book of Chronicles chapter seven and verse fourteen, but the words didn't seem to have the same effect as when you'd spoken them to me. I was confused and sad. I put my Bible down on the sofa, but suddenly I slipped down onto the floor and floods of tears poured out of me quite unintentionally. *'Oh Jesus!'* I cried fervently, *'I must find you! I need to know you because you are almighty whilst I'm just a silly old woman! Why should you have any interest in helping me, after I let you down, just as much as my own husband, for so many years! I'm so sorry Lord Jesus!'* I carried on crying and crying and then noticed that my Bible had slipped off the sofa and fallen open beside me. I found my reading glasses and picked it up. It had fallen open quite near the back cover at the Book of James chapter 4. I was very puzzled but felt prompted to read from verse 7, *'Submit yourselves therefore to God. Resist the devil and he will flee from you. Draw nigh to God, and he will draw nigh to you. Cleanse your hands, ye sinners; and purify your hearts, ye double minded. Be afflicted and mourn and weep: let your laughter be turned to mourning, and your joy to heaviness. Humble yourselves in the sight of the Lord, and he shall lift you up.'* I read those words through three times, taking them into myself like medicine. I got off the floor, stood up straight and said out loud, *'I do submit myself to you God and I do resist the devil. I know that he will flee away from me now. I want to draw near to you Lord Jesus and have clean hands and a pure heart. I'm not going to be double-minded any more! I am so sorry for what I have been. Please lift me up now!'* Well Miss Templeton, I've just come to tell you that he has! Oh, and also that Prince Salim arranged for some surveyors to sort out all the little difficulties for Mr Shulz, Mr Halleem and myself. I hope that I haven't excited you too much, but I just had to tell you! Goodbye!"

Alice Glover left room 604 unheeding her tear-streaked face, which was noticed by several of UCLH's staff on her way downstairs. "Please excuse me," said two nurses as she neared the exit. "But we know for sure who you've been visiting: it's that lady in room 604. We get all sorts of patients in here you know, our lives aren't worth living with all the terrible stuff we get from some of them, but that lady just pours out goodness without ever leaving her bed. Everybody notices it! We don't understand, but it seems to help us all somehow. Sorry to have interrupted you. Goodbye!"

***

Having no family of his own, Joshua kept Shabbat very quietly alone in his top floor flat, enjoying the peace of his own company on this well-designed day for reflection and an absence of hurry, so precious to Jewish people each week. On the other hand, Aaron Klein chose to spend at least part of Shabbat with his close relatives at Golder's Green, which decision was beginning to aid the stricken family's relationships. Joshua moved slowly and quietly around his flat all day, eating the simple food that he had prepared before Shabbat started on Friday evening. Recently he had taken more to reading in his big old Hebrew Bible, especially in Sh'mot, which book Christians referred to as Exodus. He loved especially those chapters twenty-five to thirty in which Moses wrote down God's meticulous instructions for making and furnishing the Tabernacle, including the clothes and inscribed gemstones that adorned the first High Priest, Aaron. These descriptions were packed with meaning for peoples of faith, helping Joshua to look back over his life and realise that at last he was very happy. He was beginning to recognise Alice Glover as being a most kind and gentle lady, never interfering in his own life but always ready to try to understand and tolerate his ways which were so different from her own. He thanked God that she was living just two floors down in the same house.

***

On Sunday evening, Salim phoned Aaron to say that the Council of Emirs had sanctioned his visits to Uruguay and Australia, very pleased with his initiative to introduce the FNAE into the southern hemisphere. Salim's staff would begin making arrangements for him to visit representatives of those countries, anticipating that he would fly via London to Montevideo on Sunday 3rd June, using a FNAE state aircraft. After Uruguay, he would fly across the southern Pacific to Australia, from where they would return eventually to the FNAE. Salim welcomed Aaron to be his travelling companion on this trip, suggesting that instead of being the only non-Arab, he might wish to bring his niece Ruth and a friend of hers for company, with all expenses to be paid by FNAE.

That evening, Aaron shared this tremendous news with his friend Julian Steinburg, whilst they chatted and set up their regular game of chess. Julian was amazed at Prince Salim's generosity and showed delight at Aaron's attempts to recover more of the ancient Aaronic jewels. The game was going Julian's way, even though he seemed preoccupied over something, when at a few minutes to 10.00pm his landline telephone rang. Julian answered the call immediately but spoke little. Aaron's tinnitus had given him a side-effect of greatly increased hearing ability, thus he could not avoid noticing the strong masculine voice talking to Julian, although actual speech was indistinct. Aaron also heard a church clock striking the hour and was puzzled that he thought he heard eleven chimes rather than ten. Eventually, Julian spoke firmly to his caller, "You have the wrong number, Madam. You must be more careful how you dial the numbers!" He put down the phone and returned to the chess match, but shortly afterwards, although apparently in a superior position, he abruptly knocked over his king in resignation of the game. Aaron realised that his friend had lost concentration, thus made an excuse to leave quickly to walk round to his own flat. As Julian's front door closed, Aaron heard the phone ringing again.

***

On Monday afternoon, 'AH' met with Sergeant Patel at an empty table in UCLH's busy cafeteria, eager to learn if he'd found out anything about Swarthy at Harrow. "Well, Sir, up there Swarthy was known as Mustafa Zakarian and he claimed that the lady who spent all of her time in the dry cleaners was his sister called Yeraz. In our language that means 'dream', Sir. It must have been, because local people gave me enough information to trace them to a block of flats in Rayners Lane, where all the neighbours believed her to be his wife. One of them had smelt a rat, Sir, so I used a little petty cash to sweeten him enough to give me Swarthy's forwarding address for any future mail. It's up at Walsall, Sir, but first can I tell you more about the Harrow set up please?" 'AH' sat enthralled!

"Zakarian had only rented the dry cleaners for six months and the landlord wasn't at all keen on them, Sir. They never paid the rent on time and finally disappeared without giving any notice, although that lost them the deposit they'd paid at the start. The landlord was another shifty Middle-Eastern chap with a string of small businesses and shops in Harrow, mostly gaining him a high rent for no work, Sir. He got into the dry cleaners a day or two after Swarthy had run off. He didn't like what he found inside, Sir. A little encouragement got him to show me what had been left, then to let me hire a van and clear it all out for him, Sir. There was lots of paperwork for the shop, including receipts for deliveries of all sorts of things nothing to do with dry cleaning, Sir! By cleaning out the place for him, the landlord can re-let the shop more easily, and he'd be very pleased if that could be to me, Sir, if the Met could afford his rent that is!" Harling was beginning to appreciate Waseem Patel's street-wise style, but he ignored his last comment and asked him to tell about Walsall.

"Well, Sir, you'd told me to be very careful, so I went up there and just walked around the area where Swarthy's living now." Waseem opened an envelope and showed 'AH' the contents. "You can keep these copy photos, Sir: the Harrow ones are of inside and outside of the shop, those are of his old tower block in Rayners Lane and these last ones show his new shop, which is a small photocopier's in a row of rather grubby shops in Ablewell Street, with flats above them. This long-distance shot is of the car he's driving now, Sir, an oldish dark blue 1.6 Toyota Auris 3 door hatchback, registration X 277 BSB. I watched his movements as best I could for a day or two, from a cafe down the road, but when he began to look suspicious, I cleared out quickly. I hope that's all OK for you, Sir?"

'AH' instructed the sergeant to keep well away from Harrow, Rayners Lane and particularly of Walsall, but to drive the hired van to Scotland Yard tomorrow morning and report to Sergeant Atkinson. 'AH' would have a quick look himself before the van was taken to the forensic department's garage for examination. Afterwards, Patel was to report to him at 11.00am to take matters further. 'AH' was elated as he gathered up the photos and the two men left the cafeteria without speaking and walking away in different directions.

***

When Aaron Klein checked at Acton post office on Monday afternoon, he was handed a fax received that morning from Australia. It read: *'To Glover at Box 273 Acton, UK. Topaz has similar scratchings to your previous purchases. Would accept £8,000 cash or sapphire of higher value only. Also available are stunning ruby and other necklaces priced at £15,000 to £20,000 and exotic emerald bracelet for £12,000. All items available, but this time only for collection (business hours). Kelly. Sydney Box 2650.'*

Whilst he was studying it again at a table in the post office, he was called over by the friendly assistant, "Mr Klein, I'm glad you're still here because this other fax has just arrived for Mr Glover's number." Aaron thanked her and took the single sheet of paper. It was from Montevideo Box No 759 and read as follows: *'Photo below of inscribed diamond and emerald shown. Easily recognisable tiara by serious collectors not here* shown. Prices in excess of £50,000 for tiara, and each £5,000 for jewels, from collectors in person only considered.'

Aaron phoned Sheikh Salim who was delighted to confirm that arrangements could be made for the jeweller to make private visits in Montevideo and Sydney. The prince called in his private secretary, Hasan bin Rahma and his liaison secretary, Rashid bin Mohammed, instructing them to set up arrangements for the FNAE's first diplomatic mission into the southern hemisphere.

Aaron phoned Alan Harling and discussed the 'dubious items' that he was prepared to go after. With this private foreknowledge, 'AH' expressed his excitement, albeit a little tremulous, and the encouragement of Scotland Yard for his jeweller friend to pursue this amateur yet firmly approved venture. The post office lady agreed to make copies of the two faxes, enabling Aaron to leave one of each at 'AH's Gunnersbury home before leaving Acton.

***

On Tuesday morning, the two officers were ushered into the A/C's room, "Come in Superintendents Stewart and Harling, and please sit down! The two junior men glanced at each other in amazement, as Laurence Williams was not known as a man who made slips of the tongue. Thank you both for your reports, seemingly suggesting two opposite ways forwards, which the Commissioner and I discussed yesterday. I'm sorry Stewart, but your recommendation to expand the staffing of the current Special Branch was not received favourably. You are to go immediately and organise a withdrawal from your offices. A vacant building belonging to the Met, very conveniently located near Hyde Park Corner, has been made available for those hundred and ten of your staff who you will retain for work connected to diplomatic security. Get your people onto packing up and moving immediately, so as to allow Superintendent Harling's Major Crimes Division to take over the premises on Thursday morning. Thank you, Stewart. You may go now."

After Superintendent Stewart had left the room, A/C Williams stretched out his hand to Harling. "The commissioner and I both enjoyed your report over the weekend thank you! We managed a few minutes together yesterday and decided to speed things up a bit. So instead of messing around with a confusing interim rank, accept our congratulations on your promotion Superintendent Harling! Now, I want immediate action to consolidate what we've agreed from your report. Set up your new Major Crimes Division in the building that was occupied by Stewart's people. Get your ex-Bomb Squad involved quickly with those of his officers that you think are worth keeping. You're to build up a brand new team of men and women who want to be real police officers, so you can bring in a few others up to the compliment of sixty-seven proposed in your report.

"There's an enormous amount of work to do, especially to show the politicians, media and public that we're on the job. Follow up everything you've got on this 'Swarthy' and let's get after him and the other swines who turn ordinary young people into terrorists: right!" 'AH' managed a quick 'Yes Sir' before A/C Williams continued at speed, "Here's a file we've put together on serious jewellery crime in Europe, which theoretically includes Britain of course, but we want you to concentrate on France. Apparently, there's some political need to score some points against them, so we feel it would be just right to help them solve some of their unsolved mysteries. But that must take second place to getting Swarthy — right, Superintendent?"

'AH' confirmed his understanding with a smart 'Yes, Sir' before A/C Williams sent him away to start a new chapter in his career.

***

While the meticulous sorting of materials from the plastic boxes continued at Brondesbury Road, Kilburn, Aaron and Joshua discussed the faxes received at Mr Glover's PO Box, "The word '*scratchings*' used by the Australian man is almost derogatory Mr Aaron. Surely he must be an ignorant or arrogant man!" Aaron agreed, "Clearly Joshua, as he refers to 'Glover' without the title of 'Mr' then proposes a collection rather than his previously posted sales. I've checked Mr Glover's receipts, one each for £5,500 and £6,800, from which we can be certain of the seller's identity: Logan Kelly — Chairman, Kelly Properties Inc, Kelly Towers, Castlereagh Street, Sydney, NSW. It seems as if he expects even more for the third engraved stone, showing his business acumen! Can you read what is engraved clearly enough Joshua?" The lapidorist studied the fax carefully, "Yes, I am sure that the Hebrew name equates to what in English is the tribe of Issacher, thus it is assuredly the original beautiful topaz from the High Priest's breastplate." Aaron showed the other fax to Joshua, asking the same question. "The name on the obviously coloured stone is Reuben, which identifies it as the emerald. The clear gem, apparently a perfect diamond, has the correct name of Gad inscribed. They look genuine Mr Aaron!" The jeweller was delighted with Joshua's confirmation, but decided to be discrete and did not mention the tiara, keeping such discussions between Inspector Harling and himself.

Aaron reached for two blank PO fax forms and wrote out his replies. To the Australian, he wrote: '*To L. Kelly, Box 2650 Sydney: Glover unavailable. I will visit your offices next Friday 01 June with adequate resources and high quality sapphires for mutually satisfactory business. Confirm arrangements asap. Signed A. Small.*' On the other form, he wrote: '*To Box 759 Montevideo. Must inspect highly priced items in person. Will be in Uruguay between 29 and 31 May. Send contact details asap. Signed A. Small. Box 273 Acton.*' Aaron phoned the Inspector who agreed to meet him at UCLH in an hour's time. When they were seated once again in the conveniently large and well-used cafeteria, Aaron showed the received faxes and his proposed replies, "I'm almost certain that this is the Gulchow Tiara Alan, in which case I have no idea about legal ownership, since it disappeared shortly before World War 2. Could you investigate legal status regulations for both of us please, Alan? Look at the man in Montevideo's unusual use of English. It seems 'continental' to me, possibly Germanic, which leads to a possibility of 1930s Nazi involvement, knowing that many of those intelligent brutes escaped to South America. Then this Australian businessman looks very suspicious to me. I'll send off my two fax replies this afternoon and maybe you can think about the criminality aspects, Inspector, I mean Alan?" The police officer grinned, "The inspector is no longer available my friend, but Superintendent Harling will be pleased to help you!" Aaron congratulated 'AH' on his promotion, sharing his joy and looking forwards to developing their unusually co-operative jewellery investigations. Not long afterwards, the kind assistant at Acton PO sent off Aaron's faxes, one east and one west.

***

'AH' was delighted, if a little daunted, that he'd been chosen to bring new life and direction to Special Branch, with his plans for a Major Crimes Division being so eagerly approved. There was no more speculation about his future police career, thus he was absolutely determined to show his new high-up chiefs that he could deliver what they wanted. He began preparing the first draft of a personnel structure for MCD, as it would soon become known, pencilling in his familiar Bomb Squad officers. However, he realised the unfairness of that idea, so put down his pencil and strode off to make his second visit to the crumbling Special Branch. This time he went with authority, walking up to officers and quickly assessing their attitudes and possibilities, chiefly their keenness to break out of the humdrum and into challenging serious detective work, or not. 'AH' managed enough success to refer to Stewart's staffing paperwork, before selecting some 'possibles'. Thereafter, he tried to mingle his old and ex-SB officers into 'maybe teams' based on functions of work.

His main assistants, being the leaders of those teams, needed to be officers he could really trust and work with. A difficulty concerned the unknown incoming inspector from Essex, Kevin Henderson, who was due to meet with him tomorrow. 'AH' had thoughts tumbling around his brain, but surprisingly for him he wanted to use his heart as well. He looked back at what had happened about three years ago, when a fine young DPC had been badly injured in an attempt to stop a get-away car leaving a crime scene. Peter Taylor had recovered from his injuries, but insufficiently to start back in his job; hence, had been honourably discharged and found work in The Yard's forensic department. Two years ago he had married 'AH's bright young DWPC Monique Shepard. 'AH' phoned The Yard's personnel department and asked a few private questions, after which he sent for Monique Taylor. She confirmed her husband's great love for police work, despite being thwarted in his active career. She also confirmed his excellent health and fitness, with some slight blushes. Peter Taylor had re-channelled his detective's mind into comprehensive studies in the nature of the legendary Sherlock Holmes, making Monique proud of her husband's recognised expertise in analysing physical clues such as handwriting and mental traits such as preferences and habits.

If he was to ensure one of his ex-Bomb Squad sergeant's promotion, it just had to be Geoffrey Dent, a fine all-round detective and leader. From his excursion into SB that afternoon, 'AH' selected two inspectors, Donald Spencer and Herbert Norton, as keen enough to lead new teams. But the new superintendent realised that he was thinking too rationally, so he left off work and decided to discuss further unconventional ideas at home with Mary. One of his problems was what on Earth he could do about the French jewellery issue, recognising his own ineptitude with any foreign languages and virtual absence of travelling abroad. That evening, Mary and Alan sat quietly discussing the possibilities for establishing the Metropolitan Police's Major Crimes Division, with Mary encouraging her husband to use his heart as well as his head.

***

That evening at Golder's Green, Aaron caused great excitement, "As long as your mum agrees, Ruth, I'd be delighted if you'd come with me on a trip. We'll be flying first to Uruguay on this coming Sunday, then moving on to Australia a few days later. Probably we'll fly back via Singapore and the FNAE taking about ten or twelve days in all. Prince Salim has a twenty seater plane, usually filled up with fierce Arab guards, but he's asked me to travel with him so that I can track down some more Aaronic jewels. He thought that one Jew alone amongst so many Arabs could get rather lonely, so asked if I could take my wonderful niece with me, together with a young friend for company. He believes that for an Arab prince's entourage to include a Jewish maiden and her uncle plus another young person, would demonstrate his vision to broaden his desert kingdom's aspirations enormously. It would be a great opportunity for you to practice your Spanish, Ruth, as well as seeing a few foreign places. It might be a little difficult at times, as I've got to meet with some unsavoury people, but you could help me out a lot by witnessing and recording what happens, at least in your memory, but maybe also on photos with some written notes, please."

Ruth jumped at this tremendous opportunity, "That would be brilliant Uncle Aaron, absolutely wonderful, thank you so much! What do you think Mum, and you too Aunt Esther?" Whilst Naomi Klein showed little reaction, Esther was enthralled, "Who would you invite to go with you Ruth? Isaac is too young and not in the right frame of mind to be much encouragement or support. Does anyone else spring to mind?" Ruth quickly reviewed her school friends, who were mostly other Jewish girls, but there was no-one obvious to ask.

Then she thought of Peter Templeton, who'd been working with her and the others up at Kilburn. They'd got on well, finding similarities in their temperaments and both resolving to do the best in life. Gaining her aunt's approval, Ruth phoned Peter to give him an amazing surprise, "Hi Peter, it's Ruth. Would you like to come with my Uncle Aaron and me to Uruguay and Australia, leaving on Sunday? We'll be away about ten days because Uncle and Prince Salim have some business to do and would like me to go with them. It should be fun, what do you think Peter?"

The young man had recently finished his own 'A' levels and had thought of earning some money by working in a shop, as well as continuing to help sorting out the boxes from Klein's Jewellers. But this was something else! "Yes please! Wow! I'd love to come Ruth! My parents couldn't object could they, but I'd better make sure and phone you back this evening! Thanks Ruth! Wow!" He phoned her an hour later to confirm his family's approval, leaving Ruth sad about only one thing amongst all the excitement: that her mum and brother showed no pleasure or interest in her opportunity. Ruth determined that when she got back home, she must really do something to help them come out of their lethargic nothingness. But that would be after her trip of a lifetime.

***

On Wednesday morning, Inspector Kevin Henderson reported to Superintendent Harling as arranged, hiding what had been troubling him ever since Chief Superintendent Price had offered him the job of head of the Bomb Squad. 'AH' greeted him, "Come in Henderson, sit down and tell me all about yourself!" The Essex man went through his police career of the last fifteen years since his graduate entry; unintentionally revealing his failings as well as successes, "You see, Sir, my promotions have been related more to my business and administrative abilities, rather than criminal investigations…" 'AH' was becoming disillusioned but listened politely. "… so really, Sir, it was a big surprise when Mr Price offered me this new job. I felt obliged to accept the honour of it, but could never fill your very well admired footsteps, Sir. It's not really my cup of tea Sir. I'm much more of an organiser and controller than a dashing cavalry officer. I'm sorry, Sir."

'AH' had already guessed that Henderson's appointment had been a huge blunder by Price, but gradually a new thought was developing in his head. Harling knew that efficient management and control would be vitally important in his new Major Crimes Division, yet he didn't want to get hampered by those responsibilities himself. "Look Henderson, let's be honest with each other. I really must start mixing it with senior people all over the place and I can't do that and be a man manager for a division of sixty plus people. I need them all to be fully occupied and involved in fighting crime, not filling in forms. My staffing ideas don't envisage a straight vertical hierarchy, but more a set of efficient teams charged with fulfilling differing functions. The MCD isn't going to be the regular army, but more of a Special Forces set up. It will operate successfully using smallish teams of people who trust each other, even with their lives. If I asked you to act as an adjutant officer, arranging and controlling things for me, but without responsibility for dashing around putting out fires yourself, would you be able to handle that role?"

At last, Henderson relaxed. "Surely the main thing, Sir, is that we all help each other to gain results, using unconventional methods if necessary. We might need to interfere with traditional rank order, Sir, and utilise unusual duty and leave timings instead of simplistic staff rotas, Sir."

'AH' revealed his tentative plans to this suddenly keen inspector, "I want a few specialist teams, some headed by inspectors but others by sergeants, all responsible to me but without tying me down in their management. That would be your preserve Henderson, if it would satisfy your career aspirations for the next few years."

The relieved and excited inspector replied, "It's about the most fitting job that could be offered to me, Sir! Yes I'd love to do it! Thank you, Sir!" It had been as simple as that, even though 'AH' knew that he'd need to be very diplomatic when giving Price the news.

Henderson left and 'AH' welcomed Detective WPC Monique Taylor into his office, accompanied by her husband Peter, "Now I know that your mum's French, Monique, but what about you Peter, can you speak French too? I wondered if you'd be interested in getting back into detective work, but with a different tilt to it?" 'AH' had worked out that as his bosses really wanted him to offer assistance to the French police, and that he couldn't speak a word of French himself, that he could benefit with a pair of keen young police officers who could move around over there without causing suspicion. It was obvious that the youngish man was fit and strong, with no serious health problems. 'AH' thought that it was crazy to throw good policemen onto the scrap heap just because they weren't as flexible in body after being injured in courageous action for the service. Peter explained that they both played golf and tennis, and loved walking almost as much as detective work, "I've visited Monique's family many times and I'm absolutely '*au fait*' with the language, Sir! But we know that the Met doesn't allow an officer who has been medically discharged to be recommissioned if his injury hasn't been cured, and I'll always have the metal splints in my leg, Sir."

'AH' acknowledged the regulation, "Go along to the Met's Chief Medical Officer in Harley Street at 11.00 tomorrow Peter, just to see if he could suggest anything."

***

On Thursday, Aaron Klein spent a lot of time at Acton post office, rewarded eventually by two curtly worded acknowledgements, '*To Small. Come at 10-45 with necessary. Kelly. Sydney Box 2650.*' and '*Calle Cerrito 316. Phone 72239 for morning appointment Tuesday. Rodrigo Martinez. Montevideo Box 759.*' Aaron was very satisfied!

***

Superintendent Harling convened MCD's first team leaders' briefing at 09.00 on Friday morning 25 May. "OK everybody, here we go. You're designated our Command Team and you need to get to know each other if you don't already. This meeting is formal, so listen to what I say first, but then ask as many questions as you like. We'll conclude with a buffet lunch which will be brought in here at 12-00, so take of your jackets if you want to and help yourselves to coffee or water whenever you like. First I'm going to introduce the eight of us seated around the table to each other. You all know that I've been promoted to superintendent, so watch it!" Smiles and one or two quiet 'ahs!' broke the ice. "You'll get a few surprises as the A/C has confirmed my requested promotions and changes. Inspector Henderson will pass round a copy of my draft designation of teams. The MCD will have an initial compliment of sixty-seven officers including myself, divided into six teams, each of which will be established to perform different but complimentary functions. It's most important that you don't consider this as hierarchical, but rather a set of teams being established, equipped and expected to run a practical and effective service in a very difficult business sector: investigating and stopping major crime. Kevin Henderson's been brought in from the Essex force to be my adjutant, responsible for all day-to-day communications, management and control. Whenever you can, deal with operational issues through Kevin, whilst I'm out hobnobbing with VIPs right! Henderson's team will be known as 'The Pool' as it will contain about half of our total complement, all those not included in the smaller specific teams. When you team leaders need additional resources, go to Kevin who will complement your primary staff with suitable officers from the pool."

They listened intently as 'AH' continued, "You'll notice some unusual use of team leaders of differing ranks, which is on purpose. I'm committed to achievement in MCD, rather than establishment, so you command team inspectors and sergeants will have to learn to respect and co-operate with each other. Three of the five operational teams won't have a regular function, until circumstances dictate. They'll be known as teams Amber, Beryl and Coral for simplicity. They'll be headed by Inspectors Donald Spencer and Herbert Norton, both from previous Special Branch days, and Geoffrey Dent ex-Bomb Squad; leading

Amber, Beryl and Coral respectively. Congratulations on your promotion Geoff! You'll each need to have a sergeant as deputy, plus four PCs. The other two operational teams will have a regular specific function, one called Empathy and the other Lingua. Sergeant Waseem Patel has come from the Hertfordshire force to head Empathy, a team of officers chosen for their natural abilities to move amongst peoples of differing cultures and faiths. Theirs will often be a secretive and frequently dangerous role, mixing in discretely with groups which may have radical viewpoints, sometimes opposite to each other's. Their first assignment concerns an evil character code-named 'Swarthy' who managed the Hatton Garden bombing. Team Lingua will have the joint leadership of sergeants Peter and Monique Taylor, husband and wife.

"Congratulations on your promotion Monique and your reinstatement to the force Peter! You can see that I'm enjoying the authority that being a superintendent gives me, even with the Met's doctors! The Taylors have their own family 'French Connection' with language and geography skills, but they'll need to gather other officers with different language abilities, ready for action in Europe or further afield."

'AH' fetched himself a coffee and continued, "Now let's relax a bit and talk over what I've just outlined. After lunch, I want you all to go and chat up whoever's in our offices, assessing people for your individual teams. Talk things over together between yourselves, then pencil in your chosen names for Kevin, ready for our next meeting at 10-30 on Wednesday morning, when Amber, Beryl and Coral will be given their first functional tasks. I'll do my best to accommodate your selections. MCD is a collective enterprise, so I expect you to help each other as much possible. All of your officers are to be designated 'detectives' from now onwards, with plain clothes as standard dress. Make sure that each team has a WPC in its regular complement. Let's stop there for now."

CHAPTER 11

It would be difficult to say who was most excited as the plane took off promptly at 07.30 on this drizzly Bank Holiday weekend Sunday. Crown Prince Salim was on his first mission overseas as FNAE's Deputy Foreign Minister, aiming to establish better links with nations in the southern continent. Additionally, he wanted to show the world that toleration of other's cultures and faiths would succeed, although his staff and the plane's crew were yet to be convinced, being amazed to have three persons included in his entourage, who normally would never be allowed to accompany a royal Arab diplomat. Aaron Klein was eager to recover more of the original 3,500 years old jewels worn by Israel's first High Priest, yet he recognised his responsibility to look after the two young people who were to share in this adventure. He treasured his niece Ruth even more since her father's murder and was well aware of her mother's fatalistic thoughts about her eldest child and only daughter being taken far away from her. Ruth herself was ebullient about this trip of a lifetime with Uncle Aaron and her new young gentile friend. Peter Templeton was praying silently as the plane emerged from the dismal clouds into glorious sunshine, asking his Heavenly Father for opportunities to be a wise and strong supporter to the others on this adventure.

    The others aboard composed Salim's Arab staff and the plane's crew, leaving several empty seats on the ultra-modern twenty-seater executive aeroplane as it began its very long south-westerly journey from London to Uruguay. The planned flight time of fourteen hours, including the refuelling stop at the Cape Verde Islands, would allow the passengers ample time to move around the aircraft's vacant seats to hold private discussions, with refreshments served at occasional tables. Salim firstly spent time with his staff, familiarising themselves with their plans for meeting Uruguayan government ministers and officials. The prince would focus on building relationships to benefit both of their nations, balancing FNAE's oil and its enormous revenue, with the aspirations of the relatively small South American country, so often overlooked in comparison with its powerful neighbours, Argentina and Brazil.

The three non-Arabs spent time gradually disclosing aspects of their lives that are easier to share with other persons when enmeshed together on long journeys. Ruth was unperturbed to be the only female on the aeroplane, prepared to be discrete and respectful as an interloper on this Arab male preserve. Peter found Aaron to be very different to his own father, whose interests were aimed at pursuing worldly 'gain' and personal ambitions. Money and possessions, power and importance had meant far less to Peter since his conversion to Jesus Christ, being replaced as aims by doing something really worthwhile in life. His current focus was on deciding which subject to study at university, that would lead to involvement in providing practical help for those billions of people far worse off than his own self-centred comfortable family. Aaron soon recognised that Peter loved talking about his big visions for life, whereas Ruth was more gentle about sharing important things, having equal fervour for life, but preferring listening to talking. She wanted to follow a professional career that would help people overcome their mental difficulties rather than physical limitations, thus was contemplating a degree in law as being of best value. However, because her father's death had set back her ordered timetable for university applications, Ruth was anticipating some time and opportunity on this trip to think more widely about her future.

Aaron relished this chance to travel and experience other aspects of life, after such long years focussed solely on the family jewellery business. He was determined to achieve further results concerning his accepted 'instruction' to find the ancient Aaronic jewels, and was pleased to be outside of his rather restrictive Jewish environment. He wanted to get to know the gentile Peter, seemingly a nice young man full of enthusiasm for life and energy to succeed, but with far greater opportunities than his aunt Christine. Aaron did not really expect

Christine Templeton to recover from her injuries, which made her increasingly obvious influence at the hospital even harder for him to understand. This serene lady was something of a heroine to himself and a growing number of people at UCLH, spending what was left of her ruined life passively being cared for by hospital staff, whilst he was jetting around the world on an exciting adventure. Yet people saw in her a power of fortitude and determination to live for others and not herself, which was becoming the whispered private talk of the hospital's wards and corridors.

The refuelling at Cape Verde Islands went to plan, giving them an anticipated local arrival time at Montevideo of around 18.00. On this second leg, Salim decided to spend time with his guests, hoping for some stimulating discussions. Because he had never really spent any time with Christine Templeton's nephew, he invited the young man to tell him about his school work and plans for university. Peter thanked the sheikh, "Well, Sir, my best subject by far at school is biology and within that I really prefer botany to other aspects. Somehow, it's got a grip on me and I just love it, but I'm sorry to say that most botany text books are boring, just full of stuff and without any imagination! That's never going to attract anybody to study it, is it Sir?" Salim smiled his agreement and asked Peter to go on. "My biology teacher told me that if I found things boring, then I should research something worthwhile, so I did! There are so many important problems in the world, but I decided to choose one and think about how botany could help to solve it. Because much of the world experiences extreme climatic conditions, peoples have great difficulties growing edible vegetation, so I wondered if anything simple and effective could be done to make things realistically better."

Salim's interest was aroused because the FNAE's climate was more than just difficult, with burning hot sun every single day of the year, hardly any rainfall and the entire country being a sandy desert. Life there without the hidden oilfields would be an economic impossibility, reverting to a constant struggle for survival. The crown prince wondered what on Earth this British youngster might have to say about that. Peter continued, "I began to think about plants in general and what they must have to enable growth, mainly soil, water and sunshine plus some other factors. In England, we have pretty good loamy soil that can grow most things, but in a desert that's impossible, so I looked into plants worldwide that can grow in nothing but sand. Of course there's stuff like marram grass but people can't eat that, so I wondered what would grow and be edible. We all know that weeds soon spring up on heaps of sand that are left alone, so I concentrated on some of these so-called weeds, Sir. There was a particular group that I thought looked interesting called *'urtica dioica'*, commonly known as 'stinging nettles', which gave me a big surprise because it's not only aboriginal peoples that have learnt how to cook and eat them, Sir, even sophisticated peoples have recognised their nutritional values!

"I also thought about the second main requirement: sunshine. In England it can be pretty difficult to grow plants that need a lot of sun, but in a desert there's probably too much sun and maybe no shade for less hardy plants? Next, I considered water and obviously there's not much of that in a desert, unless it can be either piped in at great cost or drawn off from expensive bore holes. But as water's chemical formula is only hydrogen plus oxygen, surely if some hydrogen was available alongside the oxygen in air, then plants could have the necessary water? Then I discovered that some plants actually make hydrogen, particularly a family called *'hydrogenous favoritem'*." Salim, with a vague recollection of a plant species with that name, began to listen more intently. "Apparently, *hydrogenous favoritem* plants have a chemical mechanism that extrudes hydrogen gas as well as nitrogen. I began to visualise a whole field of *hydrogenous favoritem*, all giving off hydrogen gas, which was somehow enabled to mix with the oxygen in the air, resulting in water, Sir! A big problem would be how to prevent the gases from escaping and instead to persuade them to combine. That might be possible in an enclosed space, but that would mean enormous expense, so I began to think about something absolutely natural instead.

"Maybe if the plant had biggish leaves, those could provide sufficient covering to keep the gases from simply blowing away, but it would be much better if the plants actually attracted the gases, enabling hydrogen and oxygen to be converted into water at source! I investigated how gases can be encouraged to remain on surfaces, which is like the opposite of ventilation, so I thought about the actual surfaces of leaves. If they had a high level of natural porosity, maybe gases would infuse into them? All you need is a porous, large-leaved version of a *hydrogenous favoritem* plant, naturally giving off hydrogen, being grown only on sand in normal open air with plenty of sunshine! If the hydrogen was absorbed naturally, rather than being dissipated, and if the oxygen in the air was encouraged to mix with it, you could produce water, although only in tiny quantities of course…"

Prince Salim interrupted him, "Do you mean that just *hydrogenous favoritem* plants, as long as they had large porous leaves and were growing in normal air, could produce water even in a desert?" Peter answered, "Certainly, Sir, in the right conditions! I discovered on the web that a variety called '*hydrogenous favoritem stratagetem*' grows naturally in Australia, and that apparently a film of water forms all over it during a normal night, rather like dew. That led me to thinking about developing a strain of '*hydrogenous favoritem stratagetem*' that is edible and could be planted in sand and just allowed to grow, but there may be something better than that!" Salim was seriously intrigued and listened avidly to this adventurous young man.

Peter continued, "My idea is 'why not grow other more-edible plants around HFS as I call it, so that any surplus water from HFS would seep into the sand and be sucked up by the neighbouring thirsty plants? Especially if such edible plants were tall enough, they could provide enough overhead shade to partially cover the HFSs and help stop the gases escaping! I'd like to research into abnormally tall varieties of lettuce plants, tomatoes and even cucumbers Sir, as they are the most frequently eaten salad plants. If a decent-sized batch of those was sown in desert conditions, with HFS deliberately encouraged to grow amongst them, then the salad plants would receive sufficient water integrally without any need at all for irrigation, or at least I think so!" Prince Salim sat back in his seat astounded.

Once he had cleared his mind, but only temporarily, of Peter Templeton's amazing hypotheses about growing food in deserts, Prince Salim invited Aaron's very demure and polite teenage niece to come and chat. He was immediately surprised at her choice of subject matter and vehemence of exposition, but gave her free rein to talk, "One of the troubles at school is that people emphasise your differences rather than acknowledging your similarities! They assume that if you have brown hair and blue eyes you must be a different sort of person to one whose hair and eyes are black! That's all very well for how you look, but what about how you feel inside or your strong beliefs? When people realise that I'm Jewish they make dozens of assumptions, most of which are ridiculous! It must be the same situation for all different cultures, which is crazy because each person is themselves, not just one of some sort of category or collection like an animal, Sir! When it comes to faith it's even harder to categorise people correctly, because nobody but themselves really knows the truth about what they believe and actually trust in, do they? It's really frustrating when Christian acquaintances, or should I say 'so-called Christian acquaintances' start saying ridiculous things that they know nothing about! Okay, so I'm Jewish and happy with that, but if you look back in history to what that means, rather than what most people assume it means, then it's perfectly all right! For instance, I believe that the world itself and every living creature in it was designed with incredible detail to be exactly what Almighty God wanted. How can anybody believe all that nonsense about some primitive creature crawling out of a dirty puddle that just happened to have been struck by lightning, then after an immensity of time changing its ugly ever-developing limbs and meddled-with internal organs, to finally become beautiful me? It's just daft and very sad, Sir!

"Therefore, if I believe in divine creation by an Almighty God and a lovely lady like Christine Templeton believes exactly the same about that, then why would we ever need to be at each other's throats about the person Jesus Christ? It's obvious that Miss Templeton believes in him as her saviour and ongoing protector, but because I'm Jewish I'm stereotyped not to be allowed to believe that even if I wanted to, which I don't! What's so silly is that Jesus was a Jew himself, as were all his family and first followers. In those days, Jewish people were used to having new Rabbis appear, become well-known and gather people around them to learn Godly principles; so that's obviously what those fishermen Peter, James and John did too. A huge difference was when Jesus started talking about himself in the same tone as God, who he called 'his father'. Such an idea causes turmoil inside any thinking Jewish person's mind.

"But if Jews decided to look much further back in time to those things perfectly well-known and accepted, they would say for sure that they were descendants of Abraham, exactly as Muslims do physically through Ishmael, and as far as I understand Christians claim to be spiritually. So why can't they all trust in their Almighty God in their hearts and leave all the mental arguments alone, Sir? Being an honestly real Christian isn't about someone who goes to a church most Sundays, any more than being an honestly real Jew isn't about someone who goes to a synagogue most Saturdays, or being an honestly real Muslim isn't about someone who goes to a mosque most Fridays, is it, Sir? That's only about religion, not real faith in God, which is in a person's heart not isolated mentally up there in his or her head!"

Ruth paused only briefly for breath, "I know that you respect Miss Templeton as much as I do, Sheikh Salim, so why can't we just try to understand about the things that join us together, instead of pulling each other apart all the time? Why do we label ourselves by what the outside of us might suggest, rather than by the inside of us which is our reality? I wasn't clever enough to take 'Pure Mathematics' at 'A level' but I was quite OK to take 'Applied Maths', so why not the same with what we believe in? I'd be very happy to sit next to dear Miss Templeton and study 'Applied Theology', even if some old bearded Rabbi told me that I was wrong! Why don't more Muslims tell their Mullahs, or whatever they're called nowadays, to go and boil their heads if they say 'kill all Jews and Christians' like Rashid's poor tormented brother was taught to do! It's not much fun for Rashid and his dad, Peter and me sorting through those boxes up at Uncle Joshua's when we come across unidentifiable bits and pieces of their Khaled, Aunt Christine and her fiancé, your brother and my dad!" Ruth Klein's tears welled up and overflowed onto Prince Salim's arm as she grasped his hand and buried her face in his shoulder.

Eventually, she sat up and spoke again, "I have great respect for you, Sir, especially after reading the speech that you made after the bombing in my dad and Uncle Aaron's shop. If I was allowed to, I'd try to do something about all this horrible religious hypocrisy and hatred, but I'm just a silly schoolgirl! I'm really sorry, Sheikh Salim, I didn't mean to get carried away and shoot off my silly mouth then blub all over you." The Arab prince kept hold of her hand and smiled tenderly, "What you said is very true, my dear Ruth, although you became a little over-heated in your exposition. It's that heat, which some people call 'fervour' that drives particular persons into ways that are clearly evil, instead of the opposite direction. Helping people to recognise and understand each other's differences, then to learn how to tolerate them, which will lead some of them even to support each other, like Mrs Glover, Rashid and his father, Peter and Mr Shulz, not to forget your own uncle and myself: that is my aim. The big question Ruth is: 'Shall you and I and the others who are coming to trust each other with our very lives, dare to acknowledge and live out this 'Applied Theology' as you so aptly call it? Let us take opportunities that present themselves on this trip Ruth. I thank you for being so honest and frank with me, and even for being a little too hot at times!"

The passengers dutifully returned to their own seats as the plane prepared to descend, reflecting on their unexpected conversations during the long flight. They landed at Montevideo just after 18.00 local time, finding respectful Uruguayan government officials waiting for them on the tarmac. They were escorted through barest customs procedures and driven to the hotel in the diplomatic district of the city. Salim had taken twelve rooms on one floor, insisting that everyone would stay close together on the entire trip. Two connecting rooms had been designated as a salon to be used to meet and talk in during their stay. The prince and his guests enjoyed a light supper there, before seeking rest after their very long day, remembering not to phone family in Britain as it was 3 o'clock in the morning there.

***

Next morning saw Salim's staff busy preparing for a series of introductory meetings with officials, before formal proceedings were to begin around midday. Aaron, Ruth and Peter hired a taxi with an English-speaking driver to take them on a sixty minute tour of the most interesting places, which included their first drive along the long Calle Cerrito in one of the city's most expensive quarters. Ruth made fair use of her Spanish language skills talking with the taxi driver, pleased that she had benefited from her school exchange visit to Spain a few months previously. She asked for the taxi to stop a little way from No 316, allowing them a glimpse of the house behind its high perimeter walls. Once back at their hotel, Aaron asked Ruth to phone the number given by Rodrigo Martinez. A woman's voice answered Ruth's hesitant Spanish in almost perfect English, "Señor Martinez will expect you tomorrow Tuesday 29 May at 3pm to negotiate the acquisition of the items discussed. My grandfather is an elderly gentleman and does not enjoy good health so I would not expect you to detain him for any longer than is necessary please." After Ruth had agreed the time of meeting, the lady gave her name as Leticia Benitez and her private phone number, then ended the purely business conversation with, "I look forward to meeting you tomorrow. Goodbye."

***

After a quiet morning and a light lunch, Aaron's party took a taxi to 316 Calle Cerrito, arriving precisely at 3 p.m.. The domophone was answered by Leticia Benitez who released the gate-lock and went downstairs to meet the visitors who walked through the mature growth of trees and shrubs to the big house's very solid front door. She escorted them upstairs to a small room lined with shelves of books, mostly concerning jewellery, "As my grandfather was expecting only Mr Small, it would be better if the young man waits here, whilst you and your niece come with me. Please recognise that elderly gentlemen tire easily and should not be over-excited, so I ask you to keep your business as peaceful as you can." Peter watched the lady, who was about the age of his Aunt Christine, as she took Aaron and Ruth into a room a few yards down the hallway and closed the door, leaving him alone amongst hundreds of expensive looking books.

Leticia introduced the two visitors to her grandfather, who did not move from his armchair as he spoke in an abrupt and unfriendly manner, "Listen Small, if that's your name, I only deal in cash! You'd better have the money with you! Leticia will bring the jewels and lay them out on the table here for you to look at, but handle them very carefully, understand! You and the girl look Jewish and I don't normally deal with Jews! You've had my prices in the faxes, so don't try negotiating! Just say if you want the jewels or not, yes or no!" Aaron hid his emotions and held out his hand, which remained unshaken. He said, "Good morning Señor Martinez. We have come a very long way to meet you and look at the items you advertised for sale. I am a jeweller by profession and will need to look carefully before any business can be discussed. You know that all jewellery of value has a history attached to it, so may I ask how long you have been in possession of the jewels and from where they were obtained?" The old man grimaced, "I know you Jews, always up to your slimy money-making ways! You'll get nowhere with me, I'm from purer blood and proud of it! These jewels were brought here from Germany by my father a long time ago. You can have five minutes to decide if you want to buy them or not? Hurry up!" Aaron turned over each item carefully, having prepared this inspection many times in his mind. He recognised the items as being described, including two more of the High Priestly jewels. Aaron caught his breath as he looked at the other items on the table, offered for sale so arrogantly despite being easily identifiable by any decent jeweller as stolen property? The old man jabbed out his finger and shrieked, "Come on Jew boy! Yes or no? If you wait any longer the price goes up!"

Aaron never managed to answer his insults or demands. At that moment, the door burst open and a man dressed in dark clothes and a balaclava sprang into the room, levelling a gun at the armchair's occupant, "OK Martinez that's enough! MOSSAD knows you by your real name 'Reinhardt Steiner' the son of the hated Nazi murderer Heinrich Steiner! We've waited a long time for this day and now I'm going to pay you back for what your evil father did to thousands of my race!" Aaron, realising in an instant that murder was the intention, jumped impulsively between the intruder and the old man, "Stop! This man is guilty for his own sins, not those of his father! You're proving your own hatred to this innocent man by your actions! Stop! Put down your gun!" The hooded man hesitated without lowering his weapon, "Keep out of this, Klein! Stick to your own business and leave me to finish mine!" Ruth had grabbed Leticia and pulled her down behind a sofa next to the armchair, from where they watched anxiously as the man spoke again. "This is going to be a comfortable execution for you Steiner, not like your father gave to those innocent…" but his sentence was never finished as he crashed to the floor directly in front of Rodrigo Martinez. Peter stood open-mouthed in the doorway, still holding the enormous black Bible that he had smashed over the assailant's head.

Ruth helped Leticia Benitez get to her feet and they all stared horrified at the armchair, as she screamed, "No! Grandfather no!" His face was pure white and rigid, like that of a living corpse, obviously caused by a massive stroke. Leticia cradled him in her arms as Ruth calmly took out her phone and called for the emergency services, explaining as best she could in her amateur Spanish that an ambulance and the police were required most urgently. After taking some quick photos with her phone, Ruth knelt down and spoke firmly to Leticia, "Señorita Martinez, you must prepare a bag ready to go to the hospital with your grandfather. My uncle and I will stay with him while you do this. The ambulance won't be long! Hurry!" Leticia ran from the room. Ruth kicked the gun under the sideboard, from where it had fallen in front of the armchair. She dropped to her knees and held one of the old man's hands, whilst Aaron recovered sufficiently from the series of shocks to take Martinez's other hand. Peter's mind came alert, "Ruth I can't speak Spanish! I'll swap places with you while you go outside to bring the ambulance men straight up here." Ruth rushed down the stairs and out to the gate, opening it wide and seeing a police car racing down the street towards the house. She waved furiously as it screamed to a halt, disgorging two burly policemen who pulled out their guns as they ran.

Inside the upstairs room, nobody had noticed that the gunman was recovering from being knocked out. Silently, he crawled backwards through the open door and ran unsteadily down the stairs, arriving at the front gate exactly as did the police. Ruth pointed straight at him and shouted, "That's the gunman! Get him quickly!" An ambulance was just arriving and the police officers took no notice of the teenage girl. She took two photos of the fleeing gunman before shouting to the ambulance men to follow her indoors. The police had pushed past Ruth, charged up the stairs to take stock instantly of the disordered room's occupants. Leticia had returned and was kneeling next to her grandfather, whilst Peter still held his other hand. Aaron was holding handfuls of jewellery, which Leticia had asked him to put into a sideboard drawer. The policemen twisted Aaron's hands behind his back and handcuffed him roughly, then were doing the same with Peter as the ambulance men rushed in and dealt efficiently with Martinez. Ruth screamed but kept enough composure to take more photos as the men were dragged outside.

Leticia got into the ambulance beside her grandfather as the police car roared away with its siren screaming. Leticia threw a bunch of keys to Ruth and shouted, "Please lock up for me and come to the Maciel Washington Hospital. I'll sort out the nonsense with the police as soon as I can!" The normally quiet young English girl was left standing alone on the pavement. Gradually, she recovered and went into the house, taking further photos before collecting the discarded jewellery and putting it into a drawer. She picked up the big black Bible and placed it on top of the same sideboard before leaving the room, now so strangely empty and silent after the drama of the last ten minutes. After locking the front door and closing the security gate, she began walking away from the town centre, taking directions from passers by and arriving a few minutes later at one of Montevideo's main hospitals.

***

At the city's police headquarters, all was shouting and confusion. The policemen had dragged the two Englishmen inside, proudly showing them to their colleagues as they pushed them roughly into the lock up. The police station's motley crowd of occupants, stirred from their bored inactivity, joined in the cacophony of shouting. Two reporters from the Montevideo Evening News jumped up to take pictures of the imprisoned men and the arresting police officers who were grinning victoriously. Scraps of English conversation were gathered haphazardly as Aaron and Peter tried in vain to explain what had actually happened. The reporters scribbled down a series of words including, 'MOSSAD, temple, uncle, Rodrigo, ambulance, Israeli, ton, jewels, kliner, Steiner, execution, flight from London, Aron, Kneese, Pete, Nazis, rich, Martinez, Jews, Germans, Ruthy, big black Bible, gunman, Reinhardt, young girl, hooded…' before rushing to their car and off to the newspaper's offices.

Their editor had been frustrated with a lack of any real local news when the reporters ran in yelling out their discoveries in a scrambled mass of incongruous and erroneous information. He reached for his pad and started immediately to compose a front-page feature article, in perfect time for the early evening edition of his newspaper. Owing to its dramatic and international nature, the Montevideo Evening News' report was recopied and published by national newspapers all around the World and featured as 'Breaking News' on major news TV and radio networks, appearing as follows:

ISRAELI EXECUTION SQUAD ATTACK IN MONTEVIDEO CENTRO!

This afternoon 29th May armed executioners from the Israeli intelligence agency MOSSAD attacked a home on the peaceful Calle Cerrito in central Montevideo belonging to 82 years old Señor Rodrigo Martinez. Two hooded gunmen and their female accomplice gained entry on the pretence of viewing jewellery recently offered for sale by Señor Martinez.

Once inside the large secluded house they announced that they were an execution squad sent to eliminate this long-term peaceful Montevideo resident, who they claimed was Reinhardt Steiner the son of a Nazi murderer named Heinrich Steiner. An unnamed person in the room where Martinez was sitting, peacefully inspecting his fabulous jewels, was attacked viciously by one of the intruders wielding a big black Bible as a weapon.

The 3 Jewish raiders are thought to have travelled to Uruguay from London, England on an unscheduled flight two days previously. The 2 male attackers were captured by the prompt and courageous action of local Police Officers Ignacio Acosta and Fernando Munez, and are now in secure custody at the Comisaria Seccional Police Headquarters. Sources there have named them as Aran Temple and Pete Kliner. Their female accomplice, using the name of Ruthy Neese, ran off from the scene of the murder attack and is being hunted this evening.

Residents of Montevideo Centro are warned to stay indoors and not to admit any young female, who may be armed and dangerous. The frail elderly jewel collector Señor Martinez was taken to Maciel Hospital on Calle Washington by ambulance where he remains in a critical condition. The Montevideo Evening News is offering a reward for information leading to the apprehension of the missing terrorist Ruthy Neese.

***

Local time in Montevideo was 5.00 p.m. when the newspaper hit the streets, causing Uruguayan and other Southern American TV and media outlets to begin pouring out reports. Uruguay's national armed forces and secret agencies were alerted. Montevideo's President was briefed to make a live TV announcement to calm the 1.4 million residents, whilst the Nation's president was being kept regularly informed of progress, which was far slower than envisaged. In Europe, the late evening news outlets carried brief but dramatic accounts. Night duty staff of major newspapers edited the text for the next day's national newspapers. In Israel, undisclosed sources claimed that the affair was being undertaken as an anti-Semitic attack by neighbouring Arab states. A spokesman for MOSSAD, shown only by a back view, denied all knowledge of any such event.

Various of these news flashes and bulletins were seen by TV watchers throughout England, where particular interest was aroused in the Hampstead, Golder's Green, Kilburn and Gunnersbury districts of London. Middle Eastern interest was keenest in Israel and the FNAE. The Uruguayan Ambassador to Great Britain, at a late evening city event, was called to visit the Foreign Office immediately. His British counterpart in Montevideo was at a function in Buenos Aires, from which he asked politely to be excused in order to return to his embassy in Uruguay's capital. On his arrival there, he was briefed on a number of calls received from London, including one from a business executive named Roland Templeton who claimed to recognise one of the MOSSAD attackers shown brandishing his hand-cuffs behind the bars of a police cell.

***

It was a long evening and night for many people, caused by conclusions pulled down from an empty sky by sensation-seeking media. Craving street drama to fuel the public's insatiable appetite for 'entertainment', they encouraged accusations, denials, anger and fear to spread like wildfire around the world. Meanwhile, oblivious to the masquerade of this 'news', a teenaged Jewish girl sat quietly at the bedside of Rodrigo Martinez talking to his granddaughter Leticia Benitez. The two women each held one of the old man's hands, smoothing the wrinkled skin and giving him as much comfort and support as they could. He was conscious but unseeing, unable to speak or move, but was thought to be able to hear.

Leticia spoke Spanish words of long familiarity, but devoid of any love, to her hateful grandfather; interspersed in excellent English to Ruth with an account of her very troubled life. She unfolded a long sad story, confirming that her great-grandfather had indeed been the Nazi officer Heinrich Steiner, famous for his life of butchery against Jews and Poles in Warsaw. He had stumbled across the old-established jewellers named Potrzecki, then by alternately threatening them and pretending to help them escape the regime of horrors, he had learnt of their deep involvement in the Central European jewellery business.

Steiner hid his secret dealings with the Potrzeckis from his Gestapo bosses, until in 1943 he arranged a final meeting promising them a safe escape route in return for a treasure trove of jewellery. That night he sold them for immediate transportation by cattle wagon to a death camp, passing his Nazi chiefs a selection of diamonds in return for their stamped authority for him and his family to take a month's leave at a Gestapo officers holiday resort on the Adriatic coast. From there it was easy to bribe his way to Libya and then in stages until he arrived in Uruguay a year later, with his ten year old son Reinhardt and a fortune in stolen jewellery including the Gulchow Tiara, but without his wife who had died and been buried at sea in the South Atlantic. He assumed a quiet life, learned Spanish, changed his name to Ignacio Martinez and renamed his son Rodrigo, before marrying a wealthy Uruguayan widow Sofia Rojas. As an established citizen of Montevideo, he began to accumulate wealth by a variety of dubious investments and extortions. In 1953, his wife Sofia and their young daughter were killed in a hit and run accident with a lorry which the police never identified.

At seventeen, Rodrigo was developing similar character and skills to his father, who waited a further two years before marrying again, this time selecting the aristocratic Lucia Sanchez to become his third wife. Two years later Lucia died with her baby in childbirth. Rodrigo was then aged twenty-one and eager to branch out on his own in the family's nefarious business. His father unintentionally assisted those efforts by dying painfully of stomach cancer in 1959, leaving Rodrigo an extremely wealthy man. Within a year he had joined Montevideo society by marrying the heiress Fernanda Ortiz who was aged just twenty-two. Their daughter Agustina was born two years later and they continued a secretive, comfortable and profitable life. In 1984, Agustina married Joaquin Benitez and gave birth a year later to Leticia.

Grandmother Fernanda died aged forty-nine of a heart attack when Rodrigo was aged fifty-one. He never remarried and in 2001 Agustina and her husband Joaquin were killed in a car crash, leaving their sixteen-year-old Leticia as an orphan. It seemed a natural thing for the young girl to move into her rich grandfather's home and provide more private help to augment that of his servants. Thus, Leticia had lived with him for the last seventeen years, growing steadily more and more embarrassed as she watched her unscrupulous grandfather's activities unfold. Now aged thirty-three and unmarried, Leticia Benitez looked back remorsefully on a long line of her predecessor's early and tragic deaths, brought on she believed as due punishment for her great grandfather's involvement in murder and extortion. She told Ruth her cheerless life story, whilst sitting with her sole remaining relative, whose evil hand she held and stroked very gently.

***

Leticia and Ruth, complete strangers an hour ago, were fast becoming trusted confidantes despite their differences in age, culture, nationality and faith. As Leticia's own anguish softened, she listened to this foreigner's tragic story with compassionate ears, as Ruth disclosed the calamity in her father and Uncle Aaron's shop in Hatton Garden. The ladies drank balm sub-consciously into their afflicted souls, sharing their lives with each other as doctors and nurses made brief professional visits to their confessional room. Leticia heard descriptions of unknown persons: Alice Glover, Joshua Shulz and the Halleem family, who had overcome their misconceptions and prejudices in willing support of each other's needs and desires. Ruth described their horrific work of sorting through the fragments collected from the bombed shop, knowing that family remains were included in the blood-soaked rubbish. Leticia saw that sharing in such a revolting task had helped their mutual understanding and respect to grow.

Ruth revealed her admiration for Prince Salim, engaged even now on his diplomatic activity elsewhere in Montevideo, describing his publicly-declared intentions to strive for understanding and tolerance between peoples of different cultures and faiths. Leticia recognised the glaring contrast to the life that she had simmered through in her grandfather's house for so many years. She divulged that her only real pleasure was that of sewing; mentioning different techniques and materials which were an absolute mystery to the teenager. Leticia told the young Jewess about her life-long Catholic religious observance, which had gained her no solace but only layers upon layers of guilt and shame. She told Ruth how she longed to be free of her inner turmoil and dissatisfaction with the life that she had been forced to live in support of her grandfather. As best she could do, Ruth described Christine Templeton's markedly different Christian life, with its faith-filled influence which now was emanating from her hospital bed at UCLH.

Leticia told Ruth that she had been the one sending and receiving post office box number faxes, strictly as dictated by her grandfather then asked why the girl's uncle was interested in buying inscribed jewels. Ruth explained about Aaron's hospitalisation at UCLH, when boredom led him to look at a Christian Bible, where he found that the early books mirrored the Jewish Torah exactly. She described the Garden Society's bookmark falling from Exodus chapter twenty-eight at the description of the High Priest's garments with exotic bejewelled breastpiece, then her uncle's discovery of the pencilled note: '*You must find these jewels*' which he eventually accepted as a divine commandment for himself to fulfil. Ruth enlarged her story to include the amazing way that Inspector Harling, Alice Glover, Joshua Shulz and the Halleems had become involved with his quest and with each other's lives. When she explained about Christine's nephew, Peter, who Ruth had invited to come to Montevideo, they recalled seeing him knock out a gunman executioner with a big black Bible. The touch of humour in this very recent memory, was so different to the friendless old man consumed with pride, conceit and prejudice, whose hands they sat holding.

***

The gradual opening of their hearts to each other, accompanied by cleansing tears of releasing power, was interrupted by an Inspector Aranjues. He had returned from a long lunchtime meeting to his police station to discover two Europeans handcuffed behind the solid bars of the lock-up cage. His English was sufficient enough for him to listen to Aaron and Peter with some understanding, but no initial belief. The two arresting officers were away assisting at a road accident in the north-east of the city, whilst none of the other police officers seemed to understand what had actually happened on Calle Cerrito. As it was only a two hundred metres walk to the hospital, Inspector Aranjues had decided to go quickly himself to visit the elderly man Rodrigo Martinez and find out what was going on. The doctor announced that Señor Martinez had had a stroke and could be of no assistance to any police enquiries, but that he believed the man's granddaughter was at his bedside and could be spoken with.

Inspector Aranjues knocked and entered the room respectfully, surprised at the positions of the two women one on either side of the old man's bed and each holding one of his hands. Within ten minutes, Aranjues had noted the exactly corroborated accounts of what had happened less than four hours ago at the house on Calle Cerrito. He was alarmed that two Europeans had spent that time handcuffed and locked into a cage reserved for staggering drunks and brawling family disputants. The inspector asked the younger woman if she would go with him to the other's home, to help him understand what had occurred. They walked the short distance to the house, completely oblivious of the van-loads of newspapers being delivered to the street sellers who were eager to sell the day's sordid news to avid public appetites. Once inside, the evidence of what had actually happened there was discerned easily by the inspector: pushed-back empty armchair, sideboard with its drawer full of jewellery, big black Bible resting serenely on its top and unfired revolver on the floor beneath it. They went outside and Ruth locked up, while the inspector checked along the pavement where she said the gunman had fled. He returned almost immediately carrying a dishevelled grey balaclava. As he escorted Ruth back to the hospital, they passed a kiosk displaying its hastily scrawled message:

'*ISRAELI EXECUTION SQUAD ATTACK IN MONTEVIDEO CENTRO!*'

They purchased four copies of the Montevideo Evening News then ran in opposite directions: Ruth returning to the hospital bedside of Rodrigo Martinez, and the inspector to his police headquarters. It was nearly 7pm when her very shaken but relieved Uncle Aaron and Peter Templeton were brought by Inspector Aranjues to join Ruth and Leticia at the hospital. The policeman was being inundated with enquiries and demands from his own bosses, Uruguayan officials from many departments, and copious media outlets. His denials of the story portrayed by the Montevideo Evening News were disbelieved by most senior people, who insisted on investigating the circumstances, including interrogating the main characters, themselves. Aranjues met quickly with the hospital's alarmed authorities, whose switchboard was becoming jammed by an escalating stream of telephone calls, and whose car park was totally unable to accommodate the influx of excited press and TV reporters, city and government officials. They opened up an unused building in their grounds to be turned into a temporary media studio, and in consideration for Leticia Benitez and her companions, they equipped two empty rooms with beds and chairs for them to take any meagre periods of respite from the onslaught of the media's barrage.

The persons gathered around Rodrigo Martinez's bed shared in horrified disbelief at how easily an innocent situation could have been so misconstrued to tell the opposite story to the truth, simply to satisfy the paying public's craving for excitement. They thought themselves to be powerless against the world-wide media machine that was pouring out its misinformation, building up crashing waves of belief or disbelief, excitement, anger or humour, hatred or sympathy, all around the globe. Before long they were joined by Prince Salim and his very anxious Arab guards who were trying desperately to shield him from all and sundry.

During that evening and on through the frantically disturbed hours of the night, Leticia, Aaron, Salim, Ruth and Peter grew into a team defending truth and righteousness in front of the glaring lights of the predominantly cynical press. Slowly, these tired 'actors' succeeded in changing the atmosphere, by demonstrating their support of each other, despite their natural differences of age, culture and faith. Aaron, Peter and Ruth graciously waved away all suggestions for them to make complaints against the city's police, amazing many of the hard-headed media personnel.

As the reporting moved from an untrue story of crime and terrorism, into a true story with human interest, it was picked up on by government and city officials and embassy staff from several countries. They recognised the opportunities for concord that were being made available and so convened at the hospital, where diplomats and officials started to see potential benefits in a friendship with the previously unheard of nation of the Federation of Non-aligned Arab Emirates. New angles of reporting were sought out and seized on by the media, including accounts of the Hatton Garden terrorist bombing with its religious murder of these visitors' family members. A copy of Sheikh Salim's inaugural speech as crown prince was re-aired on TV and radio, stimulating practical discussions on how to incorporate recognition and tolerance for acknowledged differences between dissimilar peoples around the world. Ex-statesmen and political pundits were interviewed ad nauseam, airing their lofty comments on such worthy goals and promising to introduce them 'whenever circumstances would allow' which phrase was quickly lampooned by clever interviewers who exposed the hypocrisy and demanded honest actions from their embarrassed interviewees.

Eventually, as Wednesday morning began to dawn, the media circus moved its trappings to other locations, officials switched off their dutiful expressions and headed for home, and the hospital once again concentrated on providing medical attention to patients. Señor Martinez had made no response to the treatment being given him, remaining simply alive but with no apparent recognition of people or his situation. Slowly, the changing rotas of his bedside companions were diminished, as the temporary beds and chairs provided for his visitors became more frequently occupied. It was at 8.15 that morning that he died, absolutely alone with no opportunity to turn away from his long-embittered life of accumulating wealth, in ignorance of such God-given delights as peace and joy.

***

As Prince Salim and his travelling guests would have only another twenty-four hours in Montevideo, the three men returned to their hotel to have a few hours' sleep, but Ruth insisted on staying with Leticia at the hospital. After the post-mortem and funeral preparatory formalities had been seen to, they walked back to the big empty house on Calle Cerrito. Throughout the rest of the day, they talked, cried, ate, exchanged confidences, dozed and became well acquainted. Ruth slept in a spare bedroom that night, to be collected very early the next day by the others.

On this same Wednesday afternoon and evening, Prince Salim attended a series of diplomatic and economic meetings with Uruguayan and city authorities, all of whom were very favourably disposed to establishing firm links with the FNAE.

***

At UCLH Doctor Chaudhary sat pondering over the latest results of Christine Templeton's internal medical tests, which were becoming alarming. As she was an exceptionally brave lady, he decided to go to Room 604 and talk with her straight-away, "Miss Templeton, I am sorry to say that your recent test results have not been good, and must change your and my perspectives on your injuries. I am very sorry that your internal organs are struggling to cope with the tremendous forces placed on them by the explosion. Your blood supply systems, which are designed to assist recovery, have started to relax into their normal mode which is not helping your organs. We will continue to keep a close check on all this of course, but I thought that you should know that things do not look so good as we had hoped. I am very sorry, Miss Templeton."

***

Superintendent Harling convened MCD's second team leaders' meeting at 10.30am on Wednesday 30th May, "OK everybody, let's get on with it shall we! Henderson and I have reviewed your proposals and agreed the following list of approved team deputies and WPCs. We'll fill in the names of the chaps later. Spencer's Team Amber will have Sergeant Noddy Foster with WPC Gail Tandridge. Norton's Team Beryl has Sergeant Stanley Atkinson as deputy and Cindy Davison as WPC. Dent's Team Coral will have Sergeant Elvin Artis as deputy and WPC Laura Lampston. Team D or 'The Pool' will have Sergeant Walter Baines as Henderson's right-hand-man. The remaining two specialist teams are a little different.

Empathy under Sergeant Patel won't have a designated deputy but will include Hippy Ipperstaff, Benjamin Jacobs, Salmud Jones, Gudakesha Mazumbar and WPC Nella Brown. Lingua headed by Sergeants Peter and Monique Taylor will include our Scandinavian hero Olaf Olaffsen, the half-German Gustav Shield, Ivan Sokol from somewhere strange in Russia, Hussain Qadir with his Middle-Eastern roots and WPC Sandra Gonzalez from some flamboyant flamenco land. I don't want any of us to be flippant about these experienced and trusted officers, who can speak a very large range of languages between them and have vast knowledge of how things work if you choose to cross the English Channel. They will also act as interpreters and translators between our own MCD and foreign forces. Every member of MCD must ensure that his or her passport and the usual courses of injections for foreign travel, at least throughout Europe, are up-to-date, also that they are physically fit and otherwise available to travel to previously unknown destinations at the drop of a hat.

The team leaders were far too engrossed in their own and each other's future situations to want to interrupt their boss's flow, but for tradition's sake Geoff Dent asked, "Excuse me, Sir, but with all these new arrangements and foreign stuff, can we be assured that cheese sandwiches will still be available in The Yard's canteen, or will it be only frog's legs and rat-at-you-too from now on?" His interjection pleased everyone by relaxing the atmosphere, as laughter and several friendly calls of 'Ah! Ah!' broke the ice and Harling called for a short 'comfort break' of five minutes only.

Suitably refreshed, 'AH' began again, "Remember that Inspector Henderson will act as an adjutant executive officer by providing instant initial answers and responses to problems, acting on behalf of myself. One of his functions is to coordinate us all, making sure that resources to and from all six teams are made available for those operations that need more than any single team. Another role will be coordinating MCD's dealings with The Yard's back room boys in forensic and other departments, to avoid us all in going as individuals to the boffins all the time." Donald Spencer asked a question, "Excuse me, Sir. All what you are telling us is very informative and exciting, such that I for one am very keen to get on with something, but please can you let us know about the actual current agenda and what you're expecting from us to start with, Sir?"

'AH' welcomed this prompt, "Yes, let's leave the academic stuff and turn to operational action. I must remind you all that we will be discussing major criminal and terrorist activity, such that no mention of these matters must be made outside of those absolutely trusted and able to keep their mouths shut, right?" Many 'Yes Sirs' assured him of their understanding of that vital point, before he continued, "The Commissioner wants action and success with the Met's name enhanced publicly and quickly. Associate Commissioner Williams and I have a strategy to concentrate on three main areas of impact: one is to get after the people who planned the Hatton Garden bombing, another is to break the deadlock of French inability to solve a series of major jewellery thefts, and the third is to uncover a criminal network which has been disposing of stolen jewellery around the world. We have agreed to take on these three very significant areas of crime, to find the culprits and have them dealt with. The inter-connections between the last two are obvious but the first one has jewellery as an aspect because of where the bomb went off. Our teams need to be concentrating on those three fronts, as well as responding to further major crimes that need our attention." There was a buzz of excitement around the room as at last they were to be advised of real work and not just ideas, as 'AH' continued, "Some of you know already about the character code-named 'Swarthy' who was caught on CCTV sussing out the Hatton Garden area and presumably selecting the particular jewellery shop owned by the Klein Brothers. This week has seen a breakthrough in identifying him through the actions of Sergeant Patel here. Well done again Waseem! Now we need to focus on more than just identifying him, but on discovering those evil people who are at the top of this religious hatred form of terrorism. I want Spencer's

Team Amber to work with Waseem's own Team Empathy, and I'll be briefing them separately very soon. Don't forget that we're dealing with totally unscrupulous murderers here."

The superintendent let that comment sink in then spoke of the next subject, "Now for the French connection which has embarrassed their force for several years and which our Commissioner wants us to come to their rescue. Team Beryl will work with Team Lingua on this project, which is also likely to be wider and dangerous work. Our third main ongoing area of activity is rather less public but is equally important to deal with. Some individual 'Moriarty' character, or some criminal organisation, thinks that they have control of selling off stolen jewels of immense value on a world-wide basis. Team Coral is to assist The Pool on researching the background stuff to this, which needs lots of brain work to find out what's been going on in recent years amongst some of these jewel thieves and their customers.

"That brings me to another vital point for all of you to understand," said 'AH' with emphasis, "I'm not going to let MCD become another big-headed agency out to take pride in its own achievements. On the contrary we are going to demonstrate to Her Majesty's Police Force and others around the world that we are professional policemen and women 'assisting' others in their own enquiries. Part of our role will require liaison with 'funny departments' and foreign forces, but we need to show ourselves to be a professional police service rather than a motley collection of spies or soldiers! We'll also be rubbing shoulders with non-police people much of the time, who we will have to learn to trust and respect if they are after the same people as ourselves."

I'll be as flexible as possible concerning periods of leave, but don't expect MCD to be a holiday assignment for any of us, Okay? You need to recognise and understand that powerful criminals don't work a five-day-week! This summer is going to be a critical time for MCD with many of us involved in desperate and dangerous situations which certainly don't shut down for the weekend. I've got to ask you to explain to loved ones that leave this month and next is out of the question. Even weekends are going to be interfered with often, so we might as well acknowledge that fact and make the best of supporting each other and getting on with the job. Please postpone all holidays until we get an inkling of how things are going to develop. The force will cover all reasonable expenses in reorganising proper times of leave for you and your teams, but just accept that it will be after we have come up with some real positive answers and accomplishments." The team leaders looked across the table at each other, realising that the last few days of relative inactivity had come to a sudden end. 'AH' concluded the meeting with, "I want the leader and deputy of Team Amber and all of Team Empathy, to report back at 2.00 for an initial briefing. Tomorrow at 09.00, I'll set up Beryl and Lingua with their first requirements, then at 11.00 Coral and The Pool leaders to get them started. That's all for now. Dismissed!" Harling's last few sentences did not anger his deputies, but gave them the necessary message that work must come first for serious policemen and women. They were determined not to let down their boss, their colleagues or themselves.

***

Inspector Donald Spencer and Sergeant Noddy Foster from Team Amber joined Sergeant Waseem Patel with his key Officers in Superintendent Harling's conference room at 2.00 p.m. as arranged. 'AH' began immediately. "You all know that MCD will involve working teams and unusual circumstances, including ranks, so let's get this straight right-away. Whilst Inspector Spencer is senior in rank to Sergeant Patel on the Met's official establishment listing, both of them are key members of MCD's Command Team and have equal status. I have deliberately put their two teams together for the practical working arrangements that we are likely to be involved in over the next couple of months. Get to know each other, respect each other's good points and tolerate each other's poorer points. You have a major police investigation to carry out, with the aim of arresting Swarthy and his backers, and stopping any future terrorist activity coming from their direction, right?" Many 'Yes Sirs!' rang out in unison. "OK. For now, Waseem mustn't let Swarthy see him, as he's the only one who's been around his new hangout in Walsall. I want you Waseem to go up there tomorrow morning taking Detective PCs Jones, Jacobs, Ipperstaff and WPC Brown with you, but leaving Gudakesha Mazumbar to stay here as liaison officer with Team Amber.

Similarly, Waseem will take WPC Gail Tandridge with him to be Amber's liaison officer. Both the girls are to support each other so get them to share a room in a Travel Inn or similar in the western part of Birmingham and masquerade as something or other. They are both of your communications links on the ground up there. Waseem is to stay in the southern part of Birmingham in another Travel Inn whilst the other three officers are to stay in a proper but modest hotel in Walsall, fairly close to Swarthy's address. Those three are to work a round-the-clock surveillance system starting immediately, reporting by phone to Sergeant Patel as first contact, but with the two WPCs as reserves sharing equal twelve hour shifts of listening in. What I want you to do is log absolutely everything about Swarthy's local movements, but don't attempt to follow his car at this stage. He's a clever chap and I don't want him spotting any of you too easily." 'AH' turned his attention to Inspector Spencer, "I want Amber to delve into every possible aspect of Swarthy's movements, habits and also his past months at Harrow, following up all you can from Waseem's van-load of evidence. Chase every lead to do with his purchases and especially his explosives and other bomb-making equipment. We need to track backwards first, to discover all we can about the Hatton Garden bombing, before we look to what he's up to in Walsall, which may be planning another terrorist attack. Whilst Waseem is out on the field, Spencer will report to me daily every early afternoon. Your liaison officers will make sure that both your teams are kept in the picture with mostly research down here at The Yard and watching Swarthy up at Walsall. However, you will both recognise that this is a terrorist link we're dealing with, so things may develop differently to how we think now. Let's go!"

***

Prince Salim, his staff and guests did not manage to sleep much that night and woke still tired after the tremendous exertions of the previous two days. However, they were collected from their hotel by smiling Uruguayans and taken quickly to Calle Cerrito to pick up Ruth and Leticia, before being whisked to Carrasco International Airport and delivered right to the steps of Sheikh Salim's aircraft. They were seen off with honour by senior staff from Uruguay's Foreign Ministry and thanked warmly for their achievements during their short stay in Montevideo. A suggestion was offered with great respect and discretion that if the Prince wished for FNAE to open a consulate in Montevideo, the city and country would be very pleased to assist its establishment.

The plane took off for the first leg of its long journey at 9am flying high over the lower range of the Andes mountains before descending to Santiago airport in Chile at 11.45. After a brief stop-over of ninety minutes, during which Chilean diplomatic officials welcomed Prince Salim and invited him to visit them when opportunity arose, the aircraft took off and cruised virtually due west for its uninterrupted flight of thirteen hours to New Zealand.

Once the travellers' initial tiredness had been dissipated, Salim invited the young Britons to continue discussing aspects of their respective faiths with him, this time asking them to come together. Firstly, he asked Ruth, whose surprising maturity he was coming to admire, to explain more about her 'Applied Theology', "I am not prepared to be a coward about my own faith, any more than about my politics or love of botany. What you said to me a few days ago Ruth was really meaningful, so please take me further amongst your thoughts on the subject of faith." Peter sat listening while Ruth began, "One trouble, Sir, is that young people follow their grown-up family members without very much thought, which risks them getting knocked sideways by the clever talk of somebody new and persuasive. I'm not knocking every type of evangelism by every faith group, but attractive talk without any accompanying honest action, causes a temptation which surely must be a danger? For us young people, our earlier parental-led teaching, if we got it, gets muddled up when we start to think and believe things for ourselves. Some of us may go quite off the rails before we've really got started, perhaps like Rashid's brother Khaled did? Stopping intolerances is not easy, because our world is full of them: whether you're a Greek Cypriot or a Turkish Cypriot, you live on the same island, don't you? Young people love to have role models who don't just sing a catchy new song, but show us how they live their lives. That may be brilliant to watch on TV or the internet, but it's not enough Sheikh Salim! We need to be actually taught how to understand and tolerate other cultures and faiths;

otherwise, we'll decide to either ignore or fight amongst ourselves. So could you help us to learn that Sir, please?"

The sudden abruptness and honesty of her question struck Salim's heart. How dare he only make clever speeches about battling religious intolerance, if he could find the way to advocate its practical education? Was this young Jewish woman challenging him in her own name only, or was he being led into something serious by the same Almighty God who guided Christine Templeton, Ruth and Peter, even if he appeared to be doing so in such diverse ways? He chose not to answer her question there and then, and asked her forgiveness for wanting time to consider her points properly. He gave her a modest bow of courtesy, which would have horrified so many of his culture and faith, then asked Peter Templeton to speak.

The young man had little experience of explaining Christianity to persons of other faiths, and did not want to use dogma to try to win an argument that required someone else to be a loser. However, he did want to show what he actually believed himself, so he decided to illustrate this through his great interest in botany, "Rather than make a theological exposition, Sir, please may I explain what I believe by discussing the normal course of all animal and vegetable life, where something apparently ridiculous happens: death occurs! Without death, no plant could continue its brief existence, which may be a matter of days as in some flowers or a few thousands of years as with sequoia trees. Therefore, as every plant must die, its designer and creator had to arrange for its continuation after death, by enabling new life to spring up from the old. In plants, this happens predominantly through the provision of a seed, which is usually buried and dies, yet allows the parent plant to ensure its future offspring's existence. Take potatoes for example: one of those must be buried under the ground and allowed to die, rotting away and becoming useless itself. Yet it's only through that awful fading away and the apparent finality of its death, that it can enable new potatoes to begin their own life and thence be available for sustaining the species, and us Sir! Different faiths have links with this practical method of procreation, including my own of Christianity. Many times in the Old Testament of our Bible, which Jewish people refer to as their Hebrew Bible, God talks to the people of that time through many different persons who were real live men and women. Each of them tells a story but in different ways, including factual accounts and symbolism, making it relevant to us, even in our generation, Sir. There are many references to a 'seed', which was especially important because of the rural nature of people thousands of years ago. There was a parallel design concerning the husbandry of animal life, which itself needed procreation through male and female sources to produce a 'seed'. In this second way, the parent does not need to die before its offspring gains life, but it was illustrated by God's requirement for the sacrificial death of particular animals, all explained with very specific instructions. As a Christian, I believe that Almighty God revealed himself and his entire character to us all, by coming in humble human form as his 'son' Jesus, who was both this promised 'seed' and prescribed sacrifice. It was Jesus who gave his life and died for us, so that we could have a new and Godly life in him! Sorry if theology is not my best subject, but that's just about what I believe. Thanks for asking me, Sir."

***

Promptly at 09.00 Inspector Norton and the Sergeants Taylor sat down in 'AH's office for their briefing, "Right, this is serious stuff and you've got to be diplomatic. Herbert, I want your Team Beryl to be The Yard's research and co-ordination section for this French exercise, whilst Peter and Monique's Team Lingua will operate mostly over there hunting for any hidden evidence. Herbert, your people need to think hard about the recent French robberies and look for parallels and any chances for the Taylors to seek out clues. I want Peter and Monique to take their whole team to France next week, get them settled in somewhere close to the Channel and become acclimatised, but be prepared to have their brief revised as more is discovered. Your first action will be to go to the last five locations of French jewellery robberies and try to dig up something tangible that we can use as evidence when the time is right. You'll all have to be very discrete, as the French police won't know anything about this to start with. Herbert, you must expect to be called on for backup and assistance at any time that the Taylors need it. All of you must get your people to practice French as much as possible and for goodness sake don't speak English in anyone's earshot whenever you're over there. Right? If that's all OK, let's get on with!"

***

At 1.00 am on this same Thursday 31st May, Inspectors Dent and Henderson met with Superintendent Harling, "The first thing I want Teams Coral and The Pool to do is concentrate on finding out what's been going on around the world concerning jewellery crime. Kevin's team can research the Met's archives and gently communicate with foreign forces. Geoff's team will research the aptly named magazine 'Jewels Worldwide'. It's full of dodgy stuff and must have all sorts of criminal activity hidden between its pages, but where and how we don't yet know. Your job will be to look for the systems and connections contained in the nearly four years of editions of the little rag that I have here. I want you to take these away, get several copies of each, and use your eyes and brains to discover what's going on. See if you can identify any cross involvements between police records and the magazine. Report back to me next Monday afternoon with your first ideas of what's happening especially in Europe, and how the criminality in the magazines may operate. Don't be too concerned with the details but concentrate on trying to help us understand the picture."

Having gained their initial understanding about 'Jewels Worldwide', Superintendent Harling opened up another subject, "You need to understand that it isn't just The Met's new MCD that is interested in jewel robberies, but that we are working together with a Mr Aaron Klein and his team of jewellery experts from Hatton Garden just up the road from here. They know far more than any of us will ever do about gemstones and how the rich and powerful use or misuse them around the world. Mr Klein's opinion is the same as my own, that the magazine's advertisements are deliberately worded in mundane and ambiguous language, so as not to attract ordinary people who want to buy or sell jewellery, but have been designed for a very particular clientele which includes the criminal fraternity. Remember that we are searching for big-time crooks and talking about sums of money that make our salaries look like peanuts, right!"

The two inspectors took due note of 'AH's comments before he continued, "Another chap you're going to get know about is an Arab Crown Prince of his own country and Deputy Foreign Minister of the Federation of Non-aligned Arab Emirates, or FNAE to use shorthand, called Sheikh Salim bin Rashid Al Nu'masiq. This guy looks rather quiet and is certainly not an extravert, but he's moving onto the world's diplomatic stage and will be in the newspapers around the globe. He and his entourage are flying to South America and onwards at the moment, with Mr Klein and some colleagues on a combined diplomatic and jewel hunting expedition. Sheikh Salim, as he likes to be called, and Aaron Klein were both injured themselves and lost a brother in the Hatton Garden bombing, so watch out how you handle them and their dealings. I must reiterate that their actions are firmly in line with our own and are mutually necessary and beneficial. Let's get stuck in now and report back to me next week."

***

Prince Salim's party landed in Auckland at 22.45, local time, and was accommodated at the airport hotel for a brief night's rest before being returned to their aircraft for a 06.30 take-off on Friday morning. The three-hour flight to Sydney was uneventful and they landed on time, but surprisingly there were no official New South Wales or city officials to meet them. They passed through customs clearance like ordinary passengers and went to the taxi rank, from where Prince Salim and his staff went straight to the hotel that they had booked. Hasan bin Rahma and Rashid bin Mohammed accomplished some scant contact with New South Wales State's Foreign Ministry officials, with whom they had made arrangements for this official visit. They received apologies for the *'unavailability of appropriate diplomats and staff, due to abnormally severe weather reports that had necessitated their attendance at strategically important visits to locations far from Sydney'*. When they attempted to push the Foreign Ministry officials, they were advised, *'As it could not be known when normal duties might be resumed, the Prince should be advised that he could wait in the city in case an opportunity arose for a meeting towards the middle of next week'*. It was obvious to

FNAE's Deputy Foreign Minister that he was not to be welcomed or even received with any diplomatic courtesies in Sydney. However, as today was the Muslim day of rest, Prince Salim and his team of staff and pilots were not disappointed at this unexpected day of freedom from duty, relishing the chance to relax in the grounds of their hotel catching up with their drained physical, mental and spiritual needs.

***

Aaron, Ruth and Peter had taken another taxi from Sydney airport directly to the impressive Kelly Towers, Castlereagh Street, arriving only minutes before the pre-arranged 10.45 meeting with Logan Kelly. Aaron had decided that Ruth and Peter should accompany him on his visit to this Australian business man, whose offer of jewellery for sale had prompted this long tiring journey across the Pacific Ocean. They walked through the glass and chromium atrium and reported in to one of the ladies at the reception desk. She checked their appointment with Mr Kelly off on her list and told the visitors to take the lift up to the eleventh floor, but that she would come up with them as some difficulty with the lift control buttons had been occurring. As Ruth felt rather faint, her uncle suggested that she should wait downstairs for the others to return. Aaron was going through the impending meeting in his mind, thus Peter took more notice than he did of the unusual juddering of the lift and that it stopped half an inch short of the exact floor level. They were shown into Logan Kelly's palatial office and introduced to his secretary Olivia Thompson, who whispered that they must expect to have a maximum of thirty minutes with the ultra-busy tycoon. While he finished a phone call, they had time to take in the rich decorations and trappings of a powerful Australian business mogul.

"Well now, you've come a long way to look at a few jewels Mr Small! I told you that I don't take cheques, so do you have the cash with you?" That was all of the acknowledgement or welcome that the visitors received, amazing Aaron that there was no handshake or smile, just plain black and white business expected of him. Without waiting for an answer to his question, Logan Kelly called out from behind his ornate antique desk, "Thompson, fetch the jewels from the safe and put them here." The woman must have been habitually used to her boss' arrogant style so she did simply as ordered — crossed to an open wall safe and brought a package across to his desk. "Come on! Open it up woman! I haven't got all day!" She kept her eyes down and did not speak as she unwrapped the cloth and laid out some sample necklaces, brooches and individual gemstones with the engraved jewel placed amongst them. "Right, Sonny Jim, take a look and let's see your money!" Aaron kept his emotions in check as he looked down on the reality of what he had seen in a fax twelve thousand miles away in London. He had prepared for this moment and firstly picked up a bright but rather ugly emerald bracelet, then he scrutinised a flamboyant ruby necklace, both of which looked as if they could be stolen items. Aaron looked only casually at the easily recognisable topaz gemstone, noting its engraving of the Hebrew name attributable to the tribe of Issacher.

Realising that he would be no match for the tycoon's fierce business style, Aaron used his sharp initiative and ignoring Logan Kelly's words he turned and spoke formally to Peter, "Mr Templeton, please remove the small package from my briefcase and then take several photos of these jewels from directly above and various oblique angles and positions before I inspect them more closely."

The Australian was so taken aback at Aaron's firm instructions to his associate, that he only managed to mutter, "Here, what's going on Sonny Jim?" but without stopping what was happening.

While Peter moved around and complied with what he'd been told to do, Aaron spoke again, "Mr Kelly, please advise me of the prices that you are actually requesting for these items, in order for me to consider making you some offers."

The Australian leapt to his feet and shouted, "Look here Sonny Jim, you know what I wrote on the faxes as well as I do! What are you playing at? Are you going to buy any of these things or not? Speak up man!"

Again, Aaron kept his composure and replied carefully, "Mr Kelly please recognise that I am a jeweller by profession. Please remind me of the prices you are requesting for the items, before I make you an offer. The prices in your faxes are at least forty percent too high, although I am prepared to negotiate with you. However, I may accept that the engraved jewel could have a value nearer to your requested £8,000. Do you wish me to purchase only that single jewel, or are you willing to negotiate some sensible prices for the other items as well? Before you answer, let me tell you that I do not walk around city streets with large amounts of cash in my briefcase, so I would need to visit a bank and return to you this afternoon."

Logan Kelly blurted out furiously, "I knew you were a dubious scheming Jew and that you'd try something on! It will get you nowhere! Tell me what you offer for the jewels or get out of here right away!" Aaron considered quietly and looked the Australian in the eyes, "I would give you £5,500 for the emerald bracelet and £7,300 for the ruby necklace. However, concerning the engraved stone, I have an alternative offer. Mr Templeton please unwrap my jewel." Peter had not been prepared for acting out charades, but was quick to sense what was going on and joined in enthusiastically. He undid the small package and handed his 'employer' a gloriously shining deep blue sapphire gemstone. Aaron spoke firmly to Logan Kelly, "I am interested in acquiring this topaz for my private collection and I am prepared to offer you this splendid sapphire, which is of far greater value, in direct exchange. Do you accept my monetary and exchange offers or not?!"

Although Logan Kelly was known to be an obnoxious person, he was also a very quick- witted businessman who could recognise a good deal when it appeared in front of his eyes. He realised that this visiting 'Mr Small' was a professional jeweller who was not going to pay his inflated asking prices, which he believed he could obtain from some other sucker. But for him to obtain an obviously valuable gemstone, in replacement for the one spoilt by some incomprehensible scribble, must be a very good deal. He proclaimed, "For the exchange item only, I agree Small! Business done! Thompson, put the other jewellery back in the safe. Then you and these others go away and leave me to get on with some work!" There was no handshake or even a 'Goodbye' as he sat back down behind his desk, however as Aaron and Peter were going out of his office door, Logan Kelly couldn't resist a final jibe, "You might think you're a professional jeweller Sonny Jim, but you're certainly no businessman! You've just given me a gemstone worth at least two thousand pounds more than the one I've given you! It's your loss Jew boy!" His raucous laugh was the last thing that they remembered about the Australian tycoon.

Olivia Thompson escorted them back to the juddering lift, then down to the reception atrium, apologising both for her boss' arrogant nature and for the peculiar noises emanating from the lift. Ruth joined them and a taxi had them back at their hotel by midday, with the anxieties of the last hour falling swiftly from their shoulders. Peter showed the others his photos, which were even better than Aaron had hoped for, showing not only close ups of the jewels, but some wider shots that included enough of Logan Kelly, his desk and the wall safe that he had wanted. He explained that the sapphire had been in his possession for a long time, although he didn't tell even them that it had been retrieved from the shop's under-floor *saved for a rainy day* compartment. He added that although it was a decent gem, it hadn't been cut very professionally and some of the facets were at bad angles, reducing its true value considerably. "But that's almost enough of jewels and business tycoons! I need to make a phone-call right-away, then as we've come to the opposite side of the world and we deserve a little time to explore some of this great city. Let's have a second breakfast here at the hotel and ask them to arrange for a taxi tour for the whole afternoon, as long as we're back here before sundown for Shabbat Ruth, if Peter will excuse us for that please?"

***

From his sun-filled hotel room, Aaron phoned Superintendent Harling who was sleeping soundly in his bed in London, "I'm sorry it's rather late for you Alan, but I had to tell you as soon as possible that Logan Kelly is undoubtedly dealing in stolen jewellery. He hardly concealed his actions in his arrogance! I have seen items from his wall safe that are assuredly worthy of police investigation. I had young Templeton take many photos which I'll send to you shortly. Oh! and by the way, I've acquired another wonderful Aaronic jewel." Although he was very sleepy, Alan managed to tell Aaron that the police had found several instances of a Tel Aviv post office box's involvement with apparently stolen jewellery, including with Sydney.

The British visitors spent the afternoon visiting famous places in

Sydney, receiving a great surprise whilst walking around a well-known street market, when a trader called out to them in his rich Australian accent, "Say you Pommies, are you of Israel's faith like me? If so and as Shabbat starts in a couple of hours, where are you going to have the meal?" Aaron explained that he and his niece were indeed Jewish but that the young man was not, however they knew him to be a sincere Christian who had a love for Jews and Israel. That settled the invitation and at 6.00pm that evening the three of them walked up to Noah Jacobson's house and were invited inside the Jewish home as very welcome guests. It was fascinating for Peter who acted very circumspectly and was included as far as possible in the weekly celebration of God's goodness to Jews in particular, and which they could extend to all persons who called on God's name with an honest heart. That late evening the three visitors walked back to their hotel tired but very happy.

***

It was much earlier half-way across the world on that same Friday when 'AH' arrived in his office, to be handed copies of Peter Templeton's photos taken at Kelly Towers. If Aaron Klein was convinced of the criminal background to Logan Kelly's activities, it was his professional duty to let the Australian police know of that possibility. The superintendent pondered about making an over-hasty decision, yet believed that he should contact someone in Sydney who had a similar role to his own. Using his new authority and growing political awareness, he composed a straightforward report, including several photographs, and sent this by fax marked 'Urgent and strictly private: For the attention of the Police Commander, Sydney.'

***

"Excuse me Sir," asked Inspector Dent. "I've been thinking about these *'Jewels Worldwide'* magazines that we're investigating. It would be very worthwhile if we could obtain any further editions as soon as they are published. Could that be arranged without causing undue attention please?" 'AH' recognised the wisdom in the proposal. He phoned Joshua Shulz and asked him to confer with Alice Glover about regularly collecting any new incoming mail and faxes to the post office in Acton. They suggested that a note addressed to the PO manager adding young Rashid Halleem to those persons entitled to have access to Box Number 273 would suffice, and that he could call in there that late afternoon. Thus, at 4.30 that afternoon, Rashid walked up to the PO counter, smiled and presented his note of authorisation with quiet confidence. The clerk read it carefully before stating in an unequivocal voice, "Certainly not! How could any official be assured of the validity of a hand-written note like that! How ridiculous to have given your address as the same that the original box number customer had! It's unbelievable! Any such request must be made in person and with proper proof of identity. Goodbye!"

***

Prince Salim joined his travelling guests at the Sydney hotel for breakfast on Saturday morning, giving them some surprising news, "The state government of Western Australia and the city council of Perth heard that we are in Australia and have sent us an impromptu invitation for us to visit them. I said 'us' because you three are invited just as much as myself, due to your exploits in Montevideo which became world-wide news! It is suggested that if we wished to fly to Perth today, they would be pleased to meet and talk with us, before we fly back towards the Middle East. What would you think my friends?" Aaron considered the traditional restrictions of travelling on Shabbat and asked if flying could be delayed until early evening. Salim, who welcomed that idea which would allow his staff some time to see a little more of Sydney, instructed Captain Najm to check with airport authorities and advise on the best timings. When his chief pilot reported that they could take off at 6pm for a four-hour flight to Perth, the Prince and his guests agreed willingly. Hasan bin Rahma and Rashid bin Mohammed were told to thank the officials in Perth and request that some private informal meetings might be arranged for tomorrow, even though that would be Sunday. Thus, their short stay in Sydney ended in late afternoon, when the Prince's aircraft took off as arranged, to fly from the east coast to the west of this vast country.

***

It had been earlier that Saturday when Chief Superintendent Tony Birde of New South Wales' police force was interrupted at his desk by an officer bearing a fax of several pages, placed in an official 'private and confidential' folder. Birde enjoyed the relative peace of working on occasional Saturday mornings at his office. He opened the folder intriguingly, to find a totally unexpected report from a Superintendent Harling far across the world in England. As he read the polite but boldly stated accusations concerning a well-known and powerful Sydney tycoon, based solely on the opinions of a Pommy jeweller, his mind became alert. How dare such Brits make such a pointed suggestion about someone that they did not know! Yet, surely, no highly-ranked professional police officer would dare to write what he was reading unless convinced of its truth? Birde knew that he would be putting his own head on the political block if he took any action, but equally he knew very well that Kelly Towers had a totally unproved reputation for not being quite as honest as its image portrayed. He put the papers back into the folder, locked them in his desk and went home to his family, but with ideas failing resolutely to disappear from his professional mind.

***

At 8.00pm local time, the plane landed at Perth and was directed to taxi to the area immediately in front of the terminal building, which appeared to be festooned in lights. When the plane's automatic steps were lowered and the door was opened, music could be heard from just outside. Salim sensed that he should quickly muster his Arabs into an entourage worthy of a Nation's Crown Prince and a desert sheikh, so grinning to Aaron and the young people, he walked to the top of the steps and stood in a dignified pose for any waiting cameramen. The smiling shairman of Perth City Council, accompanied by the Vice-President of Western Australia, welcomed Prince Salim onto the tarmac just as the military band finished its hastily-practiced rendition of FNAE's rather unknown national anthem. "Well Sir, Mr Sheikh, Prince, we're just delighted to welcome you to our city and our state. It's an honour to have you with us, Sir, so far away from your homeland!" Almost before the relaxed salutes and warm handshakes were completed, Salim knew that he had been right to come to places that were important, but not most important, in the southern hemisphere. FNAE was a very small nation in size and prestige when compared to global players, thus Prince Salim believed that he had found a kindred spirit on the tarmac of Western Australia's premier airport.

The visitors were whisked off in Range Rovers to a smart hotel, all booked and paid for by their hosts, and asked to convene around the hotel's outdoor pool for festivities and talks to begin. Because Australians like week-ending, they simply included the Arabs and the accompanying Brits in their own favourite activities: chatting, eating, drinking and in general having a relaxed informal time together. As they enjoyed the copious amounts of barbequed food, there were ample occasions for discussions of significant practical importance, which enabled so much more to be achieved by an absence of any stuffiness. Aaron, Ruth and Peter were welcomed as famous celebrities, having been seen on TV during the debacle in Montevideo, which had delighted the Aussies' temperament. These Western Australians might be considered in some more sophisticated eastern circles as being nothing but illiterate cowboys, yet nothing was further from the truth. Perth was a fine city with excellent educational and cultural facilities, which they loved to show off to northern hemisphere folk. Local people were more keen on moral and ethical aspects, than on 'politically correct' talk, being firmly on the side of honesty and tolerance, deploring the media's insistence on hyping up news to set one community of persons against another. They had loved the exposure of lackadaisical and intolerant local Montevideo cops, and vigorously applauded Peter's use of a big black Bible to fell a MOSSAD hit-man! They insisted on seeing the marks made by handcuffs on Aaron and Peter, and fell in love with the demure and delightfully misnamed 'Ruthy Neese'.

Saturday evening somehow turned into Sunday, with little time lost to sleep as Perth's councillors and senior officials, plus WA State representatives and business leaders, used all available time to seek opportunities for joint advantages of diplomacy, trade and culture between their so very different nations. A common factor came to light on Sunday afternoon when some state agricultural officials and Perth politicians happened to be discussing sheep grazing, of such fundamental importance to WA. Sheikh Salim asked Peter to join in the discussions by outlining the principles of his self-irrigation plant propagation. His idea wasn't laughed at or dismissed as a schoolboy dream, but caused great interest amongst people to whom the equation 'sheep need grass which needs water' was one of their major economic considerations. Sunday night allowed only a few hours rest for the visitors before Monday morning's slightly more formal meetings endorsed the '*welcome friend*' status for the FNAE. Many future connections were set up and the Arabs' briefcases were packed with business cards, commercial and cultural literature and small samples of Western Australian products. It was a great leave taking with the Prince's entire party escorted to the airport and given honestly grateful thanks for their visit. The aircraft took off at 1.00 p.m. to begin its long journey north towards India, with all but the pilots seeking some greatly needed sleep on the seven and a half hours flight to Mumbai.

***

Early on the previous Thursday 31st May, two cars had left a few minutes apart from Scotland Yard heading north to start a terrorist hunt. Their occupants were excited at the prospect and keen to uncover the evil that was behind a normal, decent young man becoming an advertisement for religious hatred and murder, cynically stated to be 'in God's name'.

Sergeant Waseem Patel drove one unmarked police car with DPC Salmud Jones sitting next to him, incongruous with his brown skin, strong Welsh accent and chirpy sense of humour, all gained in his Merthyr Tydfil homeland where he had been raised by his Afghan mother and Welsh father. In the back was DPC Benjamin Jacobs who came from Whitechapel in London's East End and looked about as Jewish as anyone could. His upbringing had been amongst the street markets and very mixed cultures of that very cosmopolitan area of London, where he went through the earlier years of defending himself and his faith with his fists until he settled into being something of a social reformer for peoples of all sorts of distinct backgrounds. Next to Ben was DPC Hippy Ipperstaff, a very sincere and determined detective, who was quite unable to hide his New Age Traveller dreamy looks, even though his meticulous brain and enormous heart were totally committed to upholding the Queen's Regulations. The four men alternated between laughing at each other's corny jokes and discussing strategies for their surveillance mission of unknown duration. They skirted around Birmingham and joined the M6 heading north until turning off into Walsall, driving sedately along Long Street before pulling up fifty yards away from The Railway Hotel. Waseem let his men out, giving them a cheery 'Goodbye chaps!' before driving away, crossing the motorway to his selected Travel Lodge.

The second car had been driven by Nella Brown, a typical English Rose from the Home Counties, with the Yorkshire lass Gail Tandridge sitting next to her. They drove straight up the M1 to Birmingham before making their way north to a Travel Inn in the south of Walsall. The two DWPCs booked in, making very sure that the receptionist noted their boxes and bags advertising a range of mediocre cosmetics, the aroma of which hung in the air around them both. They chatted enthusiastically about the marketing campaign that they would be setting up in this part of The Midlands. After a quick snack together nearby, they returned to their room where Gail laid down to rest whilst Nella sat alert at the room's desk to start her midday to midnight shift. She prepared a new log book, recording her first entries with the exact timings of leaving The Yard, their own arrival in Walsall and the first calls of the others who were spread around the city. She reported all of this to Gudakesha Mazumbar, their Team Empathy's liaison officer back at Scotland Yard, who settled down to begin entries in his own carefully prepared record book of communications.

Jones, Jacobs and Ipperstaff booked in, laughing and making enough commotion as possible for the musty old Railway Hotel's staff to take notice of, acting as over-loud sales reps for a London-based wines and spirits importers intent on opening up some Midlands franchises. They had already sorted out their eight-hour rota before they arrived, thus Jacobs and Ipperstaff wandered together down to the local Subway Food

Bar, while Jones took the opening shift which included his first walk around Swarthy's new neighbourhood. The suspect, who was known to be still using his Harrow name of Mustafa Zakarian, had rented a photocopier shop and lived in a flat above it with his wife or 'sister' Yeraz. This was not far from the Lidl supermarket, in whose customer car-park Jones spotted Swarthy's Toyota Auris hatchback X 277 BSB. Assuming that this meant that Zakarian was at home, Salmud Jones strolled down Ablewell Street and went idly into the 'Aroma Cafe'. He was an expert at making a cup of coffee last a very long time, so he sat at a window table reading a local newspaper, whilst he carefully watched the entrance to the photocopier shop, just as Sergeant Patel had been doing only a fortnight before. Waseem himself was setting out to meet people near his Travel Lodge, overjoyed at being back on street work as a real detective hunting down serious criminals. It was a wonderful relief after such a long time in Hertfordshire, trying to separate an endless stream of drunken domestic disputants. Although he wanted keenly to be closer to Swarthy's base in Walsall, he recognised the wisdom of discretion. He contrived some gentle discussions with locals about mosques in Walsall, becoming amazed when told that there were twenty-three of these, some of which were thriving and very popular.

Apart from having Swarthy's photograph, and knowing his current name and married status, all they really knew about him was what had been suggested by Peter Taylor's handwriting interpretation. That he was probably aged about forty, was clever but not highly educated, had the typical dominant and aggressive nature of a bad manager, and was a fluent liar. So far, the police had been unable to identify the man beyond that. The DVLA had revealed that his car was registered in the name of Yeraz Zakarian at an address in Hounslow. It was presumed that Swarthy had had a string of temporary homes before those known to be in Rayners Lane and now Walsall. Other agencies reported that no passports or driving licences had been issued in the names of Mustafa or Yeraz Zakarian.

By Saturday, Team Empathy had begun to record some definite facts about Swarthy's current movements. That morning his car had been followed from the Lidl car-park to a suburb of Birmingham where Swarthy had met and talked briefly with two young Asian men. After that, he had driven to an Islamic bookshop in the north of the city, staying inside for forty-five minutes before emerging with a large package and driving back to Walsall. Swarthy had parked back at the Lidl supermarket, strolled right along Ablewell Street, looking casually in the windows of the many shops, businesses and cafes, before crossing the street and doing the same thing all the way back to his photocopier shop. While he had been away, Yeraz Zakarian had spent the whole time in the shop dealing with a handful of customers, one of whom had been an incongruous New Age Traveller type. That dreamer had looked casually around the small shop whilst waiting for his complicated copying order to be finished. Hippy Ipperstaff's keen observation skills noted two large zipped-up rucksacks stacked on the floor, next to several strong cardboard boxes that unusually were of neither A3 nor A4 size. He mentally recorded the layout of the shop and as much of the store-room behind it as he could see into. Outside, he observed the grubby entrance-way next to the shop door, with name labels and door-opening buttons for the six flats, presumably reached by internal stairs up to the three floors above pavement level. Everything was being recorded meticulously.

***

On Monday 4th June in Sydney, Chief Superintendent Tony Birde had summoned two of his highly trusted inspectors to meet him well away from their offices, in the Centennial Park. That was where he disclosed a little from his urgently requested Sunday afternoon briefing with his boss, one of NSW's deputy police commissioners, which took place during their 'accidental' encounter at the Waverley Cemetery. "This is to be kept so close that no-one else could even sniff at what we're going to do at 9am tomorrow morning. You two will accompany me to the well-known Kelly Towers on Castlereagh Street, where we will request an interview with that big noise, Logan Kelly. If he wants to co-operate: all well and good; but if he storms off at me, just use your eyes and ears and try to remember his exact words and actions. Information has come our way that he may be involved in dealing with stolen goods, of extremely high value. This will be a courtesy call on him, rather than an official enquiry, at least at this stage. Is that clear?" The Australian officers hid their surprise and trepidation as they acknowledged the order.

***

Back at Walsall, Hippy reported that at 11.05 on Monday morning the photocopier shop had been locked up and a notice placed on the door stating that it would be closed between 11am and 1pm. Salmud Jones, who was waiting in the car-park in case Swarthy would be driving somewhere, was summoned as soon as Hippy realised that the Zakarians were walking intently downhill along Ablewell Street. It was as well that he did this, because soon afterwards Jones was able to watch the couple enter the separate men's and women's entrances to a mosque just off Corporation Street, where a New Ager would probably be easily spotted as an intruder. Swarthy and his wife returned to their shop at 12.50 and re-opened it for business shortly afterwards.

At 5.00pm, Swarthy emerged carrying the two large rucksacks that had been spotted by DPC Ipperstaff. He took them out to the flats' communal entranceway, unlocked the front door and carried them apparently upstairs. A few minutes later he came out, walked unhurriedly to his car, and drove back along the same route as last Saturday, all the way to the same Birmingham suburb. This time he was observed collecting the two young Asian men who he had met previously. They put their big rucksacks into the Toyota's boot and the three men drove to Walsall, parked back at Lidl's and walked down Ablewell Street to the entrance door next to the shop, where Swarthy took them upstairs to the flat above. At 8.15 p.m., two more young Asian men approached the doorway, rang the doorbell and were admitted immediately to the flats.

***

Later on that Monday 4th June afternoon Alice Glover made a further visit to UCLH to visit Christine Templeton. Having been briefed by the nurse to expect changes and to restrict her visit to ten minutes maximum, Alice was still shocked as she entered Room 604 and sat quietly on the bedside chair. She reached out to take Christine's better hand, "My dear it is so good to visit you once again. I mustn't stay long, but is there anything particular that I can do for you?" Alice needed to concentrate her hearing acutely to glean the whispered reply, "Pray, Mrs Glover. Pray."

The elderly lady felt totally inadequate and very fearful, yet knew that she must obey not in her own inadequate strength, but in the God-given authority as a believer in his son Jesus Christ. "Lord Jesus, you tell us to ask for our needs to be fulfilled and Miss Templeton needs to be healed. You promise to answer us and I thank you for the total healing that you will soon bring to this dearly-loved lady. Amen." There was no obvious response from the bed as Mrs Glover crept tearfully from the room.

CHAPTER 12

Salim, Aaron, Ruth and Peter had mixed emotions as their plane left Australia on Monday afternoon and set its course for India. Salim believed that he had accomplished his official mission by establishing good relationships and future opportunities in Uruguay and its capital city Montevideo, also in Western Australia and its capital Perth. Aaron sat contemplating his achievements: inspecting but failing to acquire two of the Aaronic jewels in Montevideo, his short term in jail after trying to defend a bitter old man from a MOSSAD executioner, the man's subsequent vicious stroke and lonely death, the meeting with an equally anti-Semitic Australian business tycoon from whom he'd purchased the Aaronic topaz now in his pocket, the Shabbat evening shared in Sydney and the good-natured people of Perth. Ruth dwelt mainly on her time with Leticia, wondering if they would ever meet again, and really hoping so. Peter, who had received the bad news from UCLH, prayed that he would arrive back in London in time to see his Aunt Christine before she died.

The long journey back to the FNAE required a refuelling stop, which was planned to be at Mumbai, but reports of adverse weather conditions there, persuaded Captain Hakim Najm to bring this forward, possibly to the city of Mangalore in south-west India. The airport there was radioed and the refuelling was agreed willingly and arranged for approximately 4 p.m. local time. Salim invited Aaron to join him in reflecting on the discussions that he had been having with the two young Britons, "It has surprised my intellect and gladdened my heart Aaron, to listen to the far-sighted views of Ruth and Peter. Where have they acquired such wisdom at their age my friend? How can they have learnt about things which I never did in my youth?" Aaron smiled and added, "Nor me in mine Salim! Although I have known and loved Ruth since the day that she was born, it staggers me that my only niece has risen to such maturity. Together with her Aunt Esther, my unmarried sister, she has been holding our family together since the bombing. Ruth's mother and younger brother have just gone to pieces. But what about Peter Templeton, Salim, is there anything worthwhile in his botanical theories or are they just youthful dreams?"

The Sheikh replied earnestly, "Well he does not talk nonsense, although he cannot yet know enough about biology in general, or botany in detail, to have made sound propositions. However, he has something that post-graduate researchers often fail to aspire to: confidence and zeal. Why hasn't somebody already had his ideas to consider the technical viability of growing crops in a desert, rather than just dismissing the idea? Why shouldn't a plant capable of producing hydrogen be assisted to mix that with the oxygen in air to produce even in a miniscule amount of water? Why shouldn't one variety of plant give protection and sustenance to an entirely different one? Such are the questions going around my botanically-trained mind. My country has no running water or any coastline. Soon you will see that it is more or less nothing other than sand and sunshine. If anybody needs his idea to work it would be the FNAE, so why shouldn't I put some effort into testing his boyish theories? But a bigger question for us friend Aaron, is what are we going to do with these two great young people, to stop them losing their zeal before university life swamps them with its disciplines and temptations?"

Aaron's cautious answer, 'Ruth's ideas about religion are not so easy to define or consider are they?' caused the Sheikh to speak determinedly to his friend, "If you and I were to propose a private discussion on comparabilities and differences between our faiths, would we accept the invitation or shy away because of its sensitivity? If we were not courageous enough to talk about such things together, then nobody would be. You're a Jew and I'm a Muslim, but if we chose to discuss Jesus Christ, would it be safe or would you hold a hidden dagger to my throat and would I rattle my scimitar in your face?"

Aaron asked solemnly, "Would you promise not to evangelise me, or make nonsense of my opinions, if I did the same for you?"

Salim smiled, "Yes, my friend. I promise not to win!"

They both laughed as Aaron responded, "That was a very Jewish joke for a Muslim to make!"

After some light refreshments had been brought to them, the Sheikh continued, "Well friend, Aaron, do you believe in Jesus Christ?"

Aaron smiled and replied, "I'm sorry to call a 'Point of Order' right away, but that's an erroneous question! The use of the word 'believe' can cover a multitude of meanings. If you are asking if I believe that a person with the name of Jesus of Nazareth existed and moved around Israel teaching and preaching, 2000 years ago, and afterwards was referred to as 'the Christ'; then my answer is an unequivocal 'Yes'. However, if your question meant *'Do you believe that this Jesus was the son of God and remains alive today?'* then I would answer 'No'. What if I posed the same question to you Salim?"

He replied, "My answer would be very similar to your own Aaron."

Salim was struck by the force of Aaron's pointed additional question: "Then please will you explain your reasoning?" The Muslim Prince spoke without emotion, "Almighty God, in whom I have absolute faith, is 'One' and cannot be divided or substituted for. He is supreme and only he is God. He has no son. However, the man Jesus was a revered prophet and has great respect amongst Muslims."

Aaron kept himself calm as he responded, "Our Jehovah is God of the Jews, but Jesus was only a man, perhaps a very good and worthy man, but he does not have respect or acknowledgement amongst very many Jews. Jehovah is the one and only Almighty God. He operates in body and by his spirit, which moves with divine power in individual people's lives. Jehovah is not part of a triune God as insisted on by Christians, but is an omnipotent existence."

The two men stared at each other. "But do you see what we have done Aaron? Each of us used religious words to make doctrinal statements with no attempt to answer as individuals. If we continued like that, we would soon become heated in defence of our own causes, which we must not do my friend. Ruth's honest questions deserve answers from a person's heart, not just intellectual statements from any faith group."

Aaron agreed, "Yes Salim, I admit that I was speaking 'as a Jew' rather than revealing what is in my heart and mind. How could we attempt to answer such profound questions ourselves and encourage younger persons to do the same?"

They concluded that it would be better initially to educate each other about their faith's beliefs, without giving personal opinions. "Surely, our lives must show our faith, if they demonstrate the principles in which we truly believe?" suggested Salim.

"And without trying to conquer each other." responded Aaron. "Because if I insist that I am absolutely right, then I'm declaring that you are completely wrong, which is an insult to your chosen belief."

Salim added, "Yes, friend, we must find an approach of respecting opinions without judgement, perhaps focussing more on acknowledgement and understanding, rather than dictating opinions. Could that help other persons to tolerate each other's culture and faith? Have you noticed that Ruth and Peter and Rashid have no difficulty in helping each other as they carry out the terrible task we have allotted to them: of sorting through boxes containing the remains of their beloved murder victims mixed in with broken glass and wonderful jewels?"

Aaron answered, "Absolutely and I am also filled with joy that Mrs Glover and Joshua Shulz could overcome their prejudices to the extent of choosing to have flats in the same house, when Mr Glover would never even have spoken to Joshua, or you or me either! Surely we must do all we can to follow their wonderful example."

***

As soon as the aircraft had landed at Mangalore, the passengers were invited by airport officials to disembark and stretch their legs, but told that it was forbidden for them to enter any buildings. Aaron, Ruth and Peter were very grateful for this respite from so much sitting inside the aeroplane. They strolled across the tarmac onto the scrubby brown grass alongside the perimeter fence feeling secure and peaceful, until they realised that the fence held back a crowd of impoverished people looking with despair towards them, stretching-out malnourished hands and crying out for alms. It was a shock for the comfortably-off Europeans to be in such close proximity to a hundred or more of the World's far greater proportion of the extreme poor, separated only by the sturdy steel mesh fence, topped out with razor wire to stop it being scaled. They moved hesitantly along with compassionate thoughts, but unknowing what if anything they should do for those people pleading passionately for help. About fifty yards along the fence a concrete wall prevented any beggars from going any further around the airport. Aaron, Ruth and Peter walked silently on, struck by the sight and smell of that portion of humanity which was made just as much in God's image as themselves, but found itself on the wrong side of life's fence.

Clustered up in the corner against the concrete wall, a group of three decrepit beggars, slightly separated from the rest, stared at them with eyes full of unreadable emotions. One was a scrawny youngish man with his body covered in open sores and wearing only a loin-cloth to hide his nakedness. There was a girl or woman of unfathomable age, maybe ten or maybe thirty, equally repulsive to look at, but with the additional horror of a missing left forearm. The last of this motley trio, which seemed to have some inter-relationship, was a man with a thin grey beard whose upper face was hidden under the filthy blanket that draped his body. The woman spoke first, "Missy Ruth, will you hold my hand?" Ruth Klein shivered convulsively at hearing her own name mentioned.

She dropped to her knees and reached her fingers through the fence to the offered hand, without any fear. The scrawny young man held out a scrap of paper towards Peter, "Kefa, Kefa, take this to Doctor Shuban. He will need it very soon. Afterwards, you must be a rock for your generation." Peter's mouth fell open as he took the dirty folded up note, realising that he and Ruth were each now holding filthy fingers.

With pounding hearts and trembling voices, they whispered, "Thank you."

The older beggar spoke, "My children and I have waited many months for your arrival. My great-great-great-grandfather was a high maharajah and presented the Great Empress with the pair of exquisite jewels that you must wear on your shoulders. Her descendant queen is keeping them safe, ready for you to ask her for them. Look down now at my hands and do not fear at what you see." Aaron looked down and saw the beggar's mutilated hands, with holes pierced right through them. He spoke again, throwing back his blanket to reveal a bony face with a wickedly hooked nose and without eyes: only empty sockets. "Will you look upon my face, son of Abraham?" It was the most hideous face that Aaron had ever seen, with scarred and bleeding cheeks and jaw, above an emaciated neck and chest covered in festering sores. There was nothing of beauty or attractiveness in the man, in fact only the extreme opposite of revulsion, yet Aaron listened respectfully as his articulate voice continued, "You must leave us here Rabbi Aaron, but take this old stone with you for a remembrance of us. It has belonged to my family for many generations and is now for you to use. You will recognise it as a moonstone and it is a blessing for your people." He pushed a translucent pale green jewel through the rusty wires to Aaron, who realised that Hasan bin Rahma was hovering discretely behind them, as he found sufficient composure to reply, "What shall we do? What can we say? We thank you so much, but we do not understand. If we give you money would that be of help to you?" The beggar spoke with quiet authority, "Money would be a hindrance to us Rabbi. Before your aircraft could take off, we would be attacked and robbed by the others on our side of the fence. No, it is not your money that we are beggars for, but your hearts. You cannot change our circumstances with your money or power, but only through your hearts. Tell the prince that you have all been entrusted with a great work, which will bring you many friends and enemies. You must not try to understand everything about this pathway, but simply persevere in your decisions and follow what your hearts tell you to do. Yours are voices calling out to this desolate world, as from a desert. People will listen to what you say and many will follow your directions. What you can do for them is the same as you can do for us, who must stay here on this side of the fence: look at us with recognition, try to understand and tolerate us, then support and love us. Soon you will be safely home in your own countries, surrounded by comforts, but first you must overcome an ordeal. Now go and continue what you have started, but tell the prince that he must go higher. Make him understand! Farewell!"

***

Captain Najm set Flight GL 17's compass to 280 degrees for the expected three and a half hours flight to Dubai's international airport. He climbed steadily out above the Arabian Sea, put the aircraft into automatic mode at an altitude of 28,000 feet and began to relax. In the air-conditioned luxury of the cabin behind his and his co-pilot's ultra-modern cockpit, which bristled with the latest technology that the aeronautical industry could offer, the prince's staff noticed that their sheikh and his guests had graver looks and more dignified postures since they had left Mangalore, and needed some undisturbed time together.

It was at 17.30, as they were about to leave Indian airspace, that the co-pilot drew his captain's attention to something unusual on the long-distance radar screen. A tiny dot appeared at the very extremity of the dial, apparently in line with their course. The two highly experienced pilots kept their eye on the screen as each repetitive circling highlighted the dot ahead of them. The captain spoke over his radio to North-West Indian air traffic control centre at Jamnagar, who reported that they could see nothing that far out on their screens. He contacted southern-Pakistan's equivalent based at Karachi next, who said the same thing.

Captain Najm estimated that the dot was about three hundred and twenty miles distant and was on their exactly opposite course. He told the co-pilot to keep a time check on the radar blip and work out the speed of the plane coming towards them, while he tried to find out from air traffic control at Muscat in Oman what they had seen going through their air space. Just as he was about to radio them, Muscat began putting out an urgent message: *"Warning to all aircraft flying over the north-central area of the Arabian Sea, sectors 62 to 67 easting with 15 to 20 northing. Beware of unidentified aircraft flying on course 60 degrees at altitude of 20,000 feet. That aircraft is not responding to our calls."* Captain Najm used his internal intercom, sending for the Prince's Head of Security Ahmed bin Sultan, who rushed to the cockpit, "Get everyone back in their seats and belted up quickly. Warn them that I may be taking evasive action to avoid an unidentified aircraft flying towards us. Go!"

The co-pilot gave his timing results, "Sir, it appears to be travelling at 900 mph which at our current airspeed of 500 gives us a closing speed of 1,400 mph. Estimated distance apart now is 275 miles which is twelve minutes, Sir."

The Captain snapped a reply, "That's beyond commercial aircraft speed, which means it must be military. What on earth is it doing?" Just then a further message came in from Oman's Air Traffic control, *"Danger! The object is believed not to be an aircraft. Possibility of a guided missile. Danger! Repeat Danger! All aircraft flying in sectors 63 to 66 easting with 16 to 19 northing take immediate avoiding action. Move outside of those sectors.* **Repeat! Danger!**'

Captain Najm responded in a clear voice that did not show his rising concerns, "Aircraft GL 17 calling Oman ATC - I am in those sectors. What is the object's height? Urgent! Over!" He received an instant reply, *"Object now at 23,000 feet and climbing."* The Captain hesitated to cause panic to his passengers but realised that they must be informed, "This is Captain Najm speaking to all passengers and crew. There is an unidentified object flying directly towards us, which may be a missile. Remain belted into your seats and await further instructions."

Prince Salim remembered some of the words relayed to him by Aaron less than an hour before, spoken by the elder beggar, *"Soon you will be safely home in your own Countries, surrounded by comforts, but first you must overcome an ordeal... you have all been entrusted with a great work which will bring you many friends and enemies... do not try to understand everything... persevere in your decisions and follow what your hearts tell you to do."* The Sheikh prayed briefly then unfastened his seat belt and walked steadily forwards to the aircraft's cockpit. He was admitted immediately, "Captain Najm, fly higher... now... much higher... that is an order." The pilots knew that they had the authority to argue against and disobey any passenger who was in their care, whosoever he was, but they also knew themselves to be their Sheikh's soldiers who were expected to do or die under his direct orders.

Captain Najm turned in his seat, reaching for the controls as he responded, "Yes, Sir... climbing now, Sir!" The Sheikh quickly returned to his seat, fastened his seatbelt and steadied himself for whatever would come. The Captain's voice came over the intercom, "We are now at 29,000 feet and climbing... the missile is 30 miles distant and climbing after us... I am going higher and turning 90 degrees to starboard... brace yourselves!" The aeroplane rarely performed such a manoeuvre even on training flights, but now it proved its capabilities, along with those of its pilots. "Now at 29,500 feet heading due north... missile is 5 miles distant at 27,000 feet... be ready!" No-one knew exactly what was in Hakim

Najm's mind when he used those words, and then he spoke again, "29,700... missile 2 miles away at 28,000." A few tense seconds later he continued, "We are at 29,900... horizontal collision point reached and passed... missile has dropped behind us to 26,000." Those inside the cabin calmed themselves and listened attentively as they heard their Captain speaking over the radio, "This is Captain Hakim Najm of flight GL 17 calling all ATC centres surrounding Arabian Sea... urgent... we have avoided collision with a missile which could not reach our height of 29,900 feet... we are returning now to our scheduled course and altitude... missile appears to be falling quickly... request others to locate missile's point of entry to sea... anticipated to be 65 easting with 18 northing... all from Flight GL 17... out!"

It was not until they had arrived safely at Dubai's International Airport, only 30 minutes behind schedule at 18.00 local time, that the facts became clear. The relief at being back in their Middle Eastern environment, and so close to their own Country, was a much-needed boost to the tired Arabs who wanted home and familiarity much more than newness and excitement. Prince Salim went down the aircraft's steps to be greeted by his father the Emir, the Chairman of FNAE's Crown Princes and the Foreign Secretary. Dignified salaams were given as Aaron, Peter and Ruth were introduced and welcomed. Chauffeurs bowed the visitors into their cars, but Salim spoke softly to his father before turning back to the steps of GL 17. He waited on the tarmac whilst his staff straightened their ruffled clothes and came down to join him. Many observers witnessed Sheikh Salim shaking each by the hand and giving them his personal thanks for their care and attention during the round the world trip of such significance to their Country. The last to come down, having shut down the aircraft's final systems, were the two pilots. Captain Hakim Najm answered his Prince's kind words with a short statement, "Sheikh Salim. Today, I flew your aeroplane nearly 1,000 feet higher than its designed maximum altitude of 29,000 feet. Let it be known that, at your command, I would have flown up to the heavens above, because today you heard directly from Almighty God."

***

Within an hour, the Europeans had their first experience of the Federation of Non-aligned Arab Emirates' hospitality, at a sumptuous feast served in modern desert tents, prepared in honour of the Crown Prince's return from battle. "Father!" salaamed Salim, "Let us build our own Federation's airport and not rely upon Dubai to send and receive us!"

The emir smiled back, "Welcome home my beloved son of giant thoughts! May I ask how such an enterprise could be built and sustained in our desert land without any river or lake of its own?"

Salim smiled, "Father, all will be revealed in due course of time, because Almighty God has sent persons to me with the solution to that and other dilemmas. But first, what news awaits me Father?"

The Emir's expression changed to a serious note, "When your aircraft began sending out messages of something travelling towards you at great speed, it did not take us long to think that intrigue was involved. I sent men to our military airbase where they discovered several of our armed forces imprisoned in their own barracks. They rushed to the secure zone and found your elder brother Hamad bin Rashid who had himself launched a missile intending to bring down your aircraft. His plan had awaited only the exact timing and route of your journey back to the Middle East. The murderous traitor attempting your assassination was offered a loaded revolver for his own use, which he complied with immediately." Salim nodded and said, "It is good that Hamad did not know the technical abilities of our missiles, Father, including their maximum achievable height."

Salim's staff and servants had no difficulty with providing for Aaron and Peter, but the equal status shown by the Sheikh to the teenaged girl Ruth was an enormous challenge for them. As a measure of her maturity and wisdom, Ruth did all that she could to alleviate any embarrassments and uncertainties that were bound to occur in her entering a male preserve, being modest in her ways of behaviour as well as dress code. She was exceptionally careful to show honour to her Uncle Aaron and young friend Peter, as well as to Salim and his father the emir, winning over the minds and hearts of many previously set-in-stone people. She knew very well that she could behave rather differently when back at Golder's Green, curled up on one end of the sofa with her beloved uncle at the other end!

***

Earlier on Monday, Rashid Halleem and his father collected Alice Glover and Joshua Shulz from Acton Town tube station and drove them straight to the post office. They went to the box number counter where the regular assistant greeted them, "It's so nice to see you again Mrs Glover! It's been a long time." Alice returned her greetings and introduced those accompanying her, placing the form on the counter, requesting that Rashid's name be added to the account for Box 273. "But Mrs Glover, surely there is a mistake, because you've put your own address where we need the young man's." The Halleems produced their driving licenses, bank books and even the title deeds to Mrs Glover's old home, satisfying the PO clerk officially, but without much comprehension of the recent strange re-arrangements. "Well, yes. Everything appears to be in order. In fact, something came into your box number before we opened this morning. I'll just get it for you." She returned bearing three recent incoming faxes plus today's' addition of the just-published edition of 'Jewels Worldwide'. "I'll look forward to seeing the young man from time to time then. Goodbye Mrs Glover."

The party went next to the house on Bollo Lane, where Mrs Halleem insisted on them trying her just-cooked highly-spiced delicacies, whilst Joshua was given a quick tour of the premises. It was Rashid who looked first at the magazine and drew Joshua's attention to a previously unseen advertisement: *'Ruby cabochon available immediately for purchase in US Dollars cash only. Very old jewel with inscription in ancient writing. Perm Box Number 621.'* "It sounds as if it could be one of the gemstones that Mr Aaron has not yet recovered. If so, it would represent the regal tribe of Judah, but where is Perm?" Fatima's school atlas was fetched and the city of Perm was discovered to be in Russia, about seven hundred and fifty miles roughly east of Moscow. It was agreed that Mr Aaron should be notified quickly about the advertisement, thus Rashid's phone was used and very soon Joshua was explaining the situation to Aaron Klein. He thought very quickly and dictated a response there and then. Alice wrote it meticulously on a blank fax form, as follows: *'To Perm Box No. 621. Am interested in inscribed ruby. Send details and asking price. Box 273 Acton, England.*' Rashid returned quickly to the post office and smiled politely whilst the puzzled clerk checked over the proffered fax requested for immediate dispatch.

***

On Tuesday morning, Aaron, Ruth and Peter had time at last to describe to Salim their phenomenal encounter with the beggars at Mangalore airport, beginning with Ruth, "How could that woman have known my name? Was there any significance in her having an amputated left arm?" Salim and Aaron recalled only too well the incident at the Klein's shop, but had not yet heard of Alan Harling's note passed to him from his daughter Emily. Ruth continued, "Why did the younger beggar call you 'Kefa' Peter and go on about you being a 'rock'? Why did he give you something for a Doctor Shuban? Who is he and what have you got to give him?" Peter explained the words used by Jesus Christ as recorded in the Bible's New Testament, but he was mystified about the note saying '*Koelreuteria paniculata*' to give to someone unknown called Doctor Shuban. Salim took the pencilled note, recognising it as a botanical name, and recalled that Shuban meant 'brilliant or gifted', "Peter, that is the personal name of UCLH's Head of Explosive Injuries Department Doctor Chaudhary. Undoubtedly the note is connected with your aunt's dramatically failing health and you must give it to him urgently."

Salim listened attentively as Aaron recounted what the hideous-looking older beggar had said, then expostulated, "Surely the 'Great Empress' must refer to Britain's Queen Victoria whose descendant is your current Queen Elizabeth. She must know about those particular two shoulder jewels and somehow must be expecting you to ask her for them! Such thoughts would be incredible my friend, except that we are seeing Almighty God's hands at work throughout your quest! Are you surprised that the beggar was so disfigured and that he referred to you as Rabbi?"

Aaron felt an embarrassment that he had not experienced previously. "I have always seen myself as a plain and ordinary man, destined to pass unnoticed through life, much maybe as your own position was Salim before the bomb transformed all of our lives. Why is it that we persons of such limited abilities and characteristics should be involved in what is happening? I have no credentials to justify the title of Rabbi, also I don't understand why that beggar was so articulate and calm considering his awful position in life. It does not make sense to me Salim!"

It was Peter who quietly offered a partial explanation, "Please excuse me, Sheikh Salim and Mr Aaron, but cannot you see something of the life of Jesus Christ demonstrated in that beggar? He looked Jewish or at least Semitic, he had nothing of the world's attractiveness yet spoke with knowledge and authority. Jesus too had no worldly credentials to be called Rabbi yet that is what the ordinary people entitled him. Jesus came from obscurity and poverty but was recognised by his Godly authority. Maybe both of you will be similarly used by Almighty God?"

Quickly leaving this very delicate subject, Peter asked, "Mr Aaron, please tell us about the jewel that the beggar gave to you?"

The jeweller was relieved to be able to talk on more familiar subjects, "It is a wonderful example of moonstone, perfectly translucent with a beautiful pale green blush and it has the inscription of the name of Asher, exactly in accordance with the Bible's description. Thus, I shall return from this long trip in possession of two more original Aaronic gemstones, yet two further have been seen but frustratingly not acquired in Montevideo."

His disappointed voice caused Ruth to respond, "But Uncle Aaron, Leticia was greatly moved by our visit and simply overcome with the drama that enfolded in such a short time. Perhaps she would be open for you to ask to buy those two jewels from her in the future?"

An Arab servant appeared sufficiently in sight to attract Salim's attention, who called a halt to their profound discussions by remarking, "That beggar-man certainly gave you life-saving advice Aaron, but he was instructing not only myself to 'go higher'. Let us all go forwards with humility and see how high Almighty God takes us."

***

At exactly 9.00 a.m. on Tuesday, Chief Superintendent Tony Birde accompanied by two inspectors walked up to the reception desk at Kelly Towers, surprised at seeing several other people clustered around the lift area. A white-faced receptionist answered his request in a shaken voice,

"You obviously have not heard the news Chief Superintendent, that there was a terrible accident here last evening. Mr Kelly had been working late and when he came down at about 8.00pm the lift crashed right down to the ground floor. He is in hospital and gravely ill."

Birde thought quickly and asked if Mr Kelly's private secretary might be available. "Miss Thompson is up in Mr Kelly's office now, Sir, but it's quite a climb up the stairs."

The three police officers made their way up to the top floor, knocked at the open door of the Chairman's office, and took note immediately of a lady clearly involved in sorting and packing items into boxes. "Good morning, Chief Superintendent Birde. It's a long way up by the stairs isn't it! Please excuse my activity, but last night's accident has left repercussions that I need to deal with quickly."

Olivia Thompson explained that she had been ordered to work late last night with her boss, but had then been clearing away papers thus had not gone down in the lift with him. "It was a dreadful thing Chief Superintendent, quite sickening. I heard the crashing sounds and rushed down the stairs. The porter had already phoned for the ambulance. They arrived promptly and used heavy cutting gear to open the remains of the lift. Ambulance men took Mr Kelly away and I followed them down to the hospital. It didn't take long for the diagnosis of severe multiple injuries to be obvious, apparently to include brain damage along with many broken bones and suspected ruptured major organs. It is questionable if he will live Chief Superintendent."

Tony Birde realigned his thoughts and made a short statement of sympathy. However, he could never had expected Miss Thompson's response. "Kelly was, or maybe still is, nothing but a swine Mr Birde. It had to happen one day and he's got exactly what he deserved. I don't expect to see him again, so I'm just clearing up a few of his more incriminating things, but as you're here, I might as well just give them straight to you. You probably know all about his wicked dealings, robbing people of much more than money, only to satisfy his devil's ego.

"Just look here at what I've taken from the wall-safe! I could tell you where each piece of stolen jewellery came from, and all the heart-ache of lives he destroyed in the process. He was an exceptionally evil man and I hope he lives as a cripple for years to come! I'm going straight from here to my parents farm up in Queensland, but I'm available anytime you want to hear facts and figures about my ex-boss. Now shall I just put the rest of his jewellery, which was too private to be kept in the safe, into these other cardboard boxes? You might at least try to help some of the rightful owners recover their stolen treasures, please, Chief Superintendent."

***

From Tuesday onwards, the morning watchers in Walsall registered all of the few persons who visited the shop or the next-door entrance to the flats. During the afternoons, Swarthy escorted the four young men, who were obviously staying in his flat, to a fitness club where they were observed by some envious casually-disguised police officers. When they emerged, all of them walked to a grassy park where Swarthy appeared to be evaluating their fitness further, sending them running and jumping for a whole hour. They were back in the flat by 7.00 p.m. each day and did not go out anywhere else at all.

***

Salim had been very keen to show his guests everything in and about FNAE, which really was not much more than a great deal of sand located in the 'Rub' al Khali', aptly known as the 'Empty Quarter' of the vast Arabian desert. It was a loosely defined region south of the United Arab Emirates and west of Oman, of no interest to the preserves of Yemen to the south and the enormity of Saudi Arabia to the north-west. The Arabian desert had always accommodated transient peoples, not only constantly travelling Bedouins, but the emirs of ancient times whose descendants now included Crown Prince Salim. Only the harsh conditions of the desert limited the FNAE's desires for development in their area known by all neighbouring countries to be their own, even if the boundaries were not officially defined. The one and only commodity that the FNAE had in abundance was hidden from sight beneath the sand, but when brought to the surface promised to supply all their needs for many generations ahead: oil! The prince took them out to the oilfields and the small township which housed the oil professionals and workers who came from other countries. He showed them the piped water installations, but the rulers of the FNAE could see little scope for further development.

Over the next three days, Salim spent much time with his guests, talking especially with Peter over and over the subject that the young man had raised concerning the possibilities of growing '*hydrogenous favoritem stratagetem*' alongside edible plants, even in arid desert conditions. Could it really be a feasible prospect and if so, why not test this in the FNAE?

They both realised that significant time and energy on research and trial plantings would be required, yet what was stopping them from an honest consideration of when, where and how such experimentation could be carried out? Peter had felt confident enough to show the prince something in his Bible which had struck him as being so relevant to their discussions. The passage of scripture was in verses 35 - 37 of Psalm 107: '*He turned the desert into pools of water and the parched ground into flowing springs. There he brought the hungry to live and they founded a city where they could settle. They sowed fields and planted vineyards that yielded a fruitful harvest.*' Peter asked, "Do you think Sheikh Salim that these words of God could be applicable not only to our discussions, but also to what we experienced in India?"

The prince replied earnestly, "Let us wait on God and ask him to lead us into his will, Peter."

Sheikh Salim had further private discussions with Peter and Ruth together, sounding them out over another ambitious idea that had been forming gradually in his mind and heart during their round-the-world trip, "What would you think about an opportunity to bring together groups of intelligent and willing young persons, of different cultures and faiths such as yourselves, to live and learn about life's needs and potentials in an atmosphere where each other's circumstances and situations would be recognised and respected? I am not suggesting a technical college, business institution, or anything academic; but a pool of development between cultures, races and faiths. May I ask for your first thoughts, please?" Surprised but happy faces showed their enthusiastic response to the Sheikh, before they poured out a wide range of questions to him.

Aaron kept Salim updated about contact with the mysterious advertiser in Perm and his first response asking for details, although he was puzzling over how they could ever meet up. His host stated royally, "My friends will arrive at London in the same FNAE aeroplane as they left it in thirteen days before. Also, it will stop en-route for you to meet another person about the search for jewels. My secretary, two guards and a steward will accompany you." Aaron accepted this further kindness with humble appreciation, before continuing his fax and sms contact with the mysterious Perm. The dialogue went as follows: *'To Box 273 Acton from Perm Box No. 621. Attached photo shows ruby. Price is 8000 USD. Collection arranged via tel +7 758920345 if quick.'* ... followed by Aaron's sms worded *'From Box 273 Acton. Must inspect to see if jewel is worth 4000 USD. Flying in private plane from Dubai to London on Friday 08 June. Possible stop over en route. Small.'* The reply came quickly by sms: *'To Small of Box 273 Acton. Minimum 6000 USD cash. Could meet Odessa Airport Friday morning. KR.'* Captain Najm proposed some possibilities to stop off at Odessa, enabling Aaron to answer *'To KR. Could stop 1 hour at Odessa 10 a.m. local time Friday. Price dependent on condition. Small.'*

The curt reply was: *'To Small. You will be collected on arrival in plane from Dubai at 10 a.m. Friday. Bring cash. KR.'*

***

On Wednesday Salim felt ready to discuss his bold thoughts for the future with Aaron, "My friend, may I ask for your wise counsel? I have talked a little of this with Peter and Ruth but my head is still full of questions! My strong desire is to encourage young persons, of an intelligent and co-operative nature, to expand their minds and hearts. How can people learn not to use defensive and retaliative thoughts and over-hasty actions when meeting persons of different backgrounds to themselves? Could they actually be helped to understand and tolerate others? All learning depends on positive and instructive teaching, including personal involvement. Could a way of helping young people practically be found, instead of cramming their heads with yet more academic knowledge, which they must receive at university? Could a pioneering college be established to help them?

"Many young people waste their time frivolously enjoying a 'year out' centred on pleasures, rather than taking part in an adventure. If a curriculum was formulated to permit learning to develop naturally, with a modicum of relatively informal teaching, would sequential residence in very different locations benefit learning? Could a college be based in three or four wide-apart locations, yet designed to operate as a cohesive unit? Would campuses need to be restricted to more open-minded countries such as England, Australia or USA, or would they be more effective in such challenging places as FNAE, Israel or South America? Could even the traditional segregation between the disparate peoples of the Middle East be overcome sufficiently to allow some integration amongst willing young persons? I am not proposing something inconsequential, but an honest and serious attempt at helping to develop tolerance between peoples. I would be honoured, friend Aaron, if you would consider joining me in the establishment of such a venture."

The Jewish jeweller was staggered to be asked such a question, feeling himself utterly incompetent and unworthy, yet Salim encouraged him not to think of their own inadequacies. "Could we do something positive to help young people overcome their natural intolerances, even to avoid another young Khaled choosing a supposedly religious excuse for murder?"

Next morning Aaron, Ruth and Peter conferred with Salim, pooling their ideas about the prince's proposals. All of them were in favour, but saw things from different perspectives. Peter visualised a mental laboratory for encouraging radical proposals to assist the overcoming of world-wide environmental and economic problems. Ruth was more concerned at allowing youngsters of different faiths to experience the truth of them, rather than stereotyped world views. Aaron was keen to include subjects usually seen as peripheral to university studies, each designed to broaden the minds and assist understanding of practical skills for basic needs. He suggested design concepts for affordable habitations, inexpensive clothing and enjoyable working methods. Salim favoured workshops enabling investigations and solution-finding for some of the world's flashpoints of tension, including religious and cultural precepts that had remained set in stone for centuries. A common thought was to remember the words of the beggars at Mangalore of not forgetting those whose circumstances kept them securely on the wrong side of the fence.

***

During this first week of June, Superintendent Harling was settling into his wider Major Crimes Division's duties. On Kevin Henderson's recommendation, he sent Inspector Dent's entire Team Coral to a small town on the East Anglian coast, where local police were failing to find any solution to a disturbing crime that was becoming the national media's latest description of police incompetence. It concerned the disappearance of two young children last seen buying ice-creams whilst their frantic mother waited in vain for their return to the beach. Dent was dispatched primarily to assist the local force, but was instructed to take his own initiatives to avoid a family tragedy and nationwide disenchantment with police in general. Soon afterwards, assistance was requested from the MCD for solving a particularly revolting murder in a Manchester suburb, for which the Superintendent sent Inspector Spencer and his Team Amber to investigate and hopefully solve. Thus depleted, the work on investigating French and other major jewel crimes, and the possible involvement of the magazine '*Jewels Worldwide*' was scaled down. However, Waseem's Team Empathy was continuing to dig in quietly with their work in the Midlands' town of Walsall.

***

Sheikh Salim had been restricting his FNAE duties whilst his guests were with him, but their time in FNAE was coming to an end for the three Britons. With heads and hearts full of future considerations, and determination to support each other in these, the arrangements were made for their departure. They were to take off from Dubai on Friday at 07-30 for the flight to Odessa, estimated to take just over three hours, meaning that they should land there before 10 a.m. local time. Allowing an hour for Aaron's meeting with the mysterious Russian, they would seek approval to take off at about 11.45 for the four-hour flight to

London, arriving there at about 13.45 UK time. That would enable the Jewish amongst them to prepare for the Sabbath. After the Sheikh himself had escorted Aaron, Peter and Ruth up the steps for their final 'Goodbyes', Captain Najm took off as planned at 07.30. It was a three-hour flight across desert and mountain countryside to Odessa located on Ukraine's Black Sea coast. However, they were not to enjoy a visit to this beautiful city.

As they landed and taxied to the standing area reserved for private aircraft, two large expensive cars were noticed, which cruised smoothly to a standstill a few metres from their aircraft's steps. Ruth stayed on board whilst Aaron and Peter walked to the front car, where a man gestured to them to get in quickly. Both cars sped fast across the concrete to an isolated low building four hundred yards away, into which everyone entered. Tables and chairs had been set up and a heavy-chested man wearing a black fur coat despite the warm weather, stood up holding out his hand to them and grinning, "Kuznetson Romanov, or maybe you would know me better as Box Number 621 Perm! Sit down and listen to me." The Russian was clearly someone who expected to be obeyed instantly. He acted with absolute authority, apparently unconcerned that he too was a foreigner here in Ukraine. "You're interested in my jewel and I'm interested in your money! Oh yes! Listen to me! My family has suffered ever since I purchased this damned jewel two years ago. My youngest child Ludmilla fell ill almost straight-away and succumbed within three months despite all that your expensive western hospitals could do for her. My only son Fyodorov has been unwell for the last two weeks and our doctors are puzzled as what is wrong, but I know in my heart that it is because of the accursed jewel. Now only last week my wife Svetlana collapsed, apparently with nervous strain! Doctors say she must go immediately for three months of fresh high-altitude mountain air, in Switzerland or Austria. Now Small, as you are on your way back to London, this is what you're going to do! Tell your pilot to divert the aircraft to Innsbruck Airport for refuelling. You will go inside the terminal and book a mountain chalet for three months starting from next Monday using your own name."

He reached inside his coat and pulled out an envelope. "Here are 1,000 US dollars to pay for a deposit on the chalet. Then get back into your plane and fly to London, from where you will post the chalet details and receipt for my money to this address in St Petersburg. In return I will reduce my price for the accursed jewel to only 3,000 US dollars. A very good deal for you, yes? Oh yes!"

Aaron looked at Peter as if this was some sort of a dream and spoke firmly to the Russian, "Mr Romanov, you must know that I have no authority to ask the pilot of the FNAE's plane to divert from his course."

The Russian snapped back his answer, "I did not say 'ask' but 'tell'!" Again, he reached inside his coat and took out another envelope, "Give him this 300 US dollars and tell him to keep his greasy, Arab mouth shut! OK, is this a deal or not?"

Peter had noticed that two of the men inside the room had one of their hands inside their coats and looked ready for action, but Aaron stood up and spoke calmly, "No, it is not a deal Mr Romanov. I will not do as you say, although I am very sorry about your family problems..."

The big Russian leapt around the table and grabbed Aaron's arm. "Very sorry, are you? Well if you won't co-operate, we'll see how very sorry you'll be later on shall we Jew Boy? Oh yes!" He shouted instructions in Russian and walked towards the door.

"But what about me purchasing your jewel?" exclaimed Aaron.

"No deal!" snarled Romanov angrily as he strode from the building with his henchmen close behind. Peter and Aaron were very scared but followed them outside, where they watched both cars scream away across the concrete.

They ran the four hundred yards back to the FNAE aircraft as fast as they could, which was noticed by an observant Arab guard. He alerted his colleagues who rushed to help the two Englishmen up the steps and inside. Seconds later, the plane taxied resolutely towards the far end of the runways, with Captain Najm speaking politely to the control tower requesting an immediate take off. After receiving a totally unclear answer, he spoke in a crisp voice, "Thank you for giving permission." Without hesitation, he turned onto the empty runway, opened up his engines, achieved maximum acceleration and lifted off with the faintest of a smile on his face.

***

The FNAE aeroplane landed four hours later on the Friday evening, but not at London. During the flight from Ukraine and all across Europe, Aaron and Peter had explained what had happened at Odessa airport to Ruth and to Sheikh Salim's secretary. He had told Captain Najm and together they had reported to the prince. Several recorded phone calls were made between FNAE and London during the afternoon, which resulted in the aircraft being diverted for landing to RAF Brize Norton in Oxfordshire. The hastily augmented welcome party which awaiting them included Superintendent Harling of the Metropolitan Police's Major Crimes Division and several unrecognised faces of men in anonymous suits. Alan greeted Aaron, Peter and Ruth warmly and having received confirmation that only Arabs were left on board the aircraft, he took the Britons to the reception area where their families awaited them. Peter's parents were very relieved at his safe return, not being much used to adventures themselves. Esther Klein hugged Aaron and Ruth excitedly, then stepped back to allow Naomi and Brian to come forwards and embrace their darling Ruth as if she had come back from the Moon. Tears flowed unceasingly as, at last, the terrible trauma of the last two months faded away, released by the relief of Ruth's safe arrival. Joy filled the whole family's faces as they were shepherded out to a police car, which was waiting to get them safely to Golder's Green before Shabbat should begin. Aaron managed a quick word of very sincere thanks to the sheikh's private secretary, Hasan bin Rahma and Captain Hakim Najm, before running to join the rest of the family in the car.

***

On Saturday morning 9 June in Walsall, the two young Asian men code-named Colin and David carried their big rucksacks from Swarthy's flat to his car and were driven to the railway station. David got out alone and walked inside without looking back. He caught the next train heading north, accompanied unknowingly by DPC Salmud Jones. Swarthy drove Colin to the same place in Birmingham that he and Boris had been collected from a few days previously.

The young man walked quietly away, looking very subdued, and was observed by DPC Benjamin Jacobs entering a block of council flats half a mile away. Swarthy had driven home alone and early that afternoon, accompanied by Andy and Boris, the three men were watched carefully as they walked into town visiting various shops. Swarthy did not buy very much in any one place, but spread his purchases between several small shops. This included several metres of fine gauge electrical wires in differing colours, some heavy voltage but small sized batteries, two cheap alarm clocks, an army surplus webbing belt, several rolls of best quality parcel tape and two packets of large safety pins.

On Sunday, Andy and Boris were taken by Swarthy to a different fitness gym, where they had a very strenuous workout. It was apparent that these were the two fittest of the initial four young men who Swarthy had gathered around him. Afterwards, they sat at a quiet cafe in a park with text books open before them for two hours, making it obvious that Swarthy was training their minds as well as their bodies. Andy was considerably bigger than Boris and looked to have a menacing temperament rather like Swarthy himself, whereas Boris appeared to be a quieter and more introspective young man. That evening most of Team Empathy convened in Waseem's room and reviewed their week's work. A summary report was prepared and sent off for Superintendent Harling's attention, accompanied by several photographs.

***

On Sunday afternoon, Alice Glover met Peter Templeton in UCLH's cafeteria and told him of his aunt's demise whilst he had been away travelling with Aaron, Ruth and Sheikh Salim. Alice explained with heart-felt sympathy about how Doctor Chaudhary had been very pleased with the initial treatment and Christine's responding so well, but that as he had feared, the internal injuries had so affected her organs and blood circulation that cancerous cells had developed and begun spreading at an alarming rate. The higher doses of drugs being administered to her were simply helping to lessen the steadily increasing pain from her cancer, which had transformed her into becoming entirely dependent on machines and drugs for survival. Apart from thinking of his patient's comfort during her expected last few weeks or days, Doctor Chaudhary knew that important research into the results of bomb-induced injuries was necessary, with not so many opportunities to examine this so easily. Thus, it had been decided that Christine would remain here in her room at UCLH until the very end.

When Peter saw his dearly-loved aunt, it was difficult for him not to reveal his shock at the dramatic change in her condition during his two week's absence. However, her spirit remained apparently as strong as ever, as she appeared to be listening to at least some of Peter's descriptions of his travels around the world. After they had prayed together simply, kissed very gently and parted, Peter knocked at Doctor Chaudhary's door. He was invited into this so very conscientious man's office, where he described the strange happenings at Mangalore Airport in India, concentrating on the scrawny young beggar pushing a scrap of paper towards him through the wire-mesh fence. Peter held out this paper to the Doctor and quoted his words as closely as he could recall them: *'Kefa, Kefa, take this to Doctor Shuban. He will need it very soon.'* Doctor Chaudhary turned the paper over and over and asked for another recounting of the beggar's exact words. He was looking rather less composed and professional than normal as he read the words: *'Koelreuteria paniculata'*. "This is all very strange Mr Templeton, but in this world of ours not everything relies on science and professionalism. There are realms within which we can enter only occasionally and with divine guidance. Your trip around the world was not disassociated from your wonderful aunt's moving towards her death, which I am very sorry to say is very imminent. I will think very hard about what is written on this piece of paper. It appears to be the Latin name of a tree, presently unknown to me, but which I will most certainly investigate straight-away."

"Thank you, young man. However, please do not omit to follow the third phrase that I believe the beggar would have spoken to you, probably concerning a rock? Goodbye for now."

***

At about the same time, Aaron was struggling to compose a letter to the queen, eventually settling on: *'To Your Esteemed Majesty and Revered*

Queen Elizabeth, from your subject Aaron Klein, jeweller of Hatton Garden. Greetings from a Jewish man searching to discover the 3,500 years old exotic jewels that were worn on the breastplate of Aaron the High Priest and brother of Moses. My desire is to re-establish the priestly ephod that was made to Almighty God's exact design and instructions, adorned with the entire 14 magnificent jewels bearing the names of the twelve tribes of Israel. My intention is to present it as a gift to the Nation of Israel and in order to complete the discovery and acquisition of the jewels I have travelled recently around the world. In India I received an account from a descendant of a high prince of that Country, whose ancestor had given two of the original gemstones to your own ancestor Her Majesty Queen Victoria, each inscribed with the names of six tribes, to be worn on Aaron's shoulders. Should it please Your Majesty to enable these very important jewels, that are believed to be amongst your treasures, to be included in the re-establishment of this ancient and holy garment; your subject would be honoured to accept and incorporate them along with your blessing. With kindest regards and greatest respect, I remain your subject Aaron Klein.' He walked to Buckingham Palace and handed his letter to a police officer requesting its prompt delivery to Her Majesty.

From there Aaron walked through some of London's lovely parks to Israel's Embassy in Palace Green, Kensington. He asked very politely if he might see someone to discuss a recent act of terrorism, his consequential world-wide search for Israel's first High Priest's 3,500 years old jewels, and a security issue concerning London and Tel Aviv. He was asked to wait for a few minutes until a Mr Dvorka could see him. Aaron assumed that he was being observed covertly, so he sat relaxed and glancing through a tourism brochure. Twenty minutes later, he was approached by a short man wearing glasses who introduced himself as Mendel Dvorka of the Embassy's security department. He took Aaron to an interview room, where the jeweller stated the reason for his visit, "You may have heard of the Hatton Garden bombing on 24th April in which my brother Reuben Klein was killed in our jewellery shop, along-with some other persons. Whilst recovering from my injuries in hospital, I was led to read a passage from our Holy Torah describing Aaron the High Priest's robes and its decorations. Subsequently, I began a search for the original 3,500 years old jewels that Aaron wore, which has taken me already on a search around the world. I have been partially successful in recovering these ancient jewels and..."

Mr Dvorka interrupted him abruptly, suggesting, "Perhaps you should be speaking to someone from our Religious Affairs Department rather than me Mr Klein?"

Aaron was not to be put off so continued, "Not so, thank you Mr Dvorka, as you will see if you listen to the next part of my unusual story. Some of the jewels were discovered with the assistance of the Metropolitan Police's Major Crimes Division at Scotland Yard, whose co-operation has been vital to my own enquiries. Their superintendent and myself have uncovered a network of persons involved around the world in selling stolen jewellery, believed to be operating in Tel Aviv amongst other cities. My request today is twofold: firstly, that this information of enormous historic and national value for Israel should be brought to the attention of the nation's president, and secondly for my senior police colleague and myself to discuss the ongoing criminal activity linking Britain with Tel Aviv. As these two points are interwoven, please may I request a meeting as soon as possible with persons of authority in those areas of activity? Thank you." Believing the jeweller to be partially deluded, Mendel Dvorka thanked him and escorted him rather determinedly to the embassy's outside perimeter.

***

Aaron walked in a subdued mood back to his flat in Hatton Garden, but decided instead to call in at his friend Julian's flat. He was welcomed in as usual and made to sit down in the familiar armchair with a glass of red wine. Mozart's Concerto No. 21 'Elvira Madigan' playing serenely on the stereo added to their complete contentment. They decided not to play chess that evening, preferring to give each other accounts of their recent activities over the last few weeks. Aaron began to describe his trip right around the world, free-of-charge thanks to the courtesy of Sheikh Salim, at whose name Julian wrinkled his brows and interjected, "But Aaron, surely he's an awful Muslim! You know how they plan to conquer the world and exterminate all of us Jews! How could you travel around with such a terrible man?"

Aaron started to defend the kind and peaceful Sheikh who he had come to respect so much, but as this Jewish friend would not be pacified, Aaron changed the topic. He told about his search for the Aaronic jewellery, describing the anti-Semitic son of a Nazi whose hatred of Jews and refusal to sell advertised jewels had led to a bitter end in a Montevideo hospital. Aaron followed that with the arrogant Australian tycoon who made such vitriolic comments about Jews, yet from whom he had acquired one of the ancient gemstones. Finally, Aaron told of the Russian oligarch's taunting at the Ukrainian airport, summing up with, "So the only original gemstones that I've actually come home with are these." He held out the magnificent topaz and beautiful moonstone. "These are just two representatives of the entire jewels attached to our original High Priest's garments, all of which I intend to discover and acquire, even if that takes me round the world again and at my own expense next time Julian!"

His friend inspected the precious gems with a look of awe on his face, "Are these really the original 3,500 years old gemstones Aaron? They must be worth an absolute fortune! This is all most interesting, so please keep me in touch with how your search continues my friend! How did you find out about such exotic places and arrange to meet those disgusting Jew-haters?" Julian listened keenly as Aaron explained a little about the magazine advertisements that he had been following up. The evening drew on and Aaron excused himself for needing to catch up with sleep. He left his friend to enjoy more wine and music alone, while he strolled happily to his own bachelor flat near-bye.

***

Inspector Henderson brought a thick folder of papers to his boss on Monday morning. Together they read carefully through Waseem's report and poured over about twenty photographs. "Sir, the smaller of the two boys looks familiar. Surely it must be the lad who accompanied Khaled Halleem to bomb the Hatton Garden jewellers? What was his name Sir, was it Amon something?"

'AH' kept his composure under control with difficulty, "No Kevin, his name is Ammar Sharmu, but I think that it would be best to refer to him from now onwards simply as Boris, just to keep in step with our lads up at Walsall. Check as much as you can into the other one. Look at the list of stuff Swarthy bought up there! Things are beginning to look serious. Tell Waseem to keep things as secret as possible and for Heaven's sake to stay vigilant!"

***

Now that his guests had left the FNAE, Sheikh Salim worked steadily through the correspondence that his staff had gathered to show him. He made quick decisions about accepting or rejecting many different invitations for him to speak at events spread far afield. One that caught his eye was a polite request for him to speak on Saturday 30th June at a mosque in Great Britain. His staff had made enquiries and believed it to be an establishment that was sincere in their religion, yet open-minded to other faith groups in their town of Walsall near Birmingham. "We will accept that one," said Prince Salim.

***

On Tuesday, Aaron was surprised to receive a phone call from Mr Dvorka of the Israeli Embassy, "Hello Mr Klein. We have had further communications concerning the different aspects of the points that you raised with me last Sunday and would like to invite you to visit the embassy on this Thursday at 10.30 a.m., when the appropriate persons will be available to discuss them further with you."

Aaron recognised the carefully worded diplomatic speech and replied, "If what you mean is that somebody will be able to help me to present a free gift of enormous national interest and value to Israel's president, and if Superintendent Harling and I can discuss the details of how to help your authorities stop specific organised crime emanating from Tel Aviv: then yes."

Mr Dvorka smarted a little and said, "Exactly, so Mr Klein. Goodbye until Thursday morning."

While Aaron was recovering from Dvorka's officious call, his phone rang again, "Good morning, Mr Klein. My name is Charles Lester and I'm the private secretary to Lord Bicester, who is an equerry of the queen. I wonder if you would be able to join me today for lunch at Smiley's Restaurant in Regent Street, unless you are otherwise engaged?"

Aaron's spirits perked up immediately, "I'd be delighted to, thank you very much Mr Lester."

***

As June progressed, Doctor Chaudhary instructed higher and higher doses of several drugs to be administered to Christine Templeton, simply to alleviate the increasing pain from the cancer which was consuming her body. She no longer could eat or drink, sit up or respond to even simple requests. She was becoming entirely dependent on machines and drugs for survival. Her visitors were restricted to family and close friends, who were permitted to have no longer than ten minutes at a time with her.

***

Aaron enjoyed his refreshing walk up to Regent Street and worked up an appetite for lunch at the rather exclusive Smiley's Restaurant. A middle-aged man in a smart business suit and displaying an immaculately clipped moustache greeted him with a formal handshake and invited him to share a light lunch at a secluded table, "Thanks for coming so promptly Mr Klein. Please understand that Lord Bicester, who is indeed one of Her Majesty's equerries, is also one of her oldest and most trusted friends."

Aaron swallowed hard, "I'm very pleased to meet you Mr Lester, presumably in connection with the rather presumptuous letter that I wrote to Her Majesty a few days ago?"

The man smiled, "You presume correctly Mr Klein! We're meeting today to enable me to assess you, either as a person who appears to be honest and serious in what he wrote to our sovereign, or a crank who my master would not wish to hear of ever again."

Over the course of their lunch, Aaron was able to convince Mr Lester that he was the former. He described his quest to recover the ancient Aaronic jewels, two of which he believed to be in Her Majesty's possession, helping his defence enormously when he casually produced the fantastically-banded agate gemstone from his pocket and handed it to Mr Lester for his inspection. Suitably satisfied and even impressed, the servant of a servant turned to the likelihood that the queen might actually possess the two almost clear, goshenite shoulder stones, each inscribed with six of the twelve tribes of Israel. If so, and if they could be located amongst her huge treasure house of priceless items, the question was would she be prepared to donate them to Aaron Klein's cause. "Of course I could not make any comment at all on that last point Mr Klein, but suffice it to say that we would not be meeting now if Her Majesty was totally unsympathetic to your cause or unaware of the very particular gift made to her predecessor Queen Victoria so long ago. Unless you'd like another coffee, I would say that our meeting has been successfully concluded and suggest that we each go about our own business." They rose, shook hands again and were about to depart to their respective work when Aaron, on impulse, handed the fantastically banded agate gemstone again to Mr Lester, "If it would please Her Majesty to have sight of one of the jewels under discussion, please let this ancient banded agate be shown to her."

***

Late on Wednesday morning, Aaron received a further very surprising telephone call, this time from Uruguay, "Good morning, Mr Aaron. It is Leticia Benitez with some news and a request." With amazing frankness and determination, she explained that her situation had changed dramatically since their time together in Montevideo only a fortnight ago, "My life here now is intolerable Mr Aaron, with continuous press demands for interviews, police and other official's bombarding me about my grandfather's life and property, being shunned by neighbours and even my very few friends. At the same time I am attempting to sort through rooms full of his possessions, including copious amounts of jewellery, much of it of dubious ownership. However could I start to build a proper decent life on my own? It would be impossible! Therefore, I have put the house up for sale, and made enquiries about my legal status and opportunities. It is my firm decision to leave Uruguay straight-away and come to Britain. My English language is good enough for me to obtain work and I have far too much wealth at my disposal, which would enable me to buy a home in England. My only problem, and I must tell you that my one-way aeroplane ticket is booked for Tuesday 26 June, is that I do not have anything beyond a one month's tourist's visa. When I arrive it will be with several large suitcases, only one of which will contain my personal things. The others, maybe four of them, will contain jewellery. I am phoning today, Mr Aaron to ask for your guidance and help in being allowed into Britain with an enormous amount of possibly stolen items of probably immense value, none of which I wish to have anything to do with. You are a jeweller and I would be pleased if you and the police would take all of them off my hands and return things to rightful owners, wherever that is possible, or dispose of them as otherwise. Naturally, I will be bringing those two ancient inscribed gemstones to give to you for your wonderful plans, which is the least that I could do after my grandfather's hateful display against you. Now, please will you help me, Mr Aaron?"

Unable to give Leticia any assurances, but promising to do all he was permitted to for her, Aaron arranged very quickly to meet with Superintendent Harling. An hour later, the two very different persons, but who shared a common aim concerning recovering jewellery and uncovering jewellery crime, sat and discussed the 'Montevideo issue'. However, before Miss Benitez's startling request was discussed, Alan told Aaron of the sincere thanks he had received from Sydney's police, with an account of their visit to Kelly Towers and his near-fatal accident, but their being given a large amount of mostly stolen jewellery. "They were absolutely delighted with your actions Aaron and have requested that both of us assist them with their enquiries, especially in identifying particular items and rightful ownerships. They are quite happy to keep everything in secure custody and to wait until we have time to go and help them, at their expense of course."

Aaron explained again that he had met Leticia's grandfather just before he died and believed that the old man had amassed a large hoard of stolen jewellery himself, along-with his Nazi father's stolen items from war-time Europe. The jewellery must be worth a small fortune and would almost certainly involve unsolved past crimes, huge insurance company payments, and the resolution of enormous legal difficulties of past and current ownership. They realised that an initial holding operation would be necessary, before a systematic analysis of whatever Leticia Benitez would be bringing could be undertaken. Because they were both extremely busy that work could not be a top priority and, therefore, secure temporary storage and sorting facilities would be required. They felt that Joshua's house at Kilburn would be inadequate for the overall huge exercise, but could be most useful for dealing with the items a few at a time. Alan was sure that a secure unit at Scotland Yard could be established, but the more difficult problem was how to bring a fortune of stolen jewels into Britain with the knowledge and consent of Her Majesty's extremely vigilant and strict customs service.

Alan remembered chatting with a Mr Nicholson at a joint briefing meeting in Whitehall for various heads of services. 'AH' had liked this friendly chap, who had failed somehow to mention the name of the agency that he represented, and had expressed a desire to work together with MCD if specific help was ever required, especially in working 'a little behind restrictive official regulations'. Aaron told Alan that he had obtained his sister Esther's willing agreement for Leticia to stay at the family home up at Golder's Green for as long as she wished, using its address for any official British residency requirements. He confirmed their arrangements for the next day's visit to Israel's embassy, wished Alan 'Goodbye', and walked away from UCLH towards his flat. 'AH' decided to ring Mr Nicholson immediately, about both Miss Benitez and a certain other difficulty that was troubling his mind.

CHAPTER 13

Aaron Klein, Superintendent Harling and Peter Templeton walked into the Israeli Embassy and reported in for their 10.30 appointment arranged by Mr Dvorka. He came to them looking peeved and escorted them without greeting to an upstairs meeting room where two men awaited them. "I thought you said there would be two men Mr Dvorka!" said the younger man of stocky build.

"Yes, Sir, but it appears that Mr Klein has an additional person with him."

The man spoke angrily, "Exactly Dvorka! In future, remember that our embassy does not admit 'additional' persons.' You may go!" In a smoother voice, the man introduced his colleague and himself, "This gentleman is Melech Segal from the State President's Office and I am Tzalel Chayyim Deputy Assistant Head of Overseas Security. Now please explain who is the young man." Aaron deliberately introduced the superintendent first, giving his full rank and titles, before presenting Peter Templeton as his own associate.

"Aha!" said Tzalel Chayyim, "Then this is the person who hit our renegade MOSSAD agent over the head with a big, black Bible in Montevideo! Welcome young man! He needed such a lesson and it will never be forgotten!"

Melech Segal spoke up, "Thank you, Mr Chayyim. Please sit down and let us come to the reason for your visit. Firstly, may I give you greetings from the State President's Office, where your suggestion of offering a replica of Aaron the High Priest's ephod with its breastplate and jewels has caused some interest. We thank you for making this offer Mr Klein."

Aaron accepted his thanks but qualified his statement in a polite voice, "Thank you, Mr Segal. The clothes will naturally be replicas after 3,500 years, but they will bear the original jewels." Seeing a look of unbelief on the men's faces, Aaron produced two shining jewels from his pocket and held them out, "By way of example, please recognise the inscribed tribal names of M'nasheh and Efrayim on these ancient jewels. There will be fourteen jewels in total, including the two worn on Aaron's shoulders, as you will know from the Torah." Melech Segal picked up on Aaron's 'will be' by asking for the exact timescale for the completion and proposed presentation of the ephod with its jewels. "My expectation Sir is that the remaining jewels will be recovered as soon as it pleases our Almighty God to reveal them, after which we would be pleased to bring the ephod to Israel for a formal presentation."

Mr Segal replied austerely, "Please keep us in touch if your collection increases Mr Klein, after which we will discuss timescales for appropriate opportunities at a later stage."

Aaron responded to this affront in a dignified manner, "Please understand Mr Segal that my offer is of world-wide significance for Israel. I am sure that the State President's Office would not like to see that jeopardised."

Tzalel Chayyim entered the fray, "So just where are you getting these jewels from Mr Klein?" Superintendent Harling intervened, explaining about the magazine advertisements and how some of the jewels that were being recovered had been bought and sold through its pages. He mentioned that a particular shop in Tel Aviv was involved in dealing with enormously valuable antique jewels, which should belong to the state of Israel. The superintendent's explanations were all but ignored as Tzalel Chayyim continued, "Are these stones insured Mr Klein?"

Aaron remained calm, "As I have tried to explain gentlemen, these jewels are being recovered by the direction and power of Almighty God. His 'insurance' is that his protecting right hand is uncovering them for the world's eyes. Now, may I ask for your assistance regarding opportunities when your president would be available to receive this free gift?"

Before the man could answer, and following Aaron Klein's tempo, the superintendent asked pointedly, "Do you wish for the Metropolitan Police's assistance in stopping major criminal activity taking place in and through Tel Aviv gentlemen, or do you not?" The men made limp suggestions that they would discuss matters with their senior officers, assuring the visitors that arrangements for receiving such a worthy gift and anti-criminal assistance would be properly considered. At that point, the meeting concluded in a frosty atmosphere.

***

Superintendent Harling went straight from the Israeli Embassy to the fresher atmosphere of Green Park, where Mr Nicholson had arranged to meet him. They walked briskly around the paths together for twenty minutes discussing the 'Montevideo Issue'. As they stopped to sit on an unoccupied bench, well away from eavesdroppers, another man approached and sat with them. He did not introduce himself, but spoke directly to them both, "Heathrow deals frequently with prestigious VIPs, including reigning monarchs, prime ministers and every sort of dignitary, which experience helps us very occasionally to enable persons of another category into Great Britain. On 26 June, a car will meet the plane from Uruguay on the tarmac and escort Miss Benitez to a certain room where we will all be waiting. Once the unloading of the aircraft's hold begins, the six suitcases that Miss Benitez has described, two of personal belongings and four with other items, will be removed and brought to that room for her to identify and open in the presence of ourselves. Once we are satisfied that the items are according to what you have been told, I will sign an authorisation for them to be taken immediately to Scotland Yard for detailed examination, with the requirement that a subsequent report back from Superintendent Harling to Mr Nicholson on their contents be made, even if pressure of work means that it takes a year or two to be completed. Hope that's OK for you chaps? Goodbye until then!"

***

At 10.00 a.m. on Friday 15 June, Aaron received a phone call direct from

Israel, "Good morning, Mr Klein, my name is Mordecai Leon and I am the secretary to Israel's vice president responsible for state relationships. I apologise that less senior persons have not grasped the significance of the offers that you and Superintendent Harling are making to our nation. Therefore, it is our desire that you gentlemen should be our guests here early next week — if that is not inconvenient for you — please. Arrangements would be made for you to spend time on Monday and Tuesday in Tel Aviv with the city's chief of solice and the state's deputy commissioner for crime. Then to visit Jerusalem for discussions with the state's minister of culture and antiquities and a short meeting with the vice president for state relationships himself. To assist arrangements, one of the state's aeroplanes would convey you from London early on Monday morning."

Aaron expressed his great surprise and sincere thanks for this honoured invitation, promising to confer with Superintendent Harling immediately and respond definitely before Shabbat would begin. In the event, Alan Harling was delighted with this offer and confirmed his agreement, which Aaron conveyed back to Mr Leon a few minutes later.

***

As Doctor Chaudhary worked very hard and for very long hours, like so many doctors are required to do, he relished his occasional escapes from UCLH. On this Saturday morning, he was one of the first to enter the Royal Botanical Gardens at Kew. He was not there simply to admire the beauty of these gardens, but to find a person who would know more than he had so far discovered about '*Koelreuteria paniculata*' or '*Pride of India*' as it was sometimes known in its native parts of Eastern Asia. He had phoned Kew's office earlier that week who confirmed that they had a single specimen of this tree, housed in a large atrium because it required a climate warmer than southern England could provide. Now he entered the magnificent glass house and made his way to the elderly gardener responsible for looking after the exotic trees.

"Not many people appreciate '*Koelreuteria paniculata*', Sir, so I am very pleased to show this wonderful tree to you, which has grown and thrived in this house for over one hundred and twenty years. It is now a mature specimen having attained a height of nearly nine metres. Because of the strict climatological conditions in which it is nurtured here, this specimen is very unusual in its forwardness of seasons. You have already missed the small, widely-branched flowers that project even above its crown, before its fruit contained in lovely papery bladders are formed, turn pink and herald the turning of its leaves from yellow to nearly white and then quite suddenly to their present dark green, Sir."

Dr Chaudhary duly admired the purple-brown bark with its scaly ridges and looked at the photographic displays of the flowers and fruit that had been and gone for this year, then asked, "Do you know why its common name is *'Pride of India'* in Asia, where it grows in the wild?"

The elderly attendant responded enthusiastically, "Well, Sir, obviously that name would not have been given by a gentleman of your own original country, but by a European who was struck by the merits of this wonderful tree."

Intrigued by this description, Dr Chaudhary enquired what these 'merits' might be. The man looked around cautiously and lowered his voice, "Please excuse my forwardness, Sir, but would you be a medical man?" The doctor confirmed that he was.

"Well, Sir, you know that most medicines, even if recently devised, stem from naturally-occurring plants that have survived and flourished in their originally-created state for centuries. This particular tree has probably had several common names, well before some European first saw it on his adventures in Asia. There was once an old man who had worked here at Kew for all of his life, Sir, and who I served under as an apprentice gardener. That man knew more about foreign trees than anyone else I have ever known, including many famous scientists Sir! He knew for a fact that *'Koelreuteria paniculata'* had perfectly natural abilities to cure many diseases, not by any jiggery-pokery, Sir, but simply because it did. He told me that it was the leaves that held these properties, not the flowers or fruit, and I don't mind telling you that I have sometimes made a sort of pottage of these leaves when the normal doctors, begging your pardon Sir, haven't been able to help me too much." Dr Chaudhary assured the elderly 'keeper of exotic trees' that he had not spoken out of turn and had in fact been most helpful. That assurance resulted in a gift to the doctor of about a dozen fresh leaves for his personal experimentation.

He began at home that afternoon, taking four of the leaves, adding boiling water, stirring then leaving them to cool before tasting the foul mixture. It was ridiculous even to consider administering such a revolting concoction to a dying lady. He was well aware of the ethics involving doctors trying to help terminal ill patients get through their last weeks, and he took the most serious professional views of the boundaries between treatment and desire to help.

***

Whilst the sun was shining in the British Midlands throughout this Sunday 17 June, further south it had been one of those dreadfully persistent wet days that only England seems to attract. All day long it rained and rained with the skies covered in darkness, which could have made it a depressing day in the Harling household, but it wasn't, because for Mary and the children it was the special, once-a-week set-apart day for honouring God collectively with others by attending church. They usually went by bus, but today Alan's offer to drive them there through the continuous downpour of rain was willingly accepted. He got quite wet even getting the car out of the garage and it steamed up as soon as the laughing children and their happy mum joined him in it. On arrival outside the church, his family called out their thanks as they rushed inside with the other joyful worshippers, leaving Alan feeling suddenly very flat and alone.

He drove home slowly, wondering yet again how it was that the four most-loved people in his life could exhibit such happiness at running though the rain to get inside a school building, unused at weekends, to sing and clap and dance and even to wave flags! Alan had noticed this flag-waving a few weeks previously, when he had surreptitiously peeped inside after he had arrived early to collect his family as a nice surprise for them. It appeared that he was the only restrained and normal person in the room, which had an electric atmosphere inside and was full of people of all sorts and ages going crazy as the meeting came to an end.

Now as he was returning to their empty home on his own, Alan struggled to understand what common link it could be that the other four seemed to have, yet that he just didn't comprehend or share in. His very intelligent and ordered mind told him that his avowed atheism was absolutely correct and true, whilst the others in their family had what they called 'faith in Jesus Christ' and also in the God that he heard them call 'Father', which he knew only because he sometimes overheard their prayers. He had always believed that this was something which had been invented centuries ago and hadn't yet died out, although it must do someday soon. It was a mystery to him as to why his family had all signed up to this, which Alan likened to people who joined a club such as the Gunnersbury Dramatic Society and liked to dress up to show off their talents for acting. Were his whole family and their friends at the church really acting too, or what else were they doing week after week? Yet they seemed not just to enjoy meeting together, but to actually believe in this God who they tried to explain about to him on occasions, who they said 'deserved to be worshipped'!

It was a ridiculous mystery to him, considering that no such god actually existed and had only been invented by weak-minded people as a crutch to help support their empty lives. However, Mary and their children didn't have empty lives, nor did that wonderfully brave woman Christine Templeton, who was slowly but surely dying from her injuries at UCLH. She had never complained and always spoke kindly to people including himself, trying to sympathise with her visitor's tiny little problems whilst she couldn't even blow her nose on her own. Then there was her nephew Peter, such a fit and active young man, as clever as one could wish to be, with his whole future before him packed full of opportunities. How could he too talk about 'worshipping' this God, even though Alan knew it all to be a fabrication of nonsense?

Alan found himself back outside his home, unable as always to conclude his thoughts more satisfactorily, so he turned away from such abstract thinking to the practicalities of getting from his car, through the gate and into the garage without getting drowned in the incessant rain. He decided that it would be best not to put the car inside the garage, but to leave it on the drive. He prepared himself for the run to his front door and leapt out into the rain, running along the path fearful of slipping over. He reached his porch but despite his deep gasps of relief and the cascading rain, he thought he heard something: "Geoff, Geoff!" there it was again, "Geoff, Geoff!" He peered out through the stair-rods of rain and strained his ears to listen. "Geoff, Geoff, over here Geoff!" Gradually he managed to locate the voice as coming from the other side of the road, where he began to make out a figure standing beneath an overhanging tree. Why would anyone be out there in this downpour and why would someone be calling out the name Geoff? His meticulously ordered mind suddenly recalled the name that he had assumed in Teignmouth some weeks ago when meeting with Ammar. Surely, it couldn't be him over the other side of the road calling out to him, or could it be? Managing to exercise his policeman's caution, he called back, "Tashir, Tashir is that you?"

"Yes, yes, Geoff it's me!"

In a flash, Alan grabbed a second coat hanging in the hall and ran outside and across the road to the figure standing immobile under the tree. "Quick, put this over your head and shoulders and run!" He half dragged the young man across the flooded road, up his path and indoors slamming the door shut behind them. Instantly the noise changed from a cacophony to virtual silence. Alan looked at the sodden and shivering young man, deciding to leave words of explanation for later, "Come to the downstairs toilet Tashir and take off all of your soaking clothes. Use this towel to dry yourself while I run upstairs and get some dry things for you to change into." He rushed up to Brian's room and grabbed some of his son's clothes, then another towel from the airing cupboard and his own dressing- gown. His mind was racing as he took the bundle down the stairs as fast as he could run.

Knocking on the toilet door, he called out, "Here, Tashir, just outside are another towel and some dry clothes. I'll boil the kettle while you get dried and dressed, then come and find me." Emotions were throbbing through Alan Harling as he stood in his own kitchen, doing such a familiar thing as boiling a kettle, yet everything seemed out-of-place because the young person who was most often on his mind apart from his family, was actually in his house getting himself dried out. How was it that a professional senior police officer could be so pleased that a known terrorist accomplice was here in his own home, and that he could be so very pleased to be helping him? He made a pot of tea, put some biscuits out on a plate and took them into the sitting room. "Are you all right in there, Tashir?" he called.

"Just coming Geoff," came the reply, after which he walked in looking bedraggled but at least better than he had done standing out in the pouring rain. "Come on in son and tell me what's going on?"

The young man began very slowly, "Today's my only chance you see Geoff, because after today it will be too late. I just had to come Geoff! Most of the arrangements have been made, but I don't want to do it! Its evil Geoff but what can I do? I'm trapped by that wicked Zakarian and this other chap Nizar Al Katabi and they never takes their eyes off me. Then last night he just told me, '*It's your turn Ammar. you're the next bomber and it will be on 30th June. Nizar will look after you almost up to when you do it, just like you did for Khaled, then you'll be a hero that night in Heaven Ammar, just like he was! Many true believers will be welcoming you into their presence: it will be absolute bliss for you!*' But how can that be true when everything that he says is a lie? At first, I took it all in, believing everything he said. He showed me things written in the manuals, about martyrdom for the cause being the highest honour, but as he went on and on, day after day I began to see the very opposite. Zakarian's pure evil, and I want no part of what he's doing, but how can I ever escape? I'm trapped and as good as dead already, whether I blow up myself and the Sheikh or not! There's no chance for me at all, Geoff!"

He burst into tears and grabbed at Alan's hands, "I don't want to do it! I don't want to do it! Please believe me, Geoff; I don't want to do it!"

There was not much in the policing manuals to help Alan here, so he just had to act on his own initiative and do all that he could to help this youngster not to become the next in a long line of murderers killing people '*In God's name!*' Alan found himself sitting on the floor where Ammar had sunk down inconsolable, putting one arm around his shoulders, "Right now, let's get down to the truth and some facts shall we? My name is Alan not Geoff, yours is Ammar not Tashir. I know where you're living now and what you're planning to do. The only question that matters is: are you going to do it and murder Sheikh Salim and many others, destroying all that this great man of peace is trying to do; or are you going to help me to nail the real villains who are training and pushing you and other youngsters to be their killing machines? That's the only question that you must answer Ammar. If you decide to go on with it, you can get out of my home this very minute! But if you want to avoid becoming a wicked terrorist murderer yourself, then you've got to help me stop all this! Will you help me or not Ammar? What's your answer going to be son?"

The young man suddenly calmed himself, sat up on the floor with his back against an armchair, accepted the proffered mug of tea, composed himself and spoke calmly, "Yes, Mr Alan, I will help you, but you must tell me what to do, please."

Alan Harling recalled his police officer's methods, even though he was sitting on his sitting-room floor. "The first thing is to decide to trust each other right to the end and to do all we can to help each other. Then we're going to make some plans about how to avoid you becoming a killer, but before that, you're going to write down for me all the details of what you and Khaled were trained to do and did do in Hatton Garden: right?"

The reply was amazingly calm, "Yes, Mr Alan, I can do that, but I've only got today because I must be back in Walsall tonight. He thinks I'm visiting my aunt in North London, making the last contact with my family before I do it."

Alan Harling slowed the conversation down, "Look Ammar, you're going to write a full confession now, before you leave my home. That's the only way that I could ever help you to get out of a sordid trial, obvious conviction and extremely long jail sentence for the Hatton Garden murders. Now it's my turn to trust you. I'm going to drive to Ealing to collect my wife and children, to stop them getting as soaking wet as you did. While I'm gone, you're going to sit at my kitchen table, drink your tea and eat some biscuits and write out absolutely everything that I need to know. Right?"

Ammar stared at him, "You mean that you'd trust me so much as to leave me alone in your home while you go out Mr Alan?"

The police officer heard himself say, "Yes, I will son. I'll fetch an A4 writing pad, some pens and you're going to sit down and write it all out, and I mean everything Ammar. Start with how you and Khaled got yourselves into this mess, then say what actually happened at Hatton Garden, then what you've been doing since, and then what you're up to now in Walsall. I want everything written out and you've got half an hour to do it before I get back. Do you understand and will you do it?"

Ammar replied resolutely, "Yes, I will do it." Alan Harling fetched the paper and pens, set up Ammar in his kitchen and watched him make a start before he left him alone. He went outside and got into his car, saying to himself, *'If that young chap runs away, my career's finished!'*

He drove through the incessant rain, pulling up right outside the church and shouting to his family, through the window. "Wow, Dad's here!" called Emily.

"Good old Dad!" shouted Brian as his father opened the doors for them.

"Oh, thank you so much for coming, dear," called Mary.

"Oh Daddy, Daddy, you're the very bestest daddy in the whole world!" said Pauline wrapping her arms round his neck.

"Come on you lot, get in for goodness sake!" he replied with his heart full of love and joy in his family. As they drove along, they noticed that he was going slower and slower, as he deliberately tried to enable the allotted time of half-an-hour to give Ammar as much chance as possible to finish his confession, or to run away again if that was what he decided to do. Alan gradually shared the news that there was a visitor waiting for them at home, giving them strict guidance as to what they should do when they arrived. "It's a frightened young man, so don't rush him or panic him. Don't be too familiar with him or embarrass him. Just give him some time and space to finish what he's writing for me. Let him make his own decisions and don't be too nice to him either. Just act politely and sensibly. Right?"

The children answered, "Yes, Dad!" whilst Mary squeezed his arm.

She opened the still-unlocked front door while Alan parked the car, then shepherded the children straight into the kitchen, calling out, "Oh hello Ammar!"

Brian and Emily simply said "Hi there!" in very relaxed and normal voices.

Pauline said, "Hello! Are you going to live here with us for ever and ever? I do hope so because we've got lots of rooms upstairs."

When Alan walked in, they were all talking at the same time, sitting together round the table and eating the plate of untouched biscuits. "Come on you lot!" cried out the father in a mock cross and managerial voice, "Make some room for me will you!" Mary took charge of the situation, sending Brian and Ammar upstairs to get some dry clothes on the visitor and tidy him up a bit. "You girls start getting lunch ready. Alan, tell me how long we've got and what you're going to do with him now. I'm not running a guest-house you know, but we can make room for him if that's what you want. So is he staying with us or not?"

Alan answered in a tired but not unhappy voice, "It depends on what he's written here, Love. Just give me some fresh tea and let me read what he's said, then we'll all know." Alan picked up Ammar's three double sides of hasty writing and began to read it to himself:

'This is me Ammar Sharmu and I'm with Inspector Harling of Scotland Yard although I'm not there just now because I'm in his home on my own in Guntersberry. I've decided that I don't want to be a killer although that's what's been planned for me to be by that evil Mustafa Zakarian. He told Khaled and me that we would be heroes of our faith if we did what he said, that's why Khaly went and did it in Hatton Garden because we both thought it was the right thing to do. He was to be the bomber while I made sure he didn't panic and helped him along like. We went down from Watford on the train to Harrow and Weldstone and walked down Station Road to Zakarian's dry cleaners where Khaly got fitted up in the bomb jacket. I carried the nail coat for him as it was so heavy but when we'd walked to Harrow-on-the-Hill Station we saw the guards there and thought that all that metal in the nail coat might set off some alarms so I dumped it in a bin before we walked into the station and waited for the train down to Farringdon. When we come out it wasnt far up past the pub to the Klein's shop in Hatton Garden but we had to get the timing just right didnt we becos he'd said to go in not too soon and not too late. We waited until we saw the two Arabs then the lady and last of all the tall chap get inside then I said sort of goodbye to Khaly and walked away slowly towards Euston like we'd been told but I hadn't gone far before the explosion came and I started running becos I was so scared. We'd never done anything like this in our lives that's honest. We never got into big trouble until that Zakarian started following us and buying us things and talking to us till our ears hurt. It was when he gave Khaly those new trainers that decided him to do it. They were ever so expensive really top notch ones which he could never have ifforded. I just

went along with him cos he was my best mate that's all. I knew that Khaly was dead so I ran away like I'd been told to do by that wicked Zakarian. I didnt want to go back to north London so I went to Paddington and bought a cheap ticket to Reading, but I stayed on right down to Deven where a sort of cousin of mine had a restraunt but I didn't like it much becos I'm not a waiter. Then one day this chap and his wife come in for a meal and started talking with me, treating me almost normal and inviting me to go fishing well of course I jumped at it becos I didn't have any money for going in fishing boats did I. So we went and I made up a name Tashir for this chap Geoff to call me but now I know it's not his real name either. When we were on the boat it was great at first but then I saw him going paler and paler and looking really awfull. He made the best of it but he just couldnt keep it down becos the boat was going up and down and round and round like. It was terrible and then this Geoff spewed out all over me and I don't have any spare clothes so it was disgusting and I smelt like an animal but I couldn't do much about it could I. He was just helpless wasn't he so he made a mistake and called me by my real name so I knew he was on to me then he said he was a policeman. When we got asshore I panikked and ran for it and he couldn't follow me cos he was so ill poor chap. He only wanted to help me I suppose but he just couldn't so I felt so sorry for him and right then it made me think about things and everything changed in my mind from then on. You see he was so vulnerable and helpless just like the people we was being trained up to kill so I decided that I was going to have nothing more to do with it and specially with that Zakarian so I ran off to the train station when this woman saw me the same woman who was with Geoff in the restrant and she just looked at me like a proper Mum but I never had a proper Mum and she said she wanted to help me and gave me some money cos I didn't have anything so I snatched it from her and jumped on a train that was just coming in. It was only becos she gave me a piece of paper with her name and I knew she was the Inspector's wife and it had their address on it so thats why I'm here today in The Inspector's home. I only went to Newtown Abbot and got my bag without seeing my cousin then ran straight back to the station and got on an express going up north but the guard caught me without a ticket so he put me of at Taunton where I hung around and got another more crowded train which was so busy the guard didn't get to me so I got off in Birmingham and looked for a room somewhere to hide away. This chap Mahmoud and I got talking and he wanted someone to share a room so I did and got a job washing up in a cafe to pay him and ate in the cafe. Then Mahmoud said he wanted me to meet someone who was helping him understand things about life he said so he took me along and gess what it was Zakarian. He brought me to his flat in Walsall over a fotocopy shop which was his next fiddle and he and his wife Yeraz has a big flat above it where me and Mahmoud and two other chaps have been staying in one room. Zakarian kept teaching us and checking us out but he sent Mahmoud and Mohammed away so now its just me and this chap Nizar Al Katabi. I don't like him becos he's a nutter really hooked onto all this hatred stuff and religus terrorism that Zakarian is selling so he'd do it for nothing becos he's totally like him he is. I hate all this stuff its just not true but what can I do? Yesterday Zakarian tells me that I'm definitely the next bomber which is why he's given me just this one day off before the final preparations but he's already told me when and where I've got to do it which is at the Aisha Mosque at some big do there having there on Saturday 30 June with all sorts of other religus people from Walsall. Christians and Jews and all sorts sort of coming together with a big noise coming to declare something open and making a speech all about peace. Zakarian and that wife of his Yeraz hates all that talk and this chap who believe it or not was in the Hatton Garden shop when Khaly bombed it. His name is Sulim and he's some sort of Arab Sheikh whose becoming famous all over the place so I've got to walk up to him just after he's started making his big speech at exactly 2 - 15 then blow myself and him and as many others as possible to bits so that's the plan that this Zakarian has made and each day from now on me and Nizar have got to practice it very quietly of course so that we know the route exactly and where to go.

Zakarian relaxes sometimes and tells us about what he's done in the past few years from when he killed eight people on Reading Station with a bomb he put in a rubbish bin then at Swanidge where he knifed some chap who was preaching in a park, then two women police outside a theatre somewhere like Margate by throwing a hand grenade at them and so on. He's always bragging that he's killed twenty people so far and wants to do in a lot more apart from setting us up to be human bombs ourselves that is. He's not mad but just concentraeted evil he is really. That's all I've got to say now only I don't want to do it and this policeman Inspector Alan is a good man who wants to help me stop all this stupid terror stuff. Even though he puked all over me in the boat he's as near to a dad to me as I ever knew so please God help me and him to stop Zakarian before it's too late becos this is me here in Mr Alan's house on my own on Sunday 17 June signed by me Ammar Sharmu.'

Alan finished reading Ammar's confession unable to hold back the emotions as he realised how much influence any person has on others, for either good or bad, depending on their actions. How could he and Mary have meant so much to this young Asian man, who apparently never had a 'proper' mum or dad? However, now he had some serious police work to do, as well as what he could achieve for young Ammar. Mary had just come in after having given Ammar's sodden clothes a quick hand wash and then put the whole lot into the tumble dryer, so he passed the three pages of paper to his wife to read, while he began working out possibilities. If he was to stop Britain's next well-planned act of terrorism, which would make world-wide news exactly like the terrorists wanted, then he Superintendent Alan Harling was the one who had to stop it. He would need to get approval from A/C Williams and let Sheikh Salim know a little of it, but otherwise he just had to keep going with the plans he already had in place up at Walsall, which were now confirmed to be of such vital importance. Then what was he to do about young Ammar himself, who couldn't be allowed to run off again and get indoctrinated another time. Must he be sent to jail?

Mary finished reading Ammar's report, dried her tears and spoke to her husband, "It seems to me Alan that Ammar needs to start a completely new life, rather like Rashid and Ibrahim are doing here in Gunnersbury, but which would be much more difficult to arrange for Ammar than for the Halleems who only had to move down from Watford. That evil man Zakarian obviously has to be stopped and sent to jail, but until you actually can catch them in the act, rather than just planning it, surely you couldn't arrest them could you, Dear?"

Alan considered his wife to be the wisest woman he knew and answered her, "You're dead right, Mary, but what two immense things to organise: how to help a suicide bomber not do it and to start a new free life somewhere, and how to let the murder plans continue right up to the moment when somehow they get stopped in the nick of time!"

Mary pondered, "That's right in your department, Dear, so I wonder if you should have a quiet chat with Sheikh Salim. He obviously has to be told that he's the target, so that he plays along with that and also trusts what your people will do to prevent it. I think he would understand about Ammar and agree to help him himself."

The children all came into the sitting room together, with Ammar looking very strange in his borrowed clothes that just about fitted him and made Pauline call out, "I've got another brother, Mummy, just like Brian but he's got a black skin all over him and much bigger muscles!"

Even Ammar managed a smile and looked less scared as he sat down and waited while Mary took the children into the kitchen and shut the door, leaving him alone with her husband. "Right now, Ammar, let's get down to business, shall we? You've done a great job writing out your confession and report on Mustafa Zakarian, well done! Now we've got to plan our own actions to stop that evil creature killing the sheikh, other innocent persons and yourself. You do realise that I've got to let you keep following Zakarian's plans right up to the last minute, don't you?"

Ammar nodded and said, "Yes, I understand that Mr Alan, although it'll be very scary, but how will you stop me blowing myself and others up when Zakarian and Nizar will be watching my every move? I won't have to go to prison for ever so long will I Mr Alan?"

The superintendent replied, "You'll have to leave all the arrangements to me Ammar, while you keep doing what Zakarian says. I can't tell you what's going on in Walsall but you're not completely on your own there, I've got people watching and I'll make sure that a message gets through to you, but whatever you do don't let Zakarian find out, or someone will get killed. You and I need to agree on just one code word that means something to us but not to Zakarian, have you any ideas?"

The young man had been greatly affected by the police officer's children, so he suggested, "What about if Brian, Emily and Pauline's names could be mentioned in any messages, because there's nobody up in Walsall that I know with their names?"

Alan liked the idea and turned to the subject of what could be done for Ammar himself after the murder of the sheikh had been stopped, "I must ask you a very straight question Ammar. Because you are helping me with my enquiries, if I could help you not to be sent to prison, would you be prepared to start a new life somewhere far away from all this horrible stuff? I can't promise you anything, but I'll do my best for you son." Mary called them in for dinner, which Ammar Sharmu felt was the best meal he had ever eaten, as he sat like an equal person around the family's kitchen table. Alan asked Brian to come with him, once the 'goodbyes' had been said and Pauline had stopped stroking Ammar's lovely soft black face. The others waved goodbye to the three men driving off into the still persistent rain. Alan drove all the way to the entrance of Euston Station, letting Ammar run quickly inside without a backwards look. He drove home, waited for Brian to run through the rain and indoors, then drove round the corner where he parked and took out his phone.

"I'm very sorry to disturb you on a Sunday afternoon, Sir, but please could you spare a few minutes for a private talk?"

Without any hesitation, A/C Laurence Williams replied, "Come straight round to my home Harling, pick me up in your car and we'll go for a drive." He gave Alan the address, finished the chapter of the book he'd been reading, and waited in expectation for what was so important that it couldn't wait until tomorrow at The Yard. An hour later as Alan dropped him back at home, Williams handed him back Ammar's confession and said, "You're doing all the right things, Superintendent. Don't take too many risks if this Zakarian changes his evil plans, but otherwise just follow your 'Copper's nose' as you've been doing so well. I don't want too much of this written down on an official report form right now, but I suggest that you write a few notes and leave them with a copy of Sharmu's confession in an envelope for me, after you get back from Israel. Life isn't boring Harling, is it! Goodbye and well done!"

***

At 1.00 p.m. on Sunday, Aaron was phoned by Lord Bicester, who asked if he would like to watch the ducks in St James's Park with him at 3.30.

When Aaron approached a bench overlooking the pond, an elderly man sitting next to a well-dressed woman, stood up and held out his hand, "Mr Klein! How nice to meet you. May I introduce my daughter Lady Buckingham to you?"

Aaron shook hands and the middle-aged lady said, "Now that I know you're in safe hands Pops, I'll leave you and Mr Klein to enjoy the ducks while I take some exercise. I'll return in half hour or so. Don't fall in will you Pops!"

Aaron estimated Lord Bicester's age at late-seventies, not that this hampered his mind as he quizzed the jeweller rigorously, "Firstly, may I return to you this beautiful agate gemstone that you sent for my perusal, Sir. Now what in particular is 'goshenite' and why do you refer to these jewels as 'shoulder stones' Mr Klein? Also, please tell me for what reason you believe Her Majesty should consider giving them to you, and who it was in India who gave you the information that Queen Victoria was gracious enough to accept them from an unnamed 'High Prince'?"

Despite knowing that the elderly man had fired a massive broadside of questions at him, Aaron detected a twinkle in Lord Bicester's eyes that helped to remove any antagonism. "Would I be permitted to answer your very astute questions in reverse order please Lord Bicester?"

The Queen's friend nodded his assent and sat back on the bench to listen. "Well, Sir, the information was given to me in India not by a 'High Prince', but by the very opposite. A hideously deformed beggar sitting with other 'untouchables' outside the perimeter fence of a dusty, provincial airport at which my plane had made an unscheduled refuelling stop, who claimed incredibly to have been waiting there for my arrival. He said that a far distant predecessor of his, who was a 'High Prince', had presented the jewel to Queen Victoria. By way of offering me his credentials, he handed me this amazingly pure moonstone jewel through the rusty wire fence, for inclusion on my restoration of the ephod, first worn by the High Priest after whom I am named: Aaron the brother of Moses." Aaron took the moonstone from his pocket and invited Lord Bicester to examine it. "You may notice its translucent nature and its absolute perfection of form and cut Lord Bicester, making it worthy of a place in any discerning monarch's or empress's crown?"

The elderly Peer smiled and said, "Certainly, I can recognise its attractions Mr Klein, as I am sure would do Her Majesty. Yet would that be sufficient reason for her to make a gift of the two stones in her own possession to yourself?"

Aaron recalled debating competitions with well-matched adversaries at school, "I believe not Lord Bicester, for I am simply an unworthy servant of my Queen. However, the two stones that I believe Her Majesty will give to me are not for my own possession. They are for inclusion on the restored ephod, which Almighty God will enable me to present to the President of the State of Israel in Jerusalem, that holy city which I believe has been revered by Her Majesty throughout her long and glorious reign. Her donation of the goshenite shoulder stones would complement the twelve individual gemstones, each of which represented a single tribe of Israel. On Aaron's shoulders he bore the inscribed names of six tribes on each of the two magnificent stones, all as detailed in exactitude by the God of Abraham, Isaac and Jacob. Goshenite may have been designated for that particular service Lord Bicester because of its rarity and phenomenally beautiful hexagonal crystal structure, which throughout the ages has made it of priceless value in comparison to mere diamonds and emeralds."

The elderly aristocrat acknowledged his own acceptance and approval of Aaron's answers, yet had a final question that amazed him, "Your explanations are lucid and worthy Mr Klein. When I convey them to Her Majesty, it may be a pleasure and most illuminating for her to handle an example jewel for herself. May I take your moonstone to show to the queen, Mr Klein?" What else could Aaron do but give this unique and so incredibly-acquired jewel into the safe-keeping of Lord Bicester, knowing that before it was returned to him it would have brought delight to the eyes and hands of his sovereign.

***

Superintendent Harling and Aaron Klein were at Heathrow Airport very early on Monday morning 18 June, where they were welcomed aboard an Israeli state aircraft, along with a few other passengers who were in one way or another assisting that Nation's affairs. They enjoyed the luxury of having several hours to talk together of all the activities of the last few weeks and of how they were being drawn onwards into as yet unknown results. A pleasant and efficient man named Harim Hertzel introduced himself and looked after them throughout the flight, explaining the initial arrangements with them, "We should arrive at Ben Gurion Airport at 3:30 p.m. local time and Mr Mordecai Leon, who is the Secretary to the Vice President or VP as we usually refer to him, will meet you and escort you into Tel Aviv, firstly to the police station in Dizengoff Street. There ready to meet you will be Tel Aviv's Chief of Police Jessel Menkin and it is hoped that Sakel Fischel, who is Israel's Deputy Commissioner for Crime, will join you later."

Things went smoothly at Ben Gurion where Mordecai Leon met them with handshakes and a wide smile. They were driven off to Dizengoff Street Police Station and taken straight up to the office of Jessel Menkin, who listened with interest as they acquainted their Israeli hosts about the *'Jewels Worldwide'* magazine and the connections that had been discovered through it in Britain, Uruguay and Australia. The superintendent produced the receipt given to Colin Glover for his jewels purchased through the Tel Aviv shop, which was situated near the Yerushalayim Street and Balfour Street junction. Jessel Menkin shared his surprise that it might be a centre of international activities, as the police knew it only for its reputation as where local ill-gotten gains could be exchanged discretely.

The state's Deputy Commissioner for Crime, Sakel Fischel arrived and thanked the visitors sincerely for their wanting to assist the Israeli services. Superintendent Harling explained that the timescale suggested by the magazine's periodic advertisements, meant that a person as yet unknown may have visited Tel Aviv several times, but particularly in the periods of February to May 2012, August to October 2013, March to July 2015 and most recently February to June 2017. Aaron Klein showed his hosts the sample jewel that he had brought with him, it being the one that he had purchased recently from the tycoon Logan Kelly in Sydney. Aaron suggested that this and other inscribed ancient gemstones had all passed through the Tel Aviv shop, before ending up in far off countries. When he mentioned the name of the Russian oligarch Kuznetson Romanov, Sakel Fischel and Jessel Menkin exchanged meaningful glances and wrote short notes on their pads. They asked their visitors if they would take a casual look at the shop, escorted by a suitable young lady officer to make them look like well-off tourists rather than police officers.

A few minutes later, Alan and Aaron were in an unmarked car being driven by Officer Davida Jainof who knew that area very well. She parked and strolled along with them, deliberately looking in the windows of half a dozen other shops before inspecting the window of 'Khalaily Jewellery Emporium'. A white Peugeot Partner van was parked at the side of the shop, with the name 'Jericho Builders' written on it in English, Hebrew and Arabic. Aaron's assessment of the shop's window display was of a typical collection of gaudy less-valuable items that low-class jewellers used to attract unknowledgeable collectors. They went inside and Aaron approached the young Assistant, "Good morning. Would you have any less-modern zircon and adamantine pieces for sale? I have associates who might be interested in necklaces or bracelets with those particular gemstones."

A fat man of indistinguishable Arab background aged about sixty, who was sitting on a stool in the workshop behind the counter, called out, "Why would the gentleman not want diamonds or rubies, which we have a good stock of and are far more valuable?"

Aaron replied pointedly, "Because zircons are what interest me and I am the customer. However, if you have none to show me, I will go elsewhere."

The fat man sauntered over to the counter and spoke in a low voice, "If the gentleman would like to step into my office for a moment, I might be able to help him." At the same time, he nodded to a younger Arab who had been in the workshop, but now left by the back door.

Using a loud Texan accent, Davida called out, "Oh for goodness sake Steve, not more silly jewels, you've got millions of them already! I'm going back to that dress shop down the street and Freddy can keep me company. Ciao Darling!" Davida grasped Superintendent Harling's arm, shepherded him outside and started back the way they had come. Twenty yards along she spoke firmly into his ear, "Stay outside the nearest dress shop, looking in the window. Abigail will pick you up in five minutes. Don't go back for your colleague, he'll be looked after. I need to follow that younger shop man. Go!"

The Chief of Britain's Major Crimes Division did exactly as he was told and walked nonchalantly to the dress shop about fifty yards away. Officer Jainof rushed beyond him and back to her car. A little later, he watched her drive slowly past him whilst she kept the Peugeot Partner van, that had left the side alley of the shop, in distant but clear sight. He stood there feeling rather inadequate and slightly scared for Aaron, muttering to himself, *"Oh Good God keep him safe!"* A small car stopped near him and the passenger door was opened wide for him. "I'm Abigail, jump in quick, Freddy!"

Forty-five minutes later the superintendent and Aaron Klein were back with Jessel Menkin in his office, waiting for coffee to be brought in for them. He joked, "You were told to act like tourists not undercover cops or spies! Oh well, it's taken some of my dedicated young ladies away from their more humdrum duties and given them some proper action I suppose!" Aaron was writing on an A4 pad for all he was worth, trying to recall a host of details about the shop, the jewellery he had been shown, the unusual boxes on the shelves that he had seen, and mostly of the fat man himself. "Did you know he only has one ear Mr Menkin? He's a peculiar sort of man, exactly like that slimy fat man in the Humphrey Bogart film *'Casablanca'*. He promised me absolutely anything that I might ask him for, as long as I could pay in cash and would take the goods with me. I bought some small zircon bracelets, just for the look of it, but not before he had shown me half of his stock of second-hand items kept in old boxes. They were obviously missing from actresses and rich women's necks and arms! He hadn't had time to dismantle them for his onward sales. He's got an Aladdin's Cave there just ready for the *'Jewels Worldwide'* magazine adverts and he's probably due for another visit from the unknown dealer." Superintendent Harling suggested that Chief Superintendent Menkin might get the usage of box numbers at Tel Aviv's main post office kept under observation, preferably when customers also made use of any left luggage facilities inside the building."

It was thought that the Englishmen had done enough in Tel Aviv to set the city's police on a new train of investigation, so Mordecai Leon collected the visitors and drove them up to the ancient capital city of Jerusalem. He explained that although Israel had no official position of vice president, that such a role was exceptionally useful for rather less-official involvements. Thus, a typical Jewish solution had been reached with Gershon Lazar being given the unique title of VP. That evening, after settling into their well-appointed hotel in a quiet district, they were taken for an informal dinner with Mr Lazar and Benjamin Sachs the Minister of Culture and Antiquities. During the meal, they discussed the High Priest's ephod and its attached 'jewels of glory', which would be a magnificent gift to the nation attracting world-wide attention. The whole evening was a great success, with the religious significance of a restored High Priest's ephod, the historic interest in ancient Biblical items, the cultural encouragement to Israel's citizens of all races and religions, and great interest for Jewish people around the world; all being reviewed with anticipation.

Aaron showed the magnificent banded agate representing the tribe of M'nasheh, that he had brought with him, explaining that he had acquired five of the Aaronic jewels and knew the whereabouts of a further five to date. When he stated that he was trusting the God of Abraham, Isaac and Jacob to reveal the remaining four original jewels very soon, Gershon Lazar responded to this boldly-stated expectation with similar courage, "I believe that the month of September would be appropriate for the auspicious presentation to the State of Israel. Rosh Hashana will begin the Jewish New Year on 10th, Yom Kippur the Day of Atonement is on 19th and Sukkot the Feast of Tabernacles will be celebrated between 24th and 30th." On that exceptionally positive note, the business of the evening was concluded, allowing them to relax and talk of other things. "Mr Klein and Superintendent Harling, is there anything in Israel that you would like to see on your first very short visit to our country? I promise you and those you bring with you, ample opportunity for travelling in Israel next time, but what about yourselves tomorrow? Is there anything particular that you would like to see?"

Alan Harling spoke up with excitement, "Well, Sir, my wife told me that I really had to float in the Dead Sea."

***

On Tuesday morning, Doctor Chaudhary went to work even earlier than usual. He was very perplexed because he wanted to help Miss Templeton so keenly, even to trying unorthodox methods, but his first attempts at using the leaves of '*Koelreuteria paniculata*' had simply produced a revolting mess. He decided that he must try again, so he locked his office door, took four of the remaining eight leaves of '*Koelreuteria paniculata*' and ground them into a fine mixture in a pestle and mortar. He poured on boiling water, left it for ten minutes and then tasted it. It was still nothing other than a foul mixture, which he could not attempt to drink himself let alone consider administering to a dying lady. What was he doing wrong? If some Indian beggar-man really had sent him the message through Peter Templeton, he could readily accept that as a divinely-inspired fact; but it would need to work! His patient was dying and could not last more than another week or so.

***

Aaron and Alan were collected and driven to the north-west shore of the Dead Sea, near to the Qumran National Park. Like hundreds of other tourists every day, they disrobed at the changing rooms and were shown how to smother themselves with the local mud, prior to floating in the extremely salty water. They took many photos to prove that they had really done it, then laid back looking across at the Qumran caves just behind the shore. History had been rewritten there between 1946 to 1956, with the amazing discoveries of the 'Dead Sea Scrolls' comprising nearly a thousand original Biblical texts. These had validated so much that had been believed through faith alone by millions of Jews and Christians for centuries. After bobbing around for half an hour, the intense heat of the sun became intolerable, so the two Britons left the amazingly buoyant water and washed off the soft brown mud. After showering, the hard-working police officer and the ex-jewellery shop owner sat almost in disbelief at one of the sea-edge cafes drinking freshly squeezed orange juice and relishing this perfect escape from London's city life.

Aaron had only one disappointment that morning, when he stubbed his toes under the water whilst struggling to regain his balance. Alan inspected the grazed toes and sought an attendant for some first-aid medication. "I'm really sorry, Sirs, but this does happen sometimes, more frequently since the improvements were made to the water access area three years ago."

'AH' asked the young man to explain. "Well, Sir, being such a busy place with so many tourists every day, the beach gets ruffled up and uncomfortable for bare feet. So the National Park Authority decided to make improvements, employing some contractors to smooth out the contours of the beach and the invisible area that can't be seen under the shallow water. The work was carried out by Jericho Builders, using a JCB and dumper trucks."

Aaron and Alan began to listen intently. "They were here for three weeks digging and moving stuff around every day, but not actually disposing of any material off site because they made a sort of bund about fifty metres out, to form a proper boundary to the beach area and stop tourists floating across to Jordan, Sir. Ever since then, people have been stubbing their toes on pieces of broken clay pots that used to be a few metres further out into the water out of harm's way. Jericho Builders were told to collect the biggest fragments of pottery and bury them under the sand, but it seems that some keep re-emerging, Sir."

Aaron asked, "If this has always been a beach, even though one with a rough surface, where did all the pots come from originally?"

The young man exclaimed, "That's easy! They must have come down from the Qumran caves, probably washed down in the heavy rains that occur every twenty years or so, or else simply rolling when disturbed by goat's feet scrabbling around on the slopes, Sir."

Aaron's Jewish mind raced as he pictured the Essene diehards more than two thousand years ago, hiding so many Biblical scrolls from the ravaging enemies of their God. Could they have also protected some of the sacred Aaronic jewels by hiding them in clay pots? Would some of those have been accidentally damaged by the contractors working on the Dead Sea shore? Could some workers have realised the value of what they were finding in some of the broken pots? Would they have decided to line their own pockets by selling jewels and other historic treasures instead of alerting the archaeologists?"

Alan added his own thoughts, "If 'Jericho Builders' realised that they were finding treasure, could they have secretly opened up many more pots, shattering enough of them to cause many stubbed tourist toes in the future? But what would they do with whatever they were finding inside the pots? How could they sell such ill-gotten gains without the help of some unscrupulous dealer, maybe somewhere else in Israel, preferably a long way away from here!"

When they returned to Jerusalem, they went straight to Benjamin Sachs's home where their theories, the evidence of Aaron's stubbed toes and several pieces of broken pottery were thoroughly considered. "Well you two, what can I say other than 'Thank you for coming to Israel and helping us out!' We'll start to look carefully at 'Jericho Builders' and the 'Khalaily Jewellery Emporium'. Now please try to relax and keep out of trouble tomorrow, until Abigail or Davida picks you up and takes you back to Ben Gurion. It's best to allow plenty of time to catch your 7.00pm flight back to London. Take care now and shalom!"

On Wednesday, they did exactly as Benjamin Sachs had suggested, eventually settling down for a relaxed hour or so at a small cafe a short distance from the Jaffa Road gate. However, twenty minutes later, Alan Harling's tea cup was smashed by a half-brick thrown from an area of rough ground behind the cafe. They jumped to their feet, perturbed to see that a crowd of teenagers wearing scarves across their faces, had crept up into throwing distance of them. A shout from the gang's leader resulted in volleys of objects being thrown at them and landing all around their table. Inevitably, some bricks, stones, pieces of wood and old bits of scrap iron made contact with their intended targets. The superintendent wasn't badly hurt, but Aaron fell to the ground bleeding from a nasty head wound. A car screamed up to the pavement, scaring the youths away in all directions. Abigail called, "Quick jump in!" They obeyed instantly and were driven straight to the minor injuries hospital for Aaron's head to be cleaned and bandaged up sufficiently for him to catch the plane home.

The badly shaken Englishmen continued their journey down to Tel Aviv's international airport without further incident, where their luggage was collected and put on board with only the formalities of a customs clearance needed. "Excuse me, Sir, but what is this object that my machine doesn't like? Please can you identify it for me Mr Klein?"

The superintendent helped his friend out as he was still feeling very groggy, "Yes, Officer. It's just an old piece of scrap iron that some kids must have bent into a sort of cube, to make a better weapon for throwing at tourists! I think that Mr Klein wants to take it back to London as a rather sad souvenir of Israel, that's all." The officer was satisfied and waved them through to where Harim Hertzel was waiting to help them board the aircraft. Not much was said between them on the flight back to London, as both of them were tired physically and mentally from their intensive days. As they were flying westerly, keeping time with the various time-zones that they crossed, it was still only 7.00 p.m. when they landed back at Heathrow. It was a great surprise to be met unexpectedly by Mary and all three children, rather than by yet another policeman or diplomat. They left the arrivals hall together like ordinary people, lost amongst the crowd of those seeking anxiously where they needed to go next, or waiting long hours for their delayed flights to be announced. They all caught the Heathrow Express to Paddington Station where the Harlings saw the bandaged Aaron into a taxi, wished him 'Goodnight' and travelled home to Gunnersbury on the tube. Alan felt tremendously good to be home again, in familiar circumstances and with people who you really loved.

***

On Thursday 21 June, Superintendent Harling was back in his office at Scotland Yard catching up with reports from his MCD team leaders, who had been just as active as himself during his three days away in Israel. Although he was delighted to see that Ammar, alias Boris, was back in Walsall and had not run further away, he knew that the young man was in an increasingly dangerous situation. There were reports from Sergeant Waseem Patel showing that Ammar and his minder, Nizar Al Katabi,, alias Andy, were having a fairly regular early afternoon walk from Swarthy's photocopy shop down into the centre of town, obviously checking and rechecking some sort of chosen route. Waseem had been holding back his officers from very close observation, for fear of alerting Swarthy and the young men, but two days ago he had sent Hippy Ipperstaff on a casual walk around town with a Birmingham dog handler PC Rodgers and his black Labrador 'Sooty'. They had met up at the railway station car park and walked past the I where Swarthy had been observed last Sunday meeting with two unknown middle-aged white-skinned people, one a flamboyant man and the other a severe-looking lady, neither of whom looked as if they hailed from Walsall. Sooty was taken along the same route as Swarthy and his companions had taken: firstly, back almost to Ablewell Street then downhill on roads and paths gradually changing direction, until emerging at Corporation Street and along to the Aisha Mosque and Islamic Centre on the corner with Rutter Street. PC Rodgers in plain clothes looked like any other dog-walker, except that Sooty was exceptionally well-behaved.

Realising that the route taken quite often now by Andy and Boris was of high importance, the officers took care to wander further around looking as casual as they could. They returned slowly uphill and came out behind Lidl's car-park, noticing over the fence that Swarthy's dark blue Toyota Auris hatchback was parked near its usual place. They strolled round and made sure that no-one was very close-by, before encouraging Sooty into some of the specialist work that he adored doing. Rodgers allowed him to sniff all around the car, resulting in the dog becoming much more agitated when near the boot, rear compartment and the passenger front door. He guided Sooty round the car twice more, before taking him away a safe distance to explain to Hippy Ipperstaff that the well-trained dog was clearly smelling at least the remains of explosive items in Swarthy's car. The two officers chatted casually as they walked from the car park and up Ablewell Street, past the filling station and along the pavement in front of the Methodist church, which was opposite the row of small shops and businesses including Swarthy's photocopiers. At the far end, they crossed over and strolled back down the other side until they reached the shop door and stepped inside, "Good morning!" said Hippy in a friendly voice, "Can I have four A4 colour copies of this please?"

The sullen young man code named Andy took Hippy's original, copied it and handed the papers back without a smile or a word apart from, "Forty pence." Meanwhile, Sooty had been encouraged by Rodgers to go under the counter flap and explore the untidy stack of boxes on the floor.

The dog became very excited in front of some cartons marked in hand-writing 'TONER CARTRIGGS'. "Here, what's going on?"

shouted Andy, "Get that dog out of here! Don't you know no manners!"

Rodgers apologised profusely and Sooty was pulled back to the customer's side. They all left the shop quickly, with Hippy calling out cheerily, "Thanks mate! Sorry about the dog getting a bit excited. See you again!"

'AH' read and re-read all the reports from Walsall. MCD's Officers had failed to identify the two visitors who had walked around the town with Swarthy last Sunday, but believed their involvement could be significant. What exactly was Swarthy up to now? The superintendent decided to go up himself early the next day, to follow his 'Copper's nose' once again.

***

Aaron woke late with his head throbbing with pain from the wound he had received in Jerusalem. The best reason not to think about that, was when his stubbed toes from the Dead Sea hurt even more! He decided to stay indoors and take this unexpected opportunity to review the jewels he had discovered and acquired, or failed to do. It had been on 27th April, nearly two months ago, that his personal mission had been commissioned. Since then he had travelled all around the world and then to Israel, seeking the original Aaronic jewels. He decided to prepare a diagram, showing the position of the individual gemstones in accordance with the detailed Biblical description. He drew rectangles for the twelve which represented single Hebrew tribes, in their three columns of four rows, numbering them from right to left in Hebrew notation.

Number 1 was top right, the ruby which he had tried to buy in vain from the Russian oligarch at Odessa airport. He had little conviction of ever having another opportunity to acquire it.

However, he had managed to obtain Number 2, the top-centre positioned golden yellow topaz, from the crooked tycoon Logan Kelly in Australia. The top left jewel, Number 3, should be a beryl, possibly of a carbuncle variety, of which he had no idea of its whereabouts. The second row down began on the right with Number 4, a turquoise green emerald which he tried to buy in Montevideo and believed to be there still. It might be possible to be bought later, if Leticia Benitez agreed.

The same situation applied to Number 6 on the left, a diamond, but the location of the gemstone between them, Number 5, a blue Sapphire, was a complete mystery to him.

The third-row right side jewel, Number 7, was the reddish-orange coloured zircon discovered in Alice Glover's Tupperware box, described otherwise in various Bible translations as a jacinth or ligure. Its position was next to Number 8, the reddish banded agate found in the same humble place, hidden away for the future by her late husband. On the left should be Number 9, a purple or violet amethyst, but for which he had no inkling of its whereabouts.

The bottom row began on the right with Number 10, described either as a chrysolite or another green variety of beryl, but of which he knew nothing. Adjacent to it was Number 11, recorded in the Bible as an onyx, which when handed to him so mysteriously through a wire fence by the Indian beggar, he knew to be the very rare variety of a translucent apple-green moonstone. The final jewel on the left of the bottom row was the equally-unusual clear red jasper, scarlet but not mottled as most common varieties, which dear Joshua Shulz had given to him to solve his conscience of having gained and kept it illicitly.

The two shoulder stones were to be onyx, of which he believed the variety would be almost clear goshenite, with just a delicate hint of green, about which Lord Bicester was talking to his Majesty and friend, Queen Elizabeth. Thus, Aaron could account for the locations of ten of the overall fourteen gems, leaving only four as totally unknown to him! Of these ten he had acquired five, hoped to gain another four, but believed in little chance of gaining the tenth, the Russian's ruby.

***

At 10.00 a.m. on Friday, Superintendent Harling's car stopped briefly to collect Waseem who updated him immediately, "Well, Sir, it looks as if the bomber's route is fixed because Andy and Boris have walked it using exactly the same roads and paths for each of the last three days. Their timing must also be decided because they have been walking clearly to a set timetable, checking in at various points to speed up at or to slow down. We believe that they intend to leave the shop at 14.57 and arrive at the mosque at 15.12 on the dot!" The car arrived at Walsall's railway station, where Hippy Ipperstaff and Nella Brown joined them.

Their plain-clothes dress was tailored for them to look like not very well-off visitors. Before they began walking, 'AH' reminded them that in nine days' time, the catastrophic terrorist murder of a revered Arab prince, together with anyone unfortunate enough to be close to him at the time, would happen successfully at a crowded and peaceful mosque, unless they and other officers of the MCD stopped it. "Our job is coming towards its end and we need a definite plan of action, even though we don't know exactly what Swarthy intends doing. We know enough, so let's get on with the job. Take me quietly up to Lidl's car park, but not the Ablewell Street photocopy shop, then we'll walk the route that you've seen Andy and Boris practicing, at the same walking pace as they take. One of them will be wearing a heavy and cumbersome bomb-jacket and nail-coat on the day, so they won't be able to go fast. Hippy, you and Nella stroll about twenty yards behind Waseem and me, acting like good friends while we chat and stop every now and again. Waseem, your job is to keep us as far as possible to the timings that A and B have been doing. Right, let's go!"

They reached Lidl's car park and turned down the footpath behind it at exactly 10.58, timed to be four hours ahead of the actual bomb-run. Three minutes later, they reached the Birmingham Road and New Street junction, strolled on and entered the park at 11.03.

Walking gently downhill they approached a block of public conveniences, "Slow down please, Sir, we're already a minute ahead of their schedule."

The nervous strain was getting to 'AH' who responded, "That's a good job Waseem, because I really must have a moment to relieve myself. Just wait outside a tick for me and signal to the others to hang on a bit."

When the superintendent emerged, they walked out of the park's southern entrance and down Bath Street. "We're just right for time now, Sir," whispered Waseem as they neared the crossroads. "Here we turn right, still going downhill." The two men walked along the street quaintly named 'Little Caldmore' until they reached Caldmore Road.

"Nella and Hippy are still the right distance behind us Sir," said

Waseem. "But slow down just a little." Passing Caldmore Green they arrived at the always busy Corporation Street, "It's only a hundred yards from here to the road, Sir, then you'll see the mosque off to our left." His boss was very pleased that the time was 11.15 as they passed the junction, but he didn't stop walking. Gradually, they made their way further along Corporation Street until turning to the right and beginning the slightly uphill journey back to the railway station.

The car collected all four officers and 'AH' made a quick decision, "Walsall must have a council of some sorts. Are their offices near here?"

Waseem replied, "Yes, Sir, they're quite close. Do you want to visit them?" His boss confirmed that he did, but when they arrived, he instructed the driver to park well away from the entrance and told Waseem and the others to wait inside the car. The superintendent walked quickly away from them, through the entrance and up to the reception desk, where he asked to see the council's Chief Executive Officer immediately. The well-trained receptionist looked at his clothes and explained politely but firmly that it would be impossible without an appointment, which perhaps he would like to request in writing using this particular blue form. Leaning forwards, he showed the lady his police pass and said quietly but with authority, "Just tell the Chief Executive that I've come up from Scotland Yard and need to see him for two minutes only, on a matter of life or death for Walsall. Straight-away now please!"

Ten minutes later, 'AH' returned to his car, which whisked away to drop the other officers off elsewhere, before driving him straight back to London, where he briefed Inspector Henderson sufficiently well to allow himself an uninterrupted weekend, unless Swarthy did something unexpected.

***

Dr Chaudhary could see that Christine Templeton would not survive many more days. Once again, he challenged himself over his medical ethics, being well aware that new drugs needed years of exactly-monitored testing even before any trials on animals, yet alone patients, could be undertaken. To think about himself administering some of the mess that he had been concocting, or even of mixing it with the excellent medicines being given to her, was absolutely out of the question. Thus, he found himself torn between his years of professional knowledge and duty, and his real anguish for this dear lady. He cried out to he knew not what, or who, in utter despair, forsaking his highly-respected image and languishing in that complete helplessness so often felt by the relatives of dying patients. If anyone had entered his office during these recent days, when the door was locked, they would have seen this exulted professional doctor reduced to a humbled man, destitute of any way to help Miss Templeton himself yet pouring out his heart for this woman to be allowed to live. Although the message sent so amazingly from India, even to himself by name, and showing the means to cure her using some tribal remedy that was beyond science; he just couldn't do it, he couldn't do it!

***

Alan Harling surprised his wife and children by arriving home on Friday evening at only 6.00 p.m. and calling out, "Hello Mary, Hi Em, how's it going, Bri? Hello, Pauline, sweetheart!" He put his surprisingly thin briefcase down out of sight in the hall, hung up his jacket and took off his shoes. Coming into the kitchen, he found his wife still preparing dinner, the teenagers glued to the telly and young Pauline engrossed with some Lego house building, "What a lot goes on in our great home, doesn't it, my loves!" His family looked him over to see if he might be ill, but realised that something else must be affecting Dad, perhaps his age? He made a pot of Earl Grey tea, Mary's favourite, put on an apron and started whistling Gilbert and Sullivan tunes whilst doing some washing up. His bonhomie continued all evening to the amazement of the family, until at 10.00 p.m. with Pauline asleep in bed, Brian out with friends and Emily busy with something or other in the living room; he suggested to Mary that they have a walk.

As they strolled around Gunnersbury's Garden Village area, Alan explained that the following weekend he would be away on business, therefore he had the next two days totally free. Mary was wise enough not to pry, and loving enough to go along with whatever her husband was up to. When it became too dark to see, they returned home, dimmed the living room lights, opened some chocolates and put on a favourite Dustin Hoffman DVD.

On Saturday morning, Alan was up exceptionally early, pottering around in the kitchen and humming more G&S. When the others came downstairs, there was a wonderful smell of pancakes, fried eggs and mushrooms, toast and coffee. "Morning Dad!" called out his surprised children.

"How lovely, Darling!" said Mary, putting her arms around him. After their breakfast, which was about two hours earlier and much bigger than on most Saturdays, Alan produced five named envelopes from his pocket, proudly watching as each of them read the contents inside. Emily found two tickets for the latest Star Wars film being shown that evening at North Ealing Granada. Brian was amazed to find two tickets for the Chelsea versus Arsenal match that afternoon. Pauline had a hand-written invitation voucher made out in fancy writing for her and Fatima Halleem to go to West Ealing's fairground under the supervision of Rashid that afternoon, with a whole ten pounds to spend 'each'! Mary took out a page of pale blue writing paper, filled with her husband's neatest possible hand-writing, putting it aside for reading in the privacy of their bedroom.

"Come on then, you lot, let's get doing, shall we? Who's ready for a spin out to the countryside for the morning, hey?" Half an hour later, they left the motorway and turned south towards Surrey's stock-broker belt with its big houses half-hidden behind manicured lawns and glorious rhododendrons. They stopped for lunch at 'The Red Lion' in an immaculate village green setting, before returning home in time for the kids to get to their afternoon and evening activities.

When the excited youngsters and their selected friends had all left, Mary sat down next to Alan on the sofa and began very gently to cry, "I suppose this is all about what Ammar's up to, isn't it, Darling?" During the afternoon and evening, they didn't move far from the sofa whilst he disclosed at least some of what would be happening next Saturday in Walsall.

Whilst the others were at church on Sunday morning, Alan sent out for an Indian takeaway to be delivered for 1.30. He'd gone rather over the top, but Mary had lots of room in the freezer for several meals in times ahead. The children all did their own things that afternoon and evening, allowing their parents some 'bonding time' which they had sussed out together to be necessary for some undisclosed reason.

***

On Saturday evening, Mr Lester had phoned Aaron asking if he would be able to drop into a particular Officers Club in St James' Street at about 3.00 p.m. the next day to visit Lord Bicester. Aaron enjoyed his Sunday walk to St James' Park, turned into a prestigious entrance way and was met by a uniformed concierge who checked that he was expected. He was escorted through the hallowed corridors of the exclusive club until the man stopped at a door, knocked quietly and admitted Aaron to a private room for his second meeting with Lord Bicester. "Come in and welcome, Mr Klein!" called the peer, motioning Aaron to a comfortable armchair. "Her Majesty wishes me to return this item that you loaned to me, which she admired very much. Her request now, Sir, is that she should see it once again herself, before you present the completed ephod in its anticipated entire glory to the State of Israel. Her Majesty suggests further that it would be more accurately visualised being worn by a man representing Aaron, rather than simply lying on a velvet cushion or something flippant. The queen asks that you should wear it Mr Klein, complete with all of its fourteen jewels for her private pleasure, on a date which can be arranged between us please. Thus now… these two magnificent translucent goshenite gemstones, that were received by Queen Victoria and held in trust by successive monarchs until you asked for them Mr Klein… are being given to you with Her Majesty's gratitude for your outstanding endeavours."

***

Once again Aaron walked the familiar Sunday evening route round to his friend Julian's flat, relaxed into the comfortable armchair and accepted the proffered glass of wine. Schubert's 'Rosamunde Ballet Music No. 2' came serenely through the speakers, while they chatted for a few minutes, with Julian talking about his apparently idyllic life of doing each day whatever he woke up with on his mind, without the pressures or anxieties that working people had. "What have you done to your head

Aaron, did you walk under a low doorway or something? Was it to do with your jewel collecting for those ancient high priestly gemstones that you are so determined to find?" Aaron gave a very short and innocent account of his time in Israel and followed it about Leticia Benitez's scheduled arrival in two days' time from Uruguay, with much jewellery in her luggage. His friend asked very casually, "What on Earth will she do with them Aaron? Where will be staying?" Aaron shrugged his shoulders and said that he didn't know any details, whilst Julian set up the chess pieces for the game to begin.

Playing chess gave you a good excuse for taking time over your answers, "My collection is growing rather well actually, Julian. So far, I've located ten of the fourteen, although I've only actually acquired five of those, I mean seven, but I've no idea where the other four might be."

Julian also took his time before asking, "Have you thought about what to do with them all, once they've fallen into your lap out of our Almighty God's hands that is?"

Aaron considered how best to reply, without disclosing confidences but wanting not to be unfriendly, "Well, it's early days yet, but naturally I'd like to reconstruct a complete ephod, that is if I manage to get all of the jewels. Probably it would end up in the safe custody of Israel's government."

Aaron lost the chess match and got up to go home, somehow unable to respond to Julian's smiles as he said, "Goodbye, Aaron and don't forget to keep me in touch with how your search progresses, won't you?"

CHAPTER 14

On Monday morning, Alan Harling waited until he had seen each of his loved ones away to schools and work, before driving unhurriedly to Scotland Yard. After catching up with Inspector Henderson and various reports that had come in during the weekend, the superintendent walked briskly to the out-of-the-way quarters at the back of Scotland Yard, which housed the 'technical boys'. He went up to Lenny Smithson, who knew more about explosives and how they were used by the criminal fraternity than almost anybody else, "Morning Lenny! Just step outside for a minute please." Once out of earshot, he continued. "I'd like to know if a bomb jacket that is being worn and primed to go off can be removed safely from a suicide bomber, or not?"

The man grinned, "I don't suppose you mean after he's been shot dead, do you?! Look Superintendent, when you combine high explosives, unpredictable amateur designs, stolen materials and fanatical terrorists, almost anything can happen and usually does. The most reliable experience is from certain foreign specialist forces, whose chaps usually kill the terrorist first and then only occasionally bother to remove an unexploded bomb jacket. I'm not saying that it can't be done, but it's about the most dangerous past-time that I can think of."

'AH' persevered, "Okay, Lenny, but let's say some crazy copper was determined to do it, what exactly would he need to do?"

Removing the grin from his face, Lenny Smithson escorted the superintendent back inside and took him to his private workshop, "Look, Harling, if you're mad enough to do it, I'll show you what I would do if I was crazy enough to try, which I'm not! Firstly, I'd need to be sure that the bomber wasn't just tricking me to come near to him before blowing both of us sky-high. Secondly, is he a hundred percent sane, or will he just let it off for the fun of it? Then, if I was convinced, he wanted to give himself up and stay alive in one shape, rather than in a million small pieces, I'd take absolute charge of the situation myself because the bomber would be too hyped-up to think rationally. Let's begin with the explosives, shall we? They can't be set off even accidentally without some mechanisms, usually a power source linked to a detonating device and wired up so the guy only has to press a button or pull a cord, rather like to inflate a life-jacket, but for the opposite reasons of course. Most terrorists aren't experts, so keep it very simple, using a high-power torch battery which has enough oomph to set something off. They'd connect that by normal three-core wire to a switch of some sort, but only fully across one of the terminals to ensure instant ignition, then along to any old detonator as long as it can take in the power and channel it along some wires to the explosives. But often that's where the trouble comes, especially if the bomb-master doesn't know how to change a light-bulb! Life or death depends on which of the three coloured strands the switch is fixed across. If the right colour wire is severed: Jolly good! But if you cut the wrong one first, then you're either in Heaven or Hell. There's no second chance!"

The superintendent considered that problem and asked, "OK Lenny, but surely the bomber would know which colour wire the switch is placed across?"

The reply was categoric, "Absolutely! Otherwise, he'd be dead before reaching his target!"

Keeping his emotions calm 'AH' asked, "Exactly where would someone cut the wires Lenny?"

Realising that the superintendent was being serious, he replied, "You'd have to separate the power supply from the detonator, therefore go straight to the switch, reach just above it and check which one goes all the way down to the detonator. Then you'd cut that one only, just above the switch, otherwise you're a dead man!"

Instead of sending the highly-respected superintendent away to try to remember all this, Smithson asked him to come back in twenty minutes and see him again. When 'AH' returned Lenny greeted him with a smile, "OK Alan, this is your life or death trial run, so come over here to the bench. I've rigged up a typical sort of hotchpotch arrangement that terrorists like to use. Just remember what I told you to do. If you cut the right wire nothing will happen, but if you sever the wrong one a red lamp will light up. I'm going outside for a walk while you do it. So long!" The superintendent had not expected this and was terrified of getting it wrong. He took two whole slow minutes to prepare himself, steady his hands and pick up the wire-cutters, while images of his wife, children and Ammar came in and out of his mind.

What had Lenny told him? Which wire was it that he must cut through? He slowed his heart-rate down and went through his instructions carefully, remembering that it would be the bomb-master who wired up the mechanisms and therefore only he would know which of the three wires he had fixed the switch across. With exceptional care, Harling touched the switch and moved his fingers just above it towards the torch battery. He gently prised open the strands of three wires entering the switch then did the same just below it. He could see that this was only the red wire that went right through, so he moved it as much away from the others as he could do, just above the switch, placed the blades of the cutters firmly on either side it and waited a few moments, before clamping the handles firmly together in his hand. Nothing happened. A voice spoke quietly behind him, "Well done, Alan. You can go home to your wife and kids tonight. Just remember to do the same thing again next time, won't you!"

***

Dr Chaudhary went through his options concerning the remaining four leaves of '*Koelreuteria paniculata*' for the hundredth time. He began to realise that if they were used in the wild, perhaps in some very rural Indian community, that the people there would not have the luxury of even boiling water and a pestle and mortar. What would they do, if they trusted in some age-old custom of using these leaves to treat their sick ones? He chopped them up as small as he could on a board, then marinaded them in a tiny amount of water. It looked just an awful mess, but he put the teaspoon-sized volume of green gunge into a sample jar, screwed down the top and put it into a locked drawer in his desk.

***

Waseem Patel and his team were well settled in their routine surveillance work in Walsall, registering the comings and goings of Swarthy, Andy and Boris each day. These two sets of persons were like butterflies that fluttered around each other, concentrating on their objectives, but without ever touching. At the photocopy shop, the routine continued with Yeraz the main person behind the counter in the mornings, assisted occasionally by Andy or Boris. They did not have many customers and Swarthy joined them very rarely. The afternoons were different, with the two young men following their route down into town with religious adherence. Swarthy never accompanied them, but was observed at different places along the way on occasions, obviously checking timings and searching for any hindrances to his plans. Sometimes he walked with his cohorts to a park, choosing quiet areas to sit and discuss things from books and manuals that he carried with him. After the shop's normal closing time of 5.30, no-one went out at all. Everything remained quiet, with just the flickering TV screen visible to their hidden observers, indicating that the four persons were still upstairs in the flat.

***

On Tuesday morning, Aaron travelled up to Kilburn, delighted to find the team still sorting through the boxes of stuff from his bombed shop. He was greeted warmly by Alice, Joshua, Ibrahim and Rashid who were hard at work, but very pleased to stop to hear of his further adventures. Alice fussed over his bandaged head wound, prompting him to produce the piece of scrap iron that had scared him and scarred him in Jerusalem. It was passed round for each of them to inspect, then left with Joshua to show to any other visitors. Aaron next pulled out a jeweller's black felt bag and removed the five gemstones that he had acquired so far. These were passed round eliciting great exclamations of wonder and joy at the amazing and beautiful jewels. He decided to ask if a 'general meeting' of all those involved could be held on Thursday early afternoon, to let everyone look more closely and be thanked for all their contributions to his search. Joshua and the others agreed whole-heartedly, as had Alan Harling and Sheikh Salim when he had asked them that morning. After Aaron had left, Joshua took the roughly cubic-shaped piece of metal into his workroom and began to look and think carefully. Its heavy weight, blackish colour with some dark greenish colouration, and a certain sort of purposeful design puzzled him.

***

Many persons who had had some involvement with Christine Templeton since the Hatton Garden bombing, began to realise that her time on Earth was very short. Several decided that they simply must go to be as near as possible to Room 604 at UCLH, desiring only her proximity. It was not necessary to speak with her and certainly not to bring flowers to this dying woman, which opportunity would be available sadly for them very soon. People were looking inside themselves, simply wanting to associate with this lady whose bravery and resolute faith in her God had touched them in ways that most of them could not, or would not, express in words. They came individually or in small groups to the hospital, not in pompous or religious ways of conformity with society's methods, but just as themselves, just to somehow say, 'thank you and goodbye Christine'. They did not want to push their way in, to affect the busy hospital's functioning, or to interrupt the hard-working staff's individual duties, but just to come for some moments, just as themselves.

Very many of the staff at UCLH knew that Christine Templeton was about to die, unable to resist the ravages of cancer despite her avowed faith, without complaint and simply submitting herself to her God's will and power. People died at UCLH on many days of the year, owing to its position as one of London's leading teaching hospitals, but somehow this time it was different. The management responded to this knowledge by placing two bench seats in the corridor outside Room 604, allowing anyone the opportunity to spend some brief quiet moments there. During the long days of this week they were used by her own shop staff and others from the community of Hampstead Heath, by off-duty policemen and women, by fellow worshippers from her church, by many UCLH managers and medical staff, hospital cleaners and workers from the downstairs cafeteria, by jewellers from Hatton Garden, by journalists without their cameras or notebooks, by Rashid Halleem with his parents and little sister, by Mary Harling with Emily, Brian and Pauline, by her old flat-mate Susan and many others. all of them persons who she had known well, a little or not at all, but who in their hearts really wanted to come. Some very few were allowed to step inside Room 604 for a few moments, just to stand there and remember: Aaron and Ruth Klein, Alan Harling, Sheikh Salim, Alice Glover and Joshua Shulz.

Inside herself, Christine shared in the knowledge of having her last few days on Earth, spending them gently fading away from people who she cared for, but especially her nephew, Peter, who she dearly loved. Again and again, she recalled the words spoken to him by the beggar in Mangalore: *'Kefa, Kefa, take this to Doctor Shuban. He will need it very soon. Afterwards, you must be a rock for your generation.'*

Peter had told his aunt that he had delivered the message written on a scrap of dirty paper dutifully to Doctor Chaudhary, but what had that wonderful doctor been willing and able to do about it? She was unable to ask him, nor did she want to embarrass him if he had decided that professionalism should not give way to a mystic message, however accurate it may be. She truly sympathised for his undisclosed dilemma, yet even in her last available hours she wanted to help him, just as he had been doing all that he could for her during the past few weeks. She knew that there was one thing that she could do: she prayed, *"Oh Father God, you know how close I am to death, which for me means a glorious entry into the loving arms and smiling welcome of my Lord and saviour, your beloved Son Jesus the Christ. In his name, and through the healing power which he demonstrated here on Earth, I ask you not for myself, but for that excellent man Doctor Chaudhary: oh my Father, help him! He is lost and cannot do with his mind what his heart desires to do to help me. He cannot do it Father, he cannot do it; but you can. Please help him Father. Amen!"*

***

At 4.30 p.m. on Tuesday, the superintendent's car arrived outside the cafe as arranged and stopped momentarily to allow Aaron to jump in. As they started their journey out to Heathrow Airport, they shared their recent news and expectations for Leticia Benitez's arrival. They were met at Heathrow and taken to an office where Mr Nicholson and the unnamed man were waiting for them. Aaron was introduced and the arrangements were gone through once again, until at 5.55 they were taken by car out to the aircraft arrivals area to a building marked simply: 'Security — No entry.' The plane from Montevideo landed on time and one of its cabin staff made an announcement for Miss Benitez to make herself known as she was leaving the aircraft. Leticia made her entry into Great Britain by being met at the bottom of the steps and escorted by car to meet the four men waiting patiently for her in a grey concrete outbuilding. Aaron came forward and greeted her warmly, trying to calm any fears that she might have by seeing three strangers wearing suits and looking very official. It was Mr Nicholson who made some short notes of the proceedings, confirming her own details and then asking her to explain why she wished to enter the country.

"When I met Mr Klein in my home in Montevideo, he had come a very long way to buy some jewellery from my grandfather. The meeting went disastrously after… an intruder… burst in causing my grandfather to suffer a stroke from which he died the next day. The totally incorrect reporting of what happened caused a frenzy of media interest around the world. The ridiculous publicity and his ignominious death left me with no work or life worth living in Montevideo, plus an enormous amount of my grandfather's possessions to sort through.

"When I realised how much of that was jewellery, which he had acquired in very dubious ways, I had to decide whether to go to the Uruguayan authorities with whom our family reputation was in shreds, or take the stolen jewels to Europe, where I imagine most of them originated. I have brought them here to be returned to their rightful owners or whatever else is decided by the authorities. I want nothing, absolutely nothing, more to do with these items, having never supported his evil enterprises. After having given my entire adult life to looking after my wicked grandfather, all I want now is to begin my life again, but to help people rather than damage them like he did. My grandfather left everything he possessed to me, so I am a wealthy woman without including the value of these tainted goods. I disclaim any ownership of them and I give them all to Mr Klein and the police for honourable disposal. Now will you allow me to stay or not?"

All four men were taken by surprise at Leticia Benitez's forthright speech, which was responded to initially by Mr Nicholson, "Thank you, Miss Benitez for explaining your situation so succinctly. The Uruguayan authorities have confirmed that there is no record of you having any criminal activity of your own in that country, from where you have never travelled abroad before. We recognise and thank you for your desire to help Britain's authorities investigate and resolve various criminal activities. Once we have seen what your luggage contains, we will be better able to answer officially but for now, would you like a cup of tea?" That broke the ice and tea for five was ordered for delivery as soon as possible.

Shortly afterwards, a luggage transporter arrived bearing only the six large suitcases belonging to Leticia. The unnamed man used a portable scanner to confirm that they contained no explosives or drugs, then asked her to open them. She quickly showed them that two contained only her personal items, especially clothes, whereas the other four were packed full of carefully padded bags. Examples of those from each case were opened, revealing what Aaron Klein declared to be 'an absolute fortune of jewellery'.

Mr Nicholson spoke again, "This investigation will take a great deal of effort and we acknowledge that you wish to co-operate and assist our endeavours. Owing to the considerable time that this will take, I am signing a diplomatic visa permitting you to stay in Britain for two years initially, entirely for your own reasons and at complete liberty to travel, but with the agreed stipulation for you to assist Superintendent Harling with his police enquiries." A few formalities were gone through, requiring several signatures, before hands were shaken and smiles replaced the formal expressions. Mr Nicholson concluded the meeting with, "Welcome to Great Britain, Miss Benitez!" Leticia smiled, thanked them all and allowed Aaron to shepherd her outside, with all of her six suitcases. The car took them all to the public side of the airport buildings where they transferred everything into the waiting police car. The unnamed man said 'Goodbye' to them all and walked away, but the superintendent asked Mr Nicholson if he could spare another five minutes in private.

They walked to a quiet unused corridor whilst the others waited for their return, "Thanks very much indeed for helping us all today, Mr

Nicholson. Would it be possible please for me to ask you about another matter, which concerns the town of Walsall?" Ten minutes later, they rejoined Aaron and Leticia, and the Superintendent's police car left the airport and was driven straight to Scotland Yard where the four heaviest suitcases were logged in as 'unopened' and locked away in the room that had been prepared for them. Alan Harling said 'Goodbye' and instructed the driver to take his two visitors up to the same address in Golder's Green that he had driven to previously, enabling Leticia to begin the first chapter of her new life. As she sat quietly in the back of the comfortable car, Leticia opened her handbag, took out a package and placed it gently into Aaron's hands, "These are for you, dear Aaron, as I somehow forgot to put them in a suitcase with the other things. Thank you for all of your wonderful help in setting me free." He felt through the thin tissue paper and knew without needing to look, that what he had travelled all that way to Montevideo to buy, had now been graciously given to him by this vibrant lady.

***

When Prince Salim arrived back in London on Wednesday morning, he was told that Superintendent Harling wished to meet him as soon as possible. They decided to meet in UCLH's cafeteria at 11.10 a.m., which would allow the sheikh a few minutes to pay his own last respects to Christine Templeton. Whilst several highly-anxious Arab guards hovered inside and outside the lifts and cafeteria, Alan Harling shared the news that the prince was the target for Britain's next act of terrorism. With scant details available to them, other than the date was the coming Saturday 30th June and the precise time was to be 3.12 p.m., the two men talked in soft voices which hid their determined and brave hearts. "My speech at the mosque is scheduled to begin at 3.10 p.m., being watched there by crowds expected to be in their many hundreds, and seen or listened to on TV and radio perhaps by millions around the World. I will leave all of the counter arrangements to yourself Superintendent Harling, telling my staff nothing of what has been planned by the culprits. I am quite content for myself, but must advise you that there will be persons known to you alongside me, not to mention many leading persons of various faith groups from in and around Walsall." Alan Harling was puzzled and then alarmed when told that Ruth Klein and Peter Templeton would be flanking the prince whilst he made his speech.

Not long afterwards, Peter Templeton and Aaron escorted Leticia Benitez to the bench outside Room 604, waiting a few moments whilst the Montevidean lady was allowed her first and probably last sight of Christine, before they in turn stood at her bedside in quiet contemplation.

***

Superintendent Harling was very surprised and even more annoyed to receive a phone call from his old boss, Chief Superintendent George Price on Wednesday afternoon, inviting him to join him that evening at the exclusive fitness and leisure club where he had been a member for many years. In attempting to decline, it was made clear to him that it was a subtle order, rather than an invitation, "I'll meet you in the foyer at 6.30 and don't forget to bring your swimming trunks!"

Thus, a few hours later, 'AH' was greeted cordially by the Chief Superintendent, "Glad to see you've brought your swimming trunks Alan! Please call me George this evening as we're definitely off duty! I'll take you through to the pool and we'll do a few lengths first shall we?" Alan was mystified at this first ever such invitation from his ex-boss, but he decided to play along and wait to see what happened. He wasn't a strong swimmer and after twenty minutes of thrashing noisily up and down the pool he was pleased when George Price suggested that they have a sauna. As they entered one of the three cabins, he noticed that Price spoke discretely to an attendant, who placed an 'Unavailable' sticker on the outside of their door.

It was in this very private meeting room, with the steam relaxing and replenishing their bodies that George Price revealed the purpose for his strange invitation, "I'd like to tell you a story Alan which has a bearing on the new work that you've been promoted to do, and have started doing so well I hear. Next year will see my retirement from the Met after a long and mostly-satisfactory career and I want to have a perfectly clean ending. That's why I've decided to tell you of an incident that occurred more than twenty years ago, before I had even reached the rank of inspector and when I too was involved in investigating jewellery robberies. As part of our team's enquiries I was sent over to Amsterdam to interview a shop owner there who had some insurance connection with a recent robbery here in Bond Street. It was meant to be a purely routine exercise, but when I met this man, I thought him to be a very untrustworthy character. I went through the usual formalities of interviewing him and taking his detailed written statement, which was mainly that he had no prior or subsequent knowledge of the robbery, nor any connection with that prestigious shop, nor the current whereabouts of the missing articles which were known to be worth a very great deal of money."

George Price paused to change position on the hard slatted wooden benches, before continuing his story, "After the man had read and signed the statement that I had prepared, he handed me back my pen, smiled and said, *'Thank you for your very professional treatment of this sordid business. Before we wish each other 'Goodbye' I should like to ask you please to accept this small souvenir of Amsterdam, which you might like to keep until your very far- distant retirement from police work.'* Then he handed me this trinket which was in a pretty little Dutch box at the time. I've kept it, although it was scratched, amongst other such inconsequential things gathered on holidays in Bournemouth, then Majorca and further afield as my promotions came along. Now my wife and I are gradually sorting through all the stuff that you collect and then don't really know what to do with. I had decided to take the trinket down to our local jewellery shop to see what it was worth, if anything. However, The Yard's grapevine informs me of what you've been up to recently, working in conjunction with the Jewish chap whose shop was bombed out and who is trying to locate some old jewels." He unwrapped a corner of his towel and extracted a small package which he placed very deliberately into Alan Harling's right hand, "Please give this to your Jewish colleague for his collection Alan, but of course without mentioning anything at all of what I've just told you."

Once he was back in his car, Alan unwrapped the pale green 'trinket' which looked very similar to the other precious jewels that Aaron had been gradually accumulating. He phoned his friend straight-away, "I've had rather an unusual evening Aaron, which I'll tell you about tomorrow up at Joshua's. I'll be bringing you an unexpected little extra! Goodnight!"

***

On Thursday morning, Alan and Mary Harling took a morning off from their respective jobs, travelled up to UCLH and went hand-in-hand together for a few moments to Room 604. They came down to the cafeteria, where nowadays he was greeted with a friendly smile, then went to his usual quiet table at the far end to enjoy unhurried coffee and cake together. From UCLH they strolled along Euston Road, turned north into Albany Street and entered the east side of Regent's Park. Selecting cones of ice-cream from the kiosk, they took these to a shaded bench amongst flower beds and sat relishing their freedom. A little later Mary walked off to the conveniences two hundred yards away, leaving Alan alone on the bench. His solitude was disturbed, according to prior arrangements, when Mr Nicholson joined him for the necessary few minutes to confirm Saturday evening's events.

Mary rejoined her husband and they travelled further north to Kilburn. Before joining the gathering of involved persons at Joshua's house, Alan had decided to wait in sight of the tube station entrance and escort his injured friend on the walk to Brondesbury Road. They saw Aaron emerge from the station amongst quite a crowd of people and begin walking towards them. Suddenly, when he was about fifty yards away, he waved a greeting but almost immediately fell to the ground. Alan rushed forward in time to see a man wearing a black coat dash across Kilburn High Road and run down a side-street. He helped Aaron to his feet, who was shaken up but managed to say, "Did you see that chap Alan? He was in my carriage on the train, but I came out before him. He must have just charged into me from behind for some reason and then run away. It's crazy what some people will do to a Jew if they don't like them, isn't it!" Mary joined them and they walked together along to Joshua's house, where they were invited first into Alice's convenient ground-floor flat for a preliminary cup of tea.

Gradually, the others arrived and everyone convened in the first-floor workroom, which had a dozen chairs arranged around a low central table. Leticia and Mary were introduced very cordially to those who had not met them previously. Sheikh Salim was delighted to see Ruth and Peter and thanked them again for agreeing to accompany him to Walsall the next day, where they would stay overnight in preparation for their joint guests-of-honour appearance whilst he made his Saturday afternoon speech. Ibrahim and Rashid had changed out of their habitual working clothes, vital for their extremely dirty work sorting the contents of the boxes in the garden, into their best clothes. Aaron thanked Joshua and Alice for their hospitality, then thanked each of the others individually for the wonderful assistance they had been giving him in his search for the ancient jewels.

Alan Harling was keen to tell the cleverly-made-up story that he had been concocting, of how the 'trinket' had come into his possession yesterday. However, Aaron was determined to begin his account of how the seven, specific, breast-piece jewels had been acquired. He took a large black satin cloth from his pocket and placed it carefully on the table. "My friends, please may I now lay out these wonderful gemstones in the positions that they occupied on the very first High Priest Aaron's ephod?" Alice wanted to make a small interruption, but thought it was out of place. Aaron explained the design and how each individual stone must be placed in accordance with the detailed Biblical description. He showed that there would be three columns of four rows for the twelve jewels which represented single Hebrew tribes, numbering them from right to left in Hebrew notation. He began his carefully rehearsed account, referring to each jewel in numerical order, "Number 1 at top right would be a ruby, which I tried to buy from the Russian oligarch when Peter was with me at Odessa airport. I failed in that exercise and I doubt if there will ever be another opportunity for me to acquire it. However, Number 2 in the top centre position is..." he paused and reached into his black jeweller's bag, rather like a magician. "This glorious golden yellow topaz, which I acquired in exchange for one of my own stones from the crooked tycoon Logan Kelly in Australia, again in the presence of Peter. That man fell in a faulty lift almost to his death very soon afterwards, just before the New South Wales police launched a criminal investigation against him, thanks to Alan who had alerted them."

The friends around the table began to really enjoy Aaron's surprisingly theatrical account, as he continued, "Number 3 at top left would be a carbuncle or another variety of beryl, but I have no knowledge of its whereabouts. The second row down includes Number 4 on the right and Number 6 on the left, which I travelled courtesy of Prince Salim's generosity, but in vain to buy from Leticia's grand-father in Montevideo. However, that dear lady who is happily now amongst us, has most graciously donated this... beautiful turquoise green emerald and this... fabulous diamond, to our venture!" The location of the gemstone between them, Number 5 a sapphire, is still a complete mystery to me".

He waited for the others to admire the three wonderful jewels now positioned on the black cloth, before continuing, "On the third row right hand side is jewel Number 7... this gleaming reddish-orange zircon, revealed in this very room by Ibrahim and Rashid after they discovered it inside Alice's long-missing Tupperware box. That had been hidden inside her late-husband's tool box, where he had secreted it for future sale and their benefit, together with... its neighbouring Number 8, an amazingly banded red agate. Those two jewels represented Ephraim and Manasseh, two sister tribes being the sons of Joseph. Surely this discovery of hidden treasure shows us the powerful hand of Almighty God at work! On the left of this row, would be Number 9, a purple or violet amethyst, but of which I have no knowledge of its ownership or location."

There were now five brilliant gemstones lying spaced apart on Aaron's cloth as he began to describe the fourth and bottom row, "Number 10 on the right would be a green variety of beryl, possibly a chrysolite, but I have no idea of its whereabouts. However, the adjacent jewel Number 11, recorded in the Bible as an onyx... is this fantastic translucent apple-green moonstone! It was handed to me with such humble drama through the wire fence at Mangalore airport, by the blind and hideously disfigured Indian beggar, with dear Ruth and Peter watching enthralled with me. This final position, Number 12 on the bottom left, is occupied by... this most rare clear red jasper, almost scarlet and not mottled as are most jaspers. It had been kept safe for me unknowingly for many years by dear Joshua, who had associated it with sadness and trouble, although in fact it was for Almighty God's future perfectly-designed plans. Its incarceration had been fully-intended, as was the case with our ancestor Joseph who was sold into slavery, then thrown into an Egyptian prison for many years until he was released and honoured by the king, also becoming the saviour of Israel!

"Thus, my friends, you see before you seven of the individual jewels from the twelve, each of which bears the name of a tribe inscribed on it. However, in addition to these, there were two stones that the original Aaron wore on his shoulders, each engraved with the names of six of Israel's tribes. Now friends, please look… here they are… two almost clear goshenites, a very rare type of onyx, which were given once to Queen Victoria, but have now been presented to me with such grace by our most honourable sovereign Queen Elizabeth!"

The gathered friends were astounded with the present collection of nine of the fourteen ancient gemstones, shown here in front of their own eyes, together with such accounts of their miraculous acquisition. Aaron sat down, humbly quiet in the awed room. After a pause, a polite cough from Alan Harling heralded his long-held back announcement, "My friends, these are not quite all the jewels that have been discovered…"

He followed his friend's example, "Because… this tenth gemstone is an anonymous gift to you Aaron." Alan passed the sea-water coloured aquamarine, a beautiful type of green beryl, into the astonished jeweller's hands, "… for placing on the right side of the bottom row, representing Dan the tribe associated with the judiciary, unless I'm mistaken!" Everyone was amazed and uttered cries of delight. Aaron smiled widely and called, "Now we have ten! How wonderful! Let's celebrate with the tea and cakes that I know dear Alice has prepared especially for this auspicious occasion!"

People moved around while Alice went about her refreshment duties with many willing helpers. She handed something quietly to Aaron explaining, "When you arrived and took off your jacket, I noticed that this screwed-up newspaper fell out, but I didn't want to disturb you at the time. It's probably only rubbish but I'm not sure." Aaron took it from her and saw immediately that it was indeed a newspaper, but the print was not in English. He took it over to Alan, "What do you think this language is? I can't make it out."

Ruth and Peter joined them and the young man said, "It's Russian! Where did you get it from?"

Aaron had no idea but Alan's policeman's brain sprung into action, "I bet it was that chap in the black coat who knocked you down. Perhaps it's some sort of message for you?" By now, with cups of tea and plates in their hands, people were returning to their places around the table. Aaron unfolded the several pages and opened them out.

Ruth pointed, "It's a photo of a crowd of people walking along, all looking very sad. Look Uncle, some of them are carrying a large box on their shoulders."

Peter exclaimed, "It's not a box Ruth… it's a coffin!" Beneath the picture, some rough hand-writing had been scrawled, '*I hope that you are cursed by this evil stone as much as my family has been. KR*' Aaron lifted up the top two sheets of paper and revealed a rather dirty but obviously glorious bright red ruby. Joshua asked permission and took the ruby away, washed, dried and polished it, before returning it bright and shining to Aaron, after which he stood with a dignified expression on his face. "My friends, I have waited until this moment before requesting your indulgence for me to make an 'elder statesman's' speech. Please help yourselves to more tea and cake as I explain." They all replenished their refreshments and sat back intrigued at what the old lapidorist wanted to say.

"It may be apparent to many of us that Mr Aaron's search was initially commissioned in a most unusual way, beginning by a note erroneously ascribed to dear Alice's late husband: '*You must find these jewels*'. However, when she confirmed that it was not in his handwriting, then the question remains: 'whose was it?'" Alan kept resolutely silent as he remembered Peter Taylor's interpretation that the writing found by Aaron in the Gideons Bible, also that strange personal note that Emily had received from a one-armed man and delivered to her father, were unusual in not being attributable readily to either a male or female hand. Joshua continued, "All of us have had involvements with Mr Aaron's search, witnessing the many unexpected turns and amazing ways that these eleven magnificent 3,500 years old jewels in front of us were acquired. Surely this has been an exploration and discovery of immense strangeness and importance, which to me at least can only be described as divinely inspired and orchestrated. From that standpoint, I am not content that Mr Aaron has no inkling of the whereabouts of the remaining three jewels." Those gathered in the room were staggered at Joshua's statement and suggestion.

He spoke on with surprising boldness, "Surely the ephod is to be fully completed, not left with unholy gaps! Two days ago, Mr Aaron left me this rough metal missile that was thrown at him last week in Israel. My supposition is that the seemingly wicked act of hooliganism and hatred, was in fact part of Mr Aaron's mission!" People around the table frowned and puzzled over old Joshua's amazing interpretation of events. "With my lapidary training and understanding, I have examined this piece of apparently scrap metal that has scarred Mr Aaron slightly, but I believe to be permanently." Joshua paused to pass the roughly cubic lump of metal around, asking people to feel the weight and note the texture, "We can see that it is of heavy weight, blackish in colour with some dark green staining, and a certain sort of cubic design about it. You may notice that it appears to have been hammered all over, with obvious thoughtfulness, especially at the corners between two of its sides. Someone has tried to construct a sort of box out of a piece of old metal, with integral flaps cut with slots and then overlapped to make a seal." He paused again for effect, "My friends, it is not a worthless piece of scrap iron!"

Aaron looked more carefully and saw what the old jeweller meant, "Well, Joshua, if it was once hammered into this sort of box shape, it must have been a very long time ago, before machines. Why would anyone have gone to so much trouble to make a crude box out of old metal and what is it made of, if not iron?"

Joshua retained a serious and dignified expression as he asked, "I believe that it is made of bronze, rather than iron, and is a deliberate container. Do you wish to keep this strange souvenir as it is Mr Aaron, or are you intrigued enough to allow it to be opened up?" Aaron gave his approval, allowing Rashid to assist Joshua in his workroom. They put whatever it was into a vice and began sawing it very gently along two sides and then across the bottom front. By now, everyone else had crowded into the doorway, intent on not missing what was taking place. They clustered as close as possible as Joshua and Rashid gradually began to separate two of the hammered-down flaps, which very slowly began to come apart. Slowly but surely these were released sufficiently and pulled a very little away from the sides. Joshua whispered, "Don't worry if you break it, Rashid, because the metal may be very brittle; but let us try to pull the flaps wide open and see what might be revealed to us inside." The young man took utmost care, as did many of the others with photographic films taken on their phones, as two rough sides of the cube began to be prised apart, allowing sight of some sort of cloth material inside. As the delicate operation continued, Alice saw that this was not just an insignificant rag, but appeared to be of finely-woven fabric. Eventually, the box was opened sufficiently to allow the cloth to be removed, with everyone wondering if the material was more important than the box or what it contained. It was carried very carefully to the table, where Leticia commented on the extremely delicate nature of the weave, so similar to the linen that she had used to wrap her grandfather's jewels and she had brought to England with her.

The others stood back to allow Aaron to inspect what was clearly a largish piece of material that had been very carefully folded over many times to completely fill the space inside the box. Alice and Joshua teased the edges of the cloth away and eased them apart, spreading them partially opened on the table. Aaron was invited to finish the unveiling, using his jeweller's delicately-tuned fingers to reveal whatever had been so carefully wrapped up. They all peered down as one by one Aaron unwrapped three shining jewels from their ancient prison, still with their gold fittings in place. In an awed voice he exclaimed, "This isn't just an old cloth! These are three of the Aaronic inscribed jewels! They have been wrapped so meticulously in what I believe to be part of the original ephod!" The rest of that day was spent in photographing, examining and admiring the workmanship of the items and of the ingenious method of concealment.

However, Joshua had not completed his exposition, "Where exactly were you when it was thrown at you Mr Aaron?"

He conferred with Alan before replying, "We were near to the point where the ancient Jaffa Road leaves the city of Jerusalem, close outside its present gate."

The elderly Jewish man smiled widely as he explained, "This metal container was very purposely designed to hold treasure and keep it from the enemy's hands. Look at these marks on the very edge of this piece of the ephod. Can you discern them Mr Aaron?" His ex-employer looked very carefully using a powerful magnifying glass, gradually recognising some Hebrew words written in a rough hand, which he asked Joshua to translate and read them out. The old man's face was shining with tears as he spoke in a determined voice, "*May Almighty God protect these holy jewels being saved from God's enemies by me, King Zedekiah. May they be brought back into the light of Almighty God's glory on a day of His choosing.*"

Mary Harling and Peter Templeton had Bible knowledge to match that of the two Jewish men who were staring dumbfounded at each other. Mary spoke, "Joshua, Aaron! Do you remember in the Tanach, what we as Christians call the Old Testament, when Jerusalem was finally overthrown by Nebuchadnezzar of the Babylonians, that King Zedekiah was blinded and led as a captive with his remaining population into exile? Could he, in the last days of the nation's freedom, have ordered for the most precious holy ephod and its jewels to be separated into parts and placed inside metal boxes, believing that they could survive for centuries in the dry climate?"

The old man agreed, "Yes and perhaps all of the fourteen jewels were once put into such boxes, which would have been thrown over the city wall before the ruthless Babylonians destroyed Jerusalem? Maybe other similar boxes have been found since that day 2,600 years ago and have been opened by inquisitive people. These ingenious containers, with their hidden High Priest's jewels, may have passed through the hands of kings, princes, thieves, emperors, beggars, the rich and the proud, righteous men and otherwise, right down through the long centuries until you, Mr Aaron, were instructed by Almighty God to rediscover and collect them, enabling them once again to be displayed together for God's glory!"

Aaron sat down exhausted by the impact of what had happened and the revelations made in this humble house in north London. Alan Harling held his wife's hand very tightly, pondering over the intricacy of the astonishing and inexplicable workings that had taken place during the last two months. Even that he himself, an atheist policeman, should have been taken with this Jewish jeweller Aaron Klein to Israel, where his friend had been attacked by modern-day enemies. Yet one of the weapons used had not been innocent, but the exact opposite as it contained these most carefully preserved and ancient holy items, which

Aaron had been sent there to collect! Alan looked across at Sheikh Salim, who alone knew the secret plans that were to unfold on Saturday. Then he glanced at young Ruth and Peter, full of excitement and wonder at the beginnings of their lives. Would he and his officers be able to stop the violent murder of these people and countless others with them in only two days' time?

***

Detective Constable Salmud Jones went into Swarthy's photocopier shop about midday on Friday and found Boris there on his own. Being careful not to speak too openly, he asked his loaded question, "Morning Mate! Please can I have six copies of this advert, no wait a minute, let's have seven so that I can give one to Pauline in the office."

Ammar's heart leapt as he registered the code-word. He did the job quickly, handed the copies to Jones in exchange for his forty-two pence, "Bye!" was all that Ammar said, although he smiled broadly at who he expected was an incognito policeman leaving the shop. A few minutes later, Zakarian came in and looked around, checking things over for himself.

Going to the copier machine, he lifted the lid and saw an A4 paper on it, "Look, Ammar! How many times do I have to tell you to remember to check that you haven't forgotten to give the original back to the customer! You've done it yet again!"

The young man apologised, but Swarthy couldn't resist a final jibe as he took the advert that Jones had forgotten to ask for, "Well you won't have to remember for much longer will you Ammar!"

Returning to his flat above the shop, Zakarian looked at the advert he had brought from the copier machine. It was for a firm of wines and spirits importers in London, showing a list of what would be on offer next week. He felt uneasy and decided to phone the number shown on the advert. Getting only an 'unavailable' tone, he switched on his computer and typed in the website address, which Google failed to recognise. Swarthy went back down to the shop brandishing the advert, "Who gave you this Ammar? What did he look like?"

The young man realised that his error might be important, so he gave only a nondescript description, "He was an Asian man aged about thirty wearing normal clothes and looking quite ordinary really. He didn't have glasses. He's been in a few times recently."

Swarthy didn't smile, "OK, but don't make any more mistakes today, Ammar. Tomorrow is our big day."

***

During Friday's long night-shift at UCLH, a nurse knocked at the sister's open door along from Room 604 and walked in smiling politely, "Good evening, Sister. Because Doctor Chaudhary knew that he would be off duty this evening, he told me before he left to wait until midnight before bringing you this note to give you, along-with his prescription for a specialist drug that he has instructed me to administer to a Miss Christine Templeton. Which is her room please, Sister?" The sister took the proffered note, satisfied herself that it was indeed from Doctor Chaudhary, recognising his unusually legible handwriting and the rather quaint way that he had of expressing things. It read: "Sister, please enable the nurse who is bringing to you my instructions, to give my prescribed medication to Miss Templeton in Room 604 by injection as soon as possible. Be enough kind to please let me know, Sister, the anticipated outcome of this analgesic treatment, after the recording of its desired effects of which I have certainty of anticipation." As it was signed by the doctor, who had instructed immediate action, the sister took the nurse along to Room 604, exposed Christine Templeton's passive arm herself and watched the nurse as she gave the injection in a proper professional way. "Thank you, Sister. Goodbye!" said the nurse as she left the room. Telling the patient's usual nurse to remain seated at the bedside, and to take care in monitoring any results, the sister returned to her own office.

Shortly after 4 a.m. that nurse left Room 604 to run the few yards to the sister's office, where she stood ashen-faced and silent in the doorway. "Whatever is it, Nurse? What is the matter with you? For goodness sake speak to me, Nurse!"

The young woman sat down uninvited onto a chair and said, "Miss Templeton is asking for a cup of tea, Sister."

The motherly sister came round her desk and put an arm around the young nurse's shoulder, "Look, dear, it affects everyone, even us professional nurses and doctors when we witness a fine person dying. You must just accept the fact that it happens. Now just tell me simply and properly. Has she gone?"

The nurse looked up with her eyes streaming with tears, "No, Sister, she wants a cup of tea, and without sugar she says!"

The sister strode magisterially along to Room 604 with the young nurse trailing behind her. Pushing the door wide open she saw Christine Templeton sitting up in bed, smiling and apologising, "Oh, I'm so sorry to be a further trouble to you, Sister, and so very early in the morning, but I do so fancy a proper cup of tea please and this dear young lady didn't quite seem to understand me. I am sorry." The sister recalled her training, did not attempt to understand or even to speak, but reached out and pulled the alarm cord to summon the duty doctor.

A minute later, a young houseman joined them and shared the same look of unbelief as he stammered out, "But what has happened, Sister, what is going on here?"

It fell to Christine Templeton herself to take the initiative away from the perplexed medical professionals as she explained, "Please don't be alarmed. Simply, share my own joy at being healed by my faithful God. Now please, one of you, may I have a cup of tea, without sugar?" Despite the time of day, Doctor Chaudhary was phoned and asked to joined them in Room 604 as quickly as he could do.

The ever-professional doctor, even though his heart was pounding with joy, knew categorically that he was not responsible for achieving the medical solution to this glorious event. He examined the prescription and note purporting to be from himself, recognising his own writing and style implicitly. He quizzed the sister and the young nurse rigorously, who could only repeat the words and actions that they had heard and witnessed. They agreed their description of the nurse who had come with his own hand-written prescription and who they had observed administering the injection soon after midnight, "*She was aged about thirty, looked clean, smart and very professional, and had a skin colour not unlike your own, Doctor. She had just one distinguishing feature in that she had only one arm, her left one apparently having been amputated at some time.*" They added their own assurance that the nurse had managed to make the injection perfectly adequately without a second arm, which had pleased their professional eyes. Doctor Chaudhary tried not to run on his way to his own office, but as he unlocked his desk drawer and took out the empty jar from where he had placed it, he failed totally to stop his tears flowing and his heart rejoicing.

The news spread around UCLH like wild-fire: *'Christine Templeton is alive and has been healed not by the doctors but by her God!'* It was handed on from person to person, it was phoned and texted outside, it was marvelled at, disbelieved until others confirmed it, believed then as having happened: *'A miracle! A miracle!'* was echoed in the corridors, the wards, the staff rooms and the cafeteria. Nobody at all could deny it. It was true and had been witnessed by more and more staff who peered into Room 604 to see with their own eyes. A miracle had taken place that early morning at UCLH!

***

On Friday morning, Superintendent Harling had convened a Command Team meeting of the MCD where discussions over the deployment of specialist groups of officers was agreed upon, after-which he issued his final instructions before travelling up to Walsall himself.

Sergeant Waseem Patel and his Team Empathy were responsible for all ongoing arrangements in Walsall, whilst Inspector Donald Spencer's Team Amber were to give them direct support on Saturday afternoon, handling the aftermath of the terrorist's attempts, assisting in arrests of involved parties, and being responsible for specific transport arrangements. Inspectors Kevin Henderson with selected officers from The Pool and Herbert Norton with his Team Beryl were to travel up to Wolverhampton's main Police Station straight after today's meeting, where 'AH' had arranged for temporary HQ facilities to be placed there at MCD's disposal. That would enable him to co-ordinate activities in Walsall and hold additional officers in reserve for deployment as dictated by changing events.

Inspector Geoffrey Dent and his Team Coral were to be prepared for making further arrests if necessary, elsewhere in the country. Once the assembled team leaders had understood and acknowledged their roles fully, they departed to brief their own officers and begin the countdown operations to the dramatic events scheduled for tomorrow afternoon.

Superintendent Harling enjoyed his cheese sandwiches, wrote out several pages of notes by hand, and took them along for his mid-afternoon briefing meeting with A/C Laurence Williams. After that, he cleared his desk with great care, packed away all superfluous items into filing cabinets and drawers, took a long look around and left Scotland Yard. He went straight to Walsall for a private meeting with Sheikh Salim, at which the fine details for tomorrow afternoon's prevention of his assassination attempt were discussed and agreed.

Saturday's events were recorded by MCD Officers from multiple angles using sophisticated sight and sound equipment deployed around Walsall and particularly along the bomber's route. Precisely at 14.57, Andy and Boris were filmed leaving the flat's entrance next to Swarthy's shop, with its 'Closed' sign still in evidence, clearly with Andy in the support role for the heavily dressed Boris. They walked conscientiously along to Lidl's supermarket and started along the footpath behind it, emerging at the far end at exactly 15.00. Andy and Boris ignored an old-style preacher who was standing on a crate holding a big Bible in one hand and extolling the few nondescript listeners, in his loud and forthright voice to: *'Repent and obey Jesus Christ's instructions,'* adding *'Let all those who have ears to hear: let them hear, Emily'*. Andy did not notice the additional final word added to the Gospel message, but Ammar picked up on it immediately.

At 15.01 they were at the Birmingham Road and New Street junction, exactly on time according to Andy's watch. Two young women, looking the worse for an excess of alcohol, were staggering across the road towards them, with one saying to the other, *"Well Pauline, my boyfriend's always telling me to hurry up, he is!"* They fell into each other's arms laughing, disgusting Nizar Al Katabi, whilst Ammar simply looked ahead and speeded up his walk a little. At 15.-03, the young men entered the park at its New Street entrance and walked downhill past the benches, on one of which sat two men-of-the road who could be heard discussing, in surprisingly clear and concise words, the merits of sleeping out at night, *"If you asks me, Brian, my favrit is always a nice cozy block of toilets, but wot about you, Brian?"* A hundred yards further on Ammar spoke to Nizar, "Look, I'm sure that we're on time and I really must go to the toilet, Nizar."

His companion replied haughtily, "You know the rules as well as I do! It's out of the question!"

Ammar persisted, "What's Zakarian going to say if I arrive at the Mosque and say 'Excuse me, where's the toilet?' just minutes before blowing up the sheikh!"

He ignored his companion's foul rebuke and walked straight into the 'Gentlemens' calling out, "Wait here, Nizar, I'll only be a moment." They never saw each other again.

Four beefy men in dark clothes, chosen partly for their size and weight, leapt straight from the 'Ladies' on top of Nizar Al Katabi, immediately wrapping a steel band around him to enclose his arms, whilst a thick black material sack was pulled over his head. He was handcuffed, shackled at the feet, tied further around all his limbs, then lifted bodily into the back of an unmarked van that arrived at that precise moment and was driven immediately up Bath Street to be parked just fifty yards up the hill.

It was at 15.06 that Ammar Sharmu had entered the block of toilets, where only one man was waiting very patiently for his arrival, "Well done, Ammar! This won't take long, so just try to relax." Ammar looked into his eyes, "What shall I do, Mr Alan?"

The superintendent reached out to the wires that could be seen disappearing inside the nail-jacket, "Just hold still while I cut a wire or two." He gently exposed the end of a switch and put his fingers on the wires leading into it. "It's important that I find the right wire Ammar, so just keep still." He opened the nail-coat and bomb jacket a fraction to try to see the other side of the switch, but that was impossible as everything was packed in much too tightly and it was dark inside the toilets. He very gently manipulated the first wires that he had found above the switch, opening them a fraction and separating them as best he could. They were so tight that he could hardly push the blades of his small but powerful wire-cutters between them, yet somehow, he wiggled them between two of the wires. "Which one? Which one?" he called aloud in an impassioned voice.

The scared reply came, "I don't know, Mr Alan, I don't know how

Zakarian joined up the wires!"

The superintendent realised that there was nothing else for him to do now other than to go on with this crazy operation. The bomb might explode whatever he did, so he pushed the blades further between two of the three strands of wire, twisted them sideways with immense care, looked up into Ammar's eyes and said, "Stand still, Ammar. I'm going to cut one wire. Don't move a muscle, Son!" The young man obeyed breathlessly, like a sheep being shorn of its fleece. Alan Harling's chest was heaving as he squeezed the handles of his cutters together.

Nothing happened at all. He breathed out and removed the tool with intricate care before reinserting it across the remaining two wires, "This is the last cut, Son!" Again, he clamped the handles tightly together and again nothing happened. He called out at the top of his voice, "Now! Now! Now!" Two men approached behind Ammar and one held the young man's shoulders whilst the other held onto the nail-coat. The superintendent said in an amazingly calm voice, "Now, just undo the nail coat for yourself, please Ammar." The young man obeyed and the sleeveless garment designed for extreme terror was slipped deftly off of him from behind. "And now for the jacket itself please Ammar. Just turn around very slowly and undo it carefully, please." Ammar did as he was told, turning to look away from the superintendent, reaching down and releasing the Velcro straps that held it in place around his chest and stomach. In the circumstances, the ripping sound of the Velcro coming apart was excruciating. Alan Harling held onto the bomb-jacket very tightly, "Now step forwards Ammar and go outside with the police officers. They'll look after you and take you somewhere safe, where I'll be seeing you later, Son. Well done!"

The young man stepped away, then turned and looking back at the superintendent in the dismal light, he whispered, "Thank you, Mr Alan. Thank you." He was accompanied from the toilets and into the waiting car which drove up the street and parked just beyond the van. A few moments later, the superintendent emerged from the toilets holding the bomb-jacket, packed solidly with its devastating explosives, so surprised at how heavy it was. He released it into Lenny Smithson's steady hands and went a few yards away to retch uncontrollably and violently into a flower bed.

At 15.10, two officers entered the 'Gentlemens' toilet and tipped out two large containers of assorted animal remains and a gallon can of blood, that had been bought that morning from a surprised worker at an abattoir a few miles away. The revolting mess was splashed generously around the floor and walls, before everyone moved systematically fifty yards away from the toilet block, leaving Lenny Smithson alone. He put the bomb-jacket down with extreme care, connected it to a cable that he began to unroll very smoothly until he joined the superintendent and his team. Lenny connected the cable to a device and began turning a handle with very steady but gradually increasing force. At 15.12, the explosion was heard over a large part of Walsall, as the block of toilets was demolished rather earlier that the council had intended. Mustafa Zakarian looked at the clock and smiled as he sat upstairs in his flat, watching TV with his wife beside him, "Exactly on time! Very good! Soon, we must move on to somewhere new and start again Yeraz!"

***

The buildings, courtyards, forecourt and pavements all around the Aisha Mosque were packed with people, all eager to learn how Sheikh Salim intended to turn his aspirations for peace and harmony into something practical. However, the assembled leaders and advocates from local and national mosques, churches, synagogues and temples were also declaring by their simple presence that they desired and supported tolerance for each other's opinions, cultures and faiths. Hundreds who were unable to gain a sight of the podium, which had been set up under an open-fronted marquee in the forecourt, were clustered around loud-speakers positioned all around the mosque. TV and radio film-crews were in position when, exactly at 3.00 p.m., the chairman's deep smile and simple message of welcome was spoken out for the world's eyes to see and ears to hear. It was, indeed, to be a happy occasion for the assembled thousands and the media audiences, who were totally unaware that an assassination attempt was in progress at that very moment, with the suicide bomber and his companion walking at a deliberately steady pace towards them. Whilst those two young men were entering the New Street Park, Sheikh Salim was introduced.

He thanked and quieted his audience and began his speech, "Ten weeks ago, an immature young Englishman of Middle-Eastern origin, walked into a peaceful shop in central London, and blew himself and some others into tiny pieces. As he did so, whilst I stood looking into his scared eyes, he called out what may be translated universally as, '*In God's Name!*' My first question to all of us here today and listening throughout the world is: 'Could indiscriminate or targeted murder and maiming of persons, ever... I repeat ever... be said truly to be '*In God's Name!*'? If you believe that it could be, may I suggest that you read your Holy books more carefully? If you listen to preachers of any faith who advocate killing '*In God's Name!*' will you listen to them and obey their injunctions, or will you dare to defy their hypocrisy and join me in declaring, '*No!*' For centuries peoples have distrusted, avoided, hated and killed each other simply because of the colour of their skin, their different culture or faith, or to steal their natural resources. We could decide to accept these evils as being normal although unfortunate patterns of life, but we could do far more than that if we had sufficient courageous. We could try to recognise each other's differences, some of which are inconsequential, but others of which go right against the treasured grain of our beliefs. Can we ever learn to understand each other's differences sufficiently to tolerate them, rather than to blow each other into pieces?"

Being aware of the exact time, Sheikh Salim hesitated briefly in his speech, enabling all those listening to him live or over TV and radio, to hear the explosion taking place 500 yards away, not knowing if it was a car backfiring, a road accident, or something more sinister. Impressed with the absolute accuracy of the superintendent's timing, the prince continued, "What if for instance that noise which we have just heard was another bomb, similar to the one that killed my own Muslim brother, and the father of this young Jewish lady sitting next to me, and the fiancé of the aunt of this young Christian man with me here today? That aunt is the dearly-loved lady Christine Templeton, who I can announce with great joy has been healed miraculously by Almighty God this very morning from her terrible bomb injuries!

"What would we say and do if that had been another bomb? Miss Templeton saved my own life in that London jewellery shop by trying to stop the bomber moments before he detonated himself. She has been slowly and painfully dying in hospital, from cancer caused by her horrendous injuries, until last night's divine healing. My question to all who are listening remains: 'What would we say and do?' Would we cheer and applaud the news that some other persons, with whom we do not agree, have been killed '*In God's Name!*' or would we say, 'No! Enough is enough!'?

"You have not come here today to hear me make a religious speech, nor have I been invited to advocate some hotchpotch of a false and universal 'common faith' that would never satisfy anybody who believed whole-heartedly in Almighty God. Rather, I have come to make known the practical way in which I intend to test and support my view that toleration can be demonstrated and taught to young persons. It is my great pleasure to announce the establishment of the 'College of Recognition', designed to assist recognition, understanding, toleration and support between such young persons of all nationalities, cultures and faiths. The one-year course is for applicants wishing to attend a pre-university-level course designed to teach understanding and harmony between different peoples." Sheikh Salim waited for the cheering and waving to diminish, before continuing, "The 'College of Recognition' will host forty students annually, who are in their so wrongly described '*Year Out*' between school and university. If the young people give it their full energy and determination, their academic year at 'COR' as it may become known, may be referred to far better as their '*Year In*'! This diploma will help to prepare young persons for their intensive studies at university, thus the curriculum will not contain academic lectures, but will be built around an atmosphere of workshop learning. Students can select subjects such as 'Relationships between foreign languages for non-linguists', 'Technical support for survival-level craft-work by non-academic people groups', 'Basic understanding of different faiths', or 'Applied Theology' as Miss Klein describes it, 'Scientific applications for arts students', and such like.

"Each of the three terms will be spent at one of three centres by rotation, one each in England, Israel and the FNAE; allowing young persons to experience very different cultures and lands. Staff will be drawn from a mixture of qualified teachers and experienced non-academic practitioners. Miss Klein and Mr Templeton have graciously accepted my invitation to be founding students who, with the other thirty-eight in the inaugural year, will be encouraged to spend time together in enabled group situations, where mind-stretching issues that are relevant to the world may be deliberated. Let us recognise and applaud the talents and abilities of our young people and assist them to develop these, rather than making them sit and obey our often-stifling regulations. Each student will be required to select one of a number of proffered research and development subjects, to be followed up at their own pace throughout the year, and with their conclusions to be published in the college year-book. Subjects aimed at finding simple practical solutions to important worldwide issues, such as 'the enabling of horticulture in desert or ice-field conditions', 'energy-conservation without technical aids to reduce wastage of natural resources', and 'recognition and development of latent opportunities in under-privileged people', will be offered. "However, with a similar approach, please will all of us who believe we are 'children of Abraham', despite our different faiths, consider how by looking back to his time and especially at his immense practical faith in God, we can learn more of Almighty God for ourselves? Rather than by concentrating on the obvious and legitimate differences between Muslims, Jews and Christians, surely our intentions should be to give Almighty God his due glory, instead of condemning those others of his children who disagree with us? Thank you for listening to me today and may I wish all of you success in opening your hearts and minds to the immense opportunities that stretch out before us, if we can dare to believe in them. Will you choose to condemn and destroy those who are different to you, or will you support me in my endeavours? Thank you for listening."

***

At 15.13, the van that had been parked in Bath Street moved off, with one of its occupants speaking in a very precise voice to another, "Wow! Did you here that? That stupid young terrorist must have set himself off too early! Just shows you that you shouldn't mess around with explosives, especially whilst you're going to the toilet eh!" They drove away with the still-bundled and strapped down 'Andy' to

Wolverhampton police station.

At the exactly same moment, two of Sergeant Patel's stronger officers smashed their way through the entrance door to the flats next to Zakarian's shop. Detective Constables Jacobs and Jones rushed up the stairs and repeated their demolition to the door to Swarthy's flat. They went straight to the source of noise, finding Zakarian sitting watching TV, but not quickly enough to stop him reaching out for a vicious kitchen knife that he always kept in reach. The first to reach him received the knife deeply into his stomach, screaming in agony and crashing in his gushing blood to the floor. Ben Jacobs put his fist into the place where blood was pumping out from alongside the knife's handle, whilst Waseem Patel smashed Zakarian to the floor. Yeraz reached into a drawer and tried desperately to hand her husband a revolver, but Nella Brown wrestled her away. Jacobs shouted downstairs for the standing-by ambulance to come immediately. Other officers joined in the melee as Zakarian fought like a whirlwind, eventually being overpowered by sheer force of numbers. Nella Brown was helping Gail Tandridge to do similarly with Yeraz, who was wielding a pair of scissors and slashing viciously at their throats. WDPC Tandridge was bleeding profusely from a deep wound in her neck, but clung onto her assailant until Brown had handcuffed her. At last an officer turned off the canned laughter accompanying the game-show blaring out from the large-screen TV. Zakarian and his wife were dragged downstairs not too comfortably and pushed to the floor of two separate vans, with police dogs and several officers waiting in readiness for the eight miles journey to Wolverhampton.

***

At the same time, other officers were making further arrests. In a suburb of Birmingham, the door of a flat was opened politely by the mother of Mahmoud, code-named 'Colin' in Walsall. When the nature of their business was disclosed, the incredulous parents sunk onto their sofa in despair at their son's well-known involvements ever since his teenage years, which they hated themselves, allowing the officers to rush to his bedroom and yank 'Colin' from his bed. A great deal of inflamed literature was gathered, along with street-fighting weapons and the young man himself, all to be dragged past the weeping parents out to the van which would take him to Wolverhampton. Meanwhile, at a terraced house in Telford, four young men were shocked into silence when several officers broke down the front door and poured into their rooms, disturbing the drug party and selecting Mohammed, also known to the police as 'David', from his mates and hurrying him away to their waiting van.

***

At 17.30, the car with blacked-out windows carrying Ammar, escorted by Detective Constable Hippy Ipperstaff, arrived at Heathrow Airport to be met by Mr Nicholson and the unnamed man who were waiting for their arrival. They were taken by a private route directly out to the apron where Sheikh Salim's official FNAE jet awaited them. Once aboard the aircraft, Mr Nicholson held out something towards Ammar, shook hands with him warmly and said, "Thank you for your bravery and very important assistance to Her Majesty's security forces young man. Here is a newly issued British passport for you to use whenever you wish, starting today on your flight to the Middle East. You may notice that it is made out in the name of Tashir Mahfuz, which I trust will help you in your new career with Sheikh Salim, as I understand that it means *'Safeguarded'*. The sheikh will be joining the aircraft in a few minutes Mr Mahfuz! Goodbye!"

At 17.50, the prince arrived straight from the celebrations in Walsall, at which he had apologised for his early departure owing to a need to return to his own country on urgent business. Superintendent Harling had flown down in the helicopter with him and were taken straight to the FNAE aircraft and quickly up the steps. They stayed only briefly before wishing each 'Goodbye', as soon as Alan and Ammar had released themselves from each other's arms.

***

The 6.15 p.m. TV News programme began, flashing 'Breaking News', by focussing onto Associate Commissioner Laurence Williams in full dress uniform with medals, standing at a podium crowded with an immense number of microphones, ready to send his words around the world.

"Good evening. It is my duty and privilege to report some important news to the British public of all backgrounds, cultures and faiths, concerning a major act of terrorist activity that took place in our country this afternoon in the city of Walsall. On account of its reputation as being a prime example of mixed communities of persons living together in harmony and peace; an attempt was made to assassinate the Deputy Foreign Minister Crown Prince Salim bin Rashid Al Nu'masiq of the Federation of Non-aligned Arab Emirates.

The assassination was planned to destroy not only the life of this man of peace, but also to ruin the worthy aspirations of a mosque that is leading the way in enabling and encouraging persons of all communities and faiths to recognise, understand, tolerate and support each other. Because of the evil nature of suicide bombings, many innocent persons would have been killed as well as Sheikh Salim.

"This act of terrorism was stopped by the selfless courage and professional skill of the officers of the Metropolitan Police's Major Crimes Division, headed by one of the bravest and reliable men that I know: Superintendent Alan Harling.

"In Walsall and at other locations, a number of armed terrorists were arrested, despite their murderous attempts on the lives of MCD's Officers, two of whom remain in hospital, with one in a critical condition. All arrested persons have been charged with attempted murder and several terrorist-related offences, including the possession and usage of explosives.

Today's suicide bomber was the only terrorist not arrested, a young man named Ammar Sharmu originating from Watford. He ceased to exist when his packed bomb-jacket and vicious nail-coat exploded prematurely, in the actual procedure of him being apprehended by MCD's Commanding Officer Superintendent Harling, for whose protection I thank God.

"I will sum up this report by re-iterating that terrorism in Britain, and indeed throughout the world, is carried out by a tiny but vicious *minority of evil persons in an attempt to intimidate the huge majority of law-abiding and peaceful citizens. Terrorism is a heinous crime and will be stopped and punished as severely as the law enables, including by the officers under my command, of whom I am immensely proud.*

It is my hope and expectation that nations around the world will support us in our determination to stamp out the hideous use of terror by such individuals and organisations. I can assure you that those evil people will not succeed while Her Majesty's Major Crimes Division of the Metropolitan Police Force is tasked with investigating and stopping such heinous activities. Thank you."

***

Doctor Chaudhary was ever the professional and whilst not being in any way sceptical, he had been determined to prove that Christine Templeton, who on Friday evening had been about to die, wasn't just improved, or maybe a little better, but was now completely and utterly healed. The physical aspects he had confirmed easily himself, even to the amazing extent of the physical restoration of her lost fingers, ear, hair and face. Although it was early on a Saturday morning, he had determined to secure the hidden internal truths, by arranging for the vigilant testing of her organs, main blood and body systems over the weekend.

Christine had smiled and chatted with the doctors, nurses and laboratory staff, all of whom were keen to check for themselves that this really had happened here at UCLH. The results were proved to be amazingly good, making all who were involved not only satisfied medically, but so overjoyed that they felt almost a part of the miracle that had taken place there themselves.

Doctor Chaudhary had also instigated enquiries throughout the staffing and contract sections of UCLH, which by early Monday afternoon had discovered absolutely no knowledge of any such nurse that fitted the description. Thus, later on Monday, he found no reason whatsoever to retain his patient and thus formally discharged her back into the world outside, so thankful himself for his secret hand-made concoction of *'Koelreuteria paniculata'*. Christine Templeton dressed herself in outdoor clothes, said her final farewells to Room 604 and the staff who had done so much for her there, and walked out of UCLH after her stay of exactly seventy days. Her bag was carried by her beloved nephew Peter who had borrowed his father's car to drive her to her own flat in Hampstead Heath, accompanied by Leticia Benitez, where they found 'Welcome Home Christine!' banners displayed prolifically in the streets.

The End